SAVING
Galahad

KIMBERLY CATES

OLIVER
HEBER
BOOKS

PUBLISHER'S NOTE: This is a work of fiction. Names, characters, places, and incidents either are the product of the author's imagination or are used fictitiously. Any resemblance to actual persons, living or dead, business establishments, events, or locales is entirely coincidental.

COPYRIGHT © Kimberly Cates

Published by Oliver-Heber Books

0 9 8 7 6 5 4 3 2 1

It was madness for fourteen-year-old Christianne Slade to sneak into a man's bed-chamber in the middle of the night, especially when Harlestone Hall was bursting with guests, but someone had to stop this disastrous wedding before Nate Rowland ruined his life.

Nate...her brother's best friend. The Galahad of all her childhood dreams. The one who had never been too puffed up with boyish dignity to show a tag-along girl how to fight with a sword, take her horse over a higher jump, or help her act out one of the hero tales she adored.

She stole down the dark corridor, drafts whisking beneath the hem of her fine lawn nightgown, light from the candlestick she clutched casting eerie shadows on the wall. The cold stone on her bare feet wasn't half so chilling as the maze of doors. Each promised ruin should she mistakenly open it—except for one.

Are you even sure you even remember which room is Nate's? Doubt whispered in Christianne's ear. She'd asked her older brothers where Nate's chamber was when they'd arrived at the estate, and they had pointed

1

it out, attributing her query to nothing more than a child's curiosity. If they'd had any idea what she planned, they would have locked her in her room.

There was nothing the members of the *haut ton* would like more than to say she was following in her mother's scandalous footsteps. They'd been staring down their noses at her from the moment Christianne had arrived, for what business did "the old Earl of Glenlyon's bastard" have attending the social event of the season—the wedding of Lord Lieutenant Nathaniel Rowland, Viscount Harlestone, to Lady Eugenie Price.

Christianne's stomach tightened as the image of the bride-to-be rose in her mind, ringlets the color of the ancient Roman coin Nate kept as a good-luck piece, dimples framing lips resembling a cupid's bow and lush curves that made Christianne feel about as womanly as her brother's cricket bat.

But it was the dissembling behind that smile that set Christianne's teeth on edge. The woman was as two-faced as almost every other female member of the *ton*. Unfortunately, even the cleverest man couldn't see beyond Eugenie's fluttering lashes and cornflower blue eyes. God help Nate once he placed a wedding band on the woman's finger.

No, Christianne told herself. She was going to stop this calamity. She had to.

Sudden pain shot through her hip as she bumped one of the tables stationed at intervals the length of the corridor. A porcelain sculpture teetered on the mahogany surface. Her hand shot out, catching the ugly thing before it could crash to the floor. She bit her lip, imagining how the sound of shattering china would have brought a raft of night-capped heads poking out of the doors to see what the disturbance was about.

She pictured those strangers' avid expressions,

heard their voices… *Isn't this exactly the kind of behavior one can expect from a by-blow? What can Lord Harlestone be thinking, allowing such a common creature to mingle with the Quality?*

"You must be even more careful than other girls," Christianne's mother had warned her when first she ventured beyond the gates of the family estate of Strawberry Grove. "Be meticulous in your behavior. Make one misstep and society will never forgive you."

It had been all Christianne could do not to point out that her mother had hardly been *meticulous* in her own morals, running away with her lover and having his children, with no wedding ring on her finger.

And wasn't saving Nate worth risking scandal?

She whisked a lock of tousled black hair over her shoulder and stared at the door she hoped was Nate's, wondering if she was about to make the worst mistake possible.

At that moment, she heard a noise somewhere down the hallway. One of Nate's beloved deerhounds? A servant? Or a noble rake sneaking out for an assignation with his mistress? She dared not wait to find out. Casting her fate to fortune, she opened the door and rushed into the room, shutting the portal behind her with a thud.

She startled herself as much as the figure lounging in the chair by the fire. Her eyes blurred at the sudden bright light from a dozen candles, unable to discern the identity of the man that rose to his feet, broad shoulders silhouetted against the bright blaze in the hearth. But a heartbeat later, Nate's deep baritone rumbled out.

"Christianne, is that you?"

Relief shot through her as her vision cleared. He was still in his shirtsleeves, his cuffs rolled past his elbows, the collar of his shirt open. A lock of tawny-brown hair threaded with strands of gold, tumbled over his brow. Christianne itched to brush it back, the way she had so many times before. It hurt to know that Eugenie might be the one to do so from now on.

"What are you doing here, Mistress Mayhem?" Nate asked with a half grin. "Is something amiss?"

She crossed to the little table beside his chair and put the candlestick down, her hand trembling. The words she'd practiced so many times became a jumble.

Nate filled her silence. "You know, I used to love it at Strawberry Grove when you'd run to me for stories when you couldn't sleep," Nate said. "But you're not a little girl anymore and the house is full of people who wouldn't understand. If someone saw you, what would they think?"

Christianne tipped her chin up at a proud angle. "I don't care what these people think!"

"No, I don't suppose you do, my brave girl. But I'd not be the cause of gossip aimed at you. Perhaps you should tell me why you've come."

Suddenly her tongue felt pinned to the roof of her mouth.

"Don't tell me that brother of yours got into a fight." Nate smiled, and Christianne's middle fluttered. "Adam and my cousin, Salway, vowed they'd keep their swords in scabbards until the wedding festivities were over."

From the time they'd been boys, her eldest brother Adam and Nate's cousin, Salway Rowland, had been at daggers drawn. But they'd forged an uneasy truce whenever Nate was around.

"No. It's not about Adam. I came to see you all on my own." A sudden draft whooshed across Christianne, and she wrapped her arms tight around her middle.

"Look at you," Nate scolded. "Wandering around in nothing but a wisp of lawn. Will you ever learn to dress

4

warmly enough?" He crossed to where his banyan lay upon the bed, and wrapped the garment around her shoulders.

The quilted satin robe smelled like Nate—cinnabar and sandalwood—whispering of exotic places where legends turned real. Christianne burrowed deep into the luxurious folds, aware of how big the garment was on her, how protected it made her feel...as Nate had always made her feel.

How many times in the past had he swept off his frock coat and settled it over her shoulders? She was forever racing off in such a hurry she didn't bother to grab her cloak. She'd always loved the freedom of the breeze swirling her skirts and tangling her hair, always so sure she'd be warm enough...

Who would laugh and make her warm now?

He scooped her up as if she were seven years old, settling her in the big chair near the fire. Kneeling down, he caught hold of her icy bare foot and chafed it gently between his rein-toughened hands. Warmth spread through her as she looked down at the crown of his head, wondering if the real Sir Galahad he'd been nicknamed for had looked just so, kneeling before his lady fair.

But she wasn't Nate's lady. With her wild ways, flashing eyes and ebony locks forever tangled, she would never be the golden, soft kind of woman to inspire knights to go on quests.

He tended to her other foot then tucked the folds of the overlong banyan around her feet. Green-gold eyes held hers as he levered himself up to stand. There were times Christianne thought she could never get enough of looking at him—his legs, so long and strong in their buckskin breeches, his narrow waist, the faint cleft in his chin. Of all her brother's friends, Nate bewitched the most feminine hearts. He reminded Christianne of the tale of Achilles, dipped in a magic pool, given every gift of beauty, strength and luck by an indulgent goddess. Possessing all that was brightest in the world and protected by an invisible shield from all harm.

Why did he suddenly seem vulnerable now?

"So, tell me, Mistress Mayhem, what matter was so important that it couldn't wait until morning?"

"I need to—to talk to you." She drew a deep breath then said in a rush, "Nate, you can't marry Eugenie."

Nate's eyes widened. "What?"

"You're making a terrible mistake."

"Come now," he chided. "Eugenie and I are exactly suited. She loves all the things I love most. I've never met anyone as much in harmony with me."

"That's the problem. She's not! In harmony, I mean. Your dogs—"

"Eugenie adores my dogs! She feeds them tidbits right from the table."

"You don't see how she prisses up her lips every time one gets a muddy paw print on her gown. When you're not looking she gets all shuddery when they lick her hand. She presses her perfumed handkerchief to her nose, as if they smell bad."

Nate chuckled. "I appreciate your defense of my hounds, but, in all fairness, there are times they *do* need a bath. As for the perils of dogs smudging gowns, the day will come when you'll be mindful of your frills and furbelows as well."

"Never!" Frustration welled up in Christianne.

"Come now, sweetheart. Objections to muddy paw prints are hardly reason enough to jilt my bride at the altar."

"She prisses up her mouth the same way when she looks at Adam," Christianne insisted.

"One of Adam's favorite pastimes is saying outrageous things that ruffle people's feathers. Eugenie says she's come to be quite fond of your brother."

"She only pretends," Christianne said, desperation building inside her. "You'd see that if you'd look in her eyes, instead of always gazing at her bosom like every other man in the room."

Nate choked out a laugh, but she could see his cheeks redden. "You can't just blurt out things like that, Christianne!"

"Why not, if it's the truth? Eugenie never says what she means. She doesn't like your dogs. She doesn't like riding horses. She doesn't like Adam." Her voice cracked. "And she doesn't like me." She blinked back tears, fiercely refusing to let them fall.

Tenderness filled Nate's eyes. "Of course Eugenie likes you. How could anyone not think you're magnificent?"

"She thinks I'm an embarrassment. Her friends hate me. Any time I'm around, they all look at me as if I'm a mouse stealing from their bowl of bonbons and they can't wait to squash me flat."

He caught her hand between both of his. "Don't you know, I'd never let that happen, and neither would my wife."

My wife...hearing Nate say those words twisted like a knife in her heart.

"You're worth a hundred of those other girls," he said. She drew a shaky breath. He meant it now. But would time and Eugenie change his mind?

"You won't be my Galahad anymore," Christianne said. "You'll be hers."

Understanding gentled that handsome, reckless face. "I'll always be on hand if you need an extra sword to slay your dragons."

"Everything will change if you marry Eugenie," she said in a small voice.

He paused to consider. It was something Christianne loved about him—the fact that he didn't brush off her thoughts and questions and doubts. He really listened and took care with his answers.

"That's true enough," he confessed at last. "Things do change. In a few years you will be the one changing. You'll have no time for me, you'll be so busy with gowns, dancing and beaus."

The moment the last word was out, his expression shifted, something haunted in his gaze before he looked away. She'd seen that expression before, as if he knew the sad ending to a story she hadn't read yet.

"Can I tell you a secret?" Nate asked. "You Slades are the reason I want to marry. I always envied Adam, having a houseful of siblings. My visits to Strawberry Grove were the happiest times of my boyhood. All that laughter and squabbling, never a dull moment. One of the first things I told Eugenie was that I want a big family just like yours. She answered that she wants a dozen babes as well."

"Let's see what she says when the first one spits up on her Mechlin lace. Oh, Nate. I'm begging you. Please, please don't do this. At least, not in such a rush. Even Gavin worries that you've known her such a short time."

Gavin Carstares, Christianne's scholarly halfbrother, was the legitimate heir to the earldom, and forever the voice of reason in their tempestuous family.

"It's no wonder Gavin worries, after the unhappiness his own mother suffered," Nate allowed slowly. "But our situations are nothing alike. Your father was forced to marry Gavin's mother so her fortune could save the earldom. And the earl was already in love with your mother at the time."

The despised countess had died when Gavin was ten. Christianne thought back to the awful day Gavin

8

had been dropped on the Slades' doorstep, fresh from his mother's funeral. He'd been so different from his half-brother and half-sisters, quiet, studious, gentle. Their father had scorned Gavin for it. What had it been like for Gavin to be handed over to the care of the very woman who had turned his mother's life into a hell of humiliation? Yet, the bastard Slade children and their legitimate half-brother had come to love each other with a fierce loyalty that still astonished anyone who knew the story.

"It might be wiser to wait to wed," Nate admitted, "but Eugenie's stepfather was determined to carry her off to the wilds of America. I'd likely never see her again, and she'd break her heart, missing me. If you'd seen her weeping before I asked her to wed me, you'd know what I say is true."

"More likely she'd be missing Ranelagh Gardens and her dressmakers."

One corner of Nate's mouth tipped up. "You don't think a woman could be madly in love with me, then?"

She looked away, her cheeks suddenly hot.

"I blush to confess, there were plenty of marriageable ladies who were most disappointed when my betrothal was announced in the society pages," Nate teased.

"Yes, yes," Christianne said with an impatient wave of her hand. "Of all the Knights of the Round Table, you're the most dashing. Everyone says so."

From the moment the sword master from the elite school of arms her brothers attended had christened their cadre of boyhood friends the Knights of the Round Table, there had been no doubt which of the five lads would be Galahad, the perfect knight.

Somehow, she'd thought their friendship would never change, but with Eugenie she knew it would. She

9

battled to keep her lower lip from trembling. "She doesn't deserve you."

"I don't deserve an angel like her. I can't believe how fortunate I am to win such a wife. Sometimes when I look at her…"

"I still say you're always looking in the wrong place." Christianne grimaced and patted her own flat bosom.

Nate threw back his head and laughed. "I promise, I look deeper into Eugenie's heart than you give me credit for. Listen, Christianne. I know how surly you get when you're proved wrong—"

"That's because I've not had much practice at it."

"I hope you'll make an exception for me, just this once. Couldn't you find it in your heart to be happy for me once you see me in the throes of wedded bliss?"

"*If* I see you in wedded bliss," she muttered the correction, picking at the fastenings on the banyan. Didn't she want Nate's marriage to be like this garment? Warm and sheltering and full of richness? *Could* she be happy for him if Eugenie was everything he believed she was?

"Please, Mistress Mayhem," he said in that voice that made her able to deny him nothing. "Won't you wish me joy?"

He looked so eager, so hopeful, stepping into this new world without her. She forced herself to nod, unable to squeeze words past the lump in her throat.

"You'll see, Christianne," he said, so certain of himself. "I intend to be blissfully happy with a dozen blond, blue-eyed boys and girls. Think of the fun you'll have teaching them mischief."

"Eugenie will never let me near them." Christianne knew for certain that Nate's new wife would banish her from her husband's life as much as possible.

She'd spent her whole life racing after Nate and her brothers and the rest of the Knights, trying to keep up with them. But she'd always known they'd leave her behind for the important world of men. A world where they could actually *do* things that mattered, instead of being trapped in boring drawing rooms and imprisoned by needlework, forced to be proper even when she wanted to run free.

"I'll always love the wildness in you," Nate said softly, kissing her on her forehead.

Who would love the wildness in her when the Knights were gone? a mournful voice asked inside her.

Maybe you're wrong about Eugenie, she tried to tell herself. *Maybe Nate will be so happy he'll be unbearable.*

"Do you remember what you used to say about me when we were children?" Nate asked. "That I was the luckiest boy in the world?"

It was true. Each of the other four Knights had some wound that had formed them, the stain of bastardy or parents who had died, marking them with secret grief. Nate's world had been as perfect as it was possible to be.

Suddenly a memory flashed in her head, a clear summer day. Nate swimming in the pond with the other lads. She'd broken her arm earlier that month and wasn't able to go in the water. He'd seen her watching them, forlorn, and he'd brought her a pretty stone.

I'm sorry you had such rotten luck, he'd said, gently touching her splinted arm. *I wish I could give you some of mine.*

No! You can't give any away, she'd said with a twinge of panic. *What if luck is like pie? You might gobble all of your luck up at once and there will be none left for later!*

His only reply was lighthearted laughter as he stretched out on the mossy bank, the sun glistening in drops of water that clung to his long, strong legs and perfectly shaped feet.

Christianne's heart squeezed as the image of that boy faded away, into the handsome face of the man he had become.

She shivered, suddenly chilled as a premonition washed over her. After tomorrow's wedding, she knew her reckless, carefree Nate would be gone. She would never see her laughing Sir Galahad again.

CHAPTER 1

1755

*I*t wasn't the first time Christianne had been forced to stand in the shadows with the wallflowers and watch the world dance past. She was under no illusions that a true gentleman would ever lower himself to dance with a bastard, even if her father had been an earl. From the day she'd attended Nate's wedding festivities eleven years before, she'd realized that nobody—from the most exalted lady to the lowliest servant—would forgive her for her scandalous birth.

But her toes *would* tap in time to the music, refusing to surrender to the fate Christianne had known awaited her even before she'd crossed the threshold to Nathaniel Rowland's drawing room this night of his birthday fete.

Christianne grimaced, wondering if she should have taken her maid's advice and pleaded one of the headaches that plagued her when people were being particularly vexing. But Nate's wife had been attempting to shove her into the shadows since the day Nate put his ring on her finger. Christianne hated the notion of letting Eugenie and her spiteful friends win.

Unfortunately, it was harder for Christianne to keep

13

her chin tipped at its accustomed devil-may-care angle when Nate was in the room to witness society's snubs.

She peered across the chamber to where he stood beside the terrace doors, looking as if he were in the midst of an army's forced march instead a celebration in his honor.

Grief squeezed her heart. How was it possible for anyone to change so much? She wondered. Ten years had passed since the Jacobite rebellion tore the Knights apart, her brothers fighting for the exiled Stuart kings, Nate for George II. That nightmare was behind them, with Nate achieving a near miracle, winning her brothers a pardon. He'd opened the way to futures Adam and Gavin hadn't dared hope for. But Nate had lost something on that battlefield no force of will could replace. A sword had severed his leg mid-calf. Unfeeling wood replaced living flesh.

In the years since, he'd flung himself into philanthropy with the passion he'd once reserved for demanding physical pursuits. Christianne knew Nate's limitations grieved her brothers, too. When they were with Nate, they concentrated on the things he could do, rather than activities he'd once loved but could no longer share.

But it wasn't only the loss of a leg that had changed Nate from the carefree young officer Christianne had adored. Another kind of pain carved deep lines into his face. An inner wound so deep that Christianne sensed even her brothers had never been allowed to see it.

How many times had she imagined being able to go to Nate, stroke his hair back from his brow and kiss away that grimness, coax out the devilish smile she loved? But he had a wife. A child. A noble title. He was forever beyond her reach.

Tonight his broad shoulders were stiff beneath a tawny-gold frock coat, the froth of lace beneath his square chin making the hard line of his lips appear even more forbidding. For hours, Nate had maintained the unyielding posture mastered during his years as a colonel in His Majesty's 10th Dragoons. Christianne knew the night had become a torment when he resorted to the cane he only used when his other choice was to fall flat. And where was Nate's wife? Flitting about, either oblivious to his predicament or choosing to ignore it so she'd not have to cut her frolics short.

Christianne glowered at the woman who was a vision in china blue satin, silver gauze gilding her lush curves. She might have forgiven Eugenie Rowland for her ability to slay men's good sense with one flutter of her fan. But the fact that Eugenie was prolonging Nate's discomfort tonight, so that she could be the center of attention, made Christianne want to dump the punchbowl full of ratafia over her head.

"It's a shame society frowns on an earl's daughter engaging in duels," a gruff voice muttered behind Christianne. "I would have made a fortune betting on you to win them."

She glanced over her shoulder, glimpsing sardonic black eyes and ink-dark hair. She drove her elbow backward, aiming for her brother's ribs. Adam dodged neatly out of her reach, his reflexes honed during years as an expert swordsman.

"I've come to ask you to dance before that glare of yours sets Eugenie Rowland's hair on fire," he teased.

Her heart warmed at his thoughtfulness. There was a time Adam had fled across the continent as a soldier of fortune to avoid the pain of seeing his sisters rejected in social situations like this one. In the years he'd been absent, he'd earned the sobriquet Sabrehawk for his bravery but only once he'd wed a bonnet-clad crusader named Juliet had he learned to face emotional tangles with the same courage.

"Eugenie Rowland might be wise to surrender the field for her own safety," he said, "Ever since the coaches started rolling up today with her 'surprise' guests for Nate's birthday fete, you've looked ready to murder her."

"The woman is insufferable, claiming she got up this nonsense as a treat for Nate. It was all I could do not to yank her hair as if I were six-years-old."

Anger shot through Christianne afresh as she recalled what had transpired earlier that afternoon. Eugenie had led the small house party of Nate's dearest friends to the carriage circle to greet a throng of unexpected guests as they arrived. She'd seemed almost feverish in her excitement, her voice high and thin.

"I know you were disappointed when your other friends were caught up in Parliamentary business and couldn't attend your birthday," Eugenie had said. "I concocted a surprise to cheer you!"

Concocted a disaster, more like, replacing Nate's trusted companions with two-dozen members of the *ton*. The arrogant herd had descended on Harlestone Hall, turning the simple gathering into exactly the kind of hurly-burly Nate had come to loathe.

He'd looked as if he'd rather face a firing squad when Eugenie caught hold of his sleeve. "It will be glorious, my darling!" Eugenie had enthused. "We'll spend the night dancing and the days traipsing through the parklands, and we'll get up theatricals." Pastimes Nate had once enjoyed as much as his wife. Pleasures forbidden to him since Culloden Moor.

In the carriage circle, Christianne had seen Nate's fingers drift to his left thigh. Now, her gaze traced down Nate's muscular body to the stiff calf beneath his stocking and the foot forever set at a right angle.

She remembered a time when she hadn't been able to take her eyes off of Nate when he was dancing or practicing with swords, riding or boxing or doing one of the hundred other things her brothers' friends were up to. Now, there was a terrible stillness in him.

"It's all I can do to keep from choking the life out of that woman," Christianne said.

"You're not the only one," Adam grumbled. "At least if someone did so, it would pluck Nate out of his misery of a marriage." Her brother straightened the up-turned cuff on his black frockcoat. "Well, someone had better try to get Nate to sit down before this crush of Eugenie's friends drives him to hang himself. They've been summoning up all kinds of storms tonight with Eugenie stirring the pot. If you'll not dance with me, maybe you can help me convince Nate to take a seat," Adam said. "When that stubborn fool gets in this mood he would stand until the last raven fled London's Tower."

Christianne swallowed hard, wishing for the child-hood days when she would have seized Nate's hand and drawn him to a chair as naturally as she drew breath. But their childhood ease was gone. "You go ahead," she told Adam.

He cuffed her under the chin. "You're worth a hundred of these snobbish misses, you know," he said. "Nate would be the first to tell you so."

Nate had told her exactly that on the night she'd boldly crept into his bedchamber, begging him not to marry Eugenie Price, Christianne thought as her brother strode off.

But the morning after, she'd had to watch the woman become Nate's wife, Eugenie's face glowing with happiness. More painful still had been the way Nate looked at his bride, as if he'd captured starlight in his hands.

Christianne felt a pang at the memory as she observed Adam waylaid by another guest before he could reach Nate.

She took cover in a curtained alcove so that Eugenie or her friends would not be able to see the chink in her armor.

A moment later she peeked through the curtain and blessed her narrow escape. Eugenie's statuesque friend, Deborah Musgrove drew near, her wide petticoats so vast they obscured the hive of ladies buzzing around her. Christianne pulled a face. Every time Deborah had crossed her path since the *ton's* arrival, the woman had held up her quizzing glass and examined Christianne with ill-concealed contempt.

"One must pity Eugenie," Deborah said, pausing an arm's length from Christianne's nook. "Who would have guessed her husband would prove to be such a trial? I'm sure she never imagined he would insist on continuing to invite those Slade people to her entertainments after she and Harlestone were wed."

Christianne's hands clenched into fists. *We've heard it all before,* she could almost hear Adam warn. *Don't kick up a fuss or it will get back to Nate. No sense making his birthday even more miserable than it already is.*

Deborah's companion, Lady Northram, fluttered her fan as if the mere thought of bastards was too shocking for her delicate sensibilities to bear. "One might be compelled to tolerate Adam Slade, though he *was* born on the wrong side of the blanket," her ladyship mused. "Men *will* insist on consorting with anyone who demonstrates such skill with a sword. But the Slade daughters are another matter entirely."

"At least the old Earl of Glenlyon had the sense not to marry their trollop of a mother once the countess was in her grave. Thank heavens for that much."

Deborah gave a delicate shudder. "Decent gentlemen visit their mistresses in secret. But Lydia Slade would not have it! La, what can that Slade chit's morals be when her mother acted as if she and the earl were man and wife, parading their bastards about?"

Goaded beyond endurance, Christianne stepped out from behind the curtain. Satisfaction filled her as she saw dismay on at least a few of the faces. "Mistress Musgrove. Lady Northram. Ladies," she said, meeting their eyes.

She was surprised to see Eugenie Rowland come forward, her face betraying something akin to alarm. "Why, Mistress Slade!" Eugenie flushed beneath the lead paint of her cosmetics, and Christianne was struck again by how strangely her reluctant hostess had been acting. In the hour since the dancing began, the tension emanating from Eugenie had grown so pronounced that Christianne half expected Nate's wife to snap.

"You sly creature," Eugenie said. "We didn't see you lurking behind curtains."

"Doubtless *creeping about* is a skill she learned aping her mother," Deborah Musgrove quipped, peering down her rather large nose. Some of the other ladies tittered.

"I find your logic a trifle bewildering," Christianne said with acid sweetness. "Weren't you just complaining to your friends that my mother *didn't* creep about? Another thing she wouldn't do—gossip about guests her hostess was entertaining."

"What quality of guests would ever be visiting *your* mother?" Deborah huffed. "The vicar, perhaps, warning of fire and brimstone. Very bad for the complexion, you know."

"As is a bitter tongue," Christianne shot back.

"You would be well acquainted with that, since everyone knows spinsters are the bitterest lot of all." Deborah Musgrove swept her skirts away from Christianne's, as if she feared contagion. "I believe I'll take a turn in the garden, dearest Eugenie. The air has grown rather stale in this corner." With that, Deborah Musgrove and the others sailed away.

Christianne seethed with rage and humiliation as she and Eugenie watched them depart. Her gaze collided with Nate's across the floor. He frowned and raised one hand as if questioning what had occurred and she wondered how much he'd been able to discern about the exchange from a distance. Before Christianne could signal back to him, Eugenie moved to block her from Nate's line of sight.

"I know Deborah and Lady Northram were naughty to say such things, but you won't carry tales to Nathaniel, will you?" Eugenie glanced a little fearfully over her shoulder in her husband's direction "He's been in a bear of a temper of late."

"I don't carry tales, and I'd certainly not ruin Nate's birthday." Christianne was sorely tempted to point out that Eugenie had already done a fine job of that herself.

Eugenie fiddled with the fan dangling from a ribbon around her wrist. "I'm grateful for your discretion. As to Deb's behavior, one cannot expect any different. The *ton* delights in gossip. That is why I was surprised you didn't make a graceful exit once I announced this new turn in our entertainment."

Christianne was fiercely glad she hadn't pleaded a headache and given Eugenie the satisfaction. "I've been looking forward to celebrating with Nate for over a fortnight."

"But once the festivities became so public, I assumed you would be more comfortable retiring to Spinster Grove, away from so many critical eyes."

"Spinster Grove?" Christianne echoed, stung.

"That is our pet name for your home."

Christianne's cheeks stung. Was it possible that Nate had named it thus? She knew the friend of her

girlhood never would, but hadn't she just been considering how much he'd changed?

"The estate is a veritable little nunnery, with all of you sisters unwed and living with your mama," Eugenie continued. "I'm certain it is quite cozy and charming. No worries about gentlemen suitors stomping about in their muddy boots, drinking brandy and tearing up your peace. Of course, beyond your front gate, people aren't nearly as liberal-minded as my husband, so I'm sure it gets uncomfortable for you to be in the public eye. But then, you need not travel anywhere beyond your village."

"We have actually traveled with our brother the earl," Christianne said, trying not to grind her teeth. "Gavin has always been kind, as you know."

"I'm sure it was helpful to our dear Glenlyon to have someone to help mind his children. They're of a most energetic disposition. Such antics would give me megrims."

"When they get out of hand, I nail them in a barrel," Christianne snapped.

For an instant, Eugenie looked mystified then she gave an awkward laugh. "You're jesting, aren't you? Nathaniel always said you had a most *unconventional* sense of humor."

Christianne tried not to wince at the memory of how hard she'd tried to make him laugh through the years. She'd loved the way he'd fling his head back as the deep, rich sound rumbled from his throat. When his eyes twinkled at her, she felt a delicious fizzing sensation in her blood. But that rare, unrestrained laughter had died.

Eugenie's eyes narrowed, and Christianne suddenly feared she might guess her thoughts.

"Shouldn't you be off dancing?" Christianne demanded, eager to be rid of the woman. "From what I

21

hear, there is nothing you enjoy more than finding a new dancing partner."

"There is no man in this room I would rather be dancing with than my husband." Eugenie surprised her with such fierceness. "But since he is not able, it would be rude of me to sit out the entire party. Even so, Nathaniel will be growling at me. It won't matter that I worked myself to a shade to make tonight perfect just for him. He's grown ever more hot-tempered. I'd hoped that fatherhood would soften him!"

Christianne had hoped Nate would find joy in being a father as well. She remembered how he'd confided his longing for a big family the night before his wedding. As a boy, he'd spent visits to Strawberry Grove playing with the younger Slades. As a man, he'd never failed to delight in her brothers' children, but he rarely mentioned his own daughter. Was Seraphina a reminder of the wife who had so bitterly disappointed him?

Sorrowful tenderness flooded Eugenie's face, tamping down the woman's spitefulness.

"Sera is six, and quite the most charming little creature. No one who comes in contact with her can resist her. Except for her father." Eugenie shifted her gaze away. "I thought Nate would be attentive to his family, but people are not always who they appear to be, are they?"

Christianne saw an echo of the vulnerable beauty Eugenie had seemed the first time she'd appeared on Nate's arm. Suddenly Eugenie's eyes widened. "Lord, my husband's coming over here. Whatever can be the matter now?"

Christianne shifted her gaze to Nate. He was limping toward them, looking like a powder keg about to explode. Even Christianne was taken aback.

"Miss Slade, perhaps you could soothe him," Eu-

22

genie pleaded, a little breathless. "He's so very attached to all of your family."

Christianne forced a smile as Nate approached. Eyes the dark green-gold of a twilight meadow sparked with anger.

"Nate!" Christianne exclaimed. "I was just about to sample some of that delicious punch. Will you come and sit with me?"

"Out of sight where my wife's friends think you belong?" Nate growled.

Eugenie laid a hand on his arm. "I don't know what you are talking about, my love."

Nate yanked away from her. He leaned his cane against the wall, as if loath to expose the slightest hint of weakness to his wife. "Another guest overheard your conversation and was kind enough to inform me that Deborah Musgrove was unspeakably rude."

Christianne wasn't certain which was more humiliating—Deborah Musgrove's barbs being gossiped about, or the knowledge that Nate had heard the nastiness the woman had spouted.

"I pay no heed to what Deb Musgrove says," Christianne told him.

"The point is that she shouldn't have dared to say it. Not with *your hostess* present."

"It's not *my* fault if Deb speaks so," Eugenie exclaimed. "Surely you can't blame me!"

"Blame you? For bringing this crowd of self-important fools down on our heads? For God's sake, Eugenie, if I'd had any idea you were plotting the devil's own scrape, I'd never have invited Christianne to Harlestone in the first place!"

Christianne knew he didn't mean to wound her, but the thought of being excluded from his celebration for any reason hurt so much she lashed out.

23

"Perhaps you'd rather I ran back to *Spinster Grove* where I belong."

"Wherever did you hear that name?" Nate's brow creased.

"It seems we're all destined to overhear things we're not meant to tonight," Christianne said. "Apparently, you believe my home is a veritable nunnery."

A muscle in Nate's jaw knotted and he glared at Eugenie, something frightening in his eyes. But before he could respond, a footman's voice boomed out, announcing late arriving guests. "The Earl of Fendale and Mister Salway Rowland."

"I must excuse myself." Eugenie said, looking as if she were escaping a flaming ship. She turned to Christianne. "Last time Salway visited he was quite under siege by Nathaniel's father, Lord Fendale. My father-in-law completely ruined Salway's tale about his adventures in the Sugar Islands. Thank goodness they have arrived before my surprise."

Christianne couldn't imagine Nate would welcome another surprise considering how disagreeable Eugenie's first one had turned out to be.

He blocked Eugenie's path, his tone steely. "Before you go anywhere, you'll apologize to Christianne for your appalling lack of manners."

For a moment, Eugenie looked defiant then she glanced toward the empty door to the room and fidgeted with the lace at her décolletage. "Even though what Deb and the others said *was* true, it wasn't kind to say it in Miss Slade's hearing."

"That is no apology," Nate snarled. "You insult my friends. You meddle in my business affairs. By God, I even caught you prying in my desk!"

Christianne stared, stunned. Nate had every right to be angry, but it wasn't like him to lambast anyone before an audience. Eugenie's face turned peony pink as

24

the nearest guests began to cast inquisitive looks their way.

"I was searching for people to add to my guest list for this party!" Eugenie hissed under her breath. "Heaven knows, you volunteer no information when I inquire."

"I didn't want this damn party and you knew it!" Nate said. "I told you I wanted quiet, a few friends. I told you to go off somewhere with Deborah Musgrove if you wished for this kind of entertainment. Hell, leave Harlestone for a month! *That* would be a gift worth having."

Christianne might loathe Eugenie, but she winced as more guests craned their necks to see what was amiss. She was so unsettled by this change in Nate that she laid her hand on his arm. "Nate, I cannot think this is helping matters."

"You, urging me to restraint? That's rich! You were right when you came to see me on the night before my wedding. This marriage is every bit the disaster you claimed it would be!"

Eugenie gaped at Christianne. "You tried to get him to jilt me at the altar? What did you hope? That he'd fall madly in love with you and forget what was due his name?"

Christianne's cheeks flamed. "Of course not! Nate is my friend."

"You always had the eye for him! But Nathaniel would die before he tainted a bloodline stretching back to William the Conqueror with that of someone baseborn!"

Her words hurt all the worse because Christianne was now experienced enough in the ways of the world to know they were true.

"Don't be absurd, Eugenie!" Nate said. "Christianne was a child when you and I were wed! She saw we were

25

unsuited, and she tried to warn me. I wish she'd succeeded in dissuading me from tangling the two of us in this hideous coil. But there's no escape for either of us now."

The new arrivals approached, Salway a somewhat washed-out copy of vivid-hued Nate, the earl looking like a Roman General ready to quell a mutiny. Eugenie unfurled her fan, fluttering the delicately painted surface to cool her hot cheeks.

"What is this nonsense about?" Lord Fendale demanded. "You're making a scene."

Salway frowned. "Whatever this disagreement is, you'd best all calm yourselves," Nate's cousin admonished. "I just saw Seraphina outside with her nurse. The little poppet is garbed in a costume, ready for some sort of performance."

"What the devil?" Nate turned an accusing glare on Eugenie. "The child is supposed to be at your sister's in Kent." The disgust on his face bewildered Christianne. It was toward Eugenie, surely, not his daughter.

Musicians struck up a spritely tune, and the guests parted. A little girl came tiptoeing in. A ripple of indulgent coos and words of praise filled the room. Those far enough away to have missed the contretemps between Seraphina Rowland's parents regarded her with delight.

Wings of silver gauze fluttered from the shoulders of a gown that floated around the child like flower petals. A wreath of blossoms crowned her golden curls. She might have looked more at home dreaming under a buttercup, were it not for the uncertainty in her face, a stark contrast to her whimsical costume. She clutched an object wrapped in cloth that was bedecked with gold fringe.

Christianne hadn't believed Nate could look worse. She saw his hands curl into fists as his gaze locked on the military insignia embroidered on the silk wrapping Seraphina was carrying. One look at Nate's face and the child froze. Christianne couldn't blame her.

Seraphina cast a nervous glance at her mama, but Eugenie's smile of encouragement was more like a stiff mask. "Come along, angel," Eugenie urged. "Do it just as we practiced."

Seraphina edged nearer to Nate then curtsied. "I am a fairy come to you from woodlands far away, to grant your dearest wish, upon this happy birthday."

Christianne was moved by how earnestly the child recited her little speech, and yet, she'd never imagined a fairy looking so somber.

It was obvious it cost Nate to smile at her. "Thank you. I didn't know you had come to Harlestone."

"Mama sent for me in secret to bring you this present." She extended the bundle. Nate uncurled his fists and took the lumpy object. He untied the cloth wrapping, part of the military uniform he'd set aside a year after Culloden Moor. Christianne remembered him wearing the sash at his wedding. During a ball Gavin held to celebrate the union, Nate had refused to let her be ignored. He'd drawn her out onto the dance floor, the satin sash glowing in the candlelight, not half so bright as his grin.

He smoothed the cloth back from the present his daughter had given him then stared down at it, silent. A carved wooden soldier peered back at him with implacable jet-bead eyes. Nate's brow creased in confusion. "This is a child's toy," he said slowly.

"It is for a boy," the girl explained.

A ghost of a smile curved the corner of Nate's mouth. "It is very fine. But perhaps I'm a trifle old for it."

"It is not for you," Seraphina said. "It is for that boy who will go into the cavalry one day, like you did."

"What boy is that?" Nate asked.

"My baby brother. I'm to tell you he's coming in the spring, right Mama?"

Christianne saw Nate's face go ghastly pale. The other guests began calling out congratulations and clapping their hands. The men nearest Nate slapped him on the back.

Christianne felt a hand curve around her elbow. She looked up to see her brother Adam looking nearly as grim as Nate. "What just happened?" she asked.

"Nate's been ambushed. That's what this whole evening has been about."

28

CHAPTER 2

Christianne stood, bewildered, a sense of unreality gripping her as she stared at Nate's stricken face. The excitement of the other guests over the news that Nate's wife was with child again seemed to crowd in on her from all sides. But Nate's was not the only one that looked unnerved by the news. Lord Fendale's features were still as stone. Salway Rowland glanced from Eugenie to Nate, something indefinable in his eyes. Eugenie scooped her daughter up into her arms and approached Nate, a pleading expression on her face. "Can this not be a new beginning, Nathaniel? For all of us?"

Nate cast her one tortured glance, then spun away. Grabbing his cane, he came face to face with Christianne. Their eyes held for one long anguish-filled moment, before she stepped out of his way. He stalked off, leaving the other guests aghast.

Christianne almost felt sorry for Eugenie. The woman was shaking so hard that Salway reached out for Seraphina. Christianne had never liked Nate's cousin more than when he gathered the little girl close and Seraphina twined her arms around his neck.

Lord Fendale snapped out an order. "My son has

gone to compose himself after such momentous news. Strike up the music. Dance. Dance."

"I'm going after Nate," Adam murmured to Christianne.

She nodded. "Will he be all right? I'm worried about him."

"I am, too." Adam gave her a bracing hug then strode away. Christianne looked around at the avid faces, the lead paint and powdered hair suddenly making her sick. Never had she seen the ugliness under the glistening satins and jewels more clearly.

Retreating to her nook, she sank down onto a chair, grateful for the curtain that hid her. She wished she were anywhere else, even Strawberry Grove with its excruciating calm.

What had happened during Eugenie's surprise? Something Christianne couldn't comprehend. Whatever it was, there was an ugly undercurrent she'd never felt before.

Eugenie's accusations still reverberated through Christianne. *You tried to get him to jilt me at the altar? Did you think he'd fall madly in love with you?*

The night she'd gone to Nate's chamber, *had* she been hoping he might wed her someday? Perhaps in the most secret reaches of her heart. But if she had ever been so naïve, the years since had taught her such dreams had no more basis in reality than her girlhood plan to run away with Adam and become a pirate.

Viscounts don't marry bastards... She could almost hear one of the rakes swirling around the dance floor mock her with a sneer.

Had any of the gossips like Deborah Musgrove heard what Eugenie had said? Between the argument Eugenie and Nate had engaged in, and Nate's reaction to the news he was going to be a father again, people would have plenty to whip up into scandal. Was it possible Christianne would be swept into the middle of it?

It doesn't matter what these people think of me, she told herself. *Nate is the one who is hurting. Please let Adam find him. Help him.*

She looked down at her little finger where a silver ring gleamed—the enameled shield scuffed in the years since Nate bought it for her at a fair. She'd been delighted when he'd told her it was Galahad's shield. But it wasn't a wedding ring. Likely, she'd never wear one or carry any man's babe...especially Nate's.

Why did that certainty suddenly leave her bereft?

NATE CLUTCHED the wooden soldier in one white-knuckled hand as he limped into the North Tower, the one place in Harlestone Hall he knew Eugenie would never follow him. She loathed what remained of the castle built by Nate's Norman ancestors, the rough ashlar stone walls devoid of the velvet hangings, gilt furnishings and porcelain monstrosities that filled the additions ensuing generations had tacked on to the ancient structure.

Nate remembered showing her his favorite part of his boyhood home when their love was new. She'd hung on his every word as he'd shared tales of the ancestors whose weapons lined the walls. Aristocratic Rowlands who had been bloodied in every major battle England had fought since William the Conqueror landed at Pevensey.

Those clashes of sword against sword were silent now, like the tender words he and Eugenie had spoken. If only Nate could quell the war raging inside his head. He stalked into the chamber that was his private retreat, each step painful where the wood met his lower leg, but grateful the servants always kept the fire burning after dark. A thick candle glowed in a sconce, for those sleepless nights when his shattered marriage, the frustrations of Parliament, or his old battle wounds bedeviled him.

His physical pain was drowned out by rage and shame. *And guilt*, he admitted, his gut twisting. The memory of Seraphina looking up at him was a burning coal in the center of his heart, her expression wary, a little hopeful. Now, there was to be another child not fathered by him who would need something Nate could never give. He looked at the implacable face of the toy soldier, a piece of hell in his hands.

He wanted to smash the plaything, cast it into the fire, watch the flames blister the paint until it curled back from the wood and all but the jet bead eyes turned to ash. He threw his cane against the wall, then crossed to the massive stone hearth, his hand shaking as he steeled himself to consign the toy to the flames. But before he could act, the door swung open, Adam Slade striding into the room.

Nate should have guessed that there wasn't a chamber secluded enough to deter Sabrehawk from finding a wounded comrade. The man had never left a soldier behind on a battlefield, even if that soldier might have been happier if he did.

"Eugenie should have been a general," Adam growled. "I've taken part in my share of skirmishes during the years I followed the drum, but this may have been the most perfectly executed ambush I've ever seen. You've had the devil of a birthday, my friend."

"Indeed." Nate stared down at the toy soldier still in his hands. "I came in here intending to throw this accursed thing into the fire."

"There's not a man alive who would blame you. To have your wife announce in front of that infernal crowd that she's having another man's...er, not that they know the truth," Adam amended hastily. Nate could hear the regret in his friend's voice, Adam bumbling into disaster like a knight in armor clomping through a castle of glass.

"Perhaps they don't know that I'm not Seraphina's father, but there are those who suspect. As for the new babe..." Nate shoved the thought away, knowing it was too soon to think of the ramifications. He felt echoes of the nightmarish haze he'd experienced right after the sword-stroke that had shattered his leg, reduced to survival, blocking out pain beyond bearing.

Adam walked to a table where a decanter of port stood amid a scattering of half-read books on seamanship, research for the Marine Society Charity. Adam removed the cut-glass stopper from the decanter and poured two draughts of liquor into heavy glass goblets. "Doubtless Eugenie was hoping you wouldn't murder her if she told you in front of an audience."

"If I were going to go mad with jealousy, it would have been when she first betrayed me. I was still in love with Eugenie then." And he had been. Or at least in lust.

He could remember the anguish of imagining his wife with another man. A man whole like Nate would never be again. But tonight's torment was worse, in its way. Eugenie peering up at him, those blue eyes that once dazzled him welling with tears as she asked to begin again. How could he explain to her that any hope of that was long dead? Especially after...no. He shoved the memory away, bile rising in his throat.

Adam grabbed up the fireplace poker and jammed it among the logs, flames leaping, wild. "Cast the infernal soldier in," he said. "You'll feel better once you do."

"I thought so, but the minute Eugenie has the servants drag the cradle down from storage, Seraphina will want to tuck this toy under the blankets. I've given little enough to the girl. Should I rob her of that pleasure as well?"

"You've done the best you can under the circumstances. You've provided a home and a nurse who adores her. She's being raised like a princess. Your mother saw to that before she died. Eugenie may be a misery of a wife, but no one questions that she's a good mother. As for you, I don't know any man who would relish having the evidence of his wife's betrayal thrust in his face every day."

"Some would see the child, not the betrayal. If Gavin were in my situation—"

Adam gave a snort of good-natured disgust. "Yes, well. If we mere mortals measure ourselves against St. Gavin, we're all dismal failures. That 'being human' nonsense gets in our way. Nate, you're as fine a man as any I've ever known. Look at all of the good you do for causes like that new Marine Charity Society you're involved with. You've funded education for the lads at the Foundling Hospital and provided dozens with the skills and equipment they need for a naval career. You have nothing to apologize for in your treatment of children."

It was true that he'd thrown himself into the cause with enthusiasm when Henry Fielding had approached him and Gavin with the revolutionary plan: Take orphaned boys and lads who had run afoul of the law, put them through school, raise them to be disciplined, then provide all the accoutrements necessary to start their career in the Royal Navy.

"You're doing the best you can, Nate," Adam said with rare gentleness. "No one could ask any more of you."

"I suppose not."

"Do you want me to call Colonel Markham out?" Adam asked. "I've not entertained myself with a duel since I wed Juliet, but there is no point letting my skills get completely rusty. It might be good to give it a go since I switched sword hands." Adam ran his thumb over the thick scar bisecting his right palm and forced a grin, trying to lighten the mood.

Nate knew his friend's fingers could no longer grip tightly enough to wield his sword with that hand. Adam had met that challenge by teaching himself to fight left-handed with nearly as much skill.

"I might not be able to use a sword as well as I once did, but I can still aim a pistol," Nate snapped. "If I wanted to call someone out, I would do it myself."

"Of course you would. It was a jest." Adam flushed, jamming his hands in his frock coat pockets.

"I don't find it amusing when my friends offer to get themselves skewered because they think I'm incapable of defending my own honor. As if I had enough left to bleed over."

"You positively reek of honor. The way you and Gavin have been fighting those arrogant lords in Parliament over the slave trade—"

"The devil a lot of good it's done." Nate crossed to the table and stood Seraphina's soldier upon it. "As for Markham, I'd have to travel to Belgium to find him. He was posted there last summer."

Adam's eyes widened in surprise.

"I don't know whose child Eugenie is bearing this time," Nate said. "Does it matter?"

Adam's silence felt heavy as a stone. Nate took up the brimming goblet and drained it in one fiery gulp.

"I'm worried about you," Adam said. "So is Christianne."

Why did the sound of her name shove a hot poker into Nate's wound? His mind filled with images—ebony eyes flashing with righteous indignation or unbridled excitement, dark curls blowing in the wind. Christianne, so unaffected and honest when Nate felt jaded, suffocated beneath his own broken body and masks of lead paint, perfumes, and lies.

It was painful enough to have a crowd witness Eugenie's announcement. But Nate was surprised to realize it was Christianne's presence that seared his pride like acid. Her dark eyes looking at him so forthright, holding something clean, fresh and whole. As if he were still the man he used to be. The thought of her knowing that he'd been cuckolded was unbearable.

And she had warned him.

"Did you or Gavin tell Christianne about Eugenie's affairs? About Seraphina?"

"What do you take us for?" Adam drew back, as if recoiling from the very thought. "That's not something a true friend discusses with anyone, especially his unwed sister."

But Christianne is no fool, a cruel voice whispered in Nate's head. *She's always been a menace when it comes to overhearing things she'd be better off not knowing. If she doesn't know already, it's only a matter of time.*

He winced inwardly, picturing the expressions that would dart across her face if—*when*—she learned the truth. Outrage. Shock.

Pity.

"Nate, this is the devil of a coil," Adam said. "I wish there was some way to untangle it."

"Aside from heaving Eugenie off the parapet or jumping myself?"

Adam sobered, and Nate sensed he was remembering the moment they'd come face to face on that blood-soaked Scottish moor. A nightmare they'd both feared when Adam had ridden off to join Bonnie Prince Charlie.

Even so many years later, Nate was haunted by the horror in Adam's face as he recognized his adversary, Adam's desperate attempt to change the lethal course of his blade mid-swing. The crack of the sword shattering bone still echoed in Nate's darkest dreams. After the blow was struck, Adam had dragged Nate behind a boulder then twisted a tourniquet around his thigh to keep him from bleeding to death.

You know there's no saving my leg, Nate had raged, trying to tear the tourniquet loose. *Let me die, damn you!*

Adam's voice jarred him back to the present. "You wouldn't do anything...drastic."

"For God's sake, you thick-headed dolt. The only question I'm struggling with now is whom I want to fling out the window first, you or my wife."

"Nate—"

"Leave me the hell alone, Adam."

"Gavin would say that you're alone too damned much," Adam grumbled.

"Parliament is overflowing with people. I have the Knights. And there are my occasional visits to The Blue Peacock." The elegant salon on the Strand provided hostesses as clever as they were lovely, the men who were their patrons eager for intellectual discussions as well as indulging in other, more secret delights.

Adam frowned, but wasn't that Nate's motive in mentioning the place? To drive a wedge between them so Adam would walk away?

"You needn't give me the gimlet eye just because you've reformed," Nate challenged. "As I recall, you were the one who introduced me to The Blue Peacock when the ladies there still called you the Prince of Sin."

But that was before Adam had met a vicar's daughter determined to provide a refuge where courtesans could reshape their lives. Since Adam's marriage, he had become as fierce a champion of the women as his Juliet was. Women whose fates were precarious... like Adam's mother's and sisters' would have been if Gavin had turned his back on them.

Nate listened to the heavy footfalls as his friend crossed the room and opened the door.

Adam paused in the entry. "After what Eugenie's put you through, I'd be the last man alive to judge you, Nate," he said. "You deserve better."

"There was a time I believed that, too. But come tomorrow that will change."

"What is going to happen tomorrow?"

"I plan to become every bit the villain Eugenie's friends believe me to be."

CHAPTER 3

*H*ow long Christianne stayed in the nook after the clamor of the entertainment resumed, she couldn't judge. An hour? Maybe more? But at last her refuge felt so confining that she had to bolt. This was exactly the kind of situation in which she'd always escaped to the outdoors, to the pastures where she could stroke the horses' velvety muzzles, or romp with the deerhounds Eugenie had exiled because of the party. Perhaps that was what she would do, Christianne reasoned. Go find Nate's dogs. She liked them far better than most people, anyway.

She ventured out from behind the curtain, hoping to go unnoticed. She needn't have worried. People couldn't care less about the impropriety of her inclusion on the guest list now. They had far richer subjects to feast upon.

Christianne looked around the room for Adam and Nate, but neither had returned. Nate's entire family was gone from the chamber as well. Christianne was grateful Seraphina had been swept away from the confusion, far from quarreling adults and nasty comments. She'd witnessed more than her share of ugly arguments as a child, when her family had encountered her mother's relatives in the village. Her proud grandparents had terrified Christianne's little sisters so much that she'd had to stand up to the frightening people who despised them. But she was tired of fighting. At least for tonight.

Grateful, for once, to be beneath anyone's notice, she skirted the edge of the room then exited onto the terrace. Orange-gold orbs spangled the darkness beyond, the glow cast by lanterns strung at intervals along the garden paths that wound through Harlestone Hall's grounds. Someone had tipped over one of the potted roses atop the wide stone railing, perhaps in their haste to escape the scene between Nate and Eugenie earlier. It was pure luck the pot hadn't tumbled off and smashed on the ground far below. Christianne felt so uprooted herself she couldn't leave the beleaguered plant to wither.

She righted the pot, scooping up a handful of dirt to cover the bared roots. A lantern dangled from a hook, illuminating the sweep of hill that plummeted beneath the raised terrace. Christianne angled the lantern closer to make sure she'd covered all of the roots when she suddenly heard a low, mournful howl.

Bemused, Christianne unhooked the lantern and lifted it high, seeing a shadowy figure disappear among the trees. One of Nate's dogs? One of the guests? She couldn't tell. But something on the ground below the terrace's rail caught her eye. Great, shimmering wings flowed out from a stemmed center, as if a giant moth had spread itself on the grass below.

Keeping hold of the lantern with one hand, she caught up her skirts with the other then crossed to one of the crescent-shaped staircases that flanked the terrace and descended to the garden. She rushed down the steps, something about the scene below putting her nerves on edge.

A couple, rumpled from love-play, stumbled out of the entry to a labyrinth made of hedgerows. Hiding their faces, they headed for the opposite set of stairs, avoiding Christianne.

Her pulse raced as she made her way toward what she could now see was a woman's blue skirt. Lantern light snagged on burnished gold curls.

"Eugenie?" Christianne called, hastening toward the crumpled figure. Had Nate's wife been so distracted by the fight earlier that she slipped on the stone steps?

Suddenly, a streak of gray bolted from the woods. Nate's favorite deerhound, Caval, raced toward her, massive jaws gaping open, teeth flashing in the lantern light. The dog grasped Christianne's petticoats and tugged, the sound of fabric tearing raking her nerves as he tried to drag her away from the figure on the ground. She stumbled, bumping Eugenie with her foot, a painted fan falling from Eugenie's fingers. Christianne reeled at the realization that Nate's wife would never object to Nate's dog again.

Eugenie Rowland's eyes stared sightless at the night sky, her mouth frozen in a silent scream.

～

CHRISTIANNE PRESSED her hand to her mouth to keep from retching, scarcely aware as Caval bolted back off into the woods. She ran toward the far side of the terrace, the lantern bobbing crazily in her hand. "Wait!" she cried out to the couple mounting the stairs. "Help!"

The lantern's glow struck their faces. Salway Rowland and Deborah Musgrove.

"Christianne?" Salway exclaimed in surprise. Deborah Musgrove's face soured.

"Salway, find Nate!" Christianne pleaded. "Something terrible has happened."

"What is it?"

"Find Nate! *Now!*"

He hesitated for a moment, then hastened into the manor house. Christianne willed Mistress Musgrove to follow him, but the contemptuous woman only stood on the stairs.

"What is this about?" Deborah demanded.

"There has been an accident." Christianne could almost taste Deborah's eagerness for some delicious gossip.

Deb Musgrove started back down the stairs. "What happened? Something with that wicked dog of Harlestone's? I heard it howling!"

"No! Caval only found her after..." Christianne blocked Deborah's path to hide the gruesome sight. The woman might despise Christianne, but she was Eugenie Rowland's best friend.

"After what? Speak clearly, Miss Slade. You are being deliberately vague."

Relief shot through Christianne as she saw Adam and Salway emerge onto the terrace, her brother's towering height and broad shoulders unmistakable. She rose up on tiptoe, straining to see if Nate followed after them, but there was no sign of him.

"Christianne!" Adam called out. "What's amiss? Are you all right?

Deborah Musgrove answered coldly. "I gather that some woman has made a spectacle of herself. Your sister won't speak like a sensible creature and say what has happened. She'd rather get attention by making a scene."

"My sister is the most sensible creature *you'll* ever know," Adam snapped, charging down the steps two at a time.

"Where's Nate?" Christianne asked when he reached her. "We need to find Nate!"

"I don't know where he got off to. I left him in the North Tower an hour ago. Now he's nowhere to be found."

She fought back tears. "Oh, Adam. It's so awful."

At that moment, Caval crashed back onto the scene, a baritone voice calling out a gruff command. Christianne spun around to see a figure limping out of the wooded area from whence the dog had come.

Nate looked as if he'd been wrestling the devil and lost. He wove toward them, even his cane unable to keep him steady on the uneven ground. His long fingers held a silver flask so loosely it seemed in danger of spilling. Perhaps it already had, Christianne thought. The smell of strong spirits emanated from Nate's clothes.

"Adam and Christianne, Salway and Mistress Musgrove," he slurred. "You're the last group I expected to be taking a stroll together in the gardens. What is the fuss about? God save me from another infernal surprise."

"It's Eugenie," Christianne choked out. "I think she fell on the terrace stairs."

Nate blinked in the frail lantern light. "I ordered repairs on that crumbling step a week ago. If I'd known there was going to be a cursed party, I would have had the gardener rope it off." He swore under his breath. "Salway, get some footmen to carry her inside, and Adam, fetch a surgeon and have him bring wraps for a twisted ankle."

"She didn't twist her ankle," Christianne stammered. "It's rather worse."

He frowned. "Where is she? Eugenie?" he grabbed Christianne's lantern, his gaze sweeping the area.

The moment he saw her, his face creased in a mixture of concern and irritation. He crossed to the figure on the ground. His shadow fell over her, his broad shoulders blocking most of the lantern's light. Nate dropped his cane and the lantern on the ground. He fell to his good knee, all but oversetting himself. "Eugenie!" He slapped his wife's cheek gently in an effort to rouse her then shook her arm. "Eugenie, it's Nate."

Christianne swallowed back tears. She touched his shoulder. "She's gone."

"She can't be!" Nate glared up at Christianne, fury and disbelief contorting his haggard features. He sat down, pulled Eugenie onto his lap, cradling her as he raked back her golden curls, his fingers searching to find a pulse in her throat. The blocked light of the lantern spilled past his broad shoulders onto the skin he'd uncovered.

Deborah Musgrove screeched. Christianne gasped in horror. A darkening bruise encircled the white column of Eugenie Rowland's neck.

NATE COULDN'T SQUEEZE air into his lungs, an aura of unreality dragging him deep. Chaos broke over him in a wave as the crowd from the drawing room poured onto the terrace, drawn by Deborah Musgrove's shrieks. Alarmed, Caval lunged between Nate and the crowd, snarling.

Nate stared at the hideous bruise, and tried to wade through the haze of alcohol and shock. Voices blurred as he fought the need to retch. But all he could see was Eugenie's blank eyes staring up at him in silent accusation.

How many times during the misery of the last years had he imagined escaping the coil of his marriage? But not like this. Never like this.

He was vaguely aware of Adam driving everyone

back inside, his gruff voice booming. When quiet fell, Nate sensed his friend beside him.

"Send someone to fetch the magistrate," Nate said. "Jasper Bascombe, on Chandler's Lane."

"I'll see to it myself." Adam dropped down on one knee. His dark eyes met Nate's. "Do you want me to move Eugenie somewhere inside?"

God, yes, Nate thought. Anywhere but here, in the heartless darkness that sheltered whoever killed her. But he shook his head. "Bascombe will want to examine the scene as it is."

"We'll need your footmen to search the area in any case. One can remain here to guard Eugenie. You go wait in your study. It's going to be a long night."

Nate wasn't sure why his arms tightened around Eugenie, but he was suddenly aware of how hauntingly familiar she felt against him. "No. I'll stay with her."

"I'll be back as soon as I can," Adam said then loped off.

As Nate shifted to watch him go, Eugenie's hand slid back toward the turf. He caught her stiffening fingers, gripped by a ridiculous fear that striking the ground might scrape her knuckles. Something sharp stuck his palm, and he was grateful for the physical pain. He looked down to see the broken sticks of a fan dangling from a loop of satin ribbon around her wrist. The wing of the fan had been torn apart during her struggles. Paint flaked off of the fan's ragged edge.

Gently, he slid her hand back so it rested on her stomach. His gut twisted as he thought of the life that had so briefly flickered in her womb. The child would never hold Sera's toy soldier, or sail a kite into a summer sky.

"Eugenie," he whispered. "How the hell did we come to this?"

He heard a faint rustling sound and looked up, expecting to see one of the footmen Adam had deployed. But it was only Christianne, a lone sentinel bathed in shadow and lantern light, watching him with eyes that saw too deeply and lips that asked too much.

CHAPTER 4

Christianne winced as slivers of sunlight pried open eyes gritty from lack of sleep. Her back ached from hours curled up on the window seat outside the suite of rooms that included Nate's study. He'd closed himself inside the chamber while a procession of guests paraded through to reach the adjoining library where they faced questions from Jasper Bascombe, the keen-eyed magistrate Adam had fetched.

Christianne grimaced. From the expressions on the parade of aristocratic faces, one would think Nate had arranged Eugenie's murder specifically to inconvenience them, a game of charades gone wrong. Deborah Musgrove and her set made no secret of the fact that speaking to "a low-born meddler of a magistrate" offended their dignity, whether their friend had been murdered or not.

As for Nate, they regarded him with almost feral suspicion, like wolves circling a wounded stag. Christianne shuddered, burying her fingers in Caval's rough coat, grateful for his sturdy body beside her.

Nate's master of hounds had tried to lead the dog away hours ago, but Caval had looked so mournfully at the door behind which Nate had disappeared that

Christianne couldn't bear to see him exiled. She knew how Caval felt, determined to stand watch outside the dark cave, even though their knight must face his ordeal alone.

Adam had attempted to get Christianne to lock herself in her chamber before he, Salway, and Lord Fendale had gone their separate ways to deal with the practical arrangements that had to be made. There was a murderer on the loose, Adam had warned. But she wouldn't budge. There was a footman posted at the end of the corridor to summon guests to be questioned and escort them back to their rooms once the interview was over. Caval was there to raise the alarm as well, and Nate and Magistrate Bascombe close by, she was safer here than anywhere else at Harlestone.

Christianne wasn't sure if her arguments convinced Adam, or he'd simply known that she was even more stubborn than he was. But in the end, Adam had surrendered the field, leaving Christianne and Caval alone to mark time by the murmurs of guests exiting after their interviews and the rattling sounds from the courtyard below, coaches quitting the scene of the murder.

Were people afraid their own necks were in danger with a maniac on the loose? Christianne wondered. Or were they eager to be the first to spread the sensational news beyond the borders of Harlestone?

Is it true that Lady Harlestone was murdered? She and Lord Harlestone were arguing... Conversations she'd overheard echoed in Christianne's head. There were those among the crowd who had insisted Nate wasn't capable of such a horror. Yet, Lord Fendale himself had said something to Adam that haunted Christianne even more.

Any man has his breaking point.

What was Nate's? Christianne wondered.

Caval raised his massive head and shifted his gaze from the door to her face. He whined so softly no one else might have heard it.

"I know, lad," she said, scratching behind his ear. "Nate has to come out sometime."

The door swung open, revealing the magistrate and Nate. Without thinking, Christianne drew deeper into the shadows. There was always something startling when one first glimpsed Jasper Bascombe. His head was out of proportion to his body, overlarge with busy, pale blue eyes that gazed out at his fellow man with frank cynicism. His sparsely powdered wig sat askew on a broad brow, as if set off-kilter by a prodigious—and somewhat alarming—brain. "I'll have more questions in the future, my lord," Bascombe said in a voice like a rake over gravel. "I want you to know I take no pleasure in interrogating you this way, after what you did for young Deacon Mathers. I've been so heartened by his progress through the Marine Society."

"One situation has nothing to do with the other. You'll do your job and bring the guilty party to justice, whomever it may be. As far as additional questions are concerned, you know where to find me."

"The coroner will arrive soon to examine the body, and there will be an inquest, of course, to determine the cause of death. Someone is responsible for that bruise on your wife's throat. It is to be hoped that the evidence gathered and these testimonies will lead us to whoever it was." Bascombe patted his frock coat, checking to see that the sheaf of notes Christianne had watched him add to during her interview was still protruding from his unadorned pocket.

"Indeed," Nate said.

Bascombe plucked at the plain neckcloth at his throat. "Before I go, allow me to offer my personal condolences one more time. Your wife was an enchanting creature. My job can be rather grim. The sight of her jaunting about in the pony cart with your daughter always cheered me. They reminded me of an image of the Madonna and child I saw as a lad."

Proof that looks can be deceiving, an uncharitable voice muttered in Christianne's head.

"Your little girl will be devastated," Bascombe continued with a shake of his head.

"She will be." The corner of Nate's mouth tightened. "It's been a long night, Mr. Bascombe. The footman will take you to the kitchen for a cup of tea and some breakfast before the coroner arrives. I had the housekeeper prepare a plate for your convenience when she delivered trays to the men you posted to guard Eugenie."

Christianne shuddered, thinking of Nate's wife, still staring sightless at the sky as the magistrate's guards ate the remains of the birthday feast.

Nate took a step forward to signal for the servant who stood at the end of the corridor. But the night had taken its toll on Nate. His bad leg slid out an awkward angle, setting him off balance. As Bascombe's arm shot out to steady him, Caval yanked his collar free of Christianne's grasp and leapt from the window seat, snarling at the magistrate.

Christianne stumbled after the dog on half-numb legs, her fingers scrabbling to regain her hold on his thick leather collar.

"Christianne," Nate said, his cheeks flushing with frustration and embarrassment when he lost his balance. "What are you still doing out here?"

"Miss Slade!" the magistrate exclaimed with a start. "Have you recalled some bit of information you wanted to share?"

"No," she said. Bascombe's gaze intensified, and she

was suddenly aware that her presence might stir more suspicion.

"I'm surprised to see a lone young lady lingering about after the violence that occurred here tonight. I'd have expected you to lock yourself behind your bed-chamber door the moment our interview was over, considering the terrible shock you had."

Her cheeks burned, and she prayed the magistrate wouldn't misconstrue it as guilt. "I was keeping Caval company. He looked so worried."

"I'd say he looks rather more as if he'd like to tear out someone's throat at present. Mistress Musgrove claims the dog might be responsible for Lady Harle-stone's demise."

Christianne stiffened, remembering Deborah Mus-grove's suggestion to another guest that Nate should shoot the deerhound, to be sure it didn't injure someone else. She'd known Nate would never allow such an abomination to occur because of some unfounded accu-sation. And yet, something about the way Bascombe looked at Caval made her leap to the dog's defense.

"Caval didn't do anything! I'm sure of it. He didn't run out of the woods until after I found Eugenie, and then he was completely confused."

"You are able to read the animal's mind then? Con-sidering all that has transpired tonight, I find it rather strange that you'd be so concerned about the beast."

"Nothing strange at all about Miss Slade's concern for Caval," Nate said. "In fact, she makes a habit of wor-rying over *the beast*. She was the one who found him with his foot caught in a snare. Her mother wouldn't let her keep him herself. Dogs make her sister Eliza sneeze."

"You are a very singular young lady," the magistrate said, giving Christianne an appraising look that helped her understand why so many of the guests had chosen to depart in haste. There was something in him that made her think of someone deftly peeling off the petals on a rosebud to see what color the heart of the bud was. "Miss Slade, we will further our acquaintance at the coroner's inquest a few weeks from now. Since you found Lady Harlestone's body, you must suffer the inconvenience of testifying."

She should have suspected as much. But it was still a shock to imagine going before a court of law. "Whatever I can do to be of help."

Thankfully, at that moment, the footman at the far end of the corridor answered Nate's summons. It always gave Christianne a bit of a start when first she saw Vickers. Footmen were supposed to be the handsomest of all household servants, and Vickers would have been exactly that, were it not for the scarring across the left side of his face. Black powder exploding at close range had left its mark while he fought at Prestonpans.

Relief shot through Christianne as Vickers led the magistrate away. She tried to ignore the fact that Bascombe turned back to look at her just before he turned the corner and disappeared.

She suppressed a shiver as Nate faced her. It hurt to see how exhausted he was. Lines carved deep at the sides of his mouth and corners of his eyes, a stubble of beard dusting his square jaw.

"I appreciate your waiting with Caval," he said, "but you should be in bed. You must be as exhausted as I am."

"I couldn't sleep. I kept thinking of all you have yet to do."

Nate rubbed the back of his neck. Christianne wished she could knead the knots out of it. "Death will have its due," Nate said. "I've got a list of necessary arrangements that could stretch from here to Brighton."

"You shouldn't have to face it all alone. I'm glad Adam could help. I thought perhaps, I might help as well. I could go with you to tell Seraphina about her mother."

Nate stiffened. "That is not necessary. I know you mean to be kind, but—"

"Please, Nate. Let me go with you. I can't bear the thought of you going to face your little girl's grief alone."

"You've barely met the child. I can't see how your presence would help."

"With all my sisters and nieces to tend, I've become good at soothing tears."

"Telling people their loved one is dead is rather different than tending a scraped knee. In my years as an officer, I got plenty of practice in shattering people's worlds with the worst possible news." The edge to his voice startled her. It was something akin to scorn. She'd experienced it before, even from Adam and the other Knights, when they thought she was intruding. But from Nate? Never. It was a sign of how much he was hurting.

"I won't say anything, if you don't want me to. Just let me be there, in case…"

"In case what? The roof collapses? The sky falls down? Because that's what is going to happen. Everything Seraphina has known and depended on is gone forever. There's not a damned thing you or I can do about it. But at least I have the sense to know it. As for you staying up all night in some misguided desire to help, your sacrifice was for naught. Seraphina is partway to Eugenie's sister's in Kent by now."

Christianne's brow furrowed. "What?"

"I informed her nurse that they were to leave immediately."

"But you didn't leave the study all night."

"I sent a note."

"A *note*?" Christianne took a step back, stunned. "You didn't even speak to her? You're her father. She needs you."

"Don't meddle in lives you know nothing about. She's gone. There's an end to it. The nurse will see to her."

She gaped in disbelief. How could Nate be so cold? "Seraphina is a six-year-old little girl who lost her mother! A mother she loved! Anyone with eyes could see that tonight."

"That's enough." His eyes narrowed in warning, but she couldn't stop herself.

"Eugenie spoke about how little interest you showed in Seraphina, but I couldn't believe it was as bad as she claimed."

"Plenty of noblemen spare little time for their children. Daughters, in particular, are left to a nurse's care."

He might as well have slapped Christianne. It was true that girls were often regarded as unimportant. A bargaining chip to wager in marriage alliances. A drain on the family income when it came to dowries.

"I'd never have believed you'd scorn Seraphina because she's a girl. If the child Eugenie was carrying was a boy would *he* have been worth your notice?"

Nate raised his hand, lips parting as if to speak, then his jaw clenched. "I'm done discussing this with you."

"I don't understand! Why would you abandon your own child?"

"For God's sake. My wife is dead, murdered under my own roof. I don't owe you—or anyone—an explanation about anything. The girl is gone from Harlestone, much to her relief as well as my own."

"This is unforgivable, Nate. Flinging her in a coach at night, casting her off."

"I will have another conveyance ready as soon as you pack so you'll not have to endure any more of my objectionable behavior."

She stared at him, tears pricking the backs of her eyes.

"What is it?" Nate demanded. "Say it, whatever is boiling up inside you. You know you could never resist speaking your mind."

This rift between them was tearing away something so precious she felt her heart would break. "You were always my hero. But after this heartless act...sending Seraphina away without so much as a word..." Her voice cracked. "You're not the man I thought you were."

"I never was," he said, his moss-green eyes a wasteland as he turned and walked away.

$\mathscr{N}$ate had attended his share of legal hearings at King's Cross Inn in the years since he'd become Viscount Harlestone. He'd helped mediate disputes over land, petty issues of the shire, and such, but this was different: Today was the coroner's inquest into the murder of his wife.

He adjusted his frock coat, his clothing as grim as his mood. The garments had been sewn when he'd gone into mourning after his mother's death fourteen months ago. Everything from his stockings to his waistcoat was unrelenting black. Even the frill that spilled from his cuffs was black, its hem brushing the mourning ring that glinted on his finger, a gift from his father. On it, words were engraved on a banner across the Rowland Family crest: *Prepare to follow me.*

When they had laid Nate's mother in the family crypt, who could have imagined Eugenie would soon do just that?

Now he wondered if the words were a subtle warning to make him aware of just how precarious his own situation could be.

Everyone in town had gathered for today's spectacle. Villagers determined to get a good seat for the sensational proceedings jostled with the servants of the Quality who were clearing the way for their masters and mistresses. Elegant bonnets from the finest milliners towered over ragged caps of cloth and braided straw from the country. Speculation ran rampant as to whether there would be an arrest at the end of the testimony. Nate couldn't blame people for hoping there would be some resolution.

God knew Nate himself would feel better knowing how this tragedy had happened. *And why.* That was the question he'd been asking during the past weeks as he busied himself with the ceremonies of death, reclaiming his wife's body from the coroner, and escorting her to her final resting place. As he'd walked in Eugenie's funeral procession, he'd been grateful for the ache in his leg, grateful to feel anything that distracted him from the image that haunted his nightmares, the delicate throat he'd once kissed with a green youth's passion encircled by an ugly bruise, Eugenie's eyes staring through him.

He shoved the memories away as he entered the room where the inquest was being held. It had been lined with chairs and makeshift benches, some from the inn, others doubtless gathered from surrounding homes and businesses in anticipation of a crowd. His father glowered from his vantage point at the north end of the chamber, Salway at his side. It had always bewildered Nate that Salway continued to shadow his father, despite the earl's obvious dislike of his dead brother's son. That animus had been even more strained the past weeks. Doubtless both men were still irritated that Nate had quashed their plan to arrive at the inquest together to provide a united front. But he couldn't bear another minute spent arguing strategy for the testimony Nate was going to have to give. He thought he'd choke if one more person warned him about the dire consequences that could result if he handled his time before the judge in a clumsy fashion.

He looked beyond his father's shoulders and saw more welcome arrivals. Adam towered above the crowd looking like a dragon guarding his horde. Beside him stood Gavin Carstares, Earl of Glenlyon, his golden hair shining, his face windburned from recent travel. Between the brothers stood the treasure they were so intent on protecting. Christianne was garbed in sober petticoats of mist gray that swept back to reveal a midnight blue underskirt. Her hair had been wrestled into submission and pinned into place with small pearls. His heart jarred at seeing her again after their contretemps over Sera. He thought of the moment he'd left the study, his astonishment at finding her there. He'd wanted to step into her arms, feel her, alive, warm. That sudden fierce need had jolted him. She'd never known what that moment meant to him. But what had it cost her?

She looked thinner than Nate remembered, the delicate bones in her face more evident, her eyes smudged with shadows. No wonder, Nate thought. Their fight about Sera had left its mark. Between that and finding Eugenie's body, Christianne's world would never feel as safe again. To make matters worse, she was going to have to recount the horror of that night before this avid crowd, questioned by men eager to trip her up, knowing that any mistake could be dangerous.

Nate felt his own protective instincts rise. The coroner would have to be circumspect in questioning him, a nobleman. However, a woman born out of wedlock would not receive the same courtesy, even with her brother, the earl, looking on.

Ignoring others who were trying to capture his attention, Nate wove through the crowd toward where his friends stood. But the instant Christianne's eyes met his, he wished he had stayed away. As long as Nate could remember, there had always been a special spark in her eyes just for him. Eagerness to share adventures. Silences that neither of them had had to fill. Oh, he'd disappointed her, made her angry in the past, yet even during the difficult years after his marriage, he'd seen her face light up when their eyes first met. Today her eyes were dull as she looked past him, avoiding his glance altogether.

"Adam. Christianne," he said with a nod of greeting. "I'd say that it's good to see you, but not under these circumstances. Gavin, thank you for coming."

"I wasn't about to let the three of you face this inquest without me," Gavin said, his expression grave. "I only wish I'd returned early enough to be of more use. If I'd been at the fete, I could testify and help put this investigation to rest. At any rate, it will be over soon, though I fear that Eugenie's death will remain as much a mystery as it ever was."

Nate turned to Christianne. "I would spare you this trial if it were in my power."

"It's an ordeal for all of us, but the adults of the party will just have to cope. Children are a different matter." Those dark eyes pierced him. "How is your daughter, Nate?"

He heard Adam's low growl and Gavin's quick intake of breath.

Nate felt a stab of guilt that hardened into defensiveness. "You would have to address your inquiries to Seraphina's aunt," Nate said coldly. He turned to Gavin. "Christianne disagreed with my handling of the situation after Eugenie's murder. As usual, she is convinced that she knows best."

"Well, it's a damned poor subject to be bringing up in the middle of a courtroom," Adam blustered.

"Isn't the prospect before Nate stressful enough

without bringing a grieving child to mind to distract him?" Gavin chided Christianne. "Nate is innocent, and he will need all his wits about him."

A sudden commotion occurred as a side door to the chamber opened and the coroner walked in, flanked by magistrates Jasper Bascombe and Addison Payne. Martin Stanhope had been the coroner in the area for a mere four years. An ambitious lawyer of some note, he had such a rigid opinion of right and wrong Nate was certain he could drop a child into Hell for stealing bread, then dump half of his own supper in the rubbish heap without a qualm.

Stanhope's milky blue eyes looked at Gavin Carstares from beneath bristly brows, and his mouth tightened like a purse string. It might have been in re-action to the policies Gavin had put forth in Parliament, or the fact that their Marine Society Charity had plucked boys out of the court system where they would have been sent on convict ships to the colonies. But Nate thought it more likely that Stanhope still saw Gavin as a traitor for serving in Charles Stuart's army, despite the royal pardon Nate had managed to secure for both of his friends.

The officiating members of the judiciary mounted the raised platform at the far end of the room. Three heavily carved chairs from the era of Charles II were arranged in an imposing row, while a line of seats for the jury was ranged off to one side where they would be able to observe the witnesses and judge their veracity.

Nate watched the jurors file in, all landholders in the area surrounding Harlestone. Most looked uncomfortable garbed in their finest clothes, but determined to do their duty. A few had a more worrisome expression, men he'd had disputes in the past regarding lands or livestock or hunting rights. Three of them had been besotted with Eugenie from afar, though Nate could hardly blame them. He'd lost his head over her himself.

Let's hope you don't lose a whole lot more upon a gallows, a voice whispered in his head. *An inquest can give way to a murder trial between one heartbeat and the next.*

It was his father who had put that warning there, entreating him to remember that innocent men had gone to the gallows before and would face the hangman's noose again. There was evidence enough of discord between Nate and Eugenie to make people wonder.

Nate made a quick bow to Adam, Gavin and Christianne then crossed to his seat in the front row of chairs where his father and Salway were already settling in for the day.

The formalities of opening the inquest were disposed of. Stanhope called witnesses who described the events of the night. Nate steeled himself as memories were raked open like a wound. Adam's testimony came first, delivered with a soldier's straightforwardness. But it was easy to see what Stanhope hoped to achieve. Adam had followed Nate to the North Tower, but Nate had sent him away. No one was with Nate for at least an hour before Eugenie's body was discovered.

Salway gave his version of the incident, earnest and eager to please. He'd taken his friend, Mistress Musgrove, walking in the garden to get some air. They'd seen nothing untoward until Miss Christianne Slade had sounded the alarm. Nate could almost pity his cousin as Salway looked from his uncle the earl, to the magistrate, to the coroner to Nate, unsure which figure of authority he should gratify today.

Next, Deborah Musgrove swept up to the stand, waving her fan under her nose as if the mere idea that a man of Stanhope's stature would question her, released an offensive odor. Nate braced himself for her testimony as she shook out crimson skirts and smoothed her black under petticoat as she faced the onlookers. Rubies winked around her wrists and neck and dangled from her ears. As Stanhope administered the oath, she spoke in arctic accents, regarding the coroner as if half-daring him to do his job.

"Mistress Musgrove, can you describe your relationship to the deceased?" Stanhope asked.

"Lady Harlestone is my dearest friend, and has been since we attended Miss Pepperton's Academy for Young Ladies." She suddenly faltered, a crack in that pretentious façade. "No, she *was* my dearest friend. I still cannot believe she is gone."

"To lose a friend of such long-standing must be devastating," Stanhope commiserated. "I will make my questions as brief as possible to spare you more pain. Regarding the night you last saw Lady Harlestone, can you give us your impression of what type of misfortune befell her?"

"Some vile beast had strangled her."

"Beast?" Stanhope raised a brow. "By that you mean an animal or a person?"

"At first I thought it might have been Lord Harlestone's abominable hound. It's a miracle that animal hasn't devoured a village child! It's huge and so fierce!"

Nate heard Christianne's muffled protest, saw Gavin curve his hand over her arm.

"I've heard reports that...what was the beast's name?" Stanhope paused and stroked his chin.

"Caval." Nate heard Christianne mutter at almost the same moment Stanhope appeared to recall the name.

"Ah, yes, Caval. Caval was quite agitated the night of Lady Harlestone's death."

"Yes. But on further consideration, I don't believe the dog attacked her. Someone murdered her."

"There can be no other interpretation, in your opinion?"

"What other opinion could there be? Eugenie's throat was a mass of bruises." Deborah pressed a hand to her neck, jarring the necklace of rubies that reminded Nate all too closely of the marks that had darkened Eugenie's skin. "She was murdered, my beautiful Eugenie! I blame myself! I can't help thinking that if we had traveled to London as Eugenie wished to, she would still be alive!"

"Lady Harlestone wished to travel to London?"

"Yes. We traveled a great deal together. Her husband had little taste for society. Her only choice was to remain isolated in the country with him or seek some measure of pleasant pastimes with her friends."

"Can you think of a reason that anyone would wish to harm your friend?"

"No! She was the belle of every assembly we attended. The moment she walked into a room everyone was enchanted by her beauty and her wit. I never met anyone who didn't love her, except, perhaps, her husband." Deborah glared at Nate, and he felt the eyes of the spectators follow her gaze, people whispering among themselves.

Nate sensed Deborah was teetering on the edge, hating him so much she'd revel in announcing he'd been cuckolded, yet wanting to protect Eugenie's reputation.

Deborah Musgrove leaned forward. "Mr. Stanhope, you *will* pursue this investigation, will you not? You will find whomever murdered poor Eugenie? She was no harm to anyone, merely a beautiful butterfly who brought charm to any life she touched."

"We must see where the inquest leads. But your concern for your friend touches me deeply. She was fortunate to have such a fond companion."

"Yes, well, she needed *someone* to lavish her affection on! She had her darling little daughter, but that was hardly enough when her husband was so cold. Even the night of the birthday fete he was intolerable. She had worked so hard to plan it for him, and he did nothing but scowl from the edge of the drawing room and make things unpleasant."

"Your observations are duly noted. You may step down."

She cast Nate a fulminating glare, but tension eased from Nate's shoulders as she returned to her seat. When Nate's turn to testify came, he mounted the dais, keeping his hands relaxed at his sides. Stanhope produced a Bible and Nate placed his palm upon it.

"Do you swear to tell the truth, the whole truth and nothing but the truth, so help you God?"

"I do," Nate answered. Yet, in that instant, images flashed through his mind. Ugly truths, damaging and shameful. Truths filled with destruction.

"Lord Harlestone, first allow me to extend my sympathies on the loss of Lady Harlestone. It must be a terrible blow to lose your wife under such tragic circumstances. Can you describe events leading up to the discovery of your wife's body?"

He'd rehearsed it a dozen times in the three weeks leading up to the inquest. His father had insisted that he not offer any more information than necessary. Saying too much could trip one up in a court's dealings. Nate looked at the jurors and answered as succinctly as possible.

"Dredging up the memories of that night cannot be pleasant," Stanhope pretended to commiserate.

"No. Recounting events that lead to a death are always painful."

"Indeed. I assume that you have done so often enough during your years as an officer in the King's

10th Dragoons. You've witnessed a great deal of death done by violence."

"Yes." He recalled the acrid taste gunpowder, the metallic stench of blood, bodies broken on a Scottish moor, including his own.

"Perhaps you could use your expertise to give us a precise description of the situation you found your wife in," the coroner said.

Nate's gut tightened as the nightmarish scene played out in his head. He could sense the breeze that had ruffled Eugenie's skirts, feel the broken sticks of her fan piercing his palm, hear Christianne's voice shaking. *She's gone.*

"I had been walking in the woods with my dog when I heard a disturbance. I found my cousin, Salway Rowland, Mrs. Deborah Musgrove, Adam Slade and his sister, Miss Christianne Slade clustered around my wife who was lying on the ground."

"What is your understanding as to how they had come to be there?"

"Miss Slade had gone onto the terrace to escape the crush in the drawing room. She saw something suspicious on the ground below and went to explore."

"Alone? Surely she wasn't wandering about without an escort of some kind?"

"It is my understanding that she was alone."

Stanhope frowned, and Nate heard murmurs ripple through the crowd. "Would it not have been wiser for her to summon a gentleman to investigate?"

Who would she have asked for help? Nate thought bitterly. He and Adam had deserted her in that drawing room full of people who held her in contempt.

"I hardly think Miss Slade was expecting to discover a dead body," he said, glancing at Christianne's pale face. "She thought someone had fallen and went to offer help. When I saw the situation, I didn't believe it could be dire, either. I thought Eugenie had tripped, maybe struck her head. Miss Slade tried to tell me my wife was dead, but I had been drinking rather heavily. I felt for my wife's pulse, but there was none. That was when I saw a bruise encircling her throat."

"Are there no accidents that could have caused the injuries you witnessed?"

"I cannot think of any. The bruises were very dark, and even in the lantern light it was obvious she'd been strangled. The marks had been made by a large hand."

"A man's hand, would you surmise?"

"I know of no woman who could exert such force."

"I agree. Judging from the angle, the depth of the bruises and so forth, I would say that the marks were the work of a man approximately six feet three inches tall."

"That seems a reasonable estimate."

Stanhope started to walk away, then turned back. "I do have a few more questions before you step down, if you are amenable. I know this must be an ordeal, your lordship."

"I will do whatever is necessary to bring Eugenie's murderer to justice."

"I am glad to hear that we are of one mind on that subject. Is it true that Lady Harlestone has been interred in Kent instead of in the Rowland family crypt?"

Nate willed himself not to stiffen, sensing that Stanhope was leading him onto precarious ground. "Yes."

"I own I am surprised. Is it not customary for a wife to be buried beside her husband?"

"I am not dead yet, so it would prove difficult to inter anyone beside me at present."

He heard a smattering of stifled laughter about the room and some grunts of disapproval. He would have to tread more carefully.

Stanhope's mouth puckered in a sour smile. "Interred in the family crypt, then, in advance of your death, which, all would hope, will not occur for a long time."

"My wife's sister, Philomena Kettering, asked that Lady Harlestone be buried beside their parents. I thought Eugenie would like that. She was very close to her father before he died."

The coroner feigned surprise. "Surely not closer than she was to her own husband?"

"It was a far different bond, and one of longer standing."

"It's not as if you were newlyweds. You'd been married for eleven years, had you not?"

"Yes."

"Was yours a happy marriage, Lord Harlestone?"

Nate had known the question was coming. It would only stir suspicion to hedge his answer. "It was happy at first. It became complicated."

One of Stanhope's bushy eyebrows shot up. "Complicated?"

"I lost my leg at Culloden Moor. It was a source of distress for Lady Harlestone."

"As it would be for any woman who loved you. Can you clarify what you mean by 'distress'?"

Nate steeled himself to answer. "She found the sight of my leg difficult to bear."

"A distressing circumstance for any man's pride. Mistress Musgrove has mentioned an unfortunate distance between you and your wife as well. That you stood off to the side during the birthday fete, and did not join in the merriment."

Nate raised one brow. "They were dancing, Mr. Stanhope. Not a pastime one such as myself can indulge in."

"I suppose not. Yet, you are a hero. You are to be

67

commended for your sacrifice for king and country. Despite Lady Harlestone's reticence about your wound, you had a daughter. According to witnesses who attended the birthday fete at which Lady Harlestone's body was found, you were to have another child come spring. She announced it before the company, is that correct?"

"It is." Nate could hear the edge in his own voice, hoped that the jury would attribute it to natural distress over the murder of his wife and child.

"I'm sure the loss of a possible heir adds weight to your grief," Stanhope said. "Where is your daughter now, Lord Harlestone?"

"With her aunt. She's spent a great deal of time in her household."

"Even before your wife's unfortunate demise?"

"Eugenie was much attached to her sister, and there were cousins for Seraphina to play with."

"I see. As an only child yourself, you are familiar with the pain loneliness inspires. I believe your own cousin, Mr. Salway Rowland, spent much time at Harlestone Hall as your boyhood companion. He is currently your heir?"

"He is." Nate looked at Salway, the expression on his cousin's face full of encouragement.

"I think that is all for now." Stanhope paced away, then suddenly stopped and turned back to look at Nate, brows raised as if he'd just thought of something pertinent. "How tall are you, Lord Harlestone?" the coroner asked.

"Six feet three inches."

"The height of your wife's murderer."

Nate felt the back of his neck prickle. "I would imagine other guests at Harlestone Hall that night are of a similar height."

"Very likely, as you say. However, they did not argue

with Lady Harlestone before a room filled with people. The night of the birthday fete, did you say that, come morning, you planned to be every bit the villain Eugenie and her friends believed you to be?"

Nate barely heard the gasps from the spectators as he fought not to show how badly Stanhope's words had stunned him. How had anyone heard the conversation he'd had with Adam? Who had informed the coroner?

Stanhope gave him a smug smile. "I could call Mr. Slade back to the stand again to confirm, but perhaps that is not necessary if you would be willing to clarify. Did you indeed say those words?"

"I said something to that effect to Adam Slade in a private conversation."

"Exactly what did you mean by it?"

"I had decided to ask my wife for a divorce."

Stanhope's eyes widened with feigned shock. "On the night she told you she might be carrying your heir?"

Nate hesitated just a moment too long. "Yes."

"It seems an extreme step. Countless people live separate lives without requesting a divorce from Parliament. Why were you were taking such drastic measures?"

"To release Eugenie and me from this coil we were trapped in. We were unhappy. Eugenie deserved something better and so did I."

Stanhope cocked his head to one side, triumph in his eyes. "You're not trapped now, Lord Harlestone. In fact, you are quite free. I have no more questions. You may stand down."

A murmur rippled from the crowd, suspicion darkening a number of faces. Nate knew that many of them were weighing his words and Deborah Musgrove's assertions. There were no other suspects, no other motive for the murder that they could see. Only an unhappy wife and a husband whose injury had left him frustrated, angry, unable to join in the kind of merriment a vital young woman would crave. Nate rose to leave the dais, determined to have the last word.

"My wife and I argued," Nate said firmly. "We were unsuited to each other but I did not want my wife dead."

"So you say, Lord Harlestone."

Nate stepped down, jaw clenched. He saw Christianne watching him, her face even paler, her eyes dark with worry.

Stanhope crossed to a small table with an ewer and glasses arranged on it. He poured himself wine and drank it, then cleared his throat and turned back to the assembly. His eyes glittered with anticipation, his mouth predatory and cold.

"Miss Christianne Slade, step forward, please," he said.

CHAPTER 6

*C*hristianne rose from her seat like a queen. Of course, she must be shaken after watching his testimony. Nate saw Gavin squeeze her hand, could tell that his friend had prepared her as best as he could for what she would face. Yet, worry lines deepened at the corners of Gavin's eyes, as if he could sense the recklessness in her.

Christianne squared her shoulders as she approached Stanhope. Nate knew she must feel the weight of everyone's gaze upon her. He tensed as someone behind him murmured, "That's a high-stepping filly if I ever saw one. I'd pay a fortune for her at The Blue Peacock."

"Might have been able to if it weren't for her brother. The Earl of Glenlyon wouldn't let his half-sister pursue such a course, even though her mother was a demimondaine."

Nate leveled the pair of dandies with a glare, but they were already silenced by Adam's fearsome expression. Red-faced, they ducked behind gilt quizzing glasses as Stanhope administered the oath.

Nate could see Christianne's quickened breath in the rise and fall of her breasts. Her cheeks flushed with

71

passionate defensiveness. The dandies' words might have made him want to knock the lascivious expressions off of their faces, but he couldn't deny that Christianne had become a beautiful woman, made even more striking by the emotion on her face. At twenty-five she had shed the last vestiges of the little girl who had trailed after him, becoming beautiful in a way he'd not allowed himself to recognize until now.

Stanhope began his interrogation with the easy questions, the location of Eugenie's body, how Christianne had discovered it. But when he asked about Nate's state of mind the night of the fete, Nate could almost hear the reins of control on her temper snap.

"If you are inferring that Lord Harlestone had anything to do with Eugenie's death, you're wrong," she insisted. "He would never lift his hand to a woman, no matter how angry he was."

"And he was very angry, according to reports," Stanhope said, eyes narrowing.

"He was exhausted. He'd been on his feet all day, and his leg was obviously paining him."

"In your opinion."

"He was using his cane, something he never does unless forced to. Also, he'd been imbibing strong spirits, I think to deaden the pain."

Nate's gut tightened, and he felt as if he'd been dueling and some opponent had stripped him of his sword.

"Would not such a condition make it *more* likely that he could lose control?" Stanhope pressed her. "He would not be the first man to attack his wife in a drunken rage."

Nate dug his fingers into his thigh, feeling the people in the room casting measuring glances his way.

"There are men who would do so," Christianne allowed, "but not Lord Harlestone."

"Some have mentioned that you and Lady Harlestone were not the best of friends."

"Our social stations were far different."

"She was a lady of Quality and you are..." He paused with a faux delicacy that set Nate's teeth on edge. "Can you enlighten us as to the circumstances of your birth?"

Nate heard a low curse from Adam, sensed Gavin's anger and knew there was nothing any of them could do to shield her.

Christianne's chin bumped up a notch. "My parents never married."

It was hardly a shocking announcement. The scandalous affair between the old Earl of Glenlyon and his beautiful mistress was widely known. Nate suppressed the urge to grab Stanhope by his neckcloth and say he saw right through his actions. Stanhope was a small-minded tyrant seizing a chance to strike out at Gavin Carstares by humiliating his sister.

"Miss Slade, can you tell us what drew you out onto the terrace that night? Alone, no less," Stanhope continued. "Did you hear a cry? Perhaps Lady Harlestone raising an alarm?"

"I heard nothing out of the ordinary. As others have testified, Lord and Lady Harlestone had been quarreling. Lord Harlestone then left the drawing room and my brother went after him. I was not widely welcomed by the other guests, so I ducked into a curtained alcove. After a time, I grew restless and decided to seek out Lord Harlestone's deerhound, who would no more bite a village child than he would sprout wings." She shot Deborah Musgrove a bitter glare.

"So you exited onto the terrace unescorted? Perhaps the other women had reason to find you not up to their standards of proper behavior."

Christianne tossed a curl over her shoulder. "With

their gossiping and petty nonsense, they're not up to *my* standards either."

Christianne the Brave, Nate thought, his heart warming as the common folk in the crowd laughed, and one or two actually dared applaud. He wished he could join them.

The frown lines bracketing the coroner's mouth deepened. "Miss Slade, can you imagine any reason why Lady Harlestone would not cry out when someone assaulted her?"

Christianne tipped her head to one side, considering. "Perhaps the attacker leapt out from behind."

"Evidence shows that Lady Harlestone was strangled from the front. I would propose another reason she did not scream."

"You are the expert in these matters," Christianne said. "What reason would you suggest?"

"She knew her attacker." He looked directly at Nate. Beyond Stanhope's shoulder, Nate could see Christianne swallow hard. Then her eyes blazed, even more defiant.

"The drawing room was full of people and Lady Harlestone knew them all," she said.

"But Lord Harlestone was the only one she was seen arguing with."

"You have no right making such accusations when you have no proof, nor ever will!" Christianne burst out, indignant.

"It's a matter of logic," Stanhope said. "I imagine I will find a judge to agree with my assessment and pursue the case."

"Even if Nate wanted to do this horrible thing he could not have done so."

"I fail to see a reason why. He towered over Lady Harlestone in height, and had experience in combat. A

74

former officer in the dragoons could easily overpower a startled woman."

"Not if he could barely stand." Christianne glanced over at Nate.

Nate went rigid. He mouthed the word *don't*. Regret filled her eyes, but she plunged on.

"When Lord Harlestone is overly tired, he loses his balance. As the night of the fete wore on, even the cane wasn't keeping him stable."

He felt stripped naked before the crowd, and the fact that Christianne was exposing his challenges made it even more painful.

"There is no way he could have choked Eugenie and stayed on his feet while she struggled," she insisted. "They would have fallen. Their clothes would have been grass-stained. The shrubs around them would have been crushed. She always pushed him beyond endurance! But even if he *had* wanted to throttle her, rational thought proves that it would be impossible."

"Impossible? Or improbable?"

"Impossible!" The word rang out through the chamber, in exactly the tone Nate sensed Stanhope would never tolerate in any woman, especially one of Christianne's background.

Stanhope's nostrils flared. "You sound peculiarly passionate about Lord Harlestone's defense. Is there something about your relationship that you would like to share that might enlighten us as to why? Considering your questionable breeding such information might also give us insight as to why you and Lady Harlestone were not on the best terms."

The blackguard was all but calling Christianne a harlot. The expression on her face tore at Nate. Outrage, but no surprise.

"Nate is my friend," she said with such dignity Nate's

throat ached. "If you're implying anything more you are greatly mistaken. I've known him since childhood and his kindness and sense of honor have never failed. I would stake my life that he did not murder Eugenie, though some of us wished we could shake her until her teeth rattled."

"You are speaking of the dead, Miss Slade. An innocent woman."

"I'm speaking of an *innocent man!*" Her hands curled into fists. "Nate Rowland had nothing to do with her death, and you and Mistress Musgrove are acting as if he did. You're grasping at nothing to try to make it seem as if you have solved a crime when you haven't!"

Nate wished he could clap his hand over her mouth as he had when she was ten and a crowd of apprentices had been tormenting a cat. She'd rushed in, practically hissing and spitting herself. Even after they'd set the poor abused creature free she'd had her claws at the ready. Since muffling her outburst was impossible, he broke protocol and spoke out instead. "Christianne, this isn't necessary. It's an inquest to determine cause of death. It's not a trial."

"You're out of order, Lord Harlestone," Jasper Bascombe said. "You are also correct. This is an inquest not a trial. Mr. Stanhope, do you have any more questions that will make the cause of Lady Harlestone's death clearer to the court?"

Stanhope's face crumpled in displeasure. "No, sir, but—"

"In that case," Bascombe cut in, "Miss Slade, you may step down."

Christianne opened her mouth, as eager to say more as Stanhope was to continue questioning her. Nate shook his head in silent plea, Bascombe leveling her a quelling glance.

"That is all, Miss Slade," he said.

Nate saw her bite her lip. Her hands trembled with

the effort it took to remain quiet. After a moment she rose and crossed to where her brothers were waiting.

Bascombe cleared his throat. "I do not believe any more testimony is needed for the court to make a decision." He turned to the disgruntled coroner. "Mr. Stanhope, can you remind those gathered here what the purpose of this inquest is?"

"To determine the cause of Lady Harlestone's death. Natural causes, a misadventure or murder."

"I think we can all agree on that at least. The jury will convene to reach their decision."

It seemed as if the jurors had barely filed out of the room before they came back in. But then, Nate thought, the verdict was never in question.

Bascombe called the proceedings to order. A portly squire spoke. "We, the jury, find that Eugenie Rowland, Lady Harlestone, was murdered," he said.

Bascombe nodded. "The court hereby rules that Eugenie Rowland, Lady Harlestone was murdered in the garden at Harlestone Hall on the fifth of April." He turned to the coroner. "Is there any solid evidence that would lead to an arrest in this case, Mr. Stanhope?"

Stanhope scowled Nate's way. "Not at this time, sir, but I trust there will be."

Bascombe arched a brow. "Isn't that what we all desire? In fact, is not Lord Harlestone financing the investigation?"

Stanhope's mouth curled, cynical. "I would argue that does not prove innocence."

"Nor does it prove guilt," Bascombe warned. "Have a care, Stanhope. It is a dangerous business throwing out baseless suspicions. May the courts grant Lady Harlestone justice, and may God have mercy on her soul."

Everyone stood as the magistrates swept from the room.

Nate wanted to shake free of his father and Salway and cross the room to where Christianne stood, defiant yet obviously still shaken. But as soon as the officers of the court exited, his father touched his arm. "You are paying for an investigation into Eugenie's death? You did not tell me."

"It's customary if one wishes an issue to be pursued. I've hired Callum MacGregor." Nate twisted the mourning ring on his finger.

"A Scotsman?" his father asked, surprised.

"I knew him when I was in the army. He will leave no clue unexplored."

"Many of these cases go unsolved." Salway frowned. "If Eugenie's murderer is not found, we know who the public will judge guilty." He gestured to the crowd that was casting suspicious glances Nate's way. "I'd hate for you to have to live under that dark cloud, cousin."

Nate's jaw clenched at the prospect of being singled out as the man who likely murdered his wife and got away with it.

"Nate is descended from the most noble bloodlines in England," his father snarled. "His life has been exemplary as an officer and a nobleman known for his sense of honor and duty. There must be some real taint of the unsavory for such a rumor to stick to a man. I defy anyone to find such a mark on my son."

The earl reached into his waistcoat pocket and withdrew his snuffbox, taking a pinch to calm himself. He sneezed into his handkerchief, and Nate noticed the forget-me-nots on the bit of fine linen. The tiny blue flowers formed the initials AR for Augusta Rowland. How many times had he seen such handkerchiefs tucked in his mother's hand? There were many who would call the Earl of Fendale a hard man. They had never seen him in private moments with his wife. Nate had imagined his own marriage would follow along the same path. But he'd not be carrying any token from his dead wife. He'd already ordered all of Eugenie's things packed away. He would have given them away were it not for Seraphina.

His mother's room was still exactly as she'd left it. It was likely to remain so until his father died.

"Excuse me," Nate said. "I wish to speak to Gavin and the Slades before they leave."

"Doubtless Glenlyon has a more useful perspective on matters than I do," his father said dryly.

"He's had greater experience in the legal system, Uncle." Salway pointed out. "Though you were the force behind winning his pardon."

It was true, Nate thought. His father had moved heaven and earth to help in Nate's quest to get Gavin back on English shores and the Glenlyon estates returned. But then, the old man had found Nate in the garden, a loaded pistol in his lap. Winning the pardon had given Nate something to fight for, to distract him from the disaster his life had become.

Nate wound through the crowd toward where his three friends stood. Christianne saw him first and took an instinctive step back. He struggled to stand even straighter, mortified that her defense of him had portrayed him in his physical infirmity. Yet, she'd been humiliated in this courtroom as well, the shame of her birth laid bare.

"Well, that was even worse than I thought it was going to be," Adam said when Nate reached them. "And I had it figured for a forced-march-in-bare-feet-in-an-ice-storm miserable. At least Bascombe put Stanhope in his place."

"Not nearly as soon as he should have," Gavin said, looking so solemn that it unnerved Nate. "Fortunately, Christianne's testimony turned the tide."

The words were like acid poured on raw skin. "The

tide of what?" Nate demanded in a tone that made Gavin start. "Deciding whether Eugenie was murdered or not? I wasn't on trial, a fact which some seem to forget."

"Because of Christianne's testimony, you never will be," Adam said.

"I wouldn't have been anyway," Nate snapped. "I didn't kill her. The investigator I hired will find whoever did. Whether or not small-minded fools at the Tidmouth Inn convict me over their flagon of ale is of no concern to me. However, the image Christianne painted of me is—"

"Nate, I was only saying that on the night of the fete—"

"I was too lame to murder my wife. I was also too drunk to protect her. You made it clear what you think of me."

"That's not fair," Christianne said. "Stanhope was trying to convict you in the minds of everyone in this room."

"Did you ever think that I might prefer that over hearing you describe me the way you did?" Nate said, low. She'd spoken the truth, but from Christianne's lips it raked something deeper than mere pride.

"That's *not* the way I see you. You had one awful night. Eugenie made it so. It's no wonder you—"

"Don't you know that you put yourself in the middle of the crossfire interfering when you had no call to? All you had to do was answer the questions as briefly as possible. I'm sure Gavin told you that."

Gavin put his arm around his sister. "What's done is done," he said. "Even though I might have advised her to do things differently but she did pull you off of Stanhope's pyre."

"I don't need saving, damn it," Nate said, low. "But Eugenie did. A man is supposed to protect his wife. But

I was too drunk, too goddamned lame to do it. I've known that from the moment I saw Eugenie dead on Harlestone's lawn. Thanks to Christianne, the whole county knows it, too."

"I did what I had to, and I'm not sorry," she said.

"I am." The pit of his stomach burned with humiliation. Yes, she'd convinced the jury he couldn't have murdered Eugenie, but was there deeper truth he couldn't face? *That there was a part of him, dark and ugly, that was glad to be free of Eugenie? That something in him had called her death into being?*

"Maybe it would be justice if I did hang. Not for what I've done, but for what I left undone."

"Nate—" Christianne began.

"I have nothing more to say to you, Christianne. Not now." He turned and walked away. Those spectators who lingered drew back. He could see revulsion in their faces, fear. The rejection would only grow worse as news from the inquest spread.

This would be his reality, until the real murderer was caught. He'd spent his life at the pinnacle of society. Now he would be an outcast, barred from the privileged world that was all he'd ever known.

GAVIN'S GIFT for silence had always raked Christianne's nerves. Anyone else would have filled the coach with observations about the weather, or discussed what might be waiting for tea when they got back to Strawberry Grove, or any one of a hundred things that would drive back the thoughts roiling in Christianne's head as the equipage jolted down the road.

But Gavin merely regarded her with solemn gray eyes, his fingers toying with the seals on a watch chain his wife, Rachel, had given him years ago.

It seemed forever until he spoke, so gently it hurt her heart. "It was very brave of you to defend Nate that way, even though he won't thank you for it."

"He was terrible to me after the inquest."

"He behaved badly. But he's been under a terrible strain."

"So have I! I kept feeling as if the person responsible for all of this was somewhere in the room, watching us."

"It's very likely." Gavin tapped his steepled fingers against his lips. "This tangle goes far beyond Eugenie's death."

"What do you mean? Tell me—"

"I can't."

If she were talking to Adam, she could badger him into telling her anything. But Gavin would remain silent and never break. "Can you at least tell me if you think Nate is in danger?" she asked. "What if the person who killed Eugenie goes after him next?"

"If Nate's enemy wanted him dead, he'd have killed him by now. I know this sounds harsh, but it's true. Unfortunately, I fear things will only get worse. I know men like whomever is tormenting Nate. Men who take pleasure in someone's suffering."

Christianne could see ghosts haunting her brother's eyes. She'd caught glimpses of them far more often in the days right after Gavin had returned from exile. Time, Rachel's love, and the children that had filled their home had lessened the past's hold on Gavin. But the horrors he'd experienced at Culloden were embedded in his blood and bone, and occasionally they'd break free of the prison he'd walled them into.

He didn't talk about what had happened between him and the English officer who had been betrothed to Rachel before Gavin took her hostage after Culloden Moor. Adam, Gavin, and Nate never spoke of the horrors they'd witnessed to those outside their circle of warriors. They protected everyone else from the unthinkable things war had done to them, or forced these good men to do to the enemy.

"You did the right thing in defending him," Gavin repeated softly, turning his gaze out the window. Christianne reached across and took her brother's hand.

CHAPTER 7

LONDON, JUNE 1756

*S*ince the year that three of the four Knights had taken seats in the House of Lords, every session of Parliament had ended at Nate's London townhouse. There, the men talked until dawn before scattering to their country estates. But tonight Nate felt strangely out of step with those he'd felt closest to, a feeling that had grown in the year since Eugenie's murder.

Nate's friends brimmed with life. Adam jested about his young son's prowess with a sword, while Myles regaled them of his plans to surprise his wife Devlin with an anniversary trip to Ireland, where they'd found adventure after Culloden Moor. Gavin seemed quiet, but that was no surprise, Nate reasoned. His earnest friend had dozens of arrangements to make before leaving on the diplomatic mission he was about to undertake. The fact that Adam was to accompany him was concern enough, Nate had remarked earlier. Sabrehawk was the last person anyone would want around during delicate negotiations.

Yet even his attempt at humor fell flat. He couldn't seem to regain the ease he'd once had with these friends he'd once taken for granted. *Whose fault is that?* he asked himself wryly. He hadn't seen nearly as much of them as before. They'd been occupied with their own growing families, their work and estates. When they *did* meet he'd found excuses not to join them. He'd observed the required period of mourning for his wife, only leaving Harlestone on pressing business. It had been a challenge to wade through the numerous complications the unsolved murder had caused. Merchants who no longer wished to do business with him. Business agreements of long-standing that were suddenly broken. Most of those who were still willing to associate with him had questions in their eyes. Questions he couldn't answer, like the ones Christianne had asked him so long ago.

"Another session of Parliament closed, and Nate and Gavin haven't managed to destroy the aristocracy as predicted by our esteemed colleagues." Myles sank into one of the large leather chairs gathered around the grand fireplace in Nate's London townhouse, his eyes twinkling. "All this taking in children who are abandoned and feeding them you two support is insufferable. Why just last week I saw another pamphlet declaring how subversive Foundling Hospitals are."

"I wish those were the only publications we had to worry about," Gavin said, shoving his spectacles up his nose. "I found this posted on the streets the other day." He drew a crumpled paper from his pocket. "Someone is stirring up the rumors about Eugenie again. Every time the scandal begins to die down, some enemy of Nate scatters these far and wide to add fuel to the fire." He handed the large sheet of cheap paper to Nate.

Nate took it from his friend and examined the lurid image portrayed there. A hulking figure more beast than man, towered over a terrified woman, his hands around her throat. It was hard to fathom that even Callum MacGregor was no closer to solving the crime. "Yes," Nate said. "I've seen this before."

Adam peered over Nate's shoulder and swore. Caval wedged his big body between the two friends regarding Adam with wary eyes.

"I'd like to get my hands on whoever spreads this rot!" Adam said. "Do you think it could be whoever killed Eugenie?"

Nate stroked the deerhound's ears.

"I don't know, but whoever is spewing it wants to harm Nate," Gavin said.

The violence the broadsheet portrayed turned Nate's stomach, but in the time since Eugenie's death, he'd grown practiced in keeping his face bland. He pointed to the smudged-ink cartoon of a savage dog tearing at the woman's skirts. "I'd like to get my hands on the artist, too," Nate said. "It's one thing to attack me, but really, maligning my dog is beyond the pale."

"Raging about this will only fan the flames," Gavin cautioned, "and that is what the author of these attacks hopes to do. Push Nate into losing his temper in public, so people can say he's mad enough to commit murder in a fit of passion."

Nate poured himself a draught of brandy from a cut-glass decanter, and took a long swallow. He'd been so drunk the night of Eugenie's death there were times even he wondered...

He'd be lying if he said he'd never been so enraged that he imagined his hands around her throat...when he'd realized during Eugenie's first pregnancy that the woman he'd been infatuated with to the edge of reason had betrayed their marriage and was carrying another man's child. He'd been wild with anger and grief. Yet, that had been a lifetime ago.

"Some people have never forgiven you for getting Gavin and me pardoned," Adam growled.

"Well, in fairness, Galahad does have questionable taste in friends." Myles elbowed Nate, but his effort to lighten the mood fell short.

"This situation is serious," Gavin said. "We know the rumor about Nate is nonsense. But people who don't know him are being goaded to a frenzy by whoever keeps dredging the scandal up. Someone threw a bottle at Nate when he was leaving The Blue Peacock last week."

Nate touched the fading bruise at his hairline, remembering. *That's Viscount Harlestone! The murderer!* The accusation had cut through the crowded street, people all around Nate staring.

"Did anyone catch the varlet?" Adam snapped.

"No." No one had come to his aid. He'd seen the look on the bystanders' faces. They'd stared at him, murmuring to each other...wondering if he was a monster.

"It might be wise to have MacGregor accompany you in the city, just in case," Gavin ventured.

"The devil I will," Nate growled. The big Scotsman had suggested the same thing when he'd given his last report. Nate had turned him down flat. Maybe he couldn't outrun an attacker, but if he got his hands on the rogue, he knew how to fight. After fate had taken Nate's leg and slashed the tendons in Adam's hand, the pair had developed combat techniques together that left them exhausted, frustrated, then triumphant.

"Do you think your life could be in danger?" Myles asked Nate.

Nate paused to consider. "I'm useful for the time being, a distraction to deflect suspicion from whoever the real villain is."

"Eugenie's murderer?" Adam asked.

"Perhaps," Nate allowed, "Or else someone who wants to hide the tracks of their own wrongdoing."

"Well, this villain sure as hell isn't you." Adam blustered. "You're honorable to the point of absurdity."

Nate had believed he was honorable once. But ever since he'd faced down Christianne, there were nights he wandered up to the deserted nursery in Harlestone Hall and wondered. Despite the passage of time, he was haunted by the harsh words they had exchanged at the inquest and fear that he could never make things right between them. How could she understand that he'd rather be in jail than have her see him as weak and vulnerable? How could he explain the reasons he had sent Sera away? Yes, there was the danger of a murderer still loose and there was a chance that Seraphina might overhear gossip from servants or farmers on the estate or some part of Bascombe or MacGregor's grisly reports.

But the most unnerving thing was that Nate couldn't endure seeing Sera's desperate longing for her mother and tell her Eugenie would never return. And more damning still was the secret he confessed to himself late at night: That he wasn't staying away from Strawberry Grove because he didn't want to see Christianne. The truth was, he wanted to see her too much.

He regarded the three men gathered around his fire. He loved his cadre of friends, but even in their boyhood days the sobriquet of Galahad had held an edge none of them understood. To be perfect, no chance to be flawed, human...

"Nate? Are you listening?" Adam's voice broke through his thoughts.

He jolted back to the present. "Yes. I mean, I am now. What did you say?"

"The Blue Peacock seems to be a link to these handbills."

Nate sat up straighter, fully alert. "How do you know that?"

"I was going through the rear door to check on that lad you placed there as a servant. A masked man raced out when he saw me," Adam said. "He crashed into me and dropped some of these fliers."

"I've found others like them posted around London and they have this rare scent as well. I know I've smelled the rare fragrance at the salon, I just don't know who wore it. It's something...remarkable. It permeated some of the handbills about me, as if someone spilled it on the pages."

"So Nate stays away from the salon," Myles said. "It's simple enough."

If only it were, Nate thought. The Blue Peacock was the one place he could go for conversation, to discuss philosophy, science, literature, debate issues and drink wine—without his father frustrating the hell out of him. It was his refuge from a house filled with reminders of Eugenie and Seraphina and the child that had never taken his first breath. Even some of the servants who tended Harlestone Hall tiptoed around him now. Suspicion went both ways... Nate wondered if someone inside the household might know more than they admitted about events leading up to Eugenie's death.

"I hate that Adam and I are sailing to the Netherlands so soon," Gavin said. "It's the worst possible time." Gavin had been planning the diplomatic mission to negotiate trade rights for ages. Adam was going as well, to visit a friend from his mercenary days.

"I wish you were coming with us, Nate," Adam said.

"I've got work to do for the Royal Marine Society." Nate raked back the lock of hair that always fell across his brow. "Captain Hind is due to reach port sometime this month. I'm determined to see Deacon Mathers installed as his cabin boy."

The charity had been a lifeline for Nate. This crop of lads was especially important to Nate. He would be proud to see them launched into a future they'd barely imagined possible when they'd starved in the London slums. The Royal Navy was no easy path but it gave the lads a fighting chance.

"God knows, you have enough on your mind Nate," Gavin continued, "but I've got one more favor to ask you. Could you look in on Mother Lydia and the girls while we are away?"

"Of course I'll watch over Strawberry Grove," Nate said, though his nerves tightened with a mixture of anticipation and dread at the thought of seeing Christianne again at last. "The girls are like sisters to me," he insisted, as much to himself as to Gavin.

And they were. All except one.

Nate bent down to scratch behind Caval's ear so he wouldn't have to meet his friend's searching gaze. "It will be good to see Mother Lydia and the girls," he evaded. "I'll stop by on my way to London at the end of the month."

You could visit Seraphina as well, Christianne's voice whispered in his head. Eugenie's sister had written to inform Nate that she and her family had moved to their home near the city for the coming months as her husband had some business in town.

Myles crossed to the table, poured wine into glasses. The friends raised them high.

"To safe journeys for our Marine Society lads and for us," Gavin said.

"To flushing out Nate's tormentors, whoever they are," Adam growled.

Myles chuckled. "And may the fates be with

Galahad as he tries to keep Christianne out of trouble while her long-suffering brothers are gone."

Nate drank deep, liquor burning his throat as he imagined walking through the door at Strawberry Grove. The simple truth was this: No matter how angry he'd been with her, no matter how shamed he'd felt at the inquest, he needed to see Christianne again.

CHAPTER 8

hristianne didn't even bother shedding her wide-brimmed straw hat before she stormed into the library at Strawberry Grove where she knew her sister would be scribbling away on her latest literary venture.

"Don't tell me you are back already!" Eliza groaned from the desk piled high with pages. She cast a baleful glare at the shopping basket slung over Christianne's arm. "I sent you on every errand I could think of."

Christianne banged her basket onto the desk. "Once I saw *this*, I couldn't endure their mindless chatter."

Christianne pulled out the ream of paper Eliza had requested. She yanked free a smudged sheet of cheap paper from the stack. "Someone stuck *this* in with your order when I gathered it at Lollyton's Stationery."

"We really must work on your adjectives," Eliza said, the scratching of her quill raking Christianne's last nerve. "I have no idea what 'this' is unless you elaborate."

"It's a broadsheet accusing Nate of murdering Eugenie. If you'd bother to look up, you'd see it for yourself. You should hear the kind of talk it's stirred up again."

Eliza glanced at the handbill and rubbed at a blot of

ink on her nose. "I know it is hard to see, but Nate is a soldier. Gossiping fools are nothing compared to the battles he's fought. Besides, we haven't seen him in forever."

Wasn't that part of this awful restlessness she felt? It was true, Gavin and Adam had been in contact with their old friend. But his absence at Strawberry Grove had been too sudden and pronounced to ignore. It had left a void in her life, despite her anger at him.

When her sisters had asked where Nate was, Gavin had gently said that Nate needed time. The brutality of Eugenie's death had left a deep wound and Nate had to piece his life together as best he could. He'd reminded them of the wounded animals Christianne had cared for over so many years. The secret was to wait for them to return to the world when they were ready. Maybe Nate would never be ready to see her or Seraphina, but as badly as that hurt, Christianne couldn't sit back and do nothing when someone was obviously trying to ruin him.

She whipped off her hat by the blue-ribbon streamers and tossed it aside, one of the faux cherries it was trimmed with tearing free of its stitches and rolling across Eliza's desk. "I'll never understand how you can sit there so calmly when the best friend this family has ever had is under attack!" Christianne exclaimed.

"My Count of Mondalvi is under attack as well. In fact, he's been trying to dispatch the evil Lord Penwillow for three days now, and his sword is growing very heavy. Not that he complains. I loathe whiners."

"Adam and Gavin are leaving the country. Myles is going off to visit friends in Ireland." Christianne waved her hands in disgust. "How can everyone just go about their lives when these lies about Nate Rowland are being spread all over the county again?"

"Exactly what would you have us do about it?" a booming voice demanded from the doorway.

She wheeled to see Adam, his head barely missing the lintel. He always arrived at Strawberry Grove like a hurricane, but she'd been too upset to hear him come in. His black hair tangled around his jaw after riding from Angel's Fall. His breeches and riding boots were spattered with mud. It annoyed Christianne to no end that he could track dirt on every Aubusson carpet in Strawberry Grove, and their mother would think he'd improved the design. Lydia Slade always delighted in visits from her eldest, and she'd be especially touched that her strapping son had taken the time to bid her farewell before setting off on his journey with Gavin.

"Adam! Thank the stars you've come!" Eliza set down her quill and went to be scooped up in her brother's bear hug. "Please take Christianne out to jump fences before every word in my head goes begging."

Adam chuckled. "Too much sisterly togetherness?"

"Someone tucked a scandal sheet in my latest order from the stationers," Eliza explained. "Christianne's been in a fury ever since."

"Look at the nonsense they're printing about Nate again!" Christianne thrust the smudged page into Adam's big paw.

He stared at the image, his good-natured expression fading. "I was just talking about these with Gavin, Myles and Nate when we gathered after Parliament closed. Gavin found some handbills posted in London as well. Gavin and I followed the trail to a salon in London, but the minute we stepped into the room, everyone acted as if I was there on some sort of raid to snap up their most accomplished employees."

"What salon are you talking about?" Christianne leaned toward him, eager.

"The Blue Peacock. I was near the salon one day

when a man in a mask came dashing out, something in his arms."

"A mask?" Eliza exclaimed. "How intriguing!"

"Yes. He crashed into me and the things he held went flying. They were handbills lambasting Nate. I swear, there was something familiar about the man, as if… I don't know…as if he was there the night Eugenie died, but he was gone before I could catch him. No one would tell me who the person was. Later, Gavin found other handbills around the city. There is a particular scent we've smelled in the salon. We don't know who uses it, but it's unforgettable. Someone must have spilled a bottle of it on a printing of the scandal sheets. Gavin recovered at least twenty that we detected the scent on. The people we questioned were either involved or too afraid to tell us. You can't stand in Parliament for the issues Nate has championed without making plenty of enemies. There is a certain Colonel Pratt who fought with Cumberland in Scotland. He's as bloodthirsty an officer as I've known. And Gavin warned us that that pinching little puritan Stanhope wouldn't let Nate's case go."

Christianne shuddered, remembering the glassy-eyed barrister who had questioned her during the inquest.

"Stanhope has hated Nate ever since he began his work with the Marine Society," Eliza said.

Christianne put her hands on her hips and glared at Adam. "Why don't you and Gavin *make* the owner of the salon talk?"

"You'd have more luck getting a sphinx to spill secrets than Marguerite Charbonneau," Adam said. "Being circumspect is her stock and trade. Men gravitate to her salon because of her strict adherence to the privacy of her patrons."

"So you just gave up?" Christianne exclaimed.

"While you were exiled, Nate never stopped fighting for you. When the crown tried to confiscate all of Gavin's property, Nate preserved it for us. We would have been homeless without him."

"I know what I owe Nate Rowland," Adam growled, and Christianne saw the guilt twist his face.

"Mother didn't believe Nate would be able to help you," Christianne pressed him. "She told me not to get my hopes up. But I *knew* Nate would work miracles to bring you back to us. Can we really do less?"

Adam flung himself into what had been their father's favorite chair. His voice rumbled with irritation. "We're not giving up. We're just pausing to reflect on the situation. Gavin and I will find a way to the bottom of this tangle once we return from this trip. But short of dressing up in petticoats and playing the courtesan, I'm out of ideas when it comes to infiltrating the salon."

He was trying to diffuse tension with humor as he often did, but the moment the words were out of his mouth, an idea flashed across Christianne's mind.

No. Adam could never pose as one of the ladies at The Blue Peacock, she reasoned, her heart pounding with determination.

But Christianne could.

Her mother would be horrified, her sisters scandalized. Her brothers—furious at her recklessness. But once she'd exposed whatever villainy was afoot at The Blue Peacock, they'd all be grateful. And she would finally have had the kind of adventure she'd longed for from the instant she'd been old enough to run to the boundary of her father's estate and look at the world beyond.

CHAPTER 9

Christianne wasn't quite sure what a hostess at a salon should wear, but she'd read enough of Eliza's precious novels to guess. For a week she'd been making secret plans. Now, a trunk lay open on Christianne's bed, packed with her prettiest gowns and a cache of jewelry, though nothing so expensive it would stir suspicion. She had to be well-dressed enough to be appealing, but not so much so that people would guess her true identity.

She suppressed a mixture of excitement and unease. She'd spent most of her youth scheming to outwit the rules and she'd become adept at it, but none of her schemes had ever held the edge of danger this one did. If her luck held, she would set her plan in motion tomorrow and it would be too late for anyone to stop her.

She jumped when she heard a tap on the door. "Who's there?" she called, trying not to betray her taut nerves.

"It's Eliza. I'm coming in."

Her sister pushed open the door and stepped inside the room. Christianne remembered the night she'd had the honor of being moved here from the nursery.

Eliza, next in line for a room of her own, had run about, stroked the beautiful bed hangings, and explored the table with Christianne's silver-backed brush and mirror, the tiny jars of cream and perfume. Most of all, she'd coveted the delicate writing desk where Christianne was supposed to keep up her correspondence.

They'd laughed and cried and shared so many sisterly confidences in this room. Suddenly, Christianne wondered if she'd ever be able to return.

Eliza eyed the trunk. "What are you doing?"

"I told everyone at dinner tonight. I've decided to accompany Kitty Wainwright to her aunt's in Bath, just like you've been hounding me to do."

"I don't believe you." Eliza regarded her with wide, worried eyes. "Last time you were at Kitty's aunt's you dumped a glass of ratafia on someone's head for saying something about Gavin. Tell me where you're really going."

"If I don't tell you, you won't have to lie." Christianne scooped up a blue satin gown, folding it with care. "You know I can take care of myself. You even used me as inspiration for Flora the Fearless. If you trusted me to take on a fleet of pirates, surely I can handle a few weeks' adventure."

"This isn't one of my stories. I can't write the end and make everything turn out well."

Christianne searched for the words to explain. "Eliza, I know you and the others are all content here. You have your writing. Maria has her art. Laura can cajole Gavin and Adam's babies into being absolute cherubs. The only thing I'm good at is arguing. It's time for me to explore my gift."

"This has something to do with Nate, doesn't it? Ever since Adam came to say goodbye, you've had that look. Like your mind is a runaway carriage."

Christianne turned away, unable to look Eliza in the eye. "Promise you won't tell anyone."

"I don't know."

Christianne grabbed her sister's hands. "I understand you love home. As long as you have your paper and ink and books, you can travel anywhere in your imagination, but I get so restless when it's just us here. The night of Nate's party, Eugenie said something that has always stuck in my mind. She said Strawberry Grove is a veritable little nunnery. And that's what I feel like sometimes. Remember the story of that woman they walled up in the abbey during medieval times? The one the boys were always pretending you were?"

"The anchorite? It was my favorite part to play. I could dream up stories in peace until they came to rescue me."

"You were supposed to be praying, and having food slipped into a little slot, but yes. I feel like a woman walled up in a nunnery, and I'm hardly suited to be a saint."

"Christianne, you're scaring me."

"I'm going to help Nate. We owe him that, don't we?"

"Yes, but how?"

"Freddy is going to drive me." She'd won loyalty unto death from the stablehand who had indulged plenty of her adventures over the years. *It is a surprise for my brothers*, she'd told him. In a way it was true. But this adventure was different. Once she'd stepped over the threshold into this world, life could never be the same again. "Just pretend I went to Bath."

"You're not going to tell me where you're going? What if something happens to you?"

"If I don't send word two weeks from now, send Nate the letter in my desk. Don't look at me that way! I knew you'd find the letter. You were bound to go rummaging around in my desk at some point. You're always scavenging paper or sealing wax."

Eliza blinked back tears. "I hate this."

"I know." Christianne hugged her sister. "But maybe by the end of this I'll be able to inspire a whole new adventure for you to write about. Just think of the ideas I can give you."

If only she knew what the ending would be.

CHAPTER 10

$\mathcal{N}$ ate strode into his father's study, the walls lined with weapons in artful displays. Swords wielded in the Wars of the Roses fanned out in perfect arcs around shields that had been dented by Frenchmen at Agincourt. Maps depicting troop movements, and portraits of historic charges had fired Nate's imagination when he was a boy. How many times had he played on the floor with his toy soldiers, listening to his father relive his glory days? How Nate had dreamed of the day he could share heroic battle tales of his own.

He'd never imagined that talking about Culloden Moor would sicken him.

At the moment, his father sat at the vast desk, his brows so fierce in concentration it seemed the papers in front of him should catch fire. Some business regarding the extensive Rowland holdings scattered across England, Nate surmised.

The Earl of Fendale had aged since the death of his wife and Eugenie's murder. Some men looked bruised and vulnerable in grief, but it had hardened his father's face instead. No lord marching to a block on Tower Hill had ever looked more resolute.

"You sent for me, sir?" Nate said.

Shaken from his concentration, his father looked up from the papers spread across his desk. "Nathaniel. Yes. How are you?"

"Busy, sir. I've got a proposal to argue in Parliament as soon as Gavin returns from his trip. We've got some reforms we're hoping to implement."

"Yes, yes. I'm certain your work is admirable. Glenlyon's efforts have always been so, except for that unfortunate episode when he joined Charles Stuart's cause. But that was his father's doing. It is not the first time that man coerced someone into mistakes that cost his family dearly."

"Yes, sir," Nate agreed. Unlike Nate and Adam, Gavin had never wanted to be a soldier. He'd wanted his books to study and lands to tend, to build things and bind up wounds. But as Gavin's father lay on his deathbed, he'd coerced his scholarly son to go to war. Gavin had done so in a last, desperate effort to win his father's love.

Nate doubted the old earl would have approved of Gavin's soldiering, but when Bonnie Prince Charlie and his other officers had fled in defeat, leaving the Scots defenseless against the Duke of Cumberland's butchery, Gavin had remained behind. He had gathered the widows and orphans of the soldiers they'd led to disaster, and had smuggled them to France where they could build a new life, instead of being hunted down and slaughtered. Gavin had shown Nate that there was more than one way to be a hero. Now Gavin championed the vulnerable here in England, and Nate was honored to fight on the same side.

"Would you care for a brandy?" The earl gestured toward the decanter and glasses that gleamed on a silver tray.

"Yes. Thank you." Nate poured himself a glass then

sat in the chair opposite his father. "You are wondering why I summoned you here, no doubt."

"Yes."

"It is time we talk about your family obligations."

A hook seemed to catch in his chest as Seraphina's poignant face flickered across his imagination. "Seraphina is well. Her aunt writes—"

"It is not Seraphina I wish to discuss." His father's mouth tightened, and Nate could see a flicker of pain at the mention of her name. "Does it not trouble you that all of the properties we hold have no true heir to inherit them?"

"Salway is heir."

"Salway is not a fit overlord for all of this and you know it," his father scoffed. "He is my younger brother's son, but he has even less gumption than Edward did. Blood will tell, and the boy has all the substance of blancmange pudding."

"He was a good friend to me when the other Knights were gone." Nate had vowed never to forget it. During the bleakest months of his life, when he'd been struggling with the loss of his leg, the shattering of his marriage, and what he'd feared was the destruction of the friendships that had been the foundation of his life, Salway had done his best to fill the void. He'd been there when Nate was relearning how to walk. He'd helped Nate convince his father to get the Knights pardoned. It had been a selfless act, Nate knew, because Salway had always been excluded from that cadre of lads. In the battle between bold young Adam and Salway, there was never any question who would win boyish admiration.

"Nathaniel, enough. I know that Salway was a help to you after you were wounded, but he is no fit heir to the position we Rowlands have held in England since William the Conqueror set foot on these shores. You know it and I know it. We have a responsibility to leave our lands to someone who can hold them in trust to pass down to the next generation. I could marry again and father a son. I may be forced to do so, if you refuse to do your duty." There was such weariness in his father's voice. "What say you?"

"Father, Eugenie has only been dead a little over a year."

"Long enough."

"Besides, what woman will want to link her fortunes to a suspected wife-murderer?"

"Perhaps flighty young things might hesitate, but there are plenty of women in England who are too sensible to get in a flutter over what is pure nonsense. Women who have already proven themselves to be good breeders."

Nate choked out an incredulous laugh. "Good breeders?"

"Is that not the most important characteristic of any woman you would wed right now? You tried marriage for love, or should I say, were led about by the front of your breeches. We saw how that ended. I'm sorry the girl died, but you must admit it was a blessing."

Nate bristled. "For a young mother to be strangled to death? Forgive me if I fail to see that as anything but a tragedy."

"You did not love Eugenie. You were miserable together. As a political hostess, she was a disaster. Important men do not wish to hear about fripperies and the latest ball."

Men seemed to find those subjects fascinating enough when they came from Eugenie's bow-shaped lips, Nate thought with a twinge of bitterness.

"You are older now," his father continued. "Wise enough to choose a partner to meet needs other than in the bedchamber."

"You and mother were a love match."

"No one was more surprised than we were. But make no mistake, had Augusta not been the perfect partner to further the fortunes of the Rowland estates, I would never have asked her to be my bride."

His father straightened the miniature brass cannon on his desk. "I have spent a good deal of time these past weeks compiling a list of widows for you to consider. Women of property, with skills that will benefit your political career. Women mature enough not to be deterred by the unfortunate circumstances regarding your leg."

Nate felt blood drain from his face. "My leg?"

"I respect you too much not to be forthright. We both know that women often have a horror of disfigurement, no matter how heroically such scars have been won. The last thing you wish to deal with when getting a son on a woman is a bout of feminine vapors."

Nate's jaw set as he remembered the first time Eugenie had seen the devastation war had left on his body. "No. I wouldn't want to horrify my wife," he said coldly.

"I want to see my son with a wife to care for him and children to carry on his name. But it is not just a selfish wish. Perhaps happiness is too ambitious a goal considering all you have gone through, but contentment is not."

Happiness is too ambitious a goal. How long ago had Nate started to believe the same thing? He'd watched his beloved friends find love as deep and true as the legends they'd once devoured. But he'd known his own chance for that kind of passion was past. Was it possible that his father was right? It was something to consider.

Nate's gaze flicked to the parchment on his father's

desk, marked with neat rows. "So who are these illustrious widows you have in mind?"

His father smiled and handed him the list. "Frances Wildermuth, Dowager Marchioness of Sheen," Nate read aloud. "Catherine Bainbridge, widow of Sir Gideon Aldbury. Olivia Nasby, Dowager Countess of Beresford."

Suddenly, he remembered his first ball, asking a pretty girl with nut-brown hair and kind green eyes to dance. He'd always liked Olivia. She'd had a way of making everyone around her comfortable. Those times she'd hosted him and Eugenie over the years he'd admired her skill at handling warring political factions with a deft touch "I was very sorry to hear Olivia's husband had died."

"An unfortunate accident that left her two boys fatherless. As I remember, you were quite fond of Olivia during her first season. Your mother was a dear friend of her family, and hoped that you might make the match."

"It's too soon," Nate said.

"I disagree. The right wife could tamp down these rumors circulating with the *ton*."

"You mean that if someone like Olivia would wed me, people might decide I cannot be the kind of beast the scandal sheets portray?"

His father looked away, and Nate realized how such notoriety distressed him.

Nate glanced down at the list, skimming the assets his father had written down for each prospective Viscountess of Harlestone. For a moment, he imagined Christianne plucking the list from his hand, her laughter ringing out. *Choosing a wife as if she was a broodmare? Perhaps your father would like to examine their teeth and the girth of their hips before you select one.*

Yet, in one way his father was right. It wasn't as if he

was going to fall madly in love and sweep some young beauty off of her feet after all that had happened to him. That time in his life was over. It was his duty to provide an heir.

A vast emptiness seemed to open inside him.

"Promise me you'll consider what I've said," his father pressed him.

Nate folded the paper, then slipped it into his waistcoat pocket.

"I will."

CHAPTER 11

 $\mathcal{C}$ hristianne had never been to London in the summer, and now she knew why. The city seethed like a cauldron, the stench and noise boiling over in the heat. A lad she'd hired to haul her things pushed a handcart carrying her trunk as she followed him from the stage stop to The Blue Peacock.

It should have been a relief to stretch her legs after hours of jouncing in the post-chaise that had brought her to the city. But London was a whole different world without sturdy footmen to clear her path and her brothers to shield her from the jostling of the crowd. Even so, excitement bubbled up inside her at the thought of seizing the reins of her own life. At any rate, she'd come prepared. Her lips curved in a secret smile, and she slipped her hand into the slit where her pocket should be, feeling the lump concealed under her petticoats—a dagger tied to her thigh with ribbons.

Adam had given the weapon to her as a jest on her fifteenth birthday. Engraved on the blade was the definition of the word their mother had forever tried to drum into her head. *Felicity—The ability to find appropriate expression for one's thoughts.*

Mama had hated Adam's gift as much as Christianne loved it. But then, she and her mother had butted heads since Christianne had been able to voice her outrage.

Adam can do it! Why can't I?

It is different for boys. The world will be just waiting for you to make the slightest mistake, her mother had warned. Christianne had decided to end the world's suspense and defy as many unfair rules as possible.

Thus far, her trespasses had only been tallied up by the people around Strawberry Grove. But the rebellion she was embarking on now reached far beyond a gaggle of village women who rarely looked past the brim of their bonnets.

No doubt some of the men who frequented The Blue Peacock opposed Gavin in Parliament, but most of them would flee the city for their country estates in summer. Still, there was no telling who might remain.

There's little chance they'd recognize you anyway, she told herself. Gavin never attempted to hide his half-siblings out of shame, but the political sphere of the Earl of Glenlyon and gatherings with the family at Strawberry Grove might as well occur on different continents. *At least I needn't worry about Adam and Gavin for the time being. It will be over a month before they return from their trip.* As for Nate, she'd have to hope that he'd stay away from the center of the intrigue.

If you can secure employment at the salon in the first place and discover who is plotting against Nate there.

She all but ran into the cart as the lad pulled it to an abrupt halt outside an imposing building. "'Ere we are, miss," he said, nodding toward a bright blue door painted with a Latin maxim in gilt letters. *Cogito, ergo sum.*

"I think, therefore I am," Christianne translated the Descartes quote aloud.

"What's that, miss?" he asked as he hefted the trunk onto the top step.

"Nothing."

"Do yer want me to wait just in case ye're turned away?"

"I won't be." There could be no turning back. Laying a coin in his grubby palm, she thanked him and watched the boy and his cart disappear in the crush of strangers.

After a moment, she sucked in a deep breath and lifted the brass lion head, letting it bang on the door. She knocked a second time, and a maid answered, scrubbing at red-rimmed eyes.

"What do you want?"

"I'd like to speak to Madame Marguerite Charbonneau."

"Let my poor mistress sleep! Didn't get to bed until nearly dawn." The maid started to shut the door, but Christianne put her foot in the gap.

"It's important."

At that moment, a striking woman in an emerald dressing gown appeared on the stairs. Sophisticated French features lent a fascinating aura to loveliness that fired the imagination. Christianne guessed at once it was the mistress of the establishment.

"Madame Charbonneau?" Christianne called out.

"Oui?" The woman brushed a strand of chestnut hair beneath a lace nightcap, turning shrewd amber eyes on Christianne.

"I tried to turn her away." The maid sputtered. "I'm so sorry we disturbed your rest, Madame!"

"No chance of that." The woman adjusted her nightcap with a wry grimace. "I was on my way to get a sleeping draught."

"This is the fourth night you've been up worrying,"

the maid grumbled. "People plaguing the life out of you."

Who was plaguing the salonnière and causing her to lose sleep? Christianne wondered. Was she tangled in whatever web the scoundrels who'd targeted Nate were spinning, or was it possible she was at the center of it?

Marguerite Charbonneau fixed Christianne with a probing gaze. "Tell me, what is your name?"

She looked down, unable to meet Madame Charbonneau's eyes. Light glanced off of the enameled ring Nate had given her. "My name is Tianne—Tianne Evelake." Evelake, the enchanted shield that had been given to Sir Galahad, to protect him on his grail quest. "I wish to secure a position here."

Madame curled elegant fingers under Christianne's chin. "You are certainly lovely, but that is hardly enough to be a jewel in The Blue Peacock's crown. What is your background and education, Miss Evelake?"

"I am the illegitimate daughter of a man of high station. The usual avenues to marriage are closed to me, unless I wish to wed someone far beneath my education and upbringing. I'm not fit to be a nobleman's wife, nor am I fit to be the wife of our groundskeeper."

"Does your father approve of the path you've chosen here?"

"My father is dead."

"I'm sorry."

"I've studied Greek and Latin, philosophy and literature, history and science."

Admiration sparked in Madame's eyes. "A rigorous program of study for a girl."

"I had older brothers, and was determined not to let them outpace me. Their tutor insisted that the female mind was not capable of retaining or understanding complex subjects."

"So you loved your studies?"

"I loved proving the tutor wrong."

The salonnière laughed, a trill so musical that Christianne could understand why so many men were in her thrall. Some of the strain in her face melted away.

"You've come at an opportune time. My most accomplished hostess has eloped with one of my patrons. It was obvious she was in love with him, but she might have done me the courtesy of leaving a note. Come back tonight and we shall see if you are clever enough to suit our patrons."

"I was hoping I could lodge here," Christianne confided. "Perhaps I could stay in the room of the hostess who has gone missing? Unless she comes back, of course."

"I can only hope she does. She was the finest of my ladies, excepting myself. Our guests will begin arriving in a few hours, so you had best get settled. Clary!" Marguerite called out.

"Yes, Madame." The maid curtsied.

"Please take Miss Evelake to Jessamyn's room."

"Miss Jessamyn's?" The maid's chapped hands fluttered. "But surely you can't..." Her gaze darted to Christianne's, so hostile it astonished her. "She's coming back! I know it!"

The salonnière grimaced. "Clary is certain that Jessamyn would not have left with some man without telling her. She has obviously not experienced the power of love." Madame turned to address the maid. "There will be time enough to sort things out if Jessamyn returns. Unless you wish to share your bed with Mistress Evelake?"

The girl's cheeks went scarlet. "No! No, Madame."

"Prepare a bath in Miss Evelake's room and tell Robin to carry up any trunks that she's brought."

Madame regarded Christianne, one winged brow sweeping upward. "You have brought more than the gown you're wearing, I hope."

"Yes. My trunk is just outside."

"You'll be lucky if it's not halfway to Thieves' Kitchen by now," the maid muttered.

"There is one question I must ask of a personal nature," Madame said, and Christianne could see the faint lines fanning from the corners of her eyes. "Is your flower still intact?"

"My flower?" Christianne echoed.

"Are you a virgin?"

The blunt question startled her. Christianne struggled to find the right words. "I—I understood that ladies here could choose..."

"That is true, but I'm astonished you know this."

She could hardly explain that she'd heard Adam and his wife, Juliet, discuss the arrangement at Angel's Fall.

"I found out what I could about various salons before choosing which to approach. Anyone with an ounce of practicality would do the same."

"Indeed." Madame regarded her through a thick veil of eyelashes. "Well, there is time enough for us to chart the right course for you. Should you wish to entertain privately, your first night would bring a rich price from the gentleman of your choice. But first, let's get the travel dust washed off of you, get you dressed appropriately, and have your hair done. Clary can aid you in that. Jessamyn had been teaching the girl how to pin and curl a lady's hair. After you are ready, we will see if your wit is sharp enough to hold your own among my guests. If so, you may stay. If not, you will leave."

"I can hold my own in any debate."

Madame's laugh was only a little strained. "You will find my clientele ruthless at times, but I can promise that you will never be bored. We've had our share of duels fought over a matter of philosophy. Everyone from dukes to playwrights to libertines and the most august members of Parliament have sought conversation here."

And who knows what else, Christianne thought, but she only smiled. "I have heard that The Blue Peacock is as fine as any salon in Paris."

"My one requirement is that you be discreet," Madame warned. "Here we believe in freedom of thought, but others are not so tolerant."

"I understand."

The maid sniffed, her nostrils curling as if she smelled the stink of travel. "I'll put the copper on the fire to heat water for her bath, and fetch the soap. But first, Madame, I'll be bringing you your sleeping draught. Mrs. Trench will take after me with a stick if you don't go back to bed."

Madame's eyes twinkled as she turned back to Christianne. "You'll find that my housekeeper is a bit of a lioness. She keeps us all marching in step. Feel free to acquaint yourself with the salon until Clary fetches you." Madame gestured to a pair of huge doors, then turned and walked back up the stairs.

Christianne pushed one of the doors open, then stepped into the room beyond.

The colors that draped walls and windows reminded her of the flock of peacocks her sister Maria insisted they keep at Strawberry Grove. Iridescent greens and blues were complemented by velvety black. Polished rosewood tables and comfortable chairs clustered in groups here and there, and gold cords swept back embroidered curtains that shimmered with hints of gilt thread. One flick of a hand could send the curtain cascading between the alcove and the rest of the salon's guests, to give privacy for a more intimate conversation.

The chamber was deserted now, but Christianne could imagine the space filled with people talking about the most fascinating issues imaginable, arguing their points, debating new ideas. Books lined shelves along one wall. Writing supplies were stacked beside them. Newspapers and other publications waited to be perused by interested parties.

She could picture Nate here so easily, seeking refuge from Eugenie's inane chatter about gowns he didn't care about and dances he couldn't participate in. Yet, Eugenie wasn't the only family Nate had been avoiding here. There was also Seraphina. The child haunted Christianne, her solemn violet eyes staring up at her father, so nervous, pleading. For what? For him to love her? A child grieving her mother, without a father who would offer comfort.

Christianne wasn't sure how long she wandered about the salon's main room before the maid reappeared, arms filled with towels and fragrant soap that scented the room with cinnamon and something citrusy. Clary's cheeks glowed bright red, though Christianne couldn't tell whether the flush was from resentment or exertion. Wispy curls stuck to skin damp from the steam of hot kettles and coppers. With a jerk of her head, the maid led Christianne up an elegant staircase to a corridor lined with doors.

Clary stopped at the last door and opened it. The room was sky blue, comfortable with a large bed. White bed curtains embroidered with stars swept gracefully back to reveal lush coverlets. Toiletries crowded the vanity table, the large mirror hanging above it sending beams of reflected light across the room. A secretary stood in the corner, the desk still filled with Jessamyn's things, and a decanter of liquor sat on a pie crust table, with two soiled glasses beside it.

"I've not had a chance to clean here," Clary explained. "The door was locked and even the mistress' keys were missing. I found them in the garden this morning when I was throwing out the dishwater."

Christianne could hardly believe her luck. The room was just as the missing woman left it. Was it possible there might be some useful clue waiting to be discovered? What if the inquiries about Nate had driven the girl and her lover to flee? Might they be tangled up in whatever Gavin and Adam had traced here?

"I'll change the bedsheets and take these glasses away before you go to bed tonight," Clary said. "But I've work of my own to do."

"Thank you. Before bed will be fine." The sooner the snippy maid left, the sooner Christianne could start searching for clues.

"Would you like me to send one of the other maids to help you unpack?"

"I can manage myself. It's obvious you care about Jessamyn very much," she ventured. "You must be worried."

Clary snapped to attention as if Christianne had pinched her. "You'll be expected downstairs at four o'clock. The salon stays open until midnight, unless you entertain a gentleman of your choosing." She glanced pointedly at the glasses on the table. "Jessamyn never did until..." She stopped and her gaze sharpened on Christianne's face again.

"Do I have mud on my cheek?" Christianne asked. "You keep looking at me strangely."

"No." The girl flushed. "It's just...you look familiar."

People had always told her she looked like a feminine version of Adam with her wild black hair and eyes. *And her irrepressible need to cross swords with people who vexed her.*

Adam might have occasionally come here with Nate

before he married, but he was far more likely to be found at the Academy of Swordsmanship.

The door swung open again, and the boy who had retrieved her trunk walked in. He was around fourteen, the barest down dusting his upper lip. Freckles spattered his face, and blue eyes looked out at her with an eager curiosity as he filled the pitcher on her washstand with water from two buckets he carried. Christianne noticed one arm was shorter, the muscles withered.

"G'day to you, Mistress," he said. "Name's Robin. I'm yer man if you want anything hauled or fetched."

Christianne's doubt must've shown on her face, for the boy broke out in a wide grin, showing a gap in his front teeth. "I know I don't look like much, but I'm stronger than you think. Can't wrestle ropes from a ship's rigging in a high wind, but I can hold my own here on shore."

"Ship's rigging?"

"I was itching to go to sea like the other lads, but Lord Harlestone brought me here when the Navy wouldn't have me."

Christianne's breath hitched. "Lord Harlestone?"

"Aye, from the Royal Marine Charity. I'm one of his crew, I am. I was real downhearted when my mates all found berth on ships and I couldn't. But his lordship brought his friend to see me. Man who got his hand cut so bad he can't close his fingers. He showed me that he can do anything with his left hand. Even fight with a sword. Well, you let me know if you need anything more. Just ring Clary when you're ready to dress and such." He darted out and shut the door, leaving her alone, the only sound the ticking of the mantel clock.

The "friend" Robin spoke of had to be Adam, Christianne thought. That was so like Nate to bring him to encourage the lad. But that meant her brother would likely visit Robin again. Her mission here was going to be trickier than she'd imagined. Was it only a matter of time before someone connected her with Adam, Gavin and Nate? What if Nate's enemy did so? she thought with a chill. Someone had already killed Eugenie Rowland. They wouldn't hesitate to eliminate Christianne, too, if they deemed her a threat.

There was no proof that whoever was stalking Nate had anything to do with Eugenie's death, she reasoned. They could be two totally separate matters. And yet, could it really be mere coincidence?

This is dangerous, Christianne, she could hear Eliza warn. But Eliza preferred her escapades folded between the pages of a book. Christianne wanted it all— the wind in her face, the fire in her veins, the heart-stopping thrill of dancing on the edge of a cliff. A surge of excitement poured through her. She'd stepped out of the cloister of Spinster Grove, and into a world where her wits and courage were sword and shield. She glanced in the mirror, her eyes flashing bright.

Finally, she could test her strength, and find out what Christianne Slade was made of.

THE SALON HAD BEEN beautiful when Christianne had entered in daylight. It was even more dazzling once night had fallen. Candles blazed in every corner. Tables shimmered with light. Crystal goblets and platters with rich pastries and other confections were positioned at various places about the room.

She glimpsed herself in a mirror just inside, but even the geranium-pink gown she'd chosen looked as if it belonged to a stranger. Perhaps because she'd spent the afternoon looking for clues among Jessamyn's belongings, rather than outfitting herself for a night she could never have anticipated a month ago.

She prayed she was up to the test. The woman reflected back to her was sophisticated, elegant, and daring. Her *robe á l'anglaise* swept down from her waist in graceful petals, revealing the white petticoat embroidered with pale green leaves beneath. The sleeves were so fitted to the elbow, she feared she'd rip a seam, a froth of white lace spilling over her hands. She'd never had patience with being bound up tight in stays, but when Clary had laced the undergarment up, she'd pulled so hard it was as if she hoped to squeeze Christianne out of existence. Yet it was the square neckline that unsettled Christianne, plunging nearly to the tops of her nipples. The panel of blush pink satin that formed the front of the bodice compressed her breasts until the tops swelled over the edge. When she'd reached for the usual ruffle of lace that she'd always worn to soften the neckline, Clary had snatched it out of her hand.

You'll not last the night here if you wear that, she'd warned.

As Christianne eyed the room before her, she knew it was true.

Marguerite was busy as a queen preparing to preside over her court, her daring gown of amber satin with green trimming revealing most of her generous bosom, a sprig of white oleander in her hair. Servants in livery bustled about her as she directed them to adjust draperies and polish invisible spots off of silver. Two other hostesses in exquisite gowns stood apart, their eyes bright with intelligence. One had hair the color of autumn leaves, a heart-shaped face and a figure designed to set men's breech-flaps burning. The other looked like a Botticelli angel with heavenly blue eyes and a seductress' mouth. Her flaxen hair gleamed silvery blond. The fluid grace of their movements made Christianne feel like Nate's deerhound about to bash his way into a china cupboard.

Christianne drew a deep breath and approached them. Madame started toward them, but some pressing matter called her away. Before Christianne could introduce herself, the red-haired woman looked at her with narrowed eyes. "So you hope to take Jessamyn's place."

"Yes."

"I'm Delilah." The star-shaped velvet patch at the corner of her lush lips rose as she smiled. "This is Aimee." She indicated the blonde.

"I'm Tianne Evelake."

"Of course you are." Delilah smirked, reminding Christianne of Deborah Musgrove. "Just because you're new, don't think you can snatch up any patron you choose. Now that Jessamyn is gone, I've been here longest. I get my choice of her gentlemen."

Christianne raised one brow. "Gentlemen choose who they keep company with, do they not? A new dish is often more tempting than a familiar one." Delilah's eyes widened in shock as Robin rushed to the door to welcome the first customers of the evening.

"Tread on my toes and I'll snap that insolent little nose of yours right off," Delilah said, showing pearly white teeth.

Christianne met her gaze. "I invite you to try it."

Delilah turned her back on them as a pair of dandies swept into the room, a rainbow of ribbons fluttering from their canes, their powdered hair piled ridiculously high. "Why, Mr. Dempsey! Sir Malcolm!" she trilled as she floated over to them on a cloud of perfume. "I've found the most intriguing translation of Homer."

Aimee regarded Christianne a long moment. "Jessamyn kept Delilah's snappishness in order. We're all a bit lost with her gone."

"I know how that feels," Christianne said, thinking of Nate. He'd been her lodestone, her North Star for as long as she could remember. When he'd sent Seraphina away, it had left Christianne hurt, bewildered and lost as well. Wanting desperately to save—not the boy she'd once idolized—but the man she'd come to know, the man who'd fought his way back from the horrific injury that had stolen his leg, whose eyes now shone with a depth of pain she wanted to ease. The Nate who was so broken he'd sent little Sera away.

She looked around at the room. Was it her imagination or did everyone seem guarded here, even some of the patrons who were beginning to fill the tables? Something was simmering beneath the glittering façade of The Blue Peacock. Simple jealousy, avarice or suspicion? Or was it something more dangerous?

CHAPTER 12

The lamplighters were hard at work as Viscount Harlestone's coach rattled over the cobblestones, but the wavering circles of light did little to drive back London's darkness. Shadows crouched like beasts waiting to pounce, and Nate's work with London's most vulnerable foundlings through the Marine Charity had shown him all too clearly the fate that awaited the sprawling city's prey. Boys determined to make their fortune. Country-bred lasses who'd dreamed of excitement and found ruin instead. Anyone deemed weaker was ripe for plucking by thieves and brothel-keepers.

A rich lord with a wooden leg had seemed like an easy target more than once, Nate mused, a grim smile playing at the corners of his lips. He'd relished the stunned expression on the blackguards' faces when he'd unsheathed his sword cane and taught them otherwise.

He almost wished for such an altercation tonight to distract him from his thoughts.

He shifted on the cushions, and Caval gave a low woof, laying his head on Nate's lap.

Salway eyed the deerhound from his seat on the opposite side of the coach with barely suppressed irritation, and picked wisps of wiry gray fur from the sleeve of his puce satin frock coat. "How was your visit to Strawberry Grove?" Salway asked.

Disappointing. The thought still surprised Nate. Ever since the inquest, he'd dreaded seeing the censure in Christianne's gaze. Yet, when his coach had wound up the oak-lined drive to the Slade manor house, he'd strained to catch his first glimpse of her. Always before she'd been the first to run out to greet him. Even as a young woman, her welcome had always made him grin. Hair that would not stay in its pins, simple gowns, suited for dashing to the tops of hills to see vistas spilling around her.

Though their first meeting was bound to be awkward, Nate had hoped he might mend the rift between them at last. Apologize for his angry outburst the night of his disastrous birthday party. And yet, how could he explain his distance from Sera and why he'd sent the child away without betraying the secret of Sera's birth? The thought of telling Christianne he'd been made a fool of, sickened him.

Eliza had greeted him instead. She'd always been quieter than Christianne, her world peopled with imaginary characters more real to her than anyone she encountered in the flesh. Yet their exchange had been more reticent than ever. "Christianne has gone off to Bath with Kitty Wainwright," she'd said, avoiding his eyes.

"Is she still angry with me?" he'd asked.

"She doesn't understand why you sent your daughter away."

The now-familiar weight of guilt had grown heavier still. *Sera's safer far away from me,* he'd told himself. He'd provided every material thing the child could want. It was as much as many aristocratic parents did.

But it's not enough, Christianne's voice whispered in his head.

At the end of his visit, he'd left Strawberry Grove without the sensation he'd always felt before—that his burdens had grown lighter.

Salway's wry chuckle drew him back to the coach and the London streets, away from his failures. "You're a braver man than I am, cousin," Salway said. "I'd not want to be responsible for that crew of spinsters. Especially Christianne."

"I'd prefer crossing swords with Christianne to the lecture my father gave me." Nate scratched Caval behind one ear. "He presented me with a list of women he found acceptable and ordered me to produce a Rowland heir."

Salway's mouth curved in a sympathetic smile. "Your father only wants what is best for you. Once you move on with your life, the gossip regarding Eugenie will fade."

"So to silence these lies, I must start accepting invitations to dinner parties and soirees I avoided as much as possible even before the investigation?"

"You can hardly sire an heir if you are barricaded in your office, writing legislation and working with beggar children."

"I thought that was my task as a member of Parliament."

"Think of this marriage as one more bit of work, then. There are far more tedious tasks in the world than bedding a comely woman. Uncle always had a knack for choosing pretty broodmares for his stables. I'm sure he'd not want his grandchild to be ugly."

Salway meant it as a jest, but the idea of exposing his leg to such a woman made Nate's fingers curl tight into his palm. Oh, he'd had sex since Eugenie abandoned the marriage bed. Women in places like The

Blue Peacock. But those exchanges had nothing to do with his emotions. They'd merely dulled troublesome urges that could never be truly satisfied—very much like the itch that sometimes tormented him on the leg that was missing.

Perhaps such a distraction would be welcome tonight.

He frowned, remembering the Knights' warning after they'd linked the slanderous handbills to the exclusive salon. *So Nate stays away*, Myles had said. *It's simple enough.*

Yet, if Nate suddenly disappeared from The Blue Peacock, would it not look suspicious and put his enemy on guard? Where else could he hope to uncover clues about whatever villainy was afoot within the salon walls?

Besides, there was comfort beyond the physical to be had there. His mind was as sharp as any man's. He smiled, thinking of Marguerite Charbonneau—one of the most sensible women he'd ever met. A shrewd businesswoman, a realist, and Jessamyn, who had a gift for distracting him when he needed it most. Yes, conversations with them would be far better than stewing over Christianne's anger and listening to Salway defend his father's insistence he wed. Nate rapped on the coach roof with his cane.

"Aye, my lord," the driver said.

"To The Blue Peacock." Nate turned to Salway. "I feel like a lively debate tonight."

Salway smiled appreciatively. "That's a fine idea. You always dazzled the ladies in your youth, but even the most dashing rake's appeal gets rusty without use."

Soon, the coach rumbled to a halt outside the tasteful building displaying a sign with an elegantly painted peacock. The coachman opened the door and lowered the step, then stood at attention as Nate climbed out. "I hope you have a pleasant evening, my lord," he said.

"I'll settle for a roaring debate, Garrity," Nate said. Such mental duels could take his mind off of the list of widows in his waistcoat pocket, and all of the logical arguments his father had put forth. Garrity chuckled, and Nate straightened his tricorn, then made his way inside.

The inviting fragrance Marguerite had developed wafted from the candles that lit the room. Tension eased from Nate's shoulders as he breathed in the combination of bergamot, jasmine, cinnamon and something unusual that he couldn't quite place. He could hear the convivial buzz of a dozen conversations, the ring of laughter, the strident tones of someone arguing a point they were passionate about.

Nate grinned as a familiar lad met him at the door to relieve him of his cloak and hat. The youth flashed a gap-toothed smile. "Welcome back, Lord Harlestone."

"Robin! It's good to see you." Nate looked from the neat black livery to the hair that had once been a rat's nest of tangles, now neatly combed and pulled back into a queue. Robin was a far cry from the boy he'd plucked off of the streets two years ago. "I think you've grown a head taller since I saw you last," Nate said.

"At least half that, since I came here, my lord."

The boy had put on weight as well, Nate observed with pleasure. When Nate had first plucked Robin from the streets, the lad had been nothing but gristle and grit.

"Is Madame about?"

"I don't think she's retired for the night yet, but she may do so soon. She's been having megrims since Jessamyn's been gone."

"Jessamyn is gone?" Nate echoed. "When will she be back?"

"Not sure she will. Eloped with that fellow she kept such a secret, we think. Hard on Madame to lose her. We're hoping Madame will feel better now that she hired a new hostess. Got a tongue like a whip, that one, and cut Colonel Pratt's arguments off at the knees not half an hour ago. I swear, I wanted to clap like I was in the pit at Drury Lane, it was that entertaining to see."

Archibald Pratt was a pompous ass who had served under the Duke of Cumberland, and taken pleasure in grinding the once-proud Scots into beggars starving on their own land. Anyone who could put Pratt in his place deserved accolades.

"I'd like to provide the lady with one of cook's finest pastries for that triumph." Nate turned to Salway. "Sal, did you hear Robin's news? Apparently Colonel Pratt has been bested by…" His voice trailed off, his eyes narrowing. "Sal?" Nate looked at his cousin, suddenly worried. "Are you all right?" Salway stared across the room, dazed as if a horse had kicked him in the head. "Sal, what's the matter?"

"Bloody hell," Salway muttered. "I don't believe it."

"Believe what? That someone taught Pratt a lesson?"

"Pratt can go to the devil. For God's sake, look over there," Salway whispered so low no one else could hear him.

Nate wheeled, looking in the direction of Salway's gaze. Christianne Slade met his eyes with a defiance that stopped his heart.

SOME LORD with a double chin was droning on about Socrates when Christianne saw Robin open the salon doors. Her pulse jumped as she glimpsed the familiar figure framed there. Nate. His caramel-colored hair was tamed back into a queue. His black frock coat was unrelieved by gold braid. Lace fell in creamy waves beneath his square jaw.

Christianne felt a sudden, inexplicable urge to tug up the bodice of her gown.

She knew the instant Nate saw her. His gaze skimmed past, then jerked back to her face, his eyes saucer-wide. Christianne wanted to dart for the stairs, but it was better to stand her ground. Fleeing would have done her no good anyway. Nate was already making his way across the room, only the slightest limp betraying his injury.

Amazing what a good head of fury can do for his balance, Christianne thought. Her heart thundered in her ears, but she struggled to appear nonchalant as she made her excuses to the lord she'd been debating. Still, there was something in Nate's eyes that made her shift to put an empty tea table between them.

"Good evening, my lady," Nate said, his green-gold eyes ablaze. "I've not seen you here before."

Madame and Delilah swept up. "Harlestone!" Madame exclaimed. "Delilah and I were just saying how much we've missed you."

"We must catch up on all the news!" The flame-haired beauty enthused, laying a hand on his arm with a familiarity that sent a bolt of jealousy through Christianne.

"I find myself intrigued by changes right here," Nate said. "You've a new hostess, I see."

Delilah gave a soft huff of irritation but Madame looked from Nate to Christianne.

"Isn't she lovely?" Madame said, seeming to measure the sizzle of intensity between the pair. "This is our newest beauty. Tianne Evelake."

"Evelake," Nate repeated.

"Yes, Tianne Evelake." Christianne force a lightness into her voice. "I am only lately arrived at this fine establishment. Whom do I have the pleasure of addressing?" She tilted her head in inquiry, aware they'd drawn curious glances from the salon's other patrons.

With the lift of one ironical brow, Nate bowed low. "Nathaniel Rowland, Viscount of Harlestone, at your service." She stared at the black ribbon tying back his hair at the nape. "It seems you've already made an impression on the company here, Miss Evelake," he said as he straightened. "Young Robin was saying you've dueled with Colonel Pratt and won."

Christianne pretended to examine the tray of delicacies on the tea table, selecting a pink cake in the shape of a rose. "I found Colonel Pratt's brain a rather dull blade."

"You'll find my wit considerably sharper. Perhaps we should put it to the test, if these ladies will be so good as to excuse us. Shall we take a turn in Marguerite's garden? It's lovely at this time of night."

"I don't think..."

His eyes glinted, hard, and he leaned toward her. "You won't be able to avoid me all night, my girl," he growled under his breath. "Better face the music."

It was true. He held out his arm and she laid her hand in the crook of Nate's elbow. She could feel his muscles knot beneath her fingers as he led her out the arched rear door into the garden, leaving the crowded salon behind. A few valiant stars fought their way through the haze of coal smoke belched by a forest of chimneys, and she felt a wave of homesickness for Strawberry Grove's wide sweeps of sky. Madame had done what she could to make this patch of green inviting. Hedges rose up in a charming maze with small wrought-iron tables and chairs positioned in intimate corners, where salon-goers could steal away for private conversations.

Here and there lanterns dangled from hooks, illuminating Nate's face. He looked like a knight about to charge in battle as he made his way through the dimly lit paths. Here and there, discreet servants delivered refreshments on trays, slipping patrons port or claret, ratafia or chocolate, then vanishing back into the shadows. It would be easy enough for Nate's enemy to conceal themselves among the servants or patrons, Christianne surmised.

She had tasted her brother's liquors in the past, and barely restrained herself from snagging a goblet from Clary's tray as she passed on their way to a table so isolated, Christianne hadn't even realized it was there. Jealousy pricked Christianne as she wondered which of Marguerite's ladies he'd escorted there in the past and what they'd done in the shadows. Delilah had certainly been anxious for his company.

When Nate reached the secluded spot, he pulled out an iron chair, and she sat down.

She tugged at her bodice, but his hard gaze gave her no quarter. "A little late for that since every man here has seen your charms," he growled. "That oaf you were talking to when I walked into the salon certainly seemed to appreciate them."

She fought the urge to cross her arms over her breasts. "We were debating Socrates."

"Of course you were!" Nate scoffed. "What the devil are you doing here? You're supposed to be in Bath, with your friend Kitty. Eliza said so."

Christianne shrugged, determined not to shiver despite the night breeze on her bare decolletage. "Yes, well, as you can see, I am not."

"I see fine. How the hell did you get here? Tell me you didn't travel alone!"

"What does it matter?" She brushed the question off, unwilling to betray Freddy's part in taking her to the stage stop near Kitty's house. "I was perfectly safe. I brought Felicity."

"Felicity?"

She lifted up the hem of her gown, and one of the lanterns gleamed on the small dagger she'd bound to her calf.

Nate swore, and pressed his fingertips to his brow. "You think that toy Adam gave you as a jest would protect a lone woman on the highway?"

"It was a far finer present than the rest of you gave me that year," she blustered. "A sewing box. Shoes with heels I couldn't run in and dresses people were forever chiding me not to tear. At least Adam's gift suited me. As for my journey to London, I'm capable of taking care of myself, you know. The people in the stagecoach were quite amiable, though the gentleman was eating raw onions. A motherly woman even shared her meat pie."

"Don't try to make light of this. I'm trying to understand what you're doing here."

"I don't expect you to." A wave of wistfulness washed over her, but she shoved it away. "Men get to forge their own paths, no matter what the circumstances of their birth are. Adam can win renown because he is a brilliant swordsman, Gavin and Myles can hie off to join Bonnie Prince Charlie in some wild scheme. You have the freedom to do anything you choose. But I'm supposed to sit in the window seat at Strawberry Grove and smile and wave, satisfied with nothing more." She shoved back the vulnerable feelings and wound every fiber of her being tight with defiance. "I got tired of watching life happen to everyone else."

Nate winced, a spark of tenderness penetrating his anger. "I know it's been difficult, watching all of us ride away to places you can't follow. But why, of all the places in England, would you come *here*?"

131

"I was fascinated when I learned about these places where women are able to speak their minds, hold conversations and debates on equal footing with men. I'd heard this salon is supposed to be one of the best. It turns out the rumors were true." She met his gaze boldly. "It's the salon *you* frequent, isn't it?"

Nate tugged at the fall of lace at his throat. "I placed Robin here. I like to see how he's doing. And I come for conversation."

"Your *conversation* is hardly why Delilah was glaring at me so fiercely."

A flush rose high on Nate's cheekbones. "All I can say is that it's a good thing I *did* come here tonight. I'll be able to bring you home before anyone realizes you were here."

Christianne curled her hands around the seat of the chair. "I'm not going anywhere."

"I'm your guardian while your brothers are away. I promised Gavin and Adam that I would look after you."

Christianne flicked a curl back over her shoulder. "I'm not a child and you're not my father or my brother. This is my life. My choice."

Nate raked his hand through his hair, tearing tawny strands loose from his queue. "You have to know if news of your time here gets out, you'll lose any place in polite society."

"Well, society is a good deal less *polite* than it seems on the surface," Christianne said bitterly. "At least, to women like me."

"It's going to get worse than you can imagine if anyone finds out you've been here. But it's not too late to stave off disaster. Pack up your things. There is a small door in the southwest corner. Slip down there after everyone is asleep and I'll take you to my townhouse. I'll have you back at Strawberry Grove before anyone guesses who you really are."

"I'm not going back."

Nate paced a few steps, then turned back to her, his gaze pleading. "Why would you destroy your chance at a decent future this way?"

"There is no future to destroy! With me in the salon, we can work together to flush out whoever is trying to hurt you."

"Evelake." Nate's face went ashen. "Sir Galahad's shield. My God. You came to the salon because of me? You have some crazed notion that you're going to catch whoever is stalking me?"

"You would do the same for us if any of the Slades were in danger. You rode to Scotland to help break Gavin out of jail when he'd been arrested. You could have been tried for treason if anyone had found out you were involved."

"That was different."

Her chin bumped up a notch. "Because you're a man?"

"Yes! And because if something happens to you, how would I ever forgive myself?"

His voice cracked with emotion and their gazes locked, held, something naked in Nate's eyes she'd never seen there before. For a moment, Christianne couldn't breathe.

When had her girlish infatuation with Nate changed into something deeper? When *he* had changed after Culloden? Or when she had seen him across the room the night of his birthday fete, watching the rest of the world dance. For a moment, Nate's gaze met hers and the brave façade he'd adopted since Culloden slipped. Longing for his old life shone in his green-gold eyes. She'd seen he was not some fantasy of Sir Galahad, but bone and sinew and flaws, with a dark edge of pain that he hid from the rest of the world. Now there were dangerous currents beneath the surface of those green eyes, pulling her in.

Suddenly she remembered the night before his wedding when she'd run through Harlestone Hall in her nightgown, how he'd knelt before her and caught her bare feet in his strong hands to warm her.

She groped for something to say that would ease the burning sensation in her breasts, the sudden tightening between her legs as she pictured him caressing her skin again. But this time, his deft fingers tracing a path up her calf, to where the bare skin was tender above the top of her stocking.

She felt a flush creep up her throat, her cheeks hot. "You couldn't bear anything happening to me? Then you understand exactly how I feel about you," she said, her voice trembling. "But even if you weren't in danger, I'd have found some way to leave home. I can't bear the thought of being stuck at Strawberry Grove forever. I refuse to spend my life scrambling for crumbs of respectability from people eager to see me make the slightest mistake. I can't be ruined, Nate. A bastard has no reputation to defend."

He grabbed her by the shoulders, his hands warm and hot on the skin bared by her dress' neckline. He pulled her so close she could feel the heat of his breath on her skin, see the intensity in his jaw. Her nipples burned where they brushed the front of his frock coat. "Damn it, Christianne, don't do this. Not for me. I'm not worth it. God, you should know that after the way I treated you at the inquest. The way I behaved after the party."

A light tinkle of laughter drifted from the other side of the hedge. Had someone heard them arguing? Defiance surged through her. Then let them think it was a lovers' quarrel.

Surrendering to instinct, she curved her hand

around Nate's nape. His eyes went wide with surprise as she pulled his lips down to hers and kissed him.

She'd dreamed of kissing Nate Rowland a thousand times, imagining it in all its possibilities—tenderness, passion. But never like this.

His mouth was warm, his full lips softer than she'd imagined, his scent so familiar and yet new. She could feel the tension that had coiled between them tighten, heat building between her thighs. For a moment, Nate kissed her back with a fierceness that stunned her, his tongue touching hers, the front of his breeches pressed hard against her. His arms twined around her waist—to keep his balance, or to pull her hips closer to his? His mouth opened, his tongue sweeping hers with a hunger that fired her blood.

She knew the instant he came to his "senses." His hands closed around her upper arms and he put space between their bodies. "What was that about?" he asked, his voice a little unsteady.

"I was afraid someone might overhear us," she whispered, breathless. "I don't want anyone to realize who I am."

The thought of that shadowy enemy sent a shiver skittering down her spine. Had that foe lurked in just such a place? If his nemesis overheard this conversation, her identity would be the perfect weapon to use against Nate.

"But that wasn't the only reason," she admitted. "I've wanted to kiss you for so long."

He swallowed hard, his hands tightening on her arms. "Come home with me," he urged, his voice thick. "I'm begging you."

She closed her eyes, imagining a different scene, a different world.

She was no courtesan, but for a moment, she wished she was one of the women who could lead Nate up to her bedchamber, with no need for propriety, nothing but heat and passion and the satisfaction that would come from finally giving in to what her body had craved so long.

Not that Nate would surrender to it.

He looked down at her, and even in the flickering lantern light, she could see that he knew what she was thinking—and that he was fighting what he'd felt in those moments her lips had been so eager against his.

Of course he felt something, a cynical voice cautioned. How long had it been since Nate had been with a woman? Was that one of the reasons he came here?

The one thing she knew was that her own world had tipped off its axis. Maybe he wasn't the hero she'd once believed him, but this kiss was the one she'd dreamed about—Nate Rowland's mouth on hers.

"I have to go," she choked out. "There are other patrons I must see to. I need to show Madame that I can hold my own."

Nate caught hold of her hand, his fingers crushing hers. "Christianne, listen to me. If any of these men press you to... You don't have to—" His voice caught.

"Don't worry," she cut in, the desperation in his voice making her throat ache. "If any of them bother me, I'll introduce them to Felicity." She pulled her hand from his and ran lightly back toward the building, through the garden full of shadows and faces she couldn't see.

"This discussion isn't over," he called after her, but she didn't answer.

She felt Nate's gaze follow her, the heat of his kiss still warming her lips. As she slipped into the salon, Delilah glared at her with open hostility from across the room. Madame pinned Christianne with a knowing gaze.

"Mistress Evelake, we wondered where you'd disappeared to," Madame said.

I've been to Avalon to kiss my Galahad, she thought. A kiss that had pierced her heart more deeply than any Excalibur ever forged.

~

WHAT THE HELL had just happened? Nate stared after Christianne as she disappeared into the shadows, feeling as if he'd just been run over by a coach. His lips were still burning from the feel of her mouth on his. She'd tasted of strawberries and oranges. Even now, that lingering tartness was far more compelling than the sweetness of any kiss he'd experienced.

She'd told him why she'd kissed him. To hide her identity from those who frequented The Blue Peacock. So she could plunge herself neck deep in danger because of him, Nate's conscience added. But it was more than that. *I've wanted to kiss you for so long*, she'd confessed.

The admission stunned him. More stunning still was the sensation he'd felt in those moments her lips were on his. Something so powerful he was still reeling, a depth of need he'd held under tight rein since Culloden Moor.

He'd never felt anything like it before.

CHAPTER 13

The last place Nate wanted to be tonight was this party at Lord Adderly's, but there was no way to escape it since his father had arranged the invitation specifically so Nate could spend time with Olivia Nasby again.

Salway sipped a glass of port as the valet put the finishing touches on Nate's attire.

"You're going to an enjoyable evening, not facing the Spanish Inquisition." Salway laughed as Nate's valet left the room.

"I *should* be at The Blue Peacock, convincing Christianne to go back home," Nate grumbled, as he shoved his signet ring on his finger.

"I doubt anyone can convince that little hellion of anything. I always knew she was rebellious, but this is a stunning indiscretion, even for her. Though it is an understandable impulse."

Nate stared in disbelief. "You can't be condoning this?"

Salway waved one hand in dismissal. "Certainly not for most women, but Christianne Slade *is* a courtesan's daughter. Perhaps she grew weary of trying so hard to

act like a perfect lady when she will be shunned regardless?"

"Christianne's presence at the salon is not what you
think."

"She has certainly been attentive to *you*," Salway
said. "Perhaps that is at least part of the reason she's at
the salon."

It was uncomfortably close to the mark.

The clock on the mantel chimed. Salway chuckled.
"Time to charm the estimable Dowager Countess
Beresford. You'd not want to keep her waiting, although I'm sure she is a model of patience after nursing
her invalid husband."

Nate smoothed the leg of his breeches, feeling the
buckles and leather that made it possible for him to
stand. For a moment, he remembered the man he'd
been, the excitement of that first London season when
the whole world had brimmed with possibilities. But
that time was gone. He and Olivia were lifetimes away
from the carefree youth they'd once shared when he'd
briefly imagined her as his wife.

LORD ADDERLY'S party had gathered in his drawing
room where some of the guests had already begun an
impromptu dance. Olivia sat quietly beside a potted
plant, her nut-brown hair gleaming. Worry had etched
lines about her eyes, but Nate saw she still had the
sweet smile that had drawn him to her side as their first
London season flew past. Their whole lives had been
ahead of them then, he thought wistfully. How much
they'd both changed!

Yet her face still brightened as she saw him approach. "Nate. How good it is to see you."

"Olivia." He took her hand and raised it to his lips. "You look lovely tonight. How is Alex's pup doing?"

"He is the size of a pony, and eating the kitchen bare, with Alex's help. Alex is half a head taller than I am now. He's fascinated with inventing things, and is working on a new irrigation system for the mill. Our steward says it is absurd, but the miller thinks it could be the most brilliant solution to our problems."

"He is clever like his father," Nate said.

"Both of my boys are. Lord Beresford would have been delighted by Alex's ingenuity—

and make certain he didn't reduce the mill house to splinters while implementing the design."

"If Alex would like me to look at his plans when next I am at Harlestone Hall, I would be pleased to do so. I have some small knowledge of such things."

A gentleman approached before the quartet struck up the next set. "Would you care to dance the gigue with me, my lady?"

"I beg you forgive me, but no." Olivia smiled. "I've just struck up a conversation with a dear friend I've not seen in far too long."

The man bowed and left them alone once more.

Nate sat down beside her. "I do hope you didn't refuse on my account. As I remember, you were a very graceful dancer when we were young."

She lifted one creamy shoulder in dismissal. "Let the younger set enjoy themselves in such a fashion. I prefer to sit quietly now. How goes your charity work? Well, I hope."

"Well enough, but there is always more to do."

A pretty young girl and a green youth swept past them, their feet flying in the intricate steps of the gigue.

A poignant smile curved Olivia's lips. "It seems so very long ago that we danced to this same song."

"Did we?" Nate asked, surprised.

She chuckled. "Yes. I had stars in my eyes the whole time. Obviously, you were not quite so smitten."

Nate's face burned. "I was young and foolish and obviously too self-absorbed to realize how fortunate I was in my partner."

She cut him off with a laugh. "You need not look so chagrinned. I was not brokenhearted overlong. So much drama in those days! Who had danced more than twice with whom, who would be engaged by the time the season was over, or who might wither on the vine. I'd not turn back time and relive it again, although there are some things I'd change now if I could. My husband alive, and you…" She looked down at his wooden leg, a shadow falling over her face. "I'd wish away your misadventure."

He was touched by her sincerity. "You're very kind. But then, you always were."

She blushed, looking far younger that her thirty-five years. "I must tell you something pleasant. I've had the chance to get acquainted with your little daughter these past months. My boys are friends with Lady Kettering's sons."

Nate lowered his gaze to his cuff and adjusted the lace. "It is good of Lady Kettering to keep Seraphina with her. I thought it best, considering the circumstances of Eugenie's death."

Her eyes softened with empathy. "It must be very difficult for you to be parted from Seraphina. She's a lovely child."

She was lovely, Nate thought with an unexpected twinge of pain. How could she not be with her mother's golden curls and heart-shaped face?

"Her doll needed a bit of mending," Olivia added. "I fear Alex's dog ran off with poor Bobo and her dress tore."

Bobo. The familiar name jolted him. Despite the

way Nate had distanced himself from Sera, he had
bought the doll when she was ill with the measles. In a
nursery full of the marvelous, ornate toys Eugenie and
his mother had provided her, somehow the doll remained her favorite.

"I'm sorry if the child troubled you," Nate said.
"Sera's nurse should have managed it."

"Nonsense. It was a pleasure to stitch Bobo up. I'd
always hoped for a little girl of my own. I love my boys,
but it must be delightful to have a child who was not
barreling about with a cricket bat and sliding down the
grand staircase on my silver trays."

Nate laughed.

"Speaking of dangerous activities, I saw your father
out riding the other day. I warned him to be cautious
when crossing the bridge over our stream. One of the
support beams has washed out. My steward was supposed to fix it months ago. But he insists the other will
hold."

"I could look at it for you next time I'm at Harlestone Hall."

Her face lit up. "Could you? I would be so grateful!
Perhaps you could stay for dinner and bring your father as well." She suddenly looked a trifle shy.

"I'm sure Father would enjoy it." The old earl would
probably be planning Nate's wedding clothes before
they got home, Nate thought wryly. "And I would enjoy
it as well." Nate knew he would. There was nothing
complicated about Olivia. Olivia would not have Nate
pacing the floor all night, wondering what an impulsive
kiss had meant.

He thought of Christianne—defiant, beautiful, infu-
riating. God knew what trouble she was getting into
right now, or if any power on earth could stop her.

NATE'S EYES felt gritty from lack of sleep as he reined his gelding, Excalibur, toward the salon. Three days. That's all it had been since he discovered Christianne at The Blue Peacock. It seemed like an eternity. He'd barely slept as he'd tried to figure out what in the devil to do about this impossible situation. Haul her back to Strawberry Grove? She'd vowed she'd just bolt for the salon again. Write to her brothers? They could hardly come running home from a diplomatic mission to fetch their incorrigible sister. Besides, it would take weeks for a letter to reach the Netherlands, then book passage on a ship to sail home. By the time either brother reached England, surely Nate could deal with the situation himself.

Or, whispered guilt, *did he have a more selfish reason for his decision?*

He'd spent more time than he cared to admit thinking about the vision Christianne had made in her gown of deep rose, her figure accented in a way he'd never seen before. She'd arched her neck so proudly as she had argued her points in the salon. But all he could think of was the lush black curl pillowed on the dainty arch of her collarbone. He'd imagined pressing his lips to the delicate hollow where that curl rested, then sliding his lips to her mouth.

She's your best friend's sister, he'd told himself as his cock stirred. But that girlish adoration she'd once lavished on him had changed to something else in the garden. A change he admitted had been creeping up on them both for a long time. She was an alluring woman now, bursting with life. While he...

He touched the place where wood met what was left of his leg. *Remember who you are,* a voice reminded him. *Maimed...broken...heir to the Rowland earldom.*

As much as it didn't matter to him, she was illegitimately born and he was already steeped in scandal. Any alliance between them was impossible. From any and all angles, he had no right to sensual thoughts of Christianne. He had to keep her safe until he could convince her to leave The Blue Peacock.

~

NATE HAD BEEN WAITING in the livery stable across the street for half an hour when he glimpsed Robin hauling a crate of oranges toward the kitchen door of the salon. "Ho there, lad," he called out, and the youngster set down his burden, and rubbed his withered arm.

"Back again already, milord? Surprised to see you here at this hour!"

"I needed to talk to you about something. Some*one*, really, and ask if you could do me a favor."

Robin shot him a gap-toothed grin. "Anything for you, sir. You know that."

Nate did. The hero-worship he sparked in Robin's eyes still made him uncomfortable, reminding him that lads just like this one had charged into cannon fire at his command. Some officers ruled by fear; others, like Nate, held sway over men's lives by their loyalty to him and to a cause.

The words of his aide echoed from the field of Culloden: *I would follow you to Hell, my lord.* Far too many men had.

"You know Mistress Evelake?" Nate asked Robin.

"You know I do, milord." The lad wiped the sweat from his brow with his sleeve. "But Clary and me don't like her much, taking Jessamyn's place the way she did." He frowned. "If you'd like us to chase her out, I could put mice in her bed an' scare her."

Nate chuckled. "Oh, I'd not start that kind of war with Mistress Evelake if I were you. She'd beat you at it

144

before you closed your eyes that night. I'd like you to keep watch over her. Make certain no one bothers her."

"Oh!" Robin gave him a look far too wise for his age. "You fancy her."

"It's not that." Nate tugged at his neckcloth, knowing he wasn't being completely honest. But he could hardly explain the circumstances. *I need to know she's as safe as I can make her. She's angry with me, reckless, but she's the truest thing in my world.*

"It's just…if you see anyone behaving in a way that's suspicious around her, I need you to tell me. Can I count on you?"

"Aye, my lord. You can count on Clary, too, though she's not going to like it."

Nate tried to suppress a prickle of unease. He knew Robin meant what he said, but there were ways to coerce boys like Robin and lasses like Clary when they'd spent time in Thieves' Kitchen. Enemies like the one after Nate were masters at turning the screw.

"Are you going to see your lady now?" Robin asked.

He hadn't intended to see Christianne. He didn't want to stir up suspicion by being too attentive, and yet his pulse quickened. "I think I will."

Nate grimaced inwardly as he approached the salon's front door. *Robin might be guarding Christianne from whatever is brewing in the salon, but you'll have to be the one to keep her safe from yourself.*

Straightening his dark green frock coat, Nate rapped on the door. Aimee answered, looking distracted. Nate caught a glimpse of a bluish shadow on her face. His jaw hardened. If one of the patrons had caused that bruise, Nate would make sure the blackguard never raised his hand to a woman again. "Have you injured yourself?" he asked gently.

"What?"

"There is a bruise on your chin."

"Oh! Oh, no!" She covered the mark with her hand, looking so guilty, he was sure he must've guessed right. "It's nothing! Just a smudge of dirt. I'm just very busy. Is there someone you're calling for?" During other visits, she and Delilah had done all they could to monopolize his attention. Today, she seemed in a hurry to be rid of him.

"I'm here to see Mistress Evelake," he said, removing the tricorn from his head.

"Good luck to you," Aimee grumbled. "She's restless as a cat with its paws afire. Delilah went to the milliner's just to avoid her. There are a hundred diversions to enjoy in the city, but she won't set foot out the door. Just pokes around the salon and glares at people as if she's trying to see right into their brain. If only Jessamyn would return, Mistress Evelake would be out on the street, and good riddance!"

That would make things easier for me, Nate thought.

"Mistress Evelake seems to have a gift for trying people's patience," Nate commiserated. "Yet, there's something about her I find engaging."

"You and the rest of the men in the salon." Aimee rolled her eyes. "I'll send Clary up for her, but don't be surprised if the maid grumbles the whole way. Clary likes her least of any of us since Miss Evelake is up before dawn, banging around."

Nate grinned. *That* sounded like the Christianne he knew.

He was examining an exquisite painting of wood nymphs in the entryway when Christianne came bounding down the stairs. The elegant hostess of the evening entertainments was gone. She wore a sky-blue *robe à la française* he'd seen her wear at Gavin's estate. She'd gathered her wild tresses back in a white ribbon.

"I hear you've been tormenting the rest of the salon's residents, clomping about when other people are trying to sleep," he said.

She brushed a wayward curl back over her shoulder. "I loathe the salon's hours. I'm weary of the city, and I long for open fields."

"I'd be happy to take you to Strawberry Grove."

"No, thank you. I haven't even begun to do what I came here for and you know how I love to have the bit in my teeth."

He couldn't help but laugh. Her blunt ways were like wind off the sea, a little raw but invigorating, challenging him where Eugenie had always seemed ready to cry at the slightest edge to his voice. Christianne would tiptoe about for no man.

"Perhaps I should just enjoy the ride," he said. Hadn't he always delighted in outings with Christianne? When she was younger, she'd had a gift for finding remarkable places. A den of fox kits. The wooded glen where newborn fawns came to drink. Her "secret" place, the top of an oak, where they could see for miles. A memory stole over him, pure and poignant. A perfect summer day, the hills of Strawberry Grove spangled with flowers. She'd pulled her horse to a stop at the top of a hill.

I'm going to go there one day, she had told him, pointing at the horizon beyond the lacework of leaves.

Where are you going? he'd asked.

Wherever you go. I'll keep up, she had added after a moment, a crease between her brows. *I promise.*

But he'd galloped his horse out the front gates without her, and ridden into a wide world where society would not allow her to follow.

She heaved a heavy sigh, bringing him back to the salon and the woman she'd become. "I'd give anything to take a ride," she confided, "but Queen Mab is in foal, so I had to leave her back home. I don't dare send for her, even after the colt is born. Mab wouldn't do well without fields to run in."

"I suppose it's futile to hope you might be so eager to see the new foal, you'll return to Strawberry Grove?"

"No such luck, I fear."

"It was worth a try," Nate said. "But Mistress Mayhem without her trusty steed is a forlorn sight indeed. Perhaps I could loan you a horse from my stable this Thursday. We could take a turn on the bridle path at St. James's Park."

"Really, Nate?" She clasped her hands. "That would be so lovely! Make sure it's one with spirit, please! Not some milksop ladies' horse with ribbons braided in its mane." She made a face. Suddenly she winced, pink coloring her cheeks. They'd always understood each other without words. He knew she was thinking of Eugenie. "I'm sorry," she said softly, touching his arm. It tugged his heart that, for an instant, she'd let him see her vulnerability.

"Don't mind it." He cradled her cheek in his hand, tracing velvety soft skin with the side of his thumb. "As for the horse—I'll see what I can do. Shall we say two days from now at one o'clock?"

Christianne beamed. "I'm not sure I can wait that long!"

CHAPTER 14

christianne was chafing and waiting for Nate's
summons when Clary rapped at her door two
days later. The maid looked as if she'd just bitten into a
rotten apple. "Lord Harlestone is downstairs waiting
for you."

Christianne took one last look at herself in the mirror, pleased by the picture she made in her cerulean
riding habit. In the past, she'd barely noticed what she
was wearing when riding with Nate. But now, she'd
spent a good hour arranging her hair and gown before
she'd settled her plumed riding hat on her curls.

He was waiting for her in the parlor, looking as
dashing as ever. Buckskin breeches clung to his muscular thighs, his broad shoulders encased in a forest
green frock coat. His hair was tied back at his nape
with a black ribbon, but she knew that it would soon be
windblown from their ride, wisps escaping to brush his
freshly shaven cheeks. His eyes twinkled as she descended the stairs, his gaze skimmed from the top of
her blue velvet riding hat with its jaunty red plume to
the soft black leather toes of her boots that peeped out
from beneath her skirts. A deliciously masculine appreciation sparked in those hazel depths.

"Good afternoon, Mistress Evelake," he greeted her with a bow. "You look particularly fetching this morning. Would you care to take a dignified trot along the bridle path today? All of London's finest will be displaying their frills and furbelows."

"Oh, bother London's finest. I intend to leave the dignified set in my dust, if your horse is up to it."

"My stable here in town is somewhat limited, but I've done the best I could."

Delilah swept in, breathless, her shopping basket trailing scarlet ribbons.

"Why, Harlestone!" she exclaimed, an overbright smile on her face. "What a lovely surprise. Have you come to take me out for some tea?"

"Not today, I'm afraid. I have a previous engagement with Mistress Evelake."

Delilah's lips pulled into a sensuous pout. "I never took you for a man so easily distracted. But it seems your eye wanders like any other man's, to the newest pretty face. Perhaps it is just as well Jessamyn isn't here to see it."

Christianne felt a jab of jealousy. Had there been something intimate between Nate and the missing woman?

"Mistress Evelake is far more than a pretty face," Nate said lightly. "Shall we go, Mistress?" he asked, offering his arm. Christianne slid her hand into the warm curve of his elbow, feeling the hard muscles beneath the dark green velvet.

She glanced back at Delilah, saw the woman's eyes go flint-hard. She'd made an enemy of the flame-haired beauty. The only question was—how dangerous of one?

He led her out onto the landing where one of the Harlestone grooms stood, holding the reins of two mounts. Nate's horse, Excalibur, pawed the dirt beside the most elegant mare Christianne had ever seen.

Christianne approached the enchanting creature, and the horse tossed her head, her white mane dancing. Liquid brown eyes, bright with intelligence, met Christianne's and she recognized just a hint of the wild in them. "Oh, Nate!" Christianne breathed. "She's exquisite."

"When she runs, she floats above the ground like the mists of Avalon," Nate said. "That's what I named her."

"Avalon," Christianne echoed as she stroked the mare's velvety nose.

"If riding Avalon suits you, I'll board her in the stable across the street. That way you can ride whenever you want."

Impulsively, Christianne flung her arms around Nate. She'd done so dozens of times over the years, but it felt so different since she kissed him that night in the garden. Nate gathered her close now, and she felt his heartbeat accelerate against the softness of her breasts.

"Thank you," she said. "Thank you, thank you, thank you!"

"A fairy queen needs her wings," he murmured against her hair.

THE PARK WAS GLORIOUS, the wind in Christianne's face blowing away the feeling of being confined as Avalon galloped across the park, Nate's roan in hot pursuit. When they reached a distant corner, she spun Avalon around to face him.

"I beat you!" she cried, reveling in the way his eyes danced beneath the brim of his hat.

He laughed, patting the roan's sweat-sheened flank. "I've not had someone test Excalibur's skill for ages," he said as he dismounted. "We'll have to make a habit of this."

He lifted her down from her sidesaddle, his hands warm and strong about her waist. Her gaze flicked to his mouth, her heart skipping a beat at the hint of that devilish smile she loved.

"Do you remember the first time I rode hell-for-leather after Culloden? I'd come to tell you Gavin and Adam were alive. You flung yourself on a horse and disappeared."

"I didn't want anyone to see me cry."

"I'd been trying to relearn how to ride, but it hurt like fire to put pressure on my injured knee. When you bolted off, no one else knew where you were going."

"You could have told someone else where to find me."

"In your secret place? Never. I seem to remember swearing a blood oath never to reveal it. I couldn't betray your confidence."

"I remember you thundering up to my tree on the bay Papa used to ride. You looked awful. Ice-white. Sweat pouring off you. Your teeth were clenched so tight your jaw should have cracked."

"Here I thought I cut a dashing figure, riding to the rescue," he jested, then sobered. "I was afraid you'd break your neck, trying to outrun your tears."

"You knew me so well." Tears pricked her eyes. "You held me tight while I sobbed against your chest. Then I felt your shoulders tremble. I knew you were crying for Gavin and Adam, too."

"There was another reason I've never told you. You gave me back my life that day." He ran his hand along the roan's arched neck, his eyes darkening with emotion. "Being on horseback with half a leg, riding at a full-out run, alone. I wasn't sure I'd ever do that again." He scooped up her hand and brushed her knuckles with his lips. Her skin tingled, even beneath her riding glove. "Everything changed for me after that," he said, low. His gaze held hers, and she felt herself falling into those hazel depths.

"Milor'?" A piping voice broke the spell.

Christianne looked down to see a girl of about six sidling toward them, her chapped hands clutching a bundle of bedraggled bouquets.

"Flowers for the pretty lady?" the child piped up, something wistful in her eyes reminding Christianne of Seraphina. Nate smiled down at the wee flower vendor, and fished a coin from his frock coat pocket. The little girl's eyes went round at the gleaming silver as he selected some charming blue blossoms. "Th-Thankee, milor'!" the little one lisped.

"Buy a meat pie with the extra, now," Nate urged, waving to a man selling pastries a ways down the path. "Promise me."

The babe bobbed a curtsey. "Oh, I will!" she exclaimed, and ran off, as if the savory scent of gravy had given her wings.

Christianne watched Nate from beneath her veil of lashes as he returned to her side. *How could he be so tender with a stranger's child and so distant from his own?* she wondered. Yet, wasn't there a sudden sadness in his face as well? For the child who was obviously hungry, or for the little girl he hadn't seen since Eugenie's death?

Everything changed, he'd told her about the ride they'd taken that awful day in the past. Might this be a chance to change things now?

"Have you heard from Seraphina?" she asked.

Nate's broad shoulders stiffened. "Her aunt writes she's doing well. They've moved to their house near Twickenham."

Christianne brightened. "Isn't that near London? You could ride over there for the afternoon. I'd love to go with you."

"I don't think disrupting the nursery routine is a good idea."

Christiane laughed. "I'm sure no one would mind! You're Seraphina's father."

Vulnerability flashed in Nate's eyes. She could see that he'd even surprised himself when he said, "Actually, I'm not."

Christianne froze mid-step. "What?"

"Seraphina was conceived after Eugenie and I were no longer sharing a bed."

The puzzle box of Nate's relationship with his daughter slid open, revealing the ugly truth. *Of course that's it,* a voice whispered inside her. *You should have guessed.* Even so, her shoulder blades pinched together.

"You *are* Seraphina's father," she asserted. "The only one the poor little mite has ever known. It's not her fault that Eugenie was a faithless fool."

"I know that. And yet, things happened that make it hard." Long, rein-hardened hands picked the petals off of the wilting blossoms he held.

"I know that the circumstances must have been painful for you," she said, "but surely a child should not pay the price for a mother who betrayed her marriage vows?"

He stared down at the petals crushed by his careless hand. "Forget-me-nots," he murmured. "These were my mother's favorites. Did you know?"

"No," she said softly, startled by his words.

"My mother was devoted to Sera. It pleased her so much to have Eugenie and Seraphina at Harlestone Hall. She had always hoped for a daughter. When Sera was born, she brought out entire layettes for the baby. I'm not sure who gave the child more dresses and playthings. I was gone a great deal at first because of my work in the army. Between Mother, Eugenie and Eugenie's sister, Philomena, Sera hardly missed me."

"How could you know Seraphina didn't miss you if you weren't there to see? Considering the way she looked up at you on the evening of your birthday fete, it certainly seemed that she wanted your affection. It was as if she were cold and waiting for just a smile from you to warm her. As for whatever love Sera had from your mother and Eugenie—death stole it from her."

Nate's fingers clenched. "Do you think it will do the child good to become attached to me, then go out into society and hear that her father may well have murdered her mother? Perhaps she would have been better off if I'd written to Colonel Markham in Belgium after Eugenie's death. Maybe he could give the child what I cannot."

"Colonel Markham?"

"Someone felt it their duty to inform me he was the object of Eugenie's indiscretions at the time of Sera's birth. I hid the truth from my parents. What good could possibly come from telling my mother that Sera was not her granddaughter by blood?"

"Maybe you don't give your mother enough credit. Maybe she would have known that what mattered was that that beautiful child was a granddaughter in her heart."

"You're wrong. Some sadistic monster exposed the truth to my mother. When she learned of it she died of a broken heart."

"My God."

"She'd been ailing for years, and Sera gave her a reason to hold on. Once that was taken away from her, she just let go."

If someone had told me such a thing, I would have fought even harder to shield Sera. I'd have loved her even more, Christianne thought, anger running hot in her veins. "Who did such a heinous thing? Tell me, Nate."

"Why? So that you can call him out?" The corner of Nate's mouth tipped up in a sad smile. "Even if I discovered who wrote the letter my mother received, the damage is done."

Christianne remembered something her own mother had said. *I knew Nate's father when I was a girl. The first time I attended a ball at Harlestone Hall, he showed me every portrait of every ancestor stretching back to William the Conqueror. He even had an artist paint one wall with a family tree with the Rowland bloodline so that he could boast to anyone who had the misfortune of straying near enough for him to collar. It is indeed as royal as any king's.*

Had Nate's mother had that same pride, layered under the warmth and love Nate had always spoken of? "I'm sorry about your mother," Christianne said. "But Sera needs you now."

"Let it go." Nate dropped the flowers from his hand. He gathered the reins of both their mounts. "We should cool the horses down." He started walking. She fell into step beside him.

She'd get no more from him now on the subject of Sera, but she couldn't "let it go." The child with her fairy wings and plaintive violet eyes haunted her almost as much as the man who was winding his way ever deeper into her heart.

"What would you have us talk about, then?" she asked.

"Anything else."

"Have you found any more leads to whomever has been printing those awful broadsheets? When I heard Adam say that clues were leading to The Blue Peacock—"

Nate ran his fingers through his hair in exasperation. "Do you think I've been sitting idly by? Whoever is behind this might have murdered my wife and her unborn babe, as well as done their best to sabotage the work I've devoted my life to."

"The question is, who would do such a thing—and why?"

"I don't know. But I don't need your help. I've already got allies, some right in the salon."

"Who are they?"

"Robin. Clary."

"Well, now you have another ally. Surely, between us, we'll be able to unravel this scheme. I'll be able to watch comings and goings, check messages left on the hall table, listen to conversations. You can't be at the salon all of the time. I'll get a chance to search the rooms here when the other women go out."

"Oh, no you don't. It's too dangerous."

"Such a warning might keep Laura or Maria in check, but it won't stop me." She met his gaze and saw an answering spark in his. "Adam said that someone had burst out of the salon and bumped into him, a man in a mask and cloak who dropped those awful handbills in his wake."

"I questioned Marguerite about it afterwards, but she didn't know who the patron might be. There have always been men who prefer to be discreet. This person is not the only one who comes wearing a mask."

"Well, I'll find out who they are. I'm not leaving The Blue Peacock until I do."

"Then will you go home?" Hell, he'd tear the salon apart brick by brick if it meant she would return to the sheltered life she'd known.

But Christianne's brow creased, suddenly thoughtful. "I don't know if I will go home. I want more out of life than to be sequestered at Strawberry Grove. I'm not sure what it is that I need."

I could teach you about need. His thought cut, bone deep. He'd done his best to suppress his reaction to her.

He couldn't do so anymore. He hadn't allowed himself to feel this kind of passion since the days leading up to his marriage. Not even then. Christianne fired his blood like no woman ever had, she made him laugh, she challenged every part of him, his mind, his heart, his body...

He'd been her Galahad when she was young, and she'd made no secret that she saw him as her own shining knight. Now he longed to be more than that. He wanted to see her face on his pillow in the morning, learn every inch of her body, hear her gasp with pleasure when he entered her. Nothing would be hidden from him, every spark of pleasure would be his to see. She was brave enough for that, to show all of herself.

He shoved back feelings, unnerving and raw.

He'd find a way to deliver her back to the brothers and sisters who loved her, and the mother who knew exactly what defying polite society would cost her. He'd find a way to protect her from the dangers of the choices she'd made—even if it meant protecting her from him and the unbridled feelings he couldn't deny.

Somehow he would rein in this need for her that had become like fever in his blood—even though he didn't want to.

CHAPTER 15

*R*ain had started to fall by the time they got back to The Blue Peacock. They turned the horses over to young Robin to rub down, then brushed past a scowling Delilah as Christianne whisked Nate up the stairs to her chamber.

"If we're to work on this together, you must give me a list of potential suspects," Christianne said. "What have you found thus far?"

Nate crossed to the small table where Clary had replenished the decanter of wine. It stung to see him pour the rich red spirits into the freshly washed glasses, as if he'd done just this in Jessamyn's room a dozen times.

"There is no need to make a list," he said. "I did so for Callum MacGregor when this all began."

"The man you hired to investigate Eugenie's murder? Has he found anything?"

"No. And I don't expect him to now. He was called back to Scotland some time ago. This might be useful, nonetheless." He drew out a piece of parchment and spread it out before her. "I've raked my memory, and come up with people who might wish me ill."

She scanned the headings, each underlined with a

159

list of names beneath. *"Thieves' Kitchen, Eugenie's Lovers."*

She hesitated, not wanting to probe an old wound, but she wasn't going to get information she needed if she didn't ask things that were painful. "What about the father of the baby Eugenie was carrying?"

"I don't know who it was. I never had the chance to ask."

"Deborah Musgrove might know."

"That's what I thought. Callum McGregor attempted to speak to her after the inquest, but apparently the lady's nerves were so shattered after giving testimony that her husband sent her to a spa in Switzerland."

"I'd like to shatter Deborah Musgrove's nerves," Christianne muttered.

Nate's mouth tipped up in that half grin that made her pulse flutter. She hesitated, fretting her lip. "I've wondered. Is it possible that Jessamyn might have something to do with this? Perhaps she said something in bed—" It hurt to think of Nate with the beauty in the bed where Christianne now slept.

"I only shared a bed with Jessamyn once," Nate said, and there was sadness in his voice. "I could tell her heart was involved. I didn't want to hurt her. She wasn't like the other women here. She hoped for something I couldn't give her."

"What do you think happened to her?"

"I hope she found what she was searching for. But love can make someone see traits in others that aren't really there. Soon after I made my position clear, a different suitor began calling on her. No one knows who he was. Perhaps he was already married. Perhaps someone who feared scandal. There are countless reasons to run away."

It hurt to see the tenderness in Nate's eyes. But then,

wasn't his empathy one of the things she'd always loved about him?

She focused on the final heading, pushing away the thought of Nate and another woman in the throes of passion. *"Political Rivals,"* she read aloud. "I've seen enough vitriol hurled at you and Gavin to know how heated those exchanges get."

Her brow furrowed. "Maybe the key is unraveling what these people want?" Christianne mused.

Nate regarded her, solemn. "Revenge of some kind."

"What about this group. *The Military,*" she pointed to the heading. "Can you tell me about your time in the cavalry? Maybe there is a clue somewhere."

Nate's eyes went dark. "You don't want to hear about this, Christianne. I spoke to Eugenie about it once when I was in my cups, and she never forgave me."

"I do want to hear about it. The battles you fought are a part of you." She laid a hand on his arm. "Please."

He waited to speak for so long, she expected him to refuse. But he walked to the window looking out onto the street below. She knew he was seeing another landscape. Scotland's rugged Highlands, battlefields peopled with ghosts. "I love my country," he said, low. "I swore an oath to my king. I was willing to fight, even against my best friends, and die if I had to. My father and his friends always talked about the glory of war. But it's blood and pain and brutality.

"There are honorable men who fight on both sides, and God knows, I admire them. But there are also men who revel in the carnage. There isn't enough death or torment in all the world to satisfy their thirst for vengeance against those on the other side. It's possible whoever is behind this plot against me is one of those men."

"What about Pratt? Or someone angry that you won my brothers a pardon?"

"Anyone angry about that could have struck the moment Gavin and Adam set foot on English shores again. Why wait so long to take revenge?"

"Maybe his anger festered... I've seen men grow more bitter over time. But not you. You grieved over the loss of your leg. But I've never once heard you say, 'Why me?'"

Nate shrugged. "Why *not* me? So many men died. I was fortunate. I had friends to support me. Important work I could devote my life to. But you don't effect real change without knocking down walls. Men like Pratt won't forgive us. They are rich and bloody comfortable with the way things are."

"Like your father?"

"He has little patience for reform work. My mother loved it." Grief pulled down the corners of Nate's lips. "She knitted scarves and mittens and hats for the lads, and gathered clothes for the Foundling Hospital."

"Your mother was very kind to me the few times I saw her," Christianne said. "When she dropped you off at Strawberry Grove, she always smiled at my mother. Most women of her station pursed their lips and turned away."

There had been something so wistful that passed between the two women during those brief encounters. Even as a young girl, Christianne had sensed it.

"I miss her," Nate said softly. "I can only imagine how much Seraphina misses her, too."

Christianne's breath caught at the mention of his daughter, the first time he'd brought up the little girl on his own. She said nothing, waiting for him to fill the silence.

"Sera and my mother were very close. To lose Eugenie and my mother in such short succession must be unbearable."

"You are the only one who truly understands Sera's loss. You could comfort her."

Nate looked down at his hands. "I don't know how."

"Do you remember when my pony was ill? You stayed up with me all night, because you were the one I wanted. Adam roared and stomped, and Gavin looked as if every tear I shed cut his heart. But you knew it was *my* pony, my grief, my loss. You didn't try to say anything stupidly comforting or thrust another pony on me. You just sat with me and let me cry, let me rage, let me be silent. Just go to Sera, Nate. You'll find the right words to say."

Nate's eyes met hers. "Perhaps I will when I'm ready. Sometimes at Harlestone I swear I can hear the echo of their laughter. My mother. Eugenie and Seraphina. Before everything came apart." He paused for a moment. "Did you know I kept the fan Eugenie carried that night? I thought Seraphina might want the image of her mother one day."

"Oh, Nate. I don't think—"

"Not the fan itself, of course. I plan to have an artist copy the picture of Eugenie and frame it. That way, as time passes, she won't forget what her mother looked like."

Christianne remembered the expression on the child's fairylike features as she made her way through the crowded ballroom, her little hands clutching the toy soldier. Seraphina had peered up at her mother as if Eugenie was an island in the sea of strangers.

"Giving Sera a portrait of her mother is a lovely idea," Christianne said.

She didn't want to feel anything but contempt for Eugenie, but her heart ached knowing the haven

Seraphina had counted on was now gone, and that she might never remember that safe harbor was once hers.

Nate grew quiet. "It's made me think of my mother as well. I'm glad she didn't live to see me under suspicion this way."

"She would have known you were innocent of these accusations, just as I do." Christianne reached out and took his strong hand in hers. "I hate feeling that you have to look over your shoulder. You can't know who to trust."

He touched her cheek, the corners of his eyes crinkled as he gave her a tender smile. "I know who to trust," he said. "The Knights. And you."

Tears stung her eyes. "We'll find this coward."

"Just promise me you'll be careful. I don't know what I'd do if something happened to you."

Her heart swelled against her ribs. "You worry too much," she said and slid her arms around him, pressing her cheek to the hard wall of his chest.

Nate chuckled. "When it comes to you, Mistress Mayhem, I doubt I worry enough."

He stroked her hair for a moment and she could hear his heartbeat begin to race. She wanted to stay in his arms forever. But Nate stepped away.

THE CLOAKED man stood in the shadows outside The Blue Peacock, where he'd waited countless times before, careful, so careful not to be seen. Nights when he'd watched that second-story window for Jessamyn to let him know it was safe. He could still remember his heart thundering as he raced up the stairs, slipping inside. Inside the room, inside her body.

He knew every inch of the chamber he watched now...the wide bed, the scent of honey that had clung to her clothes...the way the cool sheets slipped against naked skin.

But then, so did the other man who was now framed in the window. Nathaniel Rowland, Viscount of Harlestone—untouchable, no matter how dire the tempests that swirled around him. They never sucked him down where he couldn't breathe, not war, not his wife's betrayal. Not even her murder and the rumors that she'd died at his hand.

The man ran sensitive fingertips over the plume that decorated the the mask in his frock coat pocket.

"He owes me a debt," he muttered. He wasn't finished with Nathaniel Rowland yet. A second silhouette moved into the window, a woman with a nimbus of dark hair leaning close to Harlestone. "Mistress Evelake," the man in the shadows sneered. "Perhaps she will be the twist of the knife I've been hoping for."

165

CHAPTER 16

*T*ime was running out.

Christianne picked at a hangnail, trying not to fret over the letter Eliza had sent through Nate the other day, her sister's familiar handwriting warning that Gavin and Adam would return in the next three weeks. Eliza had begged Christianne to come home before they arrived. It was one thing to fool their mother, she'd written, but Adam had indulged in enough escapades of his own to sense when his sisters were up to no good.

Yet, even if Christianne wanted to spare her sister the stress of facing down Adam and Gavin, how could she leave The Blue Peacock when she'd only begun to learn about the people who made up the salon and even more important—ferret out who had killed Nate's wife?

As a girl, she'd mastered the art of sneaking out of Strawberry Grove, and her penchant for mischief aided her now as she slipped in and out of rooms, searching for clues.

Christianne mulled over the collection of possible suspects in the house. Robin and Clary shared a corner in the kitchen, drawing out their pallets when the last

166

crumb had been swept clean after the salon closed. Robin visited his best friend from the Foundling Hospital and studied navigation charts, longing for a quadrant of his own, and Clary pined for Jessamyn, who'd tried to help her exchange the scullery for the post of lady's maid.

Mrs. Trench, the housekeeper, was almost painfully predictable.

Delilah's surroundings were as fiery as her red hair, a book on the table filled with lewd etchings of naked men and women tangled together in ways Christianne had never imagined possible.

Only Aimee's room and Marguerite Charbonneau's inner sanctum remained a mystery. Both were locked the few times Christianne was able to try the door, and Madame's was only reachable by a private staircase.

But today, it seemed Christianne's luck had changed. Aimee had left the salon an hour earlier, a bundle in her arms, and Clary was cleaning the rooms, leaving them open to air. Christianne had watched as minutes ticked by, knowing she could hardly go searching through Aimee's things with the maid bobbing in and out, changing sheets and brushing clothing while Robin polished shoes. It seemed as if it took forever before brother and sister went downstairs for a cup of tea.

Quietly, Christianne slipped down the hall into Aimee's room, grateful when the knob turned. She stepped in and shut the door behind her. She looked around for a moment, surprised. Scallops of roses had been painted along one wall, the blooms looking so real it felt as if she could pluck off a petal. Clary must have been brushing dust from Aimee's wine-colored petticoat. It lay on the bed. As Christianne passed it on the way to Aimee's desk, something caught her eye. She'd thought the gown was new, but part of the skirt was folded back, exposing cloth faded and badly worn on the underside. At some time, a gifted seamstress had pulled Aimee's garment apart, then turned the pieces inside out and restitched them with the fresh side showing. Here and there, small tears had been mended, the imperfections concealed by some of the most unique trim she'd ever seen.

Bemused, Christianne explored the desk before the sunny window, finding a few letters from family. Then, her foot bumped something under the desk. She bent down, seeing a shawl concealing something. A box of some sort, she realized as she slipped the covering aside. A jewelry casket, perhaps? Or something else? She lifted it onto the desk.

Smudges of paint had been left here and there on the wood—barely visible hints of green and blue on Aimee's hands and beneath her fingernails suddenly making sense. She lifted the wooden lid and her heart skipped a beat. Pen and ink drawings had been affixed to the underside of the lid. They'd been drawn by a gifted artist, movement and emotions conveyed in bold strokes. These were of children and an older woman with kind eyes. She removed the tray of paints and brushes and examined the layer below, realizing that the floor of the box beneath it wasn't deep enough. There must be at least three inches more. She felt along the edges, finding a tiny catch, lifting out the piece of wood.

A cloth pouch had been hidden there. Christianne picked it up, feeling the weight of coins, hearing something rustle as she opened the drawstring. Paper. Crumpled into a tight ball. Carefully, she pulled it out, smoothed it open. Her heart plunged to her toes.

The hideous image of Nate strangling Eugenie stared back at her.

"What are you doing in my room?"

Christianne spun around. Aimee stood in the doorway, her face white with guilt, the basket in her hand shaking.

"I was looking for this." Christianne brandished the incriminating handbill.

Aimee didn't even seem to see it. She rushed over to Christianne, snatching away the pouch. Panic sparked in her eyes as she sifted through the money inside.

"You're the one who has been spreading this poison about Viscount Harlestone, aren't you?" Christianne accused.

The clink of coins stopped and she looked up. "Poison? Who is poisoning whom? What in the world are you talking about?"

"I know someone involved with The Blue Peacock has been spreading lies about Lord Harlestone, trying to do him harm. Now, I find this handbill with those coins of yours! You've been hiding the fact that you're an artist. Is it because you're creating things like this?" Christianne thrust the crumpled page at Aimee.

Aimee shrank back from the monstrous image, as if it turned her stomach. "I paint flowers and faces and scenes from myths on porcelain for a silversmith who uses my work to make pendants! That awful scandal sheet was posted on a wall near his shop. I ripped it down on my way to deliver my latest work and crumpled it up in my pouch. I meant to throw it in the fire when I got home, but I dropped my basket and one of the porcelain discs broke. I was so upset, I forgot about everything except the income I'd lost."

"Why should I believe you?"

"Because it's the truth! I'd never draw anything so hateful!"

"Why keep your painting secret if you've nothing to hide?"

"Madame doesn't like it. She wants me to concentrate all my efforts in the salon. Please, please don't tell her what I'm doing." Tears brimmed over Aimee's lashes. "I can't lose my position here. My mother and sisters depend on me." She looked so desperate, Christianne couldn't help but believe her.

"Your mother and sisters?" she echoed.

"They make lace, but they've not been able to sell enough to make ends meet since Mama's eyes started failing. That's how I came to work at the salon. This money is their rent. I'm determined none of my other sisters will have to join me here."

Christianne looked at the images of the family on the paintbox's open lid, and knew Aimee was telling the truth. The rush of excitement Christianne felt upon finding the handbill faded.

Disappointed as she was, empathy welled up in Christianne. She would do the same to protect Eliza, Maria and Laura if she were in Aimee's place.

"I believe you. I'm sorry I upset you. I just hoped I could finally put an end to whomever is tormenting Lord Harlestone."

"I think what's happening to him is awful, too. That's why I tore the sheet down. There are a dozen lords who deserve to be lambasted that way. I saw Colonel Pratt trample over a boy and not even slow his horse. But Lord Harlestone is as kind to Clary as he is to Madame. He doesn't deserve this ugliness."

They were quiet for a moment.

"Why do you care so much?" Aimee asked.

Christianne averted her gaze. "He helped my family when we desperately needed it." She walked toward Aimee's bed and touched the mended petticoat that lay across it. "You know, I'm always catching my lace on shrubs or fence posts," she said. "Perhaps you could bring some of your family's work back to the salon next time you visit home."

Aimee gave her a tentative smile. "I suppose I could bring some back next time I visit."

The flicker of hope in her voice warmed Christianne. Gavin's growing brood needed oceans of lace to trim shifts and cuffs and neckcloths and gowns as well. She was sure she could convince him to purchase Aimee's mother's wares.

"I loved the sketches on your paintbox lid," Christianne said. "Will you show me some of your paintings as well?"

Aimee caught her lip between her teeth, considering. After a moment, she went to a drawer and opened it. There, on a soft bed of cloth, lay an oval of porcelain the size of a small plate. It was unfinished, but the scene from mythology showed great artistic promise. "This will be framed and hung on the silversmith's wall," Aimee said. "It's a gift for his wife."

Christianne leaned closer to examine the scene. A dark-haired goddess draped her lush body across a stone bench while cupids clustered around her. "Is this Aphrodite?" she asked, then gasped in surprise. "She looks just like me."

Aimee looked as if she'd been caught trying on Marguerite's jewelry. "I steal faces. It does no harm."

Was it possible that an artist like Aimee could give insight about Eugenie's fan? Christianne pictured it again, the center of the fan leaf torn out. She still felt whatever portion of the hand-painted scene had been ripped away on the night of the murder might help them find whoever killed Nate's wife.

"Have you ever thought about painting fans?" Christianne asked. "Some are so beautiful."

"I'd love to, but there is a strict guild that controls such things. Only four apprentices a year are allowed to take up the trade. Besides, the finest fans are imported from France."

It was true, Christianne thought, discouraged. Nate had said that Eugenie and Deborah Musgrove traveled a great deal. Eugenie might have bought the fan in Paris itself.

Christianne lifted the porcelain disc carefully in her hands, holding it closer to the light spilling through the window. "You certainly have a gift for portraying children."

"I got a lot of practice drawing my sisters back in Spitalfields. There were six when Papa died, so there was always someone willing to pose for a peppermint drop."

Something about one little cupid gave Christianne a pang. The cupid had dark hair, but her wistful expression reminded her of Seraphina Rowland, her eyes asking for something the world refused to give her. Christianne understood the distance between Nate and the child better now. Yet, when he'd spoken about Seraphina's true parentage, she'd detected his deep sense of self-blame.

Now that Eugenie was no longer there to pour acid on the wound with her betrayals, might the barrier between Nate and his daughter soften? Could Christianne give that healing a little help? "Do you ever do commissions?" she asked Aimee.

"You want me to paint something?"

"I'd like to hire you to do a series of sketches of a little girl like the ones on the lid of your paintbox. Perhaps you could even paint some of them."

Interest brightened Aimee's blue eyes. "Who is this little girl?"

"Lord Harlestone's daughter. She's staying with her aunt just outside of London. If I can arrange for a carriage, will you do it? I'll pay you well."

Enough to keep the wolves from Aimee's mother's door for the time being, Christianne hoped.

Why are you doing this, Christianne? she could almost hear Eliza scold.

Because Sera needs Nate and Nate needs her as well. She'd seen the self-blame in his face. Knew that, in time, he'd see the pain he'd caused by withholding his heart and never forgive himself.

Perhaps this effort would be futile, but she had to try...for Nate and his little daughter.

CHAPTER 17

It was a risk to borrow the carriage from Gavin's townhouse. But Christianne knew it was the only way to be certain that Eugenie's sister wouldn't dare to turn her away. She'd told the startled stablemaster at Gavin's townhouse that her trip was a secret one because she was working on a surprise for Lord Harlestone. She'd sworn old Tom to remain mum and she knew he would keep his word.

But she hadn't figured that the postillion would reveal her identity to the woman sitting beside her. "You're Lord Glenlyon's sister?" Aimee's eyes went wide with disbelief as the carriage bounced along the road toward the Kettering estate.

"His half-sister. We share the same father. But my parents never married."

"Why ever would you come to the salon? Don't you realize how word of your being there could damage you even more than your current position has placed you in?"

Aimee clutched her paintbox, alarm pinkening her cheeks. "If Lord Glenlyon finds out you are working at the salon, what might he do? None of us can afford to make such an enemy. The wrath of such a powerful nobleman could destroy everything Madame has built."

"I promise, you're all safe. Gavin will understand I'm trying to help Nate."

"Does Madame know who you are?"

"No. I don't want to put anyone else on guard, or in danger. I don't mean any of you harm. I swear it. I only want to help Nate because of what he did for my brothers and because I know he didn't murder his wife. But I need proof."

"I'm glad you're trying to help him. Lord Harlestone had such sad eyes when he came to the salon, especially after he'd had too many glasses of wine."

Christianne pressed Aimee's hand. "Please don't tell anyone that I am the Earl of Glenlyon's sister," she begged.

"I won't," Aimee said. "I promise."

She could only pray Aimee would keep her word.

THE SCENE on the manicured lawn might have been plucked from a Gainsborough painting as Christianne descended from the coach in the carriage circle at Millwood Park, the ancestral home of the Kettering family. The mistress of the house sat at a table beneath the spreading branches of an ancient oak tree and sipped tea with a lady in dove gray while a flock of children frolicked and pushed each other on a swing.

Christianne pasted on her most confident smile, as she and the awestruck Aimee followed the servant racing ahead to announce them.

"A thousand pardons, Lady Kettering. May I announce Mistress Christianne Slade and Miss..." He stopped suddenly, looking over his shoulder for the second guest. But Christianne noted that Aimee's attention had been snagged by a particularly lovely fountain bubbling nearby.

It was easy to guess which of the women at the table was Eugenie's sister. Philomena Kettering had the same golden hair and delicate features as Eugenie, without the frenetic gaiety that had always bubbled beneath the surface in Nate's wife. Grief still shadowed the woman's mouth and eyes. Christianne wondered if she blamed Nate for Eugenie's death, or even thought him to be the murderer? What if Lady Kettering wouldn't allow her to have the sketches of Seraphina made at all? The possibility made Christianne a little queasy. "Good afternoon," she greeted Lady Kettering with forced brightness. "Thank you for seeing me. I'm Lord Glenlyon's sister."

Philomena Kettering frowned. "I was unaware Glenlyon even had a sister. I thought he was an only child."

Christianne cheeks grew hot. "I am his natural sister. Christianne Slade."

The stranger in gray rose, and smiled with mild surprise and interest. "My name is Lady Beresford, but please call me Olivia. It is lovely to make the acquaintance of anyone connected with Lord Glenlyon."

"It's good to meet you," Christianne replied.

"I encountered your brother on occasion, to my great pleasure. Lord Glenlyon's work with the foundlings moves any mother with a feeling heart. But I am an old friend of Glenlyon's partner in philanthropic endeavors, Lord Harlestone."

This woman knew Nate and Gavin? Christianne knew she shouldn't be surprised.

"Before my husband died, he and Lord Harlestone worked on several issues together. I've been so grieved over this cloud of suspicion that surrounds Lord Harlestone now. I could never believe he was capable of harming any woman and certainly not his wife."

Christianne saw Eugenie's sister stiffen. "I wish I were as sure," Lady Kettering said.

Olivia squeezed her friend's hand. "Of course, you are searching for answers. You grieve for your sister. They will find the real villain yet, I'm sure of it."

Olivia gestured to where a pack of boys were tumbling about in some rough game.

"The tallest two lads playing with cricket bats are my sons," Olivia said. "Philomena is kind enough to allow them to share her sons' tutor."

Philomena sniffed. "It is the least I can do. You've had a most distressing time since your husband's death." Eugenie's sister turned censorious eyes on Christianne. "Now, Mistress Slade, what is your reason for coming here?"

Aimee shrank back, her sketch pad in her arms.

"I hoped to have this artist make drawings of Seraphina at play as a gift for Lord Harlestone. We think it would do Harlestone good to see how she's grown."

Philomena's mouth drew tight as a purse string. "I can't imagine why he would want such a thing. He's barely paid attention to the child since her mother was killed. Or even before that, truth be told. No, I don't believe I can allow it."

"Oh, Mena, let her do it!" Lady Beresford exclaimed. "Perhaps she could draw the boys as well. I would so love drawings of Alexander and Richard."

"I don't believe that a drawing of his daughter would warm Lord Harlestone's heart toward her, but if she would also sketch the other children, I might allow it, I suppose. My boys *are* exceedingly handsome."

At that instant, a child came running up to them, her golden curls bouncing.

"Hello, Sera," Christianne said softly. "Do you remember me?"

"You're Caval's friend. You throw his stick. I saw you from the nursery window."

"Caval?" Philomena scoffed. "That horrible dog?"

Christianne kept all her attention on Sera. "Caval and I are good friends. I found him when he was a pup and he had his leg caught in a trap."

"Poor pup!"

"Your papa made him better."

"Papa likes Caval better than he likes me. I heard Mama say so."

Christianne thought carefully, searching for the right words. "Sometimes even the wisest grown-ups can't know another person's heart. I am going to surprise your papa with portraits of you, if you'll let Mistress Aimee draw them."

Sera tucked her chin into the ruffle on her collar, and Christianne wished she had her sister Laura's gift with children and could draw the little girl into her arms.

She waited, as if Sera was a little butterfly, poised to flutter out of reach.

At last the little girl looked up at Christianne with her whole heart in her violet eyes. "For Papa," she whispered.

~

CHRISTIANNE CURLED up on a stool next to Aimee, watching deft strokes of the sable brush bring Seraphina's face to life—rose tints, golden curls, the sweet bow-shaped lips. "I can almost hear her little voice and the rustle of her petticoats in the flowers. You've even captured that wistful expression."

Aimee stroked a highlight onto the ribbon around

Sera's waist. "Jessamyn looked sad like that after Lord Harlestone stopped going to her room," she said softly. "It hurt her when he only bedded her once, and Delilah kept taunting her about it. Then the man in the mask began to visit her. First, I thought Jessamyn was being mysterious about him just to get back at Delilah. Jessamyn seemed almost *too* happy. Like... she was brittle. She talked about the fine trips he promised to take her on to Italy and France, and how she'd take Clary with, to be her lady's maid."

"Did you ever find out who he was?"

"No. But he was always giving her gifts. We made a game of guessing what was in the packages he brought. A little silver ring with a rose carved out of coral. Shawls and fans and such. Pretty jars of scents."

Was one of them the exotic scent Gavin and Adam had detected on the handbills they'd found? Christianne wondered.

"Jessamyn even put some of the lotion on Clary's poor hands when they got too chapped," Aimee added.

"That must have meant a lot to her."

"Clary needed someone to be kind to her. The first mistress she had after she left the Foundling Hospital had no patience for the poor girl's tears. She made Clary so jumpy, she couldn't do anything right. Lord Harlestone brought her here. Mrs. Trench is strict but fair. Just the woman to help steady Clary's nerves. And Clary could walk to see Robin on Sundays. She fretted about him, though. He was desperate to go to sea, but no captain would take him with his arm that way. It hurt her to know he was yearning for an adventure he could never have."

Christianne swallowed hard. Was loving Nate so different from Robin's longing for the sea?

Aimee dipped her brush in linseed oil to thin the

paint. She dabbed a bit on a piece of wood to check the color.

"Did Clary talk about the Foundling Home much?"

"Barely said anything at all for a long time. But Jessamyn had this way about her—people were always telling her their stories. When she heard how much Clary missed Robin, Jessamyn tried to distract her, teaching Clary how to fix hair. They kept up their sessions even after Lord Harlestone brought Robin to the salon."

"No wonder Clary couldn't believe Jessamyn would leave without telling her goodbye."

"Jessamyn's problem was that she thought everyone was like her. She had some romantic notion that some dashing man would rescue her."

Nate must have seemed like just the man to make that dream come true, Christianne thought. But would someone who seemed so inherently kind lash out with these vicious handbills after those hopes were dashed? She knew Nate well enough to be sure he'd explained his reasons for resisting Jessamyn's charms as gently as any man could. Or was it possible that Jessamyn had another reason for winning people's confidences? What if she wasn't as selfless as she seemed?

"Did you notice anything strange before Jessamyn left?"

"She didn't seem like herself the last week. She seemed nervous."

"Because she was going to elope? Or do you think it was something else?"

"Clary could tell you more than I could. But that girl is warier than a cat whose tail's been slammed in a door. Part of it comes from living here. We're all rivals for the men's attention, aren't we? But Clary will never be pretty enough or clever enough to be a hostess."

Christianne pictured the maid's face spattered with

freckles, her nose too large, her mouth too wide, her brow forever puckered in an "I dare you!" scowl. She had to be in her teens, but hunger and hardship had stunted her growth, her body all sharp points. No, she'd never do more than carry coal hods and scrub floors.

"The only person Clary really trusts is Robin," Aimee said, putting the finishing touch on Sera's painted cheek.

So Robin would be the key. It shouldn't be hard to get the lad to talk to her, Christianne thought, suppressing a smile. Robin had become like the bird he'd been named for—hopping in and out to chatter with her at the most unexpected moments, his gap-toothed smile and winning ways, as unlike his sister's as it was possible to be.

She'd find some way to get Clary to trust her, Christianne resolved. She knew all about the girl's need to pretend there were no tender places in a secretly vulnerable heart.

~

CHRISTIANNE COULDN'T LOOK at the sour-faced serving girl quite the same way after her talk with Aimee. When Clary came up to her chamber to stir up the fire, Christianne noticed how the heavy coal hod bowed her shoulders, and how raw her chapped hands were from washing clothes and dishes. Clary's face was still pinched while she went about her housework, but Christianne watched more closely now, and saw how Clary's smile warmed when she passed Robin. Today, when the other women left the breakfast table, Christianne lingered while Clary moved about, clearing dishes, sweeping up crumbs. A few days earlier, she'd begun to notice the maid's habit of scooping up rolls left untouched on their plates after meals, then surreptitiously slipping them into her apron pockets.

"Robin must be busy today," Christianne ventured in yet another effort to start a conversation. She wrapped three rolls in a pristine napkin. "When you see him, will you give him this? They're still warm."

"Oh, no. I couldn't take them," Clary began to protest, but Christianne aimed a pointed look at the bulge in Clary's pocket where she could just see the telltale outline of a bun.

Clary put her hand over the bulge, her face turning scarlet.

"It's all right," Christianne said softly. "I won't tell anyone. Don't you get enough food in the kitchen?"

"Oh, yes," Clary insisted, flustered. "Plenty."

"Then why do you save the rolls?"

Clary hesitated. "It's just an old habit, I guess. Robin would get so hungry after the landlord turned us out of our cottage. Someone told us if he ate more, his arm would grow straight. Now I know it was nonsense. The man was just having fun with us. I just hate to waste good food, you know? Now, we save it for the boys at the Foundling Hospital. Robin takes it there when he goes to see his friends."

"Aren't the rolls hard and stale by then?"

"It's better than going hungry. The big boys take food from the littler ones. It's just the way of it. But it's better than being on the street."

"How long were you and Robin on your own?"

"Seemed like forever. After Mama got sick, with the consumption, she couldn't take care of us anymore. Left us at St. Andrews. We're not orphans, though. Our da was a gentleman, Mama said. Went to make his fortune in Jamaica, sailing on the *Fanny B*. Mama swore our da would return, but he never did. Da even left us something so we'd never forget he was coming back for us...but...that's lost now, just like he is." Pain creased her face. "All Robin ever wanted was to sail to Jamaica and find out what happened to him."

Christianne's heart ached for the brother and sister. How many stories had even more tragic endings? How many children were left in this sprawling city to find? Her heart squeezed as she thought of the work Nate and Gavin had done with the foundlings, and she loved Nate more than ever.

Clary eyed Christianne for a long moment, then took the rolls and hurried away.

~

THE PAINTINGS WERE DONE at last, the paint dried, the canvas carefully wrapped and stowed in a pouch attached to Christianne's saddle. Her heart raced with anticipation as she reined Avalon to a halt in front of Nate's townhouse, the Palladian façade reminding her all too sharply of the world she'd left behind. It was reckless to come here, when hiding her identity mattered so much. But even as a girl, she'd never had the patience to wait until someone's birthday to give them a perfect gift. And the roll of sketches and the painting she carried might be the most exquisite gift she'd ever given to someone she loved.

She only hoped Nate felt the same way. She dismounted and unfastened the precious bundle, hugging it against her breasts, with a mixture of anticipation and dread. She rang the bell and after a moment, the massive door swung open, a footman in livery bowing low.

"I'm here to see Lord Harlestone. Please tell him Christianne Slade wishes to see him."

The footman disappeared.

It wasn't long before she could hear the uneven

thumps of Nate's steps as he rushed down the stairs. By the time he reached the landing, the rich, caramel and tawny hair fell across his brow, his face harried above a crumpled shirt. "Christianne! Are you all right? Is anything amiss?"

"No. I'm fine," she laughed, thinking of the picture they both made. "I brought a gift and I just couldn't wait to give it to you."

He glanced at the bundle in her arms. "A *gift?*" Some of the alarm eased from his handsome features. He seemed to shake himself, as if suddenly realizing they were standing in the hall with the servants gaping.

"Come into the library," he said. He guided her through hallways lined with Tudor era chairs. An artist had painted a Greek ruin on the silk wallpaper, flowers nudging the crumbling pillars in drifts of pink blossoms.

At last, he guided her into a room where books lined the walls. She scanned the shelves, seeing volumes on military strategy, but also texts on scientific discoveries. Astronomy, the human body. Henry Fielding's *The History of Tom Jones, A Foundling* and *Gulliver's Travels* by Jonathan Swift, sat on a table beside a chair near the fire. There was something that tugged at Christianne's heart as she looked at that single chair and thought of how many nights Nate must have sat here, reading, alone.

The bang of the door shutting startled her, and she turned to see Nate framed against it, exasperation twisting his features.

"What were you thinking, coming here like this? You're already in enough danger at the salon. If someone is watching the house..." He drew a deep breath. "I'm sorry I snapped at you. When Vickers told me you were here, I thought something terrible had happened."

"I have important news."

For a moment, she clutched the precious portraits to her breast. He eyed the bundle and suddenly the corner of his mouth crooked up in that way that always made her knees feel wobbly. "Promise me it won't explode?"

Her cheeks burned as she thought of what a shock these would be. He might love the drawings, but there was an equal chance they would ignite Nate's temper. "I guess we'll find out when you open it."

Christianne handed him the package. First, he drew out the roll of pages. She'd tied them with a ribbon that had fallen out of Seraphina's hair, hoping Nate might recognize something tangible from the flesh-and-blood child who'd roamed Harlestone Hall.

Nate slipped the ribbon loose, running the bit of blue silk though his fingers, then unrolled Aimee's sketches. His body went still as he held them in his big, tanned hands.

"I took Aimee to the Kettering estate to make the sketches," Christianne explained. "She paints in secret and has a wonderful touch portraying children. Sera looks as if she should be a fairy dozing beneath a buttercup, don't you think?"

Nate's Adam's apple bobbed in his throat. Pain flashed in his eyes, and yet also, a kind of hunger. Nate leafed through the pictures: Seraphina frolicking with puppies, Seraphina in a bower of roses. Sera cradling her well-loved doll in her arms.

"Is she...is she doing well?" Nate asked after a moment, his voice low. "Philomena asked for funds to replenish her wardrobe. She said she's grown."

Christianne smiled. "Children do, you know."

"I'd imagine she's happy, surrounded by her cousins," Nate said briskly.

"Resigned is more likely. I think she misses home.

She asked how Caval is and wondered if her pony would forget her."

Nate stared down at the image of Seraphina. "She wanted to ride Caval when she was toddling about. I lifted her onto the dog's back once. She squealed in delight. But Eugenie came shrieking. She said Caval could have killed Sera. But Sera wasn't afraid. She used to watch Caval with this—this quiet longing."

"The way she looked at you the night of the birthday fete," Christianne said softly.

"Perhaps I could send her a little spaniel that can follow her about," Nate said. "I'll write to Philomena."

"Why not bring the puppy to her yourself?" Christianne urged. "I saw the way you looked at these sketches."

"She's a cunning little thing. She deserves better than I have given her."

Christianne met his gaze. "Yes. Yes she does."

Nate gave a pained laugh. "Christianne the Unflinchingly Honest."

"I'd expect no less than honesty from you if the tables were turned." Christianne drew out one of the sketches. Seraphina, curled up in a window seat with a poppet, staring out the window. "I remember you telling me once how it felt to be an only child. You always said you hoped to have a family like mine. Do you still want one?"

"I don't know. There were so many things I'd dreamt of teaching a son or daughter. Sword-fighting, how to swim in the lake, how to climb trees and dance the minuet. All the things I've watched Gavin and Adam and Myles do with their children. I thought that chance was lost to me when things with Eugenie went awry." Nate looked down at the seal ring on his finger. "You always did have a way of getting me to talk about things better left unsaid."

"Do you remember before your wedding? The night I came to your room?"

"Yes."

"You talked about how lonely you'd been as a boy. It made me sad to think of you, like a knight locked in a castle. Now, Seraphina must feel that same."

"She's surrounded by cousins."

"That's not the same as having your own place to belong. You had the Knights and Salway, but I could tell you felt different. As if you didn't belong in the same way. I was an outsider, too. Bastards always are."

He flinched at the word. "Christianne—"

"I'm just saying that I understand what that feels like, to be separate. Alone. You do, too. Sera is even more alone than you are. She doesn't even have a mother."

Nate's face contorted with savage regret. "You think I wouldn't give Sera's mother back to her if I could?"

"You can't give Seraphina her mother, but you can be a real father to her."

"You don't understand."

"Yes, I do." Christianne laid her hand on his arm. "You have a choice now, Nate. Neither you, nor Sera have to be alone."

"I *am* alone," Nate choked out. "I have to be."

Stark vulnerability showed in his face before he shuttered it away. Was that what held him back when she touched him? He had built walls around himself. Walls the maiming of his leg and Eugenie's rejection had forced him to raise higher. Was he trying to protect himself? Or her? Christianne wasn't sure. But she could sense a quicksilver heat between her body and his.

"You know you've never been able to keep secrets from me," she said. "You keep thinking about that first night in the garden at The Blue Peacock, just like I do. I know you want to kiss me again. For real, this time. Like I've wanted to kiss you for—for so very long."

"We can't. I'm older than you. Your brothers' friend."

"I'm a grown woman. If my brothers were able to choose any man for me in the world, don't you think they'd choose you?"

His face tightened in pain. "Not like this. We belong to different worlds, Christianne, and we both know it. Maybe if this could be more than—than some trifling..."

"There is nothing *trifling* about us." She ghosted her lips across the blade of his cheekbone, the corner of his mouth. "Think of it as a scientific experiment," she said, gently nipping his lower lip. "I need to practice kissing, and I've kissed you in my dreams so many times, it's the perfect test."

He was staring down at her with eyes that seemed to see right through to the center of her heart. Past the bravado and the recklessness to the vulnerable depths she hid from everyone else. "Admit it, Nate," she breathed. "You want me."

Nate's jaw clenched, his voice rough with emotion. "I want my leg back, but that's not going to happen any more than our lovemaking will."

"But we can kiss, can't we?" she urged. "Just to practice, you know? You taught me how to swim, and how to dance."

"This is nothing like that, and you know it."

She could feel his whole body, rigid with control. She wanted to break through it. Boldly, she trailed her fingertips down his chest, felt his heart thundering as she skimmed her hand down his flat belly, to the falls of his breeches.

"Don't." He ground out the word, as Christianne

traced the hard ridge of his erection with her finger-tips, but he didn't pull away and she didn't stop.

NATE FELT resistance snap inside him as her fingers skimmed his cock through the thin layer of fabric, touching him as she had in his fevered dreams since the night in the garden. He drove his fingers through her hair, taking her mouth in a kiss so hot and hungry, it threatened to consume him. She tasted like everything he'd ever wanted, like cinnamon and passion, tender-ness and fire. Christianne... His Mistress Mayhem...

Her moan of pleasure echoed his need, her lips part-ing, eager to welcome him in, and Nate plunged his tongue deep, kissing her with the pent-up longing he'd tried to deny for so long.

He raised his hand to her breast, felt her nipple harden, knowing where this would lead. She arched into his palm.

He wanted her. More than he'd ever wanted a woman before. Yet the second before he passed the point of no return, he forced himself to go still. He stared down at her face, memorizing her lips, red with his kisses, the flush of arousal in her cheeks. She was quivering in his arms, warm and willing and so very beautiful. Everything he wanted but honor and duty would never let him have.

When he could breathe again, he spoke softly. "I think that's enough of a lesson," he said.

"For now," Christianne whispered.

CHAPTER 18

"What are you whistling about today?" Christianne asked Robin three days later as he came into her room to collect shoes to polish.

"Whistling again, am I?" the boy sighed, chagrinned. "I should stop before Clary cuffs me for it."

"Your sister hates whistling?"

"No. She's having those bad dreams again. Ones she used to have at the Foundling Hospital." He gathered up Christianne's shoes. "There was this Irish girl who loved to tell stories about banshees and demon kings with black robes flowing. Clary was sure she saw them after the witching hour struck. Sees them right here when she's worried enough." He grimaced. "She's convinced that dark stair of Madame's is the perfect place for haunting."

"Poor Clary," Christianne commiserated. She was the least superstitious of the Slades, but she could imagine Eliza's imagination running wild because of such tales.

"I feel bad for her," Robin said, "but I'm too pleased for myself to stop whistling. Lord Harlestone is taking me to see Deacon, my old friend from the Foundling Home. Three weeks from now, it'll be anchors aweigh and he will be off on a new adventure, just like we always planned. I envy him more than I can say. I want to see him one last time before he leaves the Foundling Home."

"I'm glad you made such a good friend when you were there. Were people kind to you?"

"I got along all right. It was harder for Clary. She tangled with Sister Agatha from the first day."

That wasn't hard to believe, considering Clary's *sunny* disposition, Christianne thought wryly to herself, but she asked, "Who was Sister Agatha?"

"She's the one who dealt with children when they came into the home. See, the nuns take whatever you're carryin' when you walk through the door and put things in these drawers where you can't touch them. Can't be having the dormitory littered up, and orphans squabbling over private belongings, they say. They snip off bits of your clothes and pin names on them, then store them with the things you were carrying. That's the last you ever see of them."

"What did they take from Clary?"

"A bit of ivory our da carved in the shape of a heart. Had the name of the ship he was sailing out on, and initials—his and our mama's. Da strung it on Mama's best ribbon and hung it around her neck."

Christianne could picture the poignant scene all too clearly.

"Hungry as we were, Clary'd never sell it," Robin continued. "We'd grown so much, she was afraid if our papa did come back, he wouldn't remember us without it."

"They gave it to Clary when she left, didn't they?"

"No. Sister Agatha didn't like Clary because she kept sneaking over to see me when she wasn't supposed to. She told Clary she couldn't find Mama's necklace. We didn't believe her. She got this nasty look in her eye.

Like she was real pleased with herself. She wanted us to know she was lying."

Christianne scowled. "That's not right."

"No, but what could we do?" He picked up Christianne's scuffed riding boots. "I asked the old hag about the necklace the first few times I went to see Deacon there. But she never changed her mind."

He headed off to deal with the rest of his chores, but he wasn't whistling anymore. No wonder, reminded of the nun's senseless cruelty.

Christianne seethed on Clary's behalf. That little ivory heart meant nothing to anyone except Clary and Robin. Her chin jutted up a notch. Perhaps it was time someone else spoke to Sister Agatha. Christianne walked to her clothespress and selected her simplest gown. She'd always wondered about the Foundling Hospital. She'd ask to go with Nate today.

And once she got there she'd be the one to get Clary's ivory heart back if anyone could.

If she'd learned about this injustice three weeks ago, she'd have marched to the Foundling Hospital to retrieve Clary's treasure, but the reason would have been different. Of anyone at the salon, the prickly maid was the most likely to know about the goings-on here. She had access to every room, and to conversations no one else was meant to hear. Most people acted as if servants weren't even human, talking around them as if they had no more wit than a fence post. Retrieving the necklace would have been in part a way to earn Clary's trust.

But there was something deeper compelling Christianne to visit this Sister Agatha now. Sometime in the past weeks, she began to see the surly maid who had grated on her nerves in a different light. She had become Robin's sister, who quietly pocketed soft rolls so he would never go hungry. A girl who'd dared to hope, then been left behind by Jessamyn, the friend who'd promised to release her from this harsh life. Someone who also hid the raw places in her heart as Christianne had always done.

Now, Christianne felt one thing fiercely. Clary should have the ivory heart her mother had left her... and Christianne was going to see that she got it back.

~

THE COACHMAN HADN'T EVEN LOWERED the steps for Nate to descend from his coach when Christianne dashed outside to greet him.

Nate's eyes widened in surprise as he unfolded his tall body from the seat, then climbed into the crisp breeze, his claret-colored frock coat pulling over broad shoulders, black breeches skintight on his powerful thighs. He looked as if he hadn't slept, and when his eyes found hers, she could see the kiss they'd shared last time they met must have affected him as much as it had her.

"I'm here to collect Robin," Nate explained.

"I know. But come into the garden for a moment." She hooked her hand through his elbow and pulled him forward. He lost his balance for a moment, then steadied himself and let her take him to a lovely arbor. Once there, he gently removed her arm from his and put some distance between them.

"Don't look at me as if I'll fling myself at you in broad daylight." She laughed, and saw color rise above the creamy fall of lace at Nate's throat.

"You *did* kiss me in this garden once before," he said.

"And enjoyed it very much, thank you. But there is another reason I wanted to talk to you this morning."

"What is it?" Nate's brow rose at a sardonic angle. "I'm almost afraid to ask."

"I've decided to come with you and Robin to the Foundling Hospital today."

"You what?"

She smoothed her spring green petticoat as she spoke. "I'm chafing to go for a jaunt, and Robin said you were taking him there. I've always been curious about the place."

"I'd think that Gavin would have taken you long ago if you'd expressed an interest."

"He wanted to, but my mother forbade it," Christianne said. It was one of the few times Gavin and her mother had disagreed.

Nate frowned. "That doesn't sound like your mother. She supported our work there from the first."

"For you and for Gavin, yes. Not for me. I think Mama felt like it was looking in a mirror and seeing what our fates might have been." Christianne touched the enamel shield on the ring Nate had given her so long ago. "When I was a little girl, I heard my parents arguing. My mother said if something happened to our father, Gavin and his mother would turn us out on the street."

"Gavin would never be so cruel."

"Mama didn't know that then. Gavin's mother had reason to hate us, and so did he. When I look at Clary and Robin, I understand why Mama was afraid."

"So can I." Nate took her hand and ran his finger over the enameled shield. Did he guess what she was thinking? That there were things no one could protect her from now. "But you're safe. I'll keep you so." He raised her hand to his lips, kissed her knuckles. His eyes drifted shut, lashes thick on his cheekbones, his warm lips lingering a moment too long.

When he straightened, that moment was gone, his guard back up. He stepped away and smiled, the smile of the friend she'd known for so long.

"If you'd like to see the work we do, then come along. We can wait while you get ready."

"Oh, I'm ready. I've even prepared a basket to take with us as a treat for the children. Cook baked ginger nuts and they're still warm. I pilfered the morning's rolls, and added some of the oranges Colonel Pratt had delivered for me. Just let me get my hat."

She could hear Nate laugh as she ran into the salon. She returned in a moment, a basket over her arm, her broad-brimmed straw hat trailing sage green ribbons.

"You look like spring, Mistress Mayhem," he said, helping her into the equipage.

Robin was already inside. "You're coming with us to the Foundling Hospital, Mistress?" he asked, as Nate took his seat beside her.

"Yes," she said. The boy sniffed the warm, spicy scent emanating from the basket on her lap. She pulled out a ginger nut and placed the warm sweet in the boy's freshly scrubbed hand. "I'm especially eager to talk to Sister Agatha," she told him with a fierce smile. "I've heard so much about her."

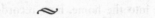

THE FOUNDLING HOSPITAL was clean but stark, the children dressed plainly in identical clothes, their caretakers rushing about. Too many children with no bright colors to delight and no loving arms to hold them, the nuns and teachers so harried there was no time—even if they wanted to. And Christianne knew from the moment she saw Sister Agatha, that the broad-faced woman had no intention of doing so. Her eyes were damp and busy, her wimple so crisp it cut into her brow.

She reminded Christianne of a tutor her brothers had had—a bitter man who had whipped the palm of

Adam's hand so that it bled—until ten-year-old Gavin had taken the switch away. What had driven Sister Agatha into the convent? she wondered. Some bitter disappointment as a young woman? It couldn't have been the love of these children that had brought her here.

"How generous, Lord Harlestone!" Sister Agatha exclaimed, regarding Christianne's basket with an avid expression. "I shall distribute the sweets after dinner time."

But Christianne had plunged into the nearest group of children, passing out ginger nuts to the little girls, and drawing the smallest ones onto her lap to make sure they could eat their treats before the bigger children snatched them away.

She glanced up to see Nate watching her, with such intense tenderness that her breath caught.

"I have some business details to attend to regarding Deacon's placement. Would you like to accompany me?" he asked.

"No. I thought Sister Agatha and I could have a comfortable talk. I'd love to see how children are welcomed into the home, how records are kept, and so forth. It must be most stringent work. I don't know how you keep everything straight." Nate shot Christianne a quizzical look, but Sister Agatha seemed delighted.

"Of course, I would be happy to show you," Sister Agatha said. Puffed up with importance, the nun led her to a room filled with serviceable furniture. A broad desk filled one end of the room, chairs faced it, looking far more uncomfortable than the larger one in which Sister Agatha now sat.

Drawers lined one wall, labeled with years.

"I've been so fascinated since my brother, the Earl of

Glenlyon, told me about your work. I can't imagine how you keep track of so many children."

"It is no small feat, but we do the best we can."

"Are they all orphans?"

"Oh, no. Often, parents leave tokens pinned to their little ones so they can reclaim their children later, when they can feed them again."

"Tokens? May I see one?"

Sister Agatha walked to the drawers. "We file them with the mother's name, and whatever trinket they leave."

"So, say, a child came in 1750? Like young Robin, the lad Harlestone brought today. What would you do if their parent came to claim them?"

"They would tell us what they left with the child, or perhaps what pattern of clothes the child was wearing the day they came here. We take snippets of the fabric if we have nothing else, and pin them to paper with the mother's name if we have it." Sister Agatha went to a drawer, opened it.

A band tightened around Christianne's chest as she looked at the keepsakes that were lined up so precisely. Each small, faded token was all that remained of a shattered family. Somewhere in this drawer was the ivory heart that should be dangling from a ribbon around Clary's neck. She examined one object after another, reading aloud a tin disk with letters pounded into it.

James Colcannon, Born December 1756

Always in my heart, though we must part.

"This is so sad," Christianne said, looking at Sister Agatha. "Do the parents ever come back?"

"Most don't. They die of sickness or hunger, or in accidents. Or time passes and the parents convince themselves that their children are better off. They have a roof over their heads and meals and clothes. The parents drown their grief in cheap gin, or find employment in brothels. Or they simply start new lives, wed new husbands or wives and are too ashamed to admit they abandoned a child or had one out of wedlock."

No wonder Mama hadn't wanted her to see this place. Always, the love story between her parents had seemed romantic, love conquering above all. Her childhood had seemed secure. But there was a darker side she hadn't fully understood until now. She and her siblings had been more vulnerable than they knew.

"What happens when a child turns sixteen?"

"We do our best to find them employment. Lord Harlestone's work with the Marine Charity helps by providing the supplies and uniforms they need. The girls, we train as servants."

Christianne ran her fingertips over the tokens, searching faded tags and writing that was cramped or overly ornate.

Suddenly, at the top of the drawer, she glimpsed the rich glow of ivory in the shape of a heart. Someone had threaded a faded ribbon through a hole bored in the heart. A rusty pin attached a scrap of paper to the wisp of faded ribbon.

Christianne picked up the heart. Someone had recorded information on brittle paper, the ink faded. *Clary Whytte, nine years of age, Robin Whytte, seven years of age. Surrendered by mother, Bess, March 7, 1750.*

Christianne held it up to the light, running her thumb over the words Clary's father had so carefully carved a lifetime ago.

RW BW I will always come back to you. On the other side, it read, *The Fanny B.*

Christianne swallowed a lump in her throat.

"These drawers are full of broken promises," Sister Agatha said. "It's rare that a parent returns. We never dispose of the relics, even after the children leave, just regardless, just in case they do."

"But if a child wants the keepsake, like that locket," she pointed to a tarnished bit of silver, "or this carved heart, surely you would return the only thing left of a father's love."

"Most of the time, yes. I swear, though, I can see why the man who carved that ivory didn't return. His daughter was nothing but trouble. Always defying the rules. She'll come to no good end, I'm sure." She held out her hand. "I'll return this token to its proper place and we can have some tea."

"No. *I* will return it to its proper place. Around Clary Whytte's neck." Christianne slipped the necklace into her pocket.

Sister Agatha's mouth dropped open. "That—that isn't allowed! I'll not—"

Christianne met her gaze, fire in her eyes. "You see, I'm a bit like Clary. I don't believe in following unjust rules either."

~

TROUBLE WAS BREWING. Nate knew the look on Christianne's face too well to doubt it. He'd only been gone half an hour, but by the time he returned to collect Christianne in Sister Agatha's office, the nun was so cold, the tea in her cup should have iced over while Christianne could well be boiling, considering the fury in her dark eyes.

Nate braced his good foot against the floor of the coach as it jounced toward The Blue Peacock. Robin filled the silence, chattering about his friend, the ship Deacon would sail on, the places he would see. Nate didn't press Christianne for explanations in front of the boy, but as soon as they alighted at the salon, he hoped to corner her and get to the bottom of whatever was going on. Apparently, she had other ideas.

"Robin, you need to bring Clary to my chamber right away," she said.

"But it's wash day, and—"

"I don't care if she's washing the queen's underpinnings. You bring her up yourself, do you understand?" Christianne said, her cheeks pink with excitement.

"That was rather imperious, don't you think? The girl has duties."

"Bother duty! Some things can't wait."

They entered Christianne's room, and Nate braced his back against the wall, rubbing the tight muscles in his left thigh. Christianne paced, her whole body seeming to vibrate with excitement. She jumped, startled when Clary stormed into the room, Robin right behind her.

Clary looked like a thundercloud with soap suds clinging to one cheek.

"What's this about? I've got a hundred things to do. Miss Delilah's been screeching like a banshee because I couldn't get a stain out of her favorite petticoat, and Madame's run out of her favorite face cream." The maid faced her with hands planted on hips. "You all think whatever you have to do is the most important."

"This isn't for me," Christianne said. "It's for you."

Clary's pinched face turned bright red when she glimpsed Nate stepping out of the shadows. "Oh, your lordship. Forgive me. Robin just said that Mistress Tianne needed something."

"Close your eyes!" Christianne said.

Clary glanced at her brother, who was bouncing on his toes in excitement. She muttered something about people being too free with the wine, then scrunched her eyes shut.

Christianne slipped her hand through the slit in her petticoat and reached into the pocket tied beneath. Her fingers closed on the ivory heart.

"Hold out your hand," Christianne said softly.

Clary did so, and Christianne pressed the necklace into the maid's chapped palm. Clary's eyelids popped open, and she stared down at the ivory heart pooled in a bed of ribbon.

For an instant, Nate feared Clary's knees might buckle. He caught her arm to keep her upright. "Where...where did you get this?" she choked out, freckles standing out like red dots on her ice-white face.

"What is it?" Nate leaned over so he could read the carving.

"My father gave this to my mother before he sailed." Clary ran her fingertips over the ivory as if trying to believe it was real. "They took it when we came to the Foundling Hospital. It's the only thing we had of them...of Mama and Da... I begged Sister Agatha to give it back to me when I left the home, but she wouldn't."

"Robin told me," Christianne said.

"You should've seen Sister Agatha when we left!" Robin enthused. "Looked so mad she was about to burst, but she was scared to death of Mistress Evelake. Didn't dare say a word to Lord Harlestone, either. She knew what he'd say if she did!"

The sour-faced expression cracked, and Nate could see who Clary must have been when the ivory heart was new and she had parents who loved her. "Thank you," Clary said. Her voice cracked. "Thank you, Mistress. I can't..." She clutched the bit of ivory against her meager chest, then ran from the room, Robin rushing after her.

Christianne stood there, staring after them, smiling softly. The green dress rippled around her, but Nate could see her again at the Foundling Hospital, distributing the treats in her basket as she cradled the smallest of the orphans on her lap.

What would it be like if that child had been one he'd planted in her womb? A little boy or girl with black curls and her mother's bold spirit? Longing filled him.

Nate closed the space between them, drew her into his arms. "You did something special today, Mistress Mayhem. I love…" He stopped himself, knowing that putting his feelings into words would only make it harder when the inevitable happened, and this interlude was done.

"I love your courage," he said, "the way you fight against things that are unfair."

But there were some injustices that were too deeply ingrained in blood and bone and the land itself, as English as Dover's chalk cliffs and the Tower of London. He had to go back to being Lord Harlestone, the heir to an earldom that traced its roots back to William the Conqueror, and she would be Christianne Slade, the daughter of scandal. An impassible gulf stretched between them and there was no way to cross it.

"My own Mistress Mayhem," he whispered. He kissed her, hoping she couldn't feel the sudden grief that knotted in his throat. His heart whispered words he could never say aloud. *I am in love with you…*

CHAPTER 19

Christianne sat before her dressing table, her eyes following Clary's reflection in the mirror as the maid moved around behind her with curling tongs and hairpins, wrestling thick black curls into an elegant coiffure.

Clary was wearing her father's ivory heart, though no one else would know it. Christianne could see the faded ribbon peeking out around her neck, the heart itself tucked beneath the bodice of her dress, as if it was still a secret too precious to share with the world. Christianne warmed as Clary's fingers fluttered to touch the hidden heart whenever she set the brush down.

"No one has ever tamed my curls so well as you do," Christianne confessed. "It's the first time anyone has kept them from falling out by the end of the night."

Clary flushed at the words of praise and anchored another curl in place. "It's just a matter of knowing where to place the pins."

Christianne hated to risk shattering this fragile connection between them, but she needed to take this chance. "Did Jessamyn teach you how to place them?"

Christianne could see the girl's shoulders tense in

the mirror. "Yes. Jessamyn taught me," Clary said in a clipped voice. She walked over to the fire to fetch the iron curling tongs she was reheating. Christianne hesitated, wondering if she should try to be subtle in her search for the information she was seeking. But she understood Clary well enough to know the maid would prefer honesty.

"I know you've wondered why Lord Harlestone paid so much attention to me from the moment he saw me," Christianne said. "The truth is, we've known each other since we were children."

The girl grabbed one long strand of black hair, wrapping it around the iron rod. "I knew there was more between you and his lordship than you were saying. Everyone has said so. Even Madame has remarked on it."

Christianne's hands curled in her petticoat. Everyone was suspicious of her link to Nate? What if his enemy discovered the truth? He'd already murdered Eugenie. Ridding himself of one more woman would hardly trouble his conscience. But that made it even more essential that she discover all she could as quickly as possible.

"I came to the salon because someone connected with The Blue Peacock is trying to destroy Lord Harlestone," she said. "What I'm telling you is a shock, and maybe it's not wise, but I need help, and you're the only one who can give it, if you are willing."

"Me? But how?"

"I know the way people behave around servants. They treat me the same way. I'm illegitimate, you see. They talk as if we're not even there. I'm hoping you've overheard something that might help me find whoever is stalking Lord Harlestone."

A strange smell emanated from the curling tongs, and Clary released the curl she was forming. "Oh, miss.

I'm sorry!" she exclaimed, smoothing out the strand. "It's only a little scorched."

"Don't mind it," Christianne soothed, then pressed on. "Will you help me, Clary? Just answer a few questions?"

"I'll try."

"Can you tell me anything about this suitor of Jessamyn's? The one who wore a mask?"

Clary set the curling tongs down, her hand suddenly shaking so hard it rattled the tin plate she rested it on. Christianne wondered if she'd just made a horrible mistake in trusting the girl. Might the man have threatened her somehow? What hold might he have over her? But it was too late to withdraw the question. There was nothing to do now but wait to see if she answered.

"I never saw the man's face," Clary admitted after a moment, "but I thought I'd heard his voice before."

Christianne's pulse jumped. "Would you recognize it if you heard it again?"

Clary's brows lowered. "I don't think so. The mask muffled the sound. There was just something that seemed familiar."

"Can you tell me anything else?" Christianne asked, eager.

"Sometimes, he had Jessamyn run errands for him. She'd pick up packages and bring them here. The bundles were always tightly wrapped and stowed under her bed. They'd be there when I cleaned, then the next time, they were gone. One day, I was chasing a mouse that had run under her bed. Jessamyn was terrified of them. I hit one of the packages with my broom and the bundle split open, scattering papers all over.

"Jessamyn came in the room while I was trying to pick them up," Clary continued. "She looked so strange when she saw me with the papers."

"What did she say?"

"She raged at me for prying in her private things. She told me never to tell a soul what I'd seen."

"Do you remember any of the words on those pages?"

"Like I told Jessamyn, I can't read. They tried to teach me at the Foundling Hospital but I couldn't master it. But every page was mostly a picture." Clary shuddered. "Like a nightmare."

"A nightmare," Christianne echoed, every muscle in her body tightening. "What did the pictures look like?"

"A madman strangling a woman. He was all slavering and savage and he had a pet wolf that was trying to tear her apart." Clary hunched her thin shoulders, and Christianne could hear echoes of the girl's terror over the Irish ghost tales. "I asked if it was advertising a play. But she said no. A lady had really been murdered and she was trying to help catch the man who did it."

A hot ball of anger lodged beneath Christianne's ribs. So it was Jessamyn who'd been given the libelous handbills falsely depicting Nate strangling Eugenie. Was she also distributing them to slander and defame him? It was clear that Jessamyn wasn't quite as innocent as people—including Nate—might presume, she thought bitterly. But she didn't say it aloud. The last thing she needed was to make Clary defensive.

Christianne crossed to the desk where she'd hidden the handbill she'd found in Aimee's room. She smoothed it out as best she could, then showed it to Clary. "Is this the picture you saw?"

Clary hugged herself. "Y-yes!"

"Did Jessamyn tell you what the words said?"

"I would have stopped her if she'd tried!"

Christianne pointed to the etching. "This monster is supposed to be Lord Harlestone murdering his wife."

Clary's eyes went saucer-wide. "Lord *Harlestone?*" she exclaimed in disbelief.

"His wife was murdered a little over a year ago, and they never caught the man who killed her. Someone has been spreading these billets around, trying to ruin him."

"B-but his lordship would *never* do such a thing. I don't believe it!"

"I don't believe it, either, but many people do. He and his wife were arguing at his birthday fete on the night she was killed."

"Where did you hear such a thing?" Clary demanded.

Christianne hesitated, but it was too late to turn back now. "I didn't hear it. I was there. I am the one who found Eugenie Rowland's body."

Clary shrank back. "You call yourself Tianne Evelake. Is that who you really are?"

"I can't tell you. But I'm trying to help Lord Harlestone like he helped my family in the past."

"Like he helped Robin and me."

"Yes. I couldn't just sit by and let this happen to him without fighting back."

Clary touched the ribbon around her neck, and Christianne knew the bit of ivory her father had carved lay against her heart.

"I wish I could ask Jessamyn where she got those handbills," Christianne said.

"You can't ask her, but I have something that might help." Clary led Christianne down to the kitchen, and pulled out the wooden chest where she and Robin kept their few clothes. She took out a slip of paper filled with writing of some kind. "I found *this* when I was doing Miss Jessamyn's wash right after she disappeared. I kept it, because I was sure she was coming back."

She pressed the scrap of paper into Christianne's hand.

~

CHRISTIANNE COULD BARELY WAIT until Nate arrived that night. The minute she saw him enter the salon, she swept over to where he stood, pretending not to see Madame motioning her to attend to a different table.

"What is so important you'd risk Marguerite's displeasure?" Nate asked as she tugged him through the crowded salon, into the garden. "She was practically waving her arm off to direct you to attend to Colonel Pratt."

"I found something that can't wait," Christianne burst out, breathless with excitement as she led him to the nook where they'd often sought privacy during the six weeks since she'd come to the salon. "We were *right*. There *is* a connection between those hideous handbills and the salon. And now I know who it was. Jessamyn."

"Jessamyn?" Nate echoed, incredulous. He sank down onto one of the iron chairs and listened, solemn as she recounted all she'd unearthed.

"Jessamyn must have told her lover that Clary had discovered those handbills beneath her bed. They didn't run to elope. They fled because they feared they'd been discovered."

"I can hardly believe it."

"I know you all think Jessamyn was all sweetness, but what if she was just a wonderful actress who was working with your enemy all along? What if she was trying to seduce you so she could ask questions about Eugenie? When you had your affair with Jessamyn, did you approach her first, or did she approach you?"

Nate shifted his feet, looking uncomfortable. "All the hostesses have approached me at one time or another," he said. Christianne winced inwardly, imagining other hands touching him, drawing out moans of pleasure. But she could tell he was shaken by Jessamyn's duplicity.

"There is more proof," she said, handing Nate the receipt.

"*J. Cotton, Print Shop*," he read, then looked up at her, his eyes burning with intensity. "Where did you get this?"

"Clary found it in one of Jessamyn's pockets after she disappeared."

CHAPTER 20

Christianne was grateful the sticks of her fan were sturdy. She'd had to rap the knuckles of Colonel Pratt three times when his hand had crept under the table to squeeze her thigh. It had been a long night, listening to him pontificate about the debating societies women could not join. She was certain she could defeat him soundly, but she'd never have the chance. She'd seated herself where she could see the door, her habit so she would know the moment Nate entered the salon.

"You're a pretty piece of muslin," Colonel Pratt said, licking puffy lips. "If we could only continue our discussion in private I would be willing to pay a high price for your time."

Relief flooded through Christianne as she saw Salway Rowland come through the door. She leaned over, expecting to see Nate right behind him. "I'm afraid I already have another engagement," she said. "If you'll excuse me."

She hurried through the crowd to where Salway was handing his cloak to Robin. Salway had obviously dressed for some occasion, Christianne thought. His rich velvet frock coat was the most elegant she'd seen him wear. His waistcoat sparkled with gold embroidery and large, ornate buttons. A ruby stickpin winked from the fall of lace at his throat.

She curtsied in greeting. "Good evening, Master Rowland. Shall I order wine for you and Lord Harlestone?"

"Lord Harlestone sends his regrets. He wasn't able to come here tonight."

She tried not to show her disappointment. "I do hope all is well with his lordship."

"Nate said he had some business to do. Something involving a print shop? He asked me to send you his regrets."

Christianne's heart skipped a beat. He must be questioning J. Cotton. Perhaps, he was even now closing in on whoever was behind the campaign of slander being waged against him. She hoped he'd be careful. Cornered rats were dangerous. She only wished he'd allowed her to come along.

"The truth is, I'm glad my cousin is otherwise occupied," Salway said. "I've been hoping for some time that I might have a chance to converse with you alone. Perhaps we might retire to a table where we can speak privately?"

Nervous that there might be more to the tale, she took a branch of candles from a sideboard and ushered him to a table, then drew the curtains around them.

"Is something wrong?" she asked.

Salway poured a glass full of spirits from the bottle on the table and sipped the amber liquid. "May I speak frankly?" he asked.

"You know I've always preferred it."

"I see how you feel about Nate. Ever since you were a little girl, you trailed after him. Now you've grown into a woman, beautiful enough so to tempt any man. But I know my cousin as well as my own face in the mirror," Salway continued. "Nate is far too honorable to deflower the sister of his best friend, Adam, when he couldn't offer marriage."

His blunt words struck like a blow. Was Salway right? Was Nate too honorable to ever bed her, no matter how desperately she wanted him to?

Christianne's cheeks burned. "My relationship with Nate is none of your concern."

Salway straightened the fall of lace at his cuff. "Don't mistake my meaning. I admire your determination to wrest Nate from this coil of scandal. We both know that your time here will come at a great personal cost. In some ways we have always been alike, you and I. Nate is the sun and we circle around him. Yet, like Icarus, if you get too close, you will fall."

Irritation flashed in Christianne. "It is my choice to make."

"I know how it feels to do everything in your power to help Nate out of dire difficulties. When he returned from Culloden, I rarely left his side after my uncle told me how he found Nate in the garden, a loaded pistol in his lap."

"Are you saying he…"

"I pushed my uncle into working to get your brothers pardoned. I knew that if Nate was fighting for them, he'd never pull the trigger."

"He wouldn't pull it anyway," Christianne asserted, then added, "I didn't know that you were so involved in getting Gavin and Adam pardoned."

Salway shrugged. "Yes, well, it was my uncle and Nate who wielded the power, though I did not believe they could really achieve the pardons in the end. I was as stunned as anyone when I heard the news." Salway set his empty glass down, turned and gave her a strange smile. "It wasn't the first time Nate had gone tilting with dragons. He likes nothing better."

"That's true," she said.

"But the thing I'd like to discuss now involves you. I've heard rumors that more than one patron who frequents here is making inquiries about purchasing the first rights to your bed."

Christianne winced inwardly, remembering Colonel Pratt's beefy hand on her thigh. "They can offer, but it would be my choice."

"I'm sure you would bring a great price, but I'm not fool enough to imagine you need the coin, not in a practical manner, anyway. Glenlyon will always see that you have whatever you need, including luxuries like that horse you have stabled across the street."

"Avalon is a gift from Nate," she said, yet what Salway had claimed was true. Gavin would let her want for nothing.

Salway traced the rim of his glass with one long finger. "To be beholden to even the most generous half-brother's charity must be galling sometimes. What would it feel like to hold the reins of your life in your own hands? To be truly independent?"

"Independent?"

"Well, you can hardly return to Strawberry Grove. There are your sisters to consider. Tales of your misadventures here are sure to get out. Once they do, even merchants won't allow their daughters to associate with the notorious Slade girls."

Christianne bit her lip. Eliza would be fine if the worst happened. She preferred the world she created with the tip of her quill. But Maria and Laura loved the society of the friends they'd found. It wasn't the social whirl Gavin's daughters would enter when they were of age. But was it possible Christianne's reckless actions would rob them of what was left?

"I have done well in the West Indies," Salway said.

"It's been a lucrative market since ladies have developed an appetite for sugar in their tea."

"Not this lady," Christianne said, bristling. "I read a tract about what the slaves who produce it suffer."

Salway rolled his eyes. "Doubtless Glenlyon gave it to you, or Adam's reformer of a wife."

"Anyone who loves freedom as much as I do could hardly help but be moved by their plight."

"Are you not bound by your own kind of chains? What if true freedom is at your fingertips? Just say the word, and you can throw off the strictures with which society binds you. Look at Marguerite. She has her own salon, a jewel box full of trinkets. You are even more alluring than she was in her prime. What if you set up your own salon?"

Christianne's eyes narrowed. "What?"

"You rival her in beauty, intelligence," Salway insisted, "and you are so regal, you could pass for any nobleman's daughter."

Christianne squared her shoulders. "I *am* a nobleman's daughter."

"I know that there are men vying to be the first in your bed." He paused. "None are more eager for that pleasure than I am."

Christianne stared, stunned. "I had no idea you desired me that way. I don't know what to say."

"Say yes." He reached across, clasping her fingers with a sweat-damp hand. "Wouldn't it be better to experience the secrets of the bedchamber with someone you can trust?"

But I don't trust you, she thought. She'd felt sympathy for Salway in the past, but trust? No. He was too eager to please to be honest.

"No. I couldn't possibly."

"You could if you were wise. It is a practical agreement. Best for everyone. You would have independence, your own salon where you could display your cleverness. Nate would no longer be tortured by desiring a woman he can never have. And I would enjoy my share in your profits, financially and physically."

The curtain concealing them was swept aside, revealing Delilah in all her sensual glory. Her flame-red hair gleamed above her emerald gown, a predatory light in her eyes. "Why, Master Salway, Aimee told me you were here! You mustn't let Mistress Evelake steal you away from the rest of us the way she does your cousin. You promised to tell me all about your sugar plantation when next you came." Delilah looked at Christianne, a hostile glint in her eye, and hooked her arm through Salway's. "Mistress Evelake will have to wait her turn."

"Of course. Do go with Delilah," Christianne urged, still stunned by Salway's proposal.

Salway leaned toward Christianne, and she could feel his breath on her face. "You will consider what I have said," he murmured. "You know what I say about my cousin is true."

"I do," she said softly. Nate, so honorable...herself, so far beyond the pale.

"I will be out of town for a week, attending to some business. When I return, we will speak again." The curtain fell back into place and she sat in silence in the alcove alone, haunted by all Salway had said.

It wasn't as if she hadn't imagined experiencing what happened between a man and woman in bed. There were times she'd run her hands over her own naked flesh, but when she did, the lover she'd dreamed of had always had Nate's face.

THE SALON HAD CLOSED its doors, and Clary had helped Christianne into her nightshift when Christianne heard a tap on her bedchamber door. She opened it to find Aimee, garbed in a flowing blue robe. "May I come in?" Aimee asked.

Christianne pressed her hand to her throbbing temple. "I'm afraid I have a headache."

"I think I know why," Aimee said, pushing past her. "I was passing by the alcove and I overheard the offer Salway Rowland made you."

Christianne shut the door, and leaned against it. "I really don't care to discuss it."

"I'm sure you don't. But it made me wonder...what are you saving your maidenhead for? It's not as if you'll marry an earl like Lord Harlestone. If you marry at all, it will be to some stolid reformer, willing to overlook the fact that you're soiled goods."

The blunt words startled Christianne.

"I'd take that offer if I had the chance; then I could paint to my heart's content."

But Christianne could never accept Salway's offer. Not for independence, or to defy the exalted society determined to rein her in.

She'd seen what happened in the salon, Delilah and the others taking lovers, but she couldn't imagine being in bed with any man but Nate. Even if they could never marry, wouldn't it be enough to know he cared for her as well? That Nate wanted her in his bed and felt the same hunger she felt for him?

She might not be able to share Nate Rowland's bed as his wife, but was it possible she might convince him to be her first? To seize this chance they'd been given, despite what the future might bring?

What was it that her brothers always said? That if conversation was a duel, she would always win. It would be no small feat to convince honorable Nate to surrender to the physical attraction they felt for each other. But she had to try.

~

NATE NEEDED TO SEE CHRISTIANNE. He'd rarely felt more disheartened, the need to see her, know she was safe, more compelling than the need for sleep.

He was surprised to find her in the kitchen, helping Clary knead bread dough as if she were attempting to pound the life out of the yeast. She looked up, a smear of flour on her cheek, and Nate felt a frisson of fear, knowing how precious she was to him. She seemed as tense as he felt, nerves drawn tight. He hated to add to whatever was troubling her, but there was no help for it.

"May I steal you away for a moment?" he asked her. Christianne shed her apron, wiped her hands on the cloth, then led him out the kitchen's back door. She closed it behind her.

"Salway said you had gone to the print shop. What did you find?"

"The print shop was burned to the ground. I found the owner sifting through the rubble." He couldn't forget the sight of the soot-smeared printer wading through the wreckage of a lifetime's work to speak to him. The tale had chilled Nate's blood, but not as much as the information he'd gathered there.

Nate told Christianne of the fire, and her eyes went round. "The print shop is full of flammable things. But they had no idea how the fire started in the middle of the night. They were lucky to get out alive."

"I don't think this fire was an accident." Christianne shuddered. "It can't have been a coincidence, can it?"

"Not likely. Especially since a woman matching Jessamyn's description provided the copper plate they used to print the handbills about me and collected the finished sheets from the shop."

Christianne looked sick. "Oh, Nate."

"Right before Jessamyn disappeared, she told the printer's daughter she was sailing off to the colonies to be a rich gentleman's wife."

"Jessamyn must have feared that once Clary saw the handbills, it was only a matter of time before she told someone. Have you seen any of the sheets posted lately?"

"A few, but nothing like before."

"If Jessamyn and this suitor of hers have really departed, maybe this nightmare is coming to an end, then," Christianne mused.

Nate shook his head. "It can't be that simple. This campaign against me isn't something Jessamyn could come up with on her own. Who put Jessamyn up to this scheme, and how did they secure her help? And the biggest mystery of all—why?"

She crossed to him, slipped her arms around his narrow waist and laid her head against his chest. "I'm sorry, Nate," she whispered. "It must hurt to know someone you were so intimate with would betray you."

He gathered her close, and pressed his lips to her hair. "Someone else is behind this. I feel it even more strongly now. That instinct I'd feel when the Scots were about to ambush us. God, I want this to be over," he said. "But whatever else Jessamyn did, she wasn't at Harlestone Hall the night Eugenie died," he said. "This won't be over until we find Eugenie's murderer. That is when this nightmare will end."

CHAPTER 21

$\mathcal{I}$t was to be a night of dancing. Robin and Clary had cleared the furniture from the center of the room. A string quartet's instruments gleamed by the light of candles, while garlands of flowers festooned the walls.

Christianne had taken pains with her gown, Clary fussing to make certain every curl was perfect. "You'll outshine them all tonight, Mistress. Lord Harlestone won't be able to take his eyes off of you."

"I doubt Lord Harlestone will come tonight," Christianne said. She'd made certain to warn him what the night's entertainment would be. She was still haunted by the dancing at Harlestone Hall, and how Nate had hung back, watching.

Salway wouldn't be attending either, to her great relief. He'd sent her a note saying he'd stopped to see his uncle to discuss some problems with one of their ships. She hoped that he'd be stuck untangling difficulties long enough in the days to come for her to convince Nate to come to her bed.

She'd tried to understand why Salway would make such an offer to trade her virginity for lifetime security under his protection. He'd always shown contempt for the Slades in general, though he'd hidden it from Nate. And he'd never seemed attracted to her before. Did he hope to get revenge on Adam somehow by deflowering her? Or did he want her because he could tell that Nate did?

"There, Mistress, you look perfect, except for the worry in your eyes. Dancing tonight will drive that away. You'll have so many partners, you'll not be able to catch your breath."

Wasn't that one of the things she'd longed for at Nate's birthday fete when Eugenie's haughty guests wouldn't escort her out onto the floor? That Christianne seemed a different person now.

She'd do her best to put aside her conflicting feelings and enjoy tonight, she resolved as she descended to the crowded salon. It didn't matter why Salway had made his offer. For the first time in the salon that evening, she was free to dance to her heart's content, as patron after patron vied for her hand. Yet despite the fact that her feet were never still, she couldn't stop glancing at the door. Searching for the gleam of tawny-brown hair, green eyes, and Nate Rowland's smile.

The clock was chiming ten when she saw a familiar figure in a shadowy alcove. She stumbled at the sight of Nate, wondering how on earth she had missed seeing him enter the room, even in this crowd. He sat alone, his hand tapping the table before him in time to the music. His eyes caught hers, and a poignant smile spread across his handsome face. She knew he was watching her and danced her best, graceful dips and swirls and leaps, catching his gaze with hers, time and again. At the end of the dance, she excused herself and went to Nate's table.

"I'm so glad you're here," she said, sinking down in the seat beside him. "I wasn't sure you would come tonight."

"Maybe I shouldn't have. But you know I've always loved watching you dance." The hint of wistfulness in his smile made her heart ache. "I should probably go."

"Please stay, Nate," she begged as another partner approached to claim a dance. "Come to my room when this is done."

He didn't answer, but every time she glanced at his alcove, he was still there, his eyes following her every move, and she knew he was remembering a time when he was dancing, too.

~

NATE WAS WAITING at her bedchamber door, his back leaned against the wall, all of his weight on his good leg. Light from the candles in the wall sconces limned the angles and planes of his face, the high cheekbones, his square jaw, the slow burn in his gaze when he saw her. She felt an answering heat in her most secret places, and knew tonight was the chance she'd been waiting for.

Her stomach fluttered with excitement, and she turned her back toward him to hide her nervousness.

"Have mercy and loosen my laces," she begged. "I swear, Clary pulls them so tight I can barely breathe!"

She'd asked him for help in the past with tangled laces and knots she couldn't reach. But that had been before they'd kissed. It felt far different as his fingertips brushed the sensitive skin of her nape now.

"It's no wonder you're breathless, the way you were dancing tonight," he said, untying the bow at the top and tugging the strings to release some of the tension. "No man there could take his eyes off of you."

She flushed with pleasure as his hands curved over her shoulders, thumbs kneading the tight muscles there. "I'd rather be here with you than dancing with any other man," she said.

He hesitated just an instant too long to reply, and his hands fell away. "It's easy for you to say that now," he said as she turned to face him. "You don't know what it's like to be chained to this leg of mine. You'd tire of sitting on the fringes of the room, just like I do. You want to believe I'm still the Nate who rode and danced and could best anyone but Adam when it came to wielding a sword. I'm not that man anymore."

She tipped her head to one side, and regarded him with unflinching honesty. "I know you're not that man. You're braver than he was. You fight harder than he did —with wit, with courage. I've seen what you've done, not just for boys like Deacon and Robin, but for the soldiers you've hired on your estates, some with wounds that you can't see with the eye."

"I would have died a dozen times on battlefields without men like those. I don't deserve any laurels for giving them a livelihood. It makes me so angry. All those people who cheered the trooping of the color— they don't want to see what war has done to those strong, young bodies."

"*I* see," she told Nate. "Your leg, yes. But more than that. I see that all you've endured has opened your eyes to the pain around you in a way most people will never understand. Of all the men I've ever met, you're still one who takes my breath away."

"Don't." His voice roughened with emotion. "We're too different now. You're so beautiful, always in motion. I will limp forever. My leg is maimed and ugly."

"It does hurt to know that you are scarred, but it doesn't change the way I feel about you.

From the time I was a little girl, the other Knights raced ahead. Even when you could run faster than any of them, you always slowed your steps to listen to me."

He cupped her cheek. Desire flared in his eyes. "I wish I could run again. I wish that I could dance with you—not as the friends we were, but as we are now."

"It was always more than a friendship to me. Remember at the Walton Assembly Hall? Deborah Musgrove and her set snubbed me and laughed behind their fans. You swept me out onto the floor and made me the luckiest girl in all that vast assembly room. My Galahad."

"I don't remember."

"I remember well enough for both of us. You were wearing a deep green frock coat that made your eyes look like forests. A lock of hair had slipped free of your queue and curled right here on your forehead." She brushed her fingertips just above his right eyebrow. "There was an emerald stickpin in your neckcloth, and you smiled as if we shared some delicious secret. I wanted you to take me into the gardens and kiss me. I pictured it so clearly that I told my sisters that you had. I described the kiss in such detail that Eliza wrote about it in one of her stories. Adam found it and was ready to bludgeon you. I had to confess the kiss was just wishful thinking." She gave a soft laugh. "Imagine my humiliation! I was certain I looked like a fool."

"Never," Nate said. His throat sounded thick. "A warrior queen, perhaps."

"Adam got angry and told me I should not break my heart over a man I could never have. The Rowland lineage was far too fine to mix with the likes of us. Later that day, I came upon him slamming fists into the stable wall. His knuckles were split and bloody. I saw the truth in Adam's eyes. I could never be a nobleman's wife. But perhaps I could be something else."

"My dearest...dearest..." Nate stumbled to a halt, and she sensed he was searching for the right word to describe the bond they shared.

She dreaded he would say *friend*... Before he could squeeze out the word, she laid her fingers on his lips and felt his breath quicken. "We are *not* friends, Nate. We both know it. There's something more between us. A bond that has always been."

Raw need flared in those eyes she'd loved forever.

"I can't be your wife," she said, "but I could be your mistress."

"Mistress?" He recoiled as if she'd slapped him, yet every muscle of his body seemed to strain toward her.

"I know that you will take your marriage vows to heart," Christianne said. "Most men in the nobility carry on liaisons, and no one minds as long as they are discreet. But you're far too honorable for that. I know you *must* marry. It is your duty to provide Harlestone with an heir. But until then, couldn't we be together?"

"No." Anguish and longing warred in Nate's face. "It would be wrong."

"Would it?" Christianne laid her hand on his thundering heart. "Or would it be wrong to turn away from this passion that we both know has always been destined? You, to go to the bed of a wife you respect, but do not love, and me into the arms of some other man who can never understand me the way you do."

"Someday, a good man will—"

She waved her hand in dismissal. "We both know the likelihood of that is small. Especially after my stay here at The Blue Peacock. It's possible Eliza will be content penning stories about imaginary loves, or that Maria will marry a fellow artist who is unconventional enough to wed her for her talent as well as her beauty. And Laura...well, who can say? But I'm not like them," she said. "I never was. I *will* run headlong into life." She looked deep into Nate's eyes. "I want to run to you."

"You deserve so much better than this," Nate protested, trying to resist the need for her that he felt in his very soul.

"You always knew the truth about my future, and now I do, too," she said. "Father may have raised his daughters like princesses, but there is no castle that would allow us through the gates."

There was no denying what she'd said was true. "I'd change the world for you if I could," Nate said.

"I know you would." She ran her fingertips along the side of his jaw. "You've been my true knight since I was a little girl."

"Which means I should protect you."

"You will...just in a different way. You can't be mine forever, but you can be my first. I want my first time to be special, something beautiful, a memory to cherish. I trust you."

Nate swallowed hard. What had it taken his proud, brave, beautiful Mistress Mayhem, to ask him this? How could he turn her away? Shouldn't making love be with someone who understood how fierce and fine she was? He remembered the night she'd come to his room on the eve of his wedding. He'd seen the hero-worship in her eyes then, knew that she adored him with a young girl's first infatuation. Despite his eagerness to wed Eugenie, he'd wanted to protect Christianne from the heartbreak he knew would come from the world he had been born to. Scoop her onto the back of his horse and ride away with her. Carry her someplace safe, like one of those mythical maids in an enchanted wood.

They were both far different now. Christianne was a grown woman, determined to send her horse pelting down a path of her own choosing. Not content accepting what scraps society would allow.

He was no perfect knight anymore. He'd been hardened by years of a loveless marriage, mistakes made.

Duties still to fulfill. Yet, he'd never wanted any woman the way he wanted her.

For years he'd dealt with his physical needs as expediently as possible. He was a considerate lover, yet never allowed his emotions to be involved. Neither Nate, nor the women he bedded had any expectations except release. Once upon a time, he'd been the most romantic of all his boyhood friends, dreaming of the kinds of love enshrined in the legends he adored. He'd wandered through the chapels in his father's castles, awed by the effigies of ladies and their knights. He'd always been moved by one couple in particular. The knight, reaching across the space between him and his wife, their stone hands entwined for eternity.

Nate had wanted to find that kind of love. Briefly, he'd even imagined he'd found it when he'd saved Eugenie from the future her stepfather had planned, but it was not to be. And Christianne... What could he offer her?

One night when they could let the passion they felt for each other break free. One night to remember forever.

"You are so beautiful," he groaned, trailing his fingers down the graceful curve of her throat, to where her breasts beckoned his hands. "If you change your mind, at any moment I'll stop."

"I've been dreaming about this forever."

He slid one ribbon-tie free, then the next. His fingers trembled as his knuckles brushed the tops of her breasts. "Your skin is so soft," he murmured, then let his hand trail to her nipples, diamond hard beneath the thin layer of silk. Her response was like everything about Christianne, no shyness or uncertainty. Oh, she was inexperienced, but she was eager to test, to try, even laughing in delight.

He pulled her against him, his mouth on hers. She

tasted of oranges, smelled of spice cake and the youth that war and disillusionment had stripped from his soul. The Nate he'd been before. The Nate he'd aspired to be.

She gasped with pleasure as he explored her mouth with his tongue, his cock hard against her. He felt her pulling at his clothes, burrowing her warm hands under his shirt until her fingers were on his skin and his body felt fiery with a need more powerful than anything he'd ever known.

They stripped away layers, waistcoat, shirt, gown, yet when her fingers went to the fall of his breeches, Nate went still, remembering the first time Eugenie saw what war had done to his leg. He tried to shove away that moment of horror, revulsion, lock the memory away where he'd hidden it for so long.

He tried not to think of others, the willing women he'd bedded since, their faces carefully blank. Yet how could he blame them for their reaction? The first time he'd seen the space where his leg should have been, he'd recoiled as well. Hell, there were times he still had nightmares.

But this was Christianne. His Mistress Mayhem. She unfastened the buttons of his breeches, and his breath hissed between his teeth as her deft fingers trailed over his cock through his linen drawers. He braced one hand on the bedpost as Christianne slid the skintight breeches and drawers down his hips. She knelt, the silk of her hair brushing his erection as she worked the fabric down his thighs, his calf, every muscle in his body tense. She paused as the breeches slid below his knees, where wood met flesh. Ever so gently, she laid her lips on the pale, twisted scar.

Tears burned Nate's eyes, and he let his lashes fall closed. "I need a minute," he said as he sat down on the bed. He expected her to draw away so he could deal with the straps that bound him to the wooden part of his leg. But Christianne would have none of it. She gently shoved his hands away and unfastened each buckle herself. The wood struck the floor and he whipped himself under the sheets as quickly as he was able, hiding his broken body from even Christianne's loving eyes.

Catching hold of her hand, he pulled her down to join him. She was soft. She was warm. Her naked skin against his eliciting a response more powerful than any passion he'd ever known.

"I'll take care of you," he murmured, kissing her throat, down to her breasts, taking one rose-tinted nipple into his mouth. He suckled her and her shoulders bucked up off of the pillow as his hand slid down the soft curve of her belly to the nest of down between her thighs. His finger touched a place that felt like fire, hot and wet and needing with a fierceness he knew she didn't fully understand yet. He would show her…

Her hands roved up and down his back, twining in his hair as it tugged loose from its queue. Slowly, he slid his finger between the petals of her center, stirring the tiny bud he found there.

Christianne gasped as he slipped his finger inside her.

His thumb rubbed soft circles on the bud above, driving her higher, drawing gasps from her. He felt her reaching for something she couldn't quite name.

Then Nate shifted his hips between her thighs. His cock nudged the part of her he longed to fill. He pushed forward, stretching her just a little, then pushed deeper.

Grasping his buttocks, she pulled him closer. He groaned with pleasure as he thrust forward. He felt her stiffen as the fragile veil between them tore. And then he was deep, deep inside her, where he'd longed to be.

"Are you...are you all right?" he asked softly. "I never want to hurt you."

She smiled at him, laughed, clutching him close. "I'm wonderful," she said. "I want...want all of you. Everything. Show me..."

He did. All of the passion and pleasure his body could give her, showed her how beautiful she was to him, how precious. He only had this night to show her...this one night...

When he came, he felt her arch against him, heard her cry out, felt, not her surrender, but her triumph. She'd won the dueling field, his Christianne. She'd asked him to teach her how to make love.

But tonight, she'd taught him something more dangerous. She'd reminded him how it felt to be whole—in body, in spirit. He'd let himself feel again.

CHAPTER 22

*N*ate came awake in stages, Christianne's body curled close against him. Her bare shoulder gleamed white in the morning sun, her hair a pool of black silk tangling over his chest. Her head was pillowed on his arm. God, what had he done? He'd taken her innocence, kissed every part of her, awakened in the middle of the night and coaxed her to passion again. He'd never felt so sated, so peaceful, as if he'd been waiting his whole life to wake up beside her.

His heart twisted with a mixture of guilt and elation. How could something that was so wrong feel so damned *right*?

She made a sound like a sleepy kitten and rolled over to face him. Her whole face lit up and the depth of trust in her smile nearly undid him.

"Good morning," she mumbled.

"Are you...all right?" he asked.

"I'm wonderful." She draped one slender, perfect leg over his hip. "I've imagined being with you like this for so long. But having you here, touching you this way...it was better than any dream I ever had."

Wasn't that what this night had been? Nate thought as he caressed her back. A dream...one doomed to end

230

when they stepped back into the world beyond her bedchamber door.

He rolled over on top of her, caressing her silky skin, kissing her throat, her lips, suckling her breasts until she was moaning and eager again. He spread her legs, settling his hips between them. Closing his eyes, he drove deep.

When she arched and shuddered and cried out, he spilled himself inside her, not sure where he ended and she began.

Tears formed in his eyes, but he buried his face in her shoulder. Long moments passed, as she held him, her fingers threading through his hair, her body so warm beneath him.

"What's wrong?" she asked, and he hated the sudden uncertainty in her voice.

"I'm afraid you'll regret this."

"Don't," she said so fiercely it startled him. "I'll *never* regret this. *Never*. Don't you know? I love you, Nate. I've been in love with you for so long, I can't remember a time when I wasn't. I wish we could stay this way forever."

"We can't." His voice cracked. "And when that time comes, I don't want to hurt you."

"I *chose* last night, Nate. It was worth any price." He could feel a sudden tension in her body and he rolled to the side.

She stood up, grabbing the nightshift she'd shed earlier, pulling it on. She walked to the window, peering out into the world that would separate them. He wanted to go to her, but he couldn't until he'd fastened on the wood and metal and leather that allowed him to stand. A hard reminder of the difference between them—the ugliness of his scars, a world away from the untamed beauty that was Christianne.

He made quick work of the straps, then wrestled his

breeches over the permanently angled foot, and pulled them up, feeling the need to cover his maimed leg.

"I should go before anyone sees me here," he said. "I'll slip out the rear door."

"Yes. That's probably best."

"Promise me you'll be careful," he pleaded. "If the person who is stalking me set the fire at the print shop, they're getting desperate. If they discovered why you're here, it would be dangerous."

She found her dressing gown and put it on, drawing it closed at her throat. "Will I see you later tonight?"

"Unfortunately, no. I have some bother of a party to attend." He felt a twinge of guilt. A party his father had arranged, one that would also be attended by Olivia Nasby. "I'll send Salway to be sure that all is well with you."

"Don't," she snapped. A muscle in her jaw jumped.

"Don't what?"

"Don't send Salway. In fact, don't tell him anything about this."

Her words stung. "I'd hardly tell him I spent the night with you."

"I just...don't want him here when you're not." She fretted her lip.

"Have you two had a falling out?"

"I just keep trying to think who might be behind this scheme against you. Salway stands to gain the most of anyone if you are ruined. If you die without an heir, he will inherit everything."

"You can't believe Salway is behind all of this," Nate exclaimed, astonished. "After I was wounded at Culloden, he never left my side. And he would never hurt Eugenie. He was half in love with her himself, and he adores Seraphina. He's visited her at the Ketterings' half a dozen times."

"Unlike you," Christianne said. "As I said, he has everything to gain. Even Sera."

Nate flinched inwardly, remembering the drawings she'd given him. He knew she'd been hoping it would inspire him to visit Sera himself. He gathered up his shirt and pulled it on, as if to hide the sudden vulnerability she'd touched.

"Maybe I'm wrong," she said, "but I keep thinking that Salway was out in the garden the night she died."

"So was I," he said, incredulous. "Salway was with Deborah Musgrove—which makes his taste in women questionable, but hardly makes him a murderer. He has always been a loyal friend to me."

Christianne's whole body stiffened, and he wondered how things had gotten so tangled between them. What the hell had driven that drowsy, well-loved look from her eyes? "Have you spoken to Deborah Musgrove since the inquest?" she asked.

"No. Callum MacGregor tried to, but her husband turned him away. The next day, they left for Switzerland, some spa to calm her nerves."

"Perhaps we should see if they're back."

"I'll make inquiries to Musgrove's friends at the club and find if they've returned."

"Nate," she said, an edge to her voice that unnerved him. "Your cousin isn't as loyal as you believe him to be." He saw her suck in a deep breath. Her eyes hardened with resolve. "Do you remember the night you were following clues at the print shop?"

His eyes narrowed. "I'm not likely to forget it."

"Salway came to see me."

"About what?"

Her cheeks flushed deep red. "He approached me with a proposition. He would set me up in my own salon if I welcomed him into my bed."

Nate felt as if someone had slammed a fence rail into his ribs. "What the devil? I can't believe it."

"It's true."

He knew it was. He could see it in her eyes. He swore. "How dare he? You're not a woman to strike so cold a bargain. I'll set him to rights."

"No, you won't." Christianne twisted the ring on her little finger, the tiny enameled shield catching the light.

Dark emotion fired in Nate's eyes. "You can't seriously be considering it!"

"Of course not! But my fate is mine to decide without answering to any man. Even you. I don't know what I hope for in the future. All I know is that you've always wanted to believe the best about people you care about—and sometimes they don't deserve it. I only told you about Salway's offer to show that even your cousin's loyalty is not as unshakeable as you might hope."

Nate clenched his fist, wanting to slam it into Salway's face, wanting to kill any man who touched Christianne.

"Don't tell him you know," she said. "He's not the first man to make such an offer. Just the most recent one."

The thought of Christianne being subjected to such advances turned Nate's stomach. Yet none of those men had deflowered this beautiful, fiercely loving woman. Nate had.

There was a clinking sound in the hall.

"You'd better leave," Christianne said. "That's Clary bringing up water for Delilah's bath. If Delilah sees you, she'll tell Marguerite."

Then what? a mocking voice demanded in his head. Would Marguerite demand payment for the most precious night of his life?

"Christianne…" He crossed to her, drove his fingers back through her hair and kissed her. "I—"

"Go!" she hissed, giving him a gentle shove. He grabbed up his frock coat and slipped through the door and limped toward the rear hallway. He hoped he'd only imagined a soft gasp from behind him as he disappeared down the stairs.

CHAPTER 23

C hristianne had ridden in a coach with Nate a hundred times in the past, but never when he had been her lover. She sat across from him, aware of every fiber of his body, yet unable to shake the awkward feelings that lingered in spite of the magical night they'd shared. The customary ease between them had stretched thin ever since she'd told him the truth about Salway. She could see the sense of betrayal darkening his eyes.

Salway's betrayal of his friendship? she wondered. Or did Nate feel their night together betrayed his own code of honor, and resolved never to do so again?

He'd seemed so guarded when he came to tell her that the Musgroves had indeed returned to England. She'd been surprised when he'd invited her to come with him in hopes that between them, they might catch Deborah in some sort of deception, or push her into revealing some detail that could help them unravel what had happened the night Eugenie died.

But as the coach rolled up the drive to the Musgrove house, Christianne couldn't conceal her surprise.

She wasn't sure what she'd expected as she and Nate drove up to Deborah Musgrove's manor house, but it was not this drab Elizabethan era building with stucco and heavy dark timbers. It might once have been impressive, but neglect had left it looking shabby. Overgrown ivy seemed determined to pry into second-story windows. Hedges tumbled over each other in desperate need of a trim, while brambles and wild roses fought for purchase on stucco that needed whitewashing.

When Nate handed her down from the coach, she cast him a puzzled look. "It's hardly as grand as I expected Deborah Musgrove's house to be."

"Mr. Musgrove is a gambler, and so is she. Besides," Nate said with fresh bitterness, "why bother keeping up your home when you're so rarely there? She and Eugenie were always running about. Of course, I paid for the lodgings the two of them stayed in. It was worth it to have peace and quiet."

"If anyone can give us more information as to what was happening in Eugenie's life, it will be Deborah," Christianne said.

The footman who answered the door ushered them in and had them sit in a withdrawing room. But as Christianne passed, she saw rooms nearly empty of furnishings and servants with liveries that had seen better days.

"Tell your mistress that Lord Harlestone has come to call," Nate said. "I will not be leaving until I see her. She knows me well enough to know that I mean what I say."

The footman flinched at his stern tone, and Christianne couldn't blame him. Nate's grim expression even gave her pause.

Christianne wandered about the room, its gilt mantel chipped, the draperies faded. Over the mantel hung a portrait of a rather foolish-looking old man and a much younger Deborah with a pet monkey on her lap.

237

Deborah kept them waiting long enough for them to grow thirsty, the set of Nate's jaw making Christianne wonder if he'd soon charge upstairs to find Deborah himself.

But at last, Mistress Musgrove blew into the room like a thundercloud.

"Jones told me that you refused to leave until I spoke to you, Harlestone, so here I am. But to bring that person as well is unconscionable." She looked at Christianne as if she was a dead mouse in the bottom of her teacup.

"Did you enjoy your sojourn to Switzerland?" Nate asked bitterly.

"Certainly not." Deborah crossed to a chair with a faded cushion and sat, her primrose skirts ballooning out around her. "I've been grieving the loss of my dear friend."

"And her unborn child, no doubt," Nate said. "While you have been taking the waters, I've been attempting to track down the man who killed her."

Deborah pinned him with a haughty glare. "I suggest you look in the mirror."

"I do. Every morning. And every morning I renew my vow to find whoever left Seraphina motherless."

Deborah gave a damp snort of derision. "As if you care about that child!"

"Someone has gone to great pains to remind me that I do." He pulled out one of the sketches Christianne had had made. Seraphina peered out from the page, so wistful, so innocent, Christianne wanted to gather the little waif in her arms. "I *will* get justice for my wife and daughter. To do that, I need to know what was happening in Eugenie's life before she died. Who fathered Eugenie's babe, Deborah? We both know it wasn't me."

Deborah blinked, then looked hastily away.

"You and Salway Rowland came out of the garden maze after I found Eugenie," Christianne said. "Were you there when she was attacked?"

"Who can guess how long poor Eugenie lay there!" Deborah exclaimed, her lips quivering. "The scene with Seraphina upset me. Anyone with eyes could see how badly you crushed Eugenie's hopes." She glared at Nate. "I fled to the terrace to wipe away my tears. Salway came upon me and was kind enough to take me into the garden to help me compose myself."

"Did Salway come from the ballroom, or was he already outside?" Christianne asked.

Deborah flung up her hands. "How should I know? I was most distressed. If you are trying to lay the blame on Salway, you should be ashamed of yourself. He *adored* Eugenie. In fact, he was in love with her."

Nate's shoulders went rigid beneath his claret-colored frock coat. "Was he the babe's father?"

Deb sniffed. "I don't know."

"She never confided in you?" Nate pressed.

"If she *did*, do you think I'd betray her secrets to *you*?" Deb sprang to her feet, her tone pure venom. "During the inquest, I prayed that they'd put you on trial and hang you. Nothing on earth could make me lift a finger to help you. Why don't you ask Salway if he bedded your wife?"

"You cruel witch." Christianne took a step toward her, and Deb skittered back.

"Don't you dare speak to me thus! Harlestone, had I known *this person* was with you, I would have had the servants throw you out. The only reason I let you in at all is that I wanted to see for myself that you'd suffered as you deserve. But you don't even have the grace to grieve your murdered wife. My God, you look as if you're glad to be rid of Eugenie, coming here with this tart on your arm."

Christianne could see Nate's cheeks darken in fury, but before he could speak, she cut in. "You claim to be Eugenie's friend. Shouldn't you want her murderer brought to justice? Are you content to let the man who killed her run free? Help us. Trust me, Nate has suffered enough, even to satisfy you."

Christianne drew Eugenie's fan out of her pocket. "I have something to show you." She splayed out the fan, revealing the remaining images. It was still exquisite, delicate and feminine, its colors so vibrant they seemed alive. "Do you recognize this?"

Deb seemed drawn to the object in spite of herself. She took it from Christianne and examined it. "The picture looks just like Eugenie…"

"She must have commissioned a fan-painter herself," Christianne reasoned. "She was carrying this on the night she was murdered."

Deborah flinched, her cheeks white even without the lead paint she so often wore.

Nate leaned forward, pointing to the jagged hole in the fan's center. "Someone cut a section out of the fan leaf. Do you remember what was painted there?"

Deborah's hand fluttered to her brow, a bracelet glittering on her bony wrist. One of the gems in her bracelet was broken in two, Christianne realized. The jewelry was paste. "The fan leaf was supposed to be an allegory of some sort," Deborah said with a wave of her hand. "Something about spring. I believe it was supposed to be Demeter in the center."

"The goddess of the harvest," Christianne said eagerly. "Do you have any idea who painted it?"

"No." Deborah touched the image of Eugenie. Real sadness touched her hard face. "She was so beautiful. So bright and gay. She should be alive right now, playing with that charming little girl of hers."

"That is something we agree on," Nate said.

Deborah's sorrow hardened again to a steely expression. "How *is* Seraphina?"

"Well cared for by her aunt," Nate replied.

"Rumor says that you may soon provide Seraphina with a mother." Christianne winced at Deborah's words. The woman's haughty gaze sharpened as she regarded Nate.

"I hear the child is spending a good deal of time with the sons of Olivia Nasby, Dowager Countess of Beresford. She is widowed, is she not?"

"Sadly, yes."

"Her estate is a lovely piece of property that borders Harlestone. I seem to remember she was quite smitten with you during her first season, and you favored her as well."

"Olivia is a kind friend."

Christianne felt a twinge of jealousy. As a girl, she'd listened as Nate, Myles and Gavin talked of society beauties and matchmaking mamas. She hadn't realized the Olivia she'd met while Aimee sketched Sera was the young woman who had once, albeit briefly, caught Nate Rowland's eye.

"Apparently you and Olivia were quite congenial at Lord Adderly's gathering a few weeks past. I warned her to beware," Deborah said with a hard glare.

"I'm sure you did," Nate said levelly.

"You expect me to betray Eugenie's secrets so that you can destroy her reputation to save your own? I can see it now—spread across *The Tattler*. No. I'll not help you do that."

"Do you really think I'd spread such ugliness about Eugenie and saddle Seraphina with such a legacy?"

"You seemed capable of any cruelty when you were wed to Eugenie."

Nate gripped the back of the settee, and Christianne could see him struggle to master his temper. "Deborah,

I know that you and I dislike each other heartily, and always have," he said with fierce earnestness. "But surely we both want whomever murdered Eugenie brought to justice."

Tears shone in Deborah Musgrove's eyes. "Will that bring Eugenie back to life?"

"Perhaps not," Nate confessed, "but you may want to consider this: What if Eugenie's lover is responsible for her death? He would be well within reason to suspect that she would confide his identity to her bosom friend. What's to stop him from silencing you if he fears you might expose him?"

"You are trying to frighten me."

"All I know is that there is something dangerous brewing. Eugenie got caught up in it somehow and she died because of it."

At that moment, the door swung open and a portly man with ruddy cheeks and crooked teeth walked in, swinging a cane bedecked with ribbons. Musgrove was thirty years his wife's senior, with a title in the offing. "M'dear, I didn't know we were ex- pecting company," Musgrove said. "How are you, Salway?"

"It is not Salway Rowland," Deborah snapped. "It's his cousin, Lord Harlestone."

"Harlestone?" The man looked through a quizzing glass. "Why, so it is you! I haven't seen you for an age. Eyes not what they used to be, what?"

Nate bowed. "Good afternoon, Musgrove."

"Forgive me for mistaking you. Your cousin has be- come a regular fixture around here." Was it possible that Salway and Deb were lovers? It surprised Nate that Deborah would have much to do with a man whose fortunes were limited.

"And who is this beauty?" Musgrove asked, grinning at Christianne. "How have I not seen you before?"

"This is Miss Slade." Deborah curled her lip in distaste. "The Earl of Glenlyon's half-sister."

"Ah, yes! The last earl's natural daughter."

Nate curved one hand protectively under Christianne's elbow. "My friend Glenlyon considers Mistress Slade his sister in every way. He loves her dearly. *As do I.*"

Musgrove had the grace to look chagrinned at Nate's censure, and Christianne guessed he was not purposely cruel like his wife, but just a bit of a fool. "My eyes don't see enough, and my mouth tumbles over itself, jabbering away, ain't that right, m'dear?" He cast a rueful glance at Deborah, then turned with an earnest smile to Christianne. "Do forgive me, Mistress Slade."

"Don't mind it," Christianne said. "I often blurt things out as well. My brother Glenlyon is always chiding me for it."

Musgrove brightened. "Stay for dinner, won't you?" he urged.

Could the doddering old man have missed the undercurrent of tension in the room, or was there part of him that enjoyed discomfiting his much younger wife?

Deborah compressed her lips as if she'd just sipped sour milk. "Harlestone and his companion were just leaving."

"Oh, don't go!" Musgrove protested, crestfallen. "This hasn't been the same lively place since Deb and Lady Harlestone frolicked about. And while we were in Switzerland, we received family news that has left my wife quite downcast."

"I'm so sorry," Christianne said. "Is someone ill?"

"La, no! Quite the opposite. It's my uncle—the one I was to inherit from. I always feared he'd outlive both Deb and me, but he dealt us one better. Married himself a seventeen-year-old bride and she popped out a son. Uncle always did love surprises. But, as Deb says, they'd best keep the boy wrapped in velvet. Babes are fragile creatures. Why, just last week, our maid's child went to sleep in its crib and didn't wake—"

Deborah cut in. "Seriously, must you run on about everything I say? Let Lord Harlestone and Miss Slade get out the door, why don't you?"

"Mr. Musgrove," Christianne broke in, quickly taking out Eugenie's fan. "One question quickly. Have you ever seen this before? We're searching for the artist. It belonged to Eugenie. Whoever murdered her tore out the center panel."

"Wasn't this painted by that French fellow who hung about here three summers ago? I don't remember his name, but I seem to recall the fan was meant to be a gift."

"A gift for whom?"

"Don't know. Only he left England right after for some outlandish place."

Deborah rapped him on the hand with her own fan so hard one of the sticks snapped. "That's enough!" The woman's eyes grew agate-hard. "This interview is done."

THE INTERIOR of the coach seemed full of questions as they jounced back toward London, tension rolling off of Nate in waves. Christianne watched his drawn face, sensing he might as well be a hundred miles away.

"Deborah knows more than she's saying," she said, longing to touch his hand. "I keep wondering who gifted Eugenie with that fan she was carrying the night she died. Did someone commission it for her? She'd have to sit for it, to have such a good likeness done of her, and of Seraphina."

Nate didn't respond.

"Do you think the father of Eugenie's child commissioned the fan? Whoever he is. Or perhaps she had an affair with the painter himself, and—did you hear me, Nate?"

He seemed to shake himself, returning to the coach, and the conversation. "If Deborah knows anything, she'll never tell me. She thinks I deserve whatever happens to me for making Eugenie miserable."

"What happened between you and Eugenie, Nate? Was it only Culloden? At least in the beginning, you convinced *me* you were in love with her."

"Neither of us were prepared for what we faced after Culloden. She'd led a sheltered life. And I... What was it I used to say when I was young? I was the luckiest boy in the world."

He kneaded the muscles of his thigh. "God, I could barely stand seeing Deborah again. She was unconscionably rude to you. At least there is some justice in the world. I'm glad Musgrove's uncle has got himself an heir. She was counting on her husband inheriting."

"If I were that babe's mother, I'd not leave him alone with her," Christianne said. "She looked like she'd happily drown him in the well."

"She was a terrible influence on Eugenie," Nate said. "I suspect Eugenie's stepfather was trying to separate the two of them when he insisted Eugenie accompany him to the colonies. Once Deborah married Musgrove, she became even more of a problem. He had a gouty leg and hated to travel, so the two women would flit from Bath to Brighton to the London shops as if they had the Royal Treasury at their disposal. Nothing satisfied Deborah for long, and Eugenie felt she had to keep up with her or be humiliated. I'm fairly certain Deborah encouraged the worst kind of flirtation as well."

He fell quiet, his words reminding Christianne of

something Deborah had said that troubled her. She glanced over at him, aching to close the space between them, feel the reassuring warmth of his shoulder brushing hers. But there was a distance between them now. Nate's world had put it there. The world in which she could not follow.

"Speaking of flirtations, Deborah mentioned the name Olivia Nasby. I seem to remember you, Myles and Gavin talking about a woman named Olivia when you started going to balls. I eavesdropped on you shamelessly, you know."

"I do hope you didn't hear anything too shocking."

"I lived for the shocking bits," Christianne confessed. "But there weren't nearly enough to satisfy Eliza. She was saving them up for her blood and thunder stories."

"We knew you were listening." Nate winked, but the smile didn't quite reach his eyes.

She tried to keep her voice light. "So, you've struck up a friendship with Olivia again?"

"The Beresford estate shares a boundary with Harlestone. Occasionally my parents and I dined there when Eugenie was off flitting about. Beresford was a good man. Alex, their eldest son, was always fascinated by Caval. When Beresford died, I brought the lad one of Caval's pups."

"How long ago was that?"

"Three, maybe four years. Olivia is one of the few who issued invitations to me after the inquest, aside from Myles and your family. She's unfailingly kind."

Christianne felt a twinge of jealousy. "She wasn't at your birthday, as I remember."

"She'd taken ill with a megrim. There have been problems with the estate, which I'm trying to help her untangle."

"Of course you are." Christianne grimaced.

Nate cast her a wounded glance. "What would you have me do?"

She shrugged. "Certainly not marry her to save the day."

She expected him to refute it, say he had no intention of doing so. Instead, he grew quiet.

"I think you'd like Olivia very much if you met her," he said.

Her heart sank. From the first, she'd known that Nate would have to marry again, and yet the prospect pained her more than she could ever show. "I did meet Olivia. When I took Aimee to sketch Seraphina."

"What did you think of her?"

"She seemed...pleasant enough." But she'd been more than that.

Olivia had been every bit the fine lady Deborah purported her to be, but warmer. There had been a tenderness when she'd looked at her sons and soft grief in her eyes as well. Had the loss of her husband left that mark? Christianne swallowed hard.

Would it be irresistible to Nate, to rescue a damsel in distress? Christianne wondered, her heart aching. That was the one thing she could never bear to be.

She always came out fighting.

CHAPTER 24

*N*ate threaded Christianne's forgotten green satin ribbon through his fingers as he mounted the steps to his townhouse, his leg aching almost as much as his head. He'd pulled the flask from an inner pocket of his frock coat to dull the throbbing, but whiskey couldn't untangle the jumble of emotions the visit to Deborah Musgrove's had unleashed.

Eugenie's friend had always cut up his peace, but rarely more than she had today, with Christianne in the room. She'd hoped to torment him with her talk of Eugenie and of the gossip about him and Olivia. But she'd managed to wound Christianne as well. It would have been easier to dismiss the rumor if it wasn't at least partially true. He needed to marry and of all the prospective viscountesses on his father's list, Olivia set him most at ease.

He only hoped Deborah hadn't seen the sudden vulnerability flash across Christianne's face, that face that had been flushed with passion for him just a few nights before. Christianne had done her best to keep the mood light the last miles of their journey back to the salon, but she couldn't fool him.

Only after she'd disappeared inside The Blue Peacock and his coach had lurched into motion again, had he found the ribbon, still holding the soft jasmine scent of her hair, the silk not half so soft as her skin.

He wound Christianne's ribbon around his hand, knowing that everything changed the night he'd gone to her bed. There could be no going back to the way things had been.

Jackson, the footman, greeted him, taking his hat. "Good evening, my lord. Mr. Salway arrived two hours ago. He is waiting for you in your room."

Nate kneaded his temple with the fingers of one hand. The last thing he wanted was to converse with Salway.

He walked into his bedchamber and found his cousin trying on the new frock coat that had just been delivered by Nate's tailor.

"I didn't expect to see you tonight."

"You should have. We bought tickets to the theater weeks ago."

"That was tonight?" Nate's hand uncurled. "My mind is so jumbled I forgot. I'm sorry."

"What can be so important that you forgot seeing the exquisite Phoebe Bracegirdle onstage?"

"I went to Deborah Musgrove's, hoping she'd tell me something about the fan Eugenie was carrying the night she died. The piece torn out of the center."

"Ah, yes. I remember."

"Deborah said the fan was a gift of some kind. We don't know from whom."

"I see." Salway walked to the mirror and admired the cut of the coat he'd tried on. "Did she say anything else?"

"Gossips claim that I'll be marrying Olivia."

Salway's smile tightened over straight white teeth.

"Uncle will be so pleased. When should I offer felicitations?"

"No time soon, if I have anything to say about it."

"Perhaps you can loan me this coat for the celebration. The cut on these lapels is very fine." A crease formed between Salway's brows and he bent down, retrieving the green ribbon from the carpet. "Don't tell me the angelic Olivia has offered you a knight's favor, Sir Galahad?"

"No. It's Christianne's." Nate pulled the ribbon out of Salway's hand, not wanting him to touch it. He folded it with care, and tucked it in his waistcoat pocket. His fingers lingered there a moment too long.

Salway's gaze sharpened. "That fiery little beauty is spirited enough to tempt any man. A fine diversion before being shackled to a suitable bride."

"Do not speak of her so." Nate clenched his fists. Jealousy burned under his breastbone, the memory that Salway had offered a price for Christianne's virginity. The thought of Salway, or any other man, taking her to bed made Nate want to throttle someone.

You bedded her, didn't you? A bitter voice mocked him. *And not just once.*

"Nate, you are my cousin. My blood. Yes, and my best friend, though I know full well you don't consider me yours. I'm telling you the truth because of that bond. The Slade girl is exquisite but she is a bastard. Bed Tianne Evelake at The Blue Peacock, if you must. But anything more than that would mean ruin."

"Leave me," Nate growled.

"I'll go, then. Just remember that I warned you." Salway paused at the door. "By the way, I visited Seraphina at her aunt's and took her the doll you sent."

"How is she?"

"She's a pretty little thing, just like Eugenie."

Salway strode from the room. Nate heard the

murmur of voices as a footman sent a lad running to the stables for Salway's horse.

Nate walked to the table where he'd spread the drawings Christianne had given him, leafing through the images. Sera playing. Sera weaving a flower crown. Sera cradling Bobo with the tenderness she'd learned from Eugenie. If Eugenie had lived, the Rowland cradle would have been carried down from the attic of Harlestone Hall by now. The delicate gowns and bonnets Nate's mother had given to Sera when she was born would be garbing another vulnerable babe. The wooden soldier Sera had given Nate would be clutched in another little hand.

He closed his eyes, remembering the wooden rocking horse in Sera's nursery, rainbow ribbons tied at the ends of plaits in its horsehair mane. He could see Eugenie bending over the daughter she'd adored, patiently teaching those small hands to fold lengths of hair one over the other, praising her, laughing with her, kissing Sera's plump pink cheeks. Somehow in these past weeks with Christianne, he'd let go of the anger that had poisoned him for so long.

So many people had said what a loving mother Eugenie had been. But then, Nate and his wife had given each other precious little affection since she'd shown her horror over his leg. Didn't that human need for love have to go somewhere? He pictured Christianne, so eager in his arms. He'd felt alive again, no longer alone after so many barren years. Had Eugenie felt that in the arms of her unborn baby's father? He hoped so.

He should have the housekeeper, Mrs. Davies, pack the toys that might remind Sera of her mother's love. Send them to the Kettering nursery. Why hadn't he already done so? Because these drawings that Christianne had given him made him remember...the way Sera's hair smelled...the way her tiny baby weight had felt in his arms. The way she'd sighed and nuzzled her head on his chest. Surely Sera wouldn't want to come back to a house with no mother to love her, Nate thought.

Or would she?

CHAPTER 25

$\mathcal{C}$hristianne sat at the small desk, penning a note to Eliza, when Delilah swept in, a spark of malice in the red-haired hostess' eye.

"Madame would like to see you in her chamber. I wouldn't want to be you."

Christianne smoothed her hair back from her forehead, wondering if Marguerite had found out somehow about the searches she'd been making of other rooms. Twice she'd nearly been caught. Had the salonnière guessed that Christianne had attempted to open the door to Madame's inner sanctum as well? Madame's room was accessible by a private staircase, far from the group of rooms the other hostesses shared. Christianne had attempted to sneak up there several times and tried the door. It was always locked tight.

At least you'll finally get a chance to see what lies behind the door, Christianne encouraged herself.

Outside the carved panel, Christianne hesitated, then knocked.

"Who is it?"

"Tianne Evelake. Delilah said you sent for me?"

"Enter," the musical voice lightly seasoned with a French accent bade her.

253

Christianne stepped inside the luxurious room. It was the hue of a ripe peach, coloring that would hide the lines that feathered from the corners of an aging beauty's eyes and around her mouth. French furnishings from the time of Louis XIV made it seem like a queen's boudoir. Draperies in a deep rose were pulled back with gold cord. A fainting couch was angled in front of the largest mirror Christianne had ever seen, and she could imagine every movement of lovers being reflected back. The dressing table was so laden with cosmetics and unguents and lotions and perfumes that the spindly legs seemed likely to crack. Did one of them hold the unique scent Adam had spoken of?

"Since the day you arrived at my salon, I sensed something was not quite what it seemed. But I believe I have worked out what has been transpiring here at last."

A chill raced down Christianne's spine. "I don't understand."

"You came here as Tianne Evelake. But that is not your name. You are Christianne Slade."

Christianne looked at Madame's eyes, once so sly, laughing at the world, now hard.

"Who—who told you—"

"Does it matter? Now I realize why you looked so familiar when you first came here," Marguerite accused. "Your brother Adam Slade was quite a fixture around here before he wed. The Prince of Sin, we called him." Marguerite's lip curled in disgust. "He'd not been doing any sinning here for years, then he returned soon after Harlestone placed Robin in my employ."

"Why should it matter that I didn't give my real name? I know I'm not the first woman to hide her real name in this kind of establishment."

"You ask why your true identity matters? Because you are the baseborn sister of one of the most powerful men in London. I wonder what the Earl of Glenlyon would think of his friend spending the night in his sister's bedchamber."

Christianne's cheeks flamed. "Lord Harlestone has spent quite a few nights in your chamber as well, has he not?" Christianne challenged her.

She'd heard Clary and others whisper that Madame knew everything that went on in the salon. Had she some way of hearing what was going on in the rooms? If so, she would know that Christianne had been prying about in The Blue Peacock...and why.

"I do not appreciate being used to facilitate this affair of yours," Marguerite said. "If Harlestone insists on taking his best friend's sister as his mistress, then let him set you up in a comfortable house and face your brother's justifiable wrath."

"It's not what you think."

"It is *exactly* what I think," Marguerite snapped. "I have made my fortune by understanding the alchemy of what transpires between a man and a woman. There is something new in your eyes when the two of you look at each other. Anyone can see the change. When Glenlyon does so—*and he will!*—I want The Blue Peacock well clear of the conflagration that follows."

Dread weighed heavy in Christianne's stomach. What *would* happen if Gavin found out? Surely she and Nate couldn't be together this way once she left this place.

"Harlestone has always been one of my favorite patrons, and the last thing I want to do is offend him and lose his commerce." Madame scooped up a fan from the table and waved it, the ringlets around her face swaying gently. "I have enjoyed my dalliances with him immensely, and would have welcomed more of them. I hope once this ridiculous melodrama between the two of you plays itself out, I shall enjoy bedding his lordship again. But for now, you will leave my establishment in the morning and not come back."

No! Christianne thought. Not when she felt as if she was finally getting close. Her hands curled into the fabric of her sea-green gown.

"What if I promise to stay away from Lord Harlestone? Have I not held my own in debates? I've already got almost as many admirers as you."

"You overestimate your power, like many women. Right now, you are a novelty at the salon. In time, the fervid attention you attract will wane. And, no. Once you've lied to me, you no longer hold my trust."

"Is that what happened with Jessamyn?" Christianne blurted out. She could see something in Marguerite's eyes...fear? Dread?

"Please, don't send me away," Christianne implored. "Something dire is brewing here and I need—"

"What? What is so dire?"

Christianne stared at the salonnière's guarded face. What if Marguerite was tangled in whatever was afoot here?

Wasn't it possible? Marguerite's room was the only one that was always locked. What was it that Clary had said? That she'd seen the man with the cloak near Marguerite's chamber. Had he been trying Madame's door as Christianne had? Or had he gone to meet with Marguerite Charbonneau since Jessamyn was gone? Might Madame herself know more about the disappearance than she let on?

"You have nothing more to say?" Madame glared at Christianne. "Then enough! My decision is made. Perhaps there are other salonnières who would risk employing the Earl of Glenlyon's sister. I will not."

Christianne could see that it was hopeless to argue. "All right then. I can pack and have my affairs here in the city finished by Friday."

"You will leave tomorrow."

"But I need to make arrangements," she pleaded, desperate to buy time. "Surely a few more days can't hurt. I won't even go down to the salon."

"Send Robin to fetch Lord Harlestone at once. Everyone knows how close his lordship is to the Earl of Glenlyon," she said with a snide curl to her lip. "I'm sure he will be *happy* to see his friend's sister home."

Christianne started to turn, glimpsed the dressing table filled with bottles, cosmetics and unguents, lotions and powder, and three bottles that were obviously perfume.

Was the remarkable scent that had been on the handbills somewhere amongst the bottles? There was only one way to find out.

Christianne clasped her hands before her and walked to the window by the table, only partly feigning agitation. "I've truly loved my stay at the salon. I was able to hold my own with men, speak as an equal." She swung around, trying to make it seem an accident when her elbow struck the three bottles of scent toward the edge of the table, knocking them over.

Madame cried out as the vials teetered, two of the three bottles tipped over, their stoppers falling out. Christianne scrambled to right them, making certain to get the scent on the lace of her cuff. Christianne eyed the third bottle as she hastened to right things, but Madame had stormed over, furious.

"Do you have any idea how expensive that perfume is?"

"You may send me a bill," Christianne said coolly. "I'll make certain to replace it."

"You may be sure I will. Now, leave before you do any more damage. Just to be clear, my door will be locked in case you feel the need to come sneaking about again."

She knew Christianne had attempted to get into her room. How much else did she know?

"I will expect you to leave in the morning and I never wish to see your face again."

~

SHE'D FAILED.

Christianne lifted the lace of her cuffs to her nose once more, despair pulling her deeper. Roses, jasmine, civet and musk, expensive, and yet, nothing exotic as she'd hoped. When Nate arrived, she would ask him if he detected whatever that elusive scent was they'd been seeking, but she had little hope it was there. Might that last vial—cobalt blue with a wide base—hold the scent they sought? Perhaps Nate could find out if he went to Marguerite's room. But the possibility of what might happen there once he did, made her feel sick to her stomach.

When would he arrive? Robin had gone off to carry her note to him. Brief, merely asking him to send his coach because she would be leaving The Blue Peacock in the morning. Would business keep him away until then, or would he come soon? She needed to see his face.

Christianne looked about the room that had been her home for the most exciting six weeks of her life. The chair pulled up to the fireplace, with the footstool she'd arranged so Nate could rest his leg. Her own chair drawn companionably close. Since their love-making, she'd even dared to massage the tight muscles of his thigh while they spoke. He'd resisted her ministrations at first. But soon it had felt so right, he'd even asked her to do it.

She'd loved the sounds of pleasure he'd made, low in his throat as she'd kneaded out the knots that had formed during the day. His eyelids would drift closed, the tension draining out of his body.

Would she at least be able to do that much when she was back at Strawberry Grove? Tears pricked her eyes. She knew every inch of Nate's body now, the pale ridge on his rib where a saber had grazed him, the place on his left shoulder where shrapnel had burned him. The scar where his leg had once been.

Here in this room were a hundred memories of the man she loved. A shawl he'd bought when they were at the park and she'd forgotten to bring a wrap. A bowl of oranges he'd gotten from a Spanish ship's captain at the waterfront. A scented pomander filled with spices Salway had brought from exotic islands.

In the weeks she'd spent at the salon, the time she and Nate had shared together had become even more important than clearing his name. Somehow, in this room, they'd managed to create their own Avalon.

But the magic was ending. Christianne folded the petticoat to the geranium gown she'd worn that first night Nate had seen her here, remembering how his gaze had heated as he looked at her. She could still feel the power of the first kiss that had set so much in motion, exposing the bone-melting attraction neither of them could deny.

She might have to leave The Blue Peacock without exposing Nate's enemy, but she'd never regret coming here, the time she'd spent free in a way she'd never experienced. Free to be herself, to defy society's strictures and become Nate Rowland's lover.

Clary entered the room, her arms weighed down with shifts and stockings. "I've fetched the rest of your things from the wash. They're dry enough, but I'll not have a chance to iron them."

"Never mind. Thank you for bringing them."

"Aimee wanted to come up here as well, but she is

afraid of Madame's temper. Madame has told everyone in the house that you are leaving and that they are not to speak to you."

Was that the real reason Aimee was staying away, or was she feeling guilty? Had she accidentally exposed Christianne's secret? The possibility stung.

Christianne cleared her throat. "Yes, well, I have no time for visitors anyway. I have a great deal to do before I leave."

Clary drew something from her apron pocket. "Aimee asked me to give you this."

Christianne took the piece of paper and spread it flat. A lump formed in her throat as she stared down at the exquisite image Aimee had sketched. Nate laughing in the salon garden, his eyes alight with love as he looked down at the woman before him. The woman's face was obscured by flowers and her curtain of dark hair, but Christianne knew it was her. One moment, one precious moment captured on paper that she could carry with her into their uncertain future.

"Mistress?"

"Yes."

"Mistress, there is one more thing I haven't told anyone."

"What is that?"

"Last night, I heard something in the night. It was coming from Madame's stairs. I thought she wanted a sleeping draught, so went to see. Someone nearly knocked me over, charging past. I didn't get a look at him. His face was turned away and it was dark. But when I was sweeping the stairs to Madame's room this morning, I found this." She reached into her pocket.

She held up a broken bit of feather. Thin and elegant, the iridescent green a color she'd never seen before.

Christianne took it, but as she lifted it to the light,

the hairs on her arms stood on end. A scent drifted from the shimmering plume. She'd never smelled anything like it before.

~

THE SKY beyond the window was growing dark, the sounds of guests arriving at the salon drifting up the stairs. Christianne had made a last, futile foray to Madame's room, but the door was solidly locked. The rest of the time she'd spent pacing, waiting for Nate to arrive.

She could tell when he came down the hall, the slight hitch in the sound of his steps because of his leg. She opened the door before he had a chance to knock. He entered the room, his brow creased with concern.

"Robin said I was to come right away," he told her. "What happened?"

"Madame knows who I am."

"Who told her?"

"I don't know," Christianne said, "but she ordered me to leave the salon in the morning." She gestured to the packed trunk. "Did you tell her, Nate? I know you've wanted me to go home."

"Of course not!"

"She knows I'm Gavin's sister. She knows that we are lovers."

Nate's jaw clenched. "Not much happens here that Marguerite *doesn't* know."

"I'm afraid she might add our liaison to the horrific rumors people are spreading about you."

Nate paused to consider. "If you're thinking Marguerite is behind those handbills, I truly doubt it," he said. "We've been friends for years."

"More than friends, considering what she told me when she summoned me up to her chamber."

Nate looked down at the floor and Christianne hated the jealousy she felt. "Marguerite helped me to deal with needs once I lost my leg. It was never more than that."

"I've something else to tell you," Christianne said. "When I was in her room, I saw perfume bottles on her dressing table. When I realized she was sending me away, I feigned clumsiness and knocked two of them over. I managed to drag my lace in each one while supposedly cleaning them up. I hoped one of them might be the scent we've been searching for."

"And was it?"

She held up the lace. He took it between his fingers, lifting it to his nose, shaking his head as he smelled each in turn. "No."

"What about this?" She crossed to the desk and retrieved the feather Clary had given her.

Nate lifted it to his nose. She knew the answer before he spoke. Deep lines carved in his brow, his gaze, knife-sharp as he met hers. "Where did you get this?"

"Clary found it in the hallway outside Madame's room," Christianne said. "Clary heard a disturbance and went to see what it was. A man almost trampled her in that tiny hall. The next day, when she was sweeping, she found the feather. Robin once told me that Clary had nightmares about a ghost in black robes haunting the stairway to Madame's room. But this is no phantom. It hurts to know I won't be here to track this person down now." Her voice dropped low. "Or to be with you."

"Shall I take you home come morning?"

"Yes." She could see pain in his eyes, the knowledge that this was the last night they'd spend together here, with no one to tell them they could not draw the bed-curtains around them and fall naked into each other's arms.

What would that mean? Going home? Now that everything had changed. Suddenly need cut, sharp. She locked the door, took his hand and led him to her bed.

They needed to be naked, in each other's arms one more time.

CHAPTER 26

*T*he coach rumbled over the familiar road, Christianne's trunk lashed to the roof above them.

Nate twined his hand in hers, fingering the cheap enamel ring she still wore on her little finger. A little shield for his shield maiden, he'd told her long ago.

"You're awfully quiet." Her voice startled him from the memory, and he looked up to see the beloved oval of her face. How could the delicate planes and angles still be the same, and yet, so changed? The plush red of her mouth had softened with his kisses. Her eyes still brimmed with intelligence and daring, but there was a depth of feeling in them now, a seeking and understanding that their lovemaking had awakened. He knew every dip and swell and curve of her body, the way she gasped when he kissed the tender skin behind her knee, the way she caught her breath when he trailed those kisses upwards until he tasted fragile petals and the pearl within.

He'd never loved a woman more thoroughly and never felt more loved himself. He knew once he left Strawberry Grove, he'd never love the same way again.

"I've wanted you to return to Strawberry Grove for

so long. I just hadn't thought how things would change once you did," he confessed. "I will miss being able to stop whenever I like, go up to your bedchamber."

She looked into his eyes, unflinching. "It doesn't have to be that way," she said.

Didn't it? What was all of his honor worth if he couldn't have Christianne? In his life, in his bed? He stared out at the land rolling by, silent.

"Nate, promise you won't say anything about this to my brothers. I don't want my family to know about my time at The Blue Peacock."

Nate swallowed hard. What could he say to his friends anyway? *I allowed your sister to stay in a salon, fend for herself among strange men. She was in danger and discovered the person plotting against me. I took her to bed because when she touched me, I needed her more than breath and light. More than honor...*

Her reputation would be ruined if anyone found out. They'd been lucky only Aimee and Marguerite had learned her true identity. "I'll say nothing."

"What will you do now?" Christianne asked.

"There is much work to catch up on at Harlestone Hall. And Olivia asked me to come to Beresford Manor as soon as may be. Apparently there is something Alexander is eager to show me that will improve the function of their grist mill. She's afraid he'll crush himself between the millstones."

"I see," Christianne said softly. He feared that she did. All too well.

"It's strange." Nate toyed with a fastening on his cuff. "I feel as if we've been in Avalon these past weeks and now it's fading back into the mist."

"I feel that, too."

He curved his hand around her nape, stared deep into those eyes in which he'd found the man he'd thought lost forever on Culloden Moor. "But it's not gone," Nate said fiercely. "Not yet." He'd hold onto this one golden moment before he had to let her go and Avalon disappeared, taking *his* Christianne beyond his reach.

~

It seemed so strange to be back at Strawberry Grove, as if Christianne's childhood home had frozen in time. Her sisters had welcomed her and Nate with delight, and dinner had been a convivial affair, with chatter about Maria's new art teacher, Laura's new kitten and how Eliza had been flinging out crumpled pages of her writing as if paper were free.

Christianne felt guilty as she glanced across the table at Eliza's face, thinner, more somber. Eliza had burst into tears when she'd walked through the door. Even their mother watched Christianne with a look that let her know a painful interview would come as soon as Nate was bundled into his coach and rattled away. Lydia Slade did not care to have conflicts with her children when guests were about. Only Laura and Maria asked her about her trip to Bath with Kitty, and she changed the subject as quickly as she could, aware of her mother's gaze upon her.

Nate had agreed to stay overnight and get a fresh start in the morning, and they'd settled him in Adam's old room, looking out over the pond where they'd swum as boys.

Nate couldn't sleep. But tonight, it wasn't his leg that was aching. Somehow, the presence of his old friend seemed all around him. The enormity of the lines he'd crossed with Christianne were more real here than they'd been before.

He'd done his best not to let anyone see how thoughts tormented him—guilt, need, loss...and love.

Yes, love. He was in love with Christianne and once his coach rolled away from Strawberry Grove, he must never touch her again.

What if you have gotten her with child? Then what would you do? a voice jeered in his head. And for a moment, he imagined what that would be like. Her belly swelling with his babe, feeling new life growing inside of her.

Wouldn't a man of honor, no matter what his lineage, marry her, then? The fierce yearning in him made him long for that moment, and yet that would be no way to start a marriage and he knew full well how impossible such a match would be. The gossip, the ugliness that would spread because of it.

No. That would be a coward's way out. Nor could he slip into her room, make love to her under her family's roof. Unable to bear the silent temptation, he moved through the house, out the door and into the garden.

At least outside, he could gaze up at Christianne's window. The fragrance of night blossoms filled his nostrils as he turned to look up at the darkened bedchamber where she lay. He ached, not being able to go to her. This was what it would be like from now on, he knew. This ache.

He'd started down the garden path when he glimpsed a figure, standing with one hand on a tree, a white nightshift wafting gently around long, slender legs. She might have been a statue, her form was so exquisite as moonlight filtered through the fragile fabric, but he knew in a heartbeat that it was Christianne.

She was staring out at the pond where they'd gone swimming on long past summer days, when she'd played his Lady of the Lake. Her waist-length black hair rippled down her back. Nate knew he should leave. To give his body what it so desperately craved felt like an even deeper breach of trust. But his cock hardened with a need so overwhelming he couldn't move.

She must have sensed his presence, too. Her voice drifted to him, soft, though she didn't turn. "Nate. I knew you would come."

He slipped his banyan off, meaning to drape it around her shoulders. But before he could, she untied the gathered neckline of her shift, and let it slide down her arms to pool around her feet.

She turned to him and for a heartbeat he couldn't breathe. The moonlight limned white breasts, rose-tipped and begging for his mouth. Long, slender legs gleamed and he wanted them wrapped around his hips, urging him to drive deep. His cock ached, rock-hard with wanting her.

"Christianne..." *We can't...we shouldn't*...the denials ran through his head. But he didn't care anymore, about honor, about breaking trust.

All he could think of was that this might be the last time he could ever bury himself inside the woman he loved.

She took his hand, drew him down the path to the edge of the pond, then without a glance at him, she dove cleanly into the water. He saw a flash of white flank, the flip of her bare feet before they disappeared beneath the surface. She rolled over in the water, and her face shone, pale and lovely in the moonlight, her hair a dark nimbus in the water around her.

"Swim with me," she said softly, and cut through the water like a mermaid. She drew him, like a siren, to cliffs he yearned to wreck himself upon.

Nate stripped off his clothes at the edge of the water, unfastening shirt and breeches, and leather straps, until he entered the chest-deep water, abandoning wood and leather and metal bracing on the shore.

He felt the water buoy him up with a freedom of movement he'd all but forgotten on land, then he cut through the water until he caught Christianne against him. Her body was slick with water, warm and supple and ripe and eager for his hands as he smoothed them over her, from her back to her waist, her buttocks, his palms gliding with a friction that made his whole body feel on fire. His mouth came down on hers, his tongue delving deep into her mouth, starving for the taste he'd thought he'd given up forever.

But not tonight, he told himself as he pressed his cock against the soft swell of her belly. Her legs drifted apart in the water and she let her thighs float up around his hips. The heat of her beckoned and she gasped and pulled him tighter, closer, until the tip of him dipped inside. He thrust deep, burying himself in her heat, feeling her envelop him, arch against him, moaning softly with need.

Nate slid his hands down to cup the lush curves of her bottom. "Christianne... Christianne..." He murmured her name over and over as he lifted her, the water buoying them up as he thrust, the damp heat gripping him so tight he'd never felt anything more powerful, so sensual, wringing every sensation out of him. Her mouth took fierce kisses along his throat, her teeth catching at the cords of his neck, her nails scraping in a sensual path over his shoulders, down his back, to his buttocks.

They held each other, gasping, reaching for that fulfillment. Suddenly it burst through his whole body, and he heard Christianne's cry.

I love you... The words rose in his mind, but he couldn't say it. It would only make it harder to leave her.

They got out of the water and lay together under the stars, wrapped in his banyan, clinging to the last moments they could be together until pink stained the sky. At last they dressed, Nate strapping on buckles and brace, the leg he'd hated for so long...the flaw whose sting her tender touch had taken away.

"I love you, Nate," she whispered to him, kissing him one last time.

He stood by the shore of the lake, watching her run lightly to the house, her nightshift rippling around her, her hair loose. His Lady of the Lake, carrying all of the stars in his sky with her.

~

NATE WAS GONE. That morning, Christianne had caught back her hair with a blue ribbon, her stays once again loose, her petticoats and bodice and sleeves roomy enough to move in. She'd stood in the carriage circle with her sisters and mother, offering hugs as if he were still like a third big brother. He'd come to her last of all, looking down into her eyes with such tenderness. "Goodbye, Mistress Mayhem," he'd said, a choke in his voice.

"Goodbye, Galahad."

He'd gathered her close, holding her only heartbeats longer than he'd hugged Eliza, but it had been long enough.

Christianne had felt her mother's gaze on them and sensed that a reckoning was coming. Not long after his coach rumbled away, her mother sent a maid to fetch her to the "Jewel Box."

Filled with light and the colors Lydia Slade loved, the personal parlor had been created for her by the earl when he was young and besotted. As if within its confines he could protect her from the world that would sling its arrows at the woman who had surrendered everything—her chance at marriage, her parents, her friends, an illustrious future—to be with the man she loved.

Now, as Christianne walked into that familiar room, where she'd been praised and scolded, had laughed and cried, she wondered what would it be like to step out the door into that uncertain future, knowing the man she loved had to wed another woman. That he had chosen not to surrender to the passion they'd shared because of society's conventions.

Her mother sat in a sea-green chair, beautiful despite her years. Her face had softened with age, but her complexion was still creamy. Her head still had that proud tilt that no censuring curate had ever caused her to lower in shame.

Christianne wasn't sure why she should feel guilty for her own actions these past six weeks, after her mother's rebellious past. She'd only followed in Lydia Slade's footsteps by doing something scandalous. Yet facing her mother made her uncomfortable. Perhaps because Lydia had been defiant herself, she had a gift for sensing rebellion in her brood of children.

A silver tray sat on the pie crust table before her. Two teacups waited to be filled from the Meissen teapot that gleamed in the light streaming in the window.

"Please do close the door," Lydia said. "Would you care for tea? It seems as though much has happened since we had a comfortable prose."

Often in the past, Christianne had complained that her mother's "comfortable proses" were rarely "comfortable," but she was in no mood to jest. "Yes. I would love tea."

Her mother poured, and added a touch of cream. "You look rather peaked, dear."

"I'm still quite tired from the journey."

"From Bath? That is where you happened upon Nate? Or so you said."

She'd cobbled together a story as best she could. "Yes. He was taking the waters for his leg." Christianne raised the cup to her lips. "Kitty and I encountered him—"

"I know that you were not with Kitty."

Christianne choked on the scalding liquid. "Wh-what?"

"Kitty's aunt sent a lovely note, mourning that you'd been called away at the last minute. She wanted to know if Gavin's children were getting better with you helping to nurse them through their illness." Her mother leveled her with the glare that made even Adam squirm.

"I pressed Eliza. She would not tell me where you were, but she assured me that you were safe and well, and that Nate was looking after you."

"Eliza didn't know where I was."

"Christianne, I doubt you will tell me what you've been doing. You were always my wild, headstrong girl, thinking you know best. But something seemed very different between you and Nate when he brought you here."

Different? Yes...I thought I was in love with him before I left. But that was merely the shadow of what I feel for him now, when we've shared so much, spent evenings together where we talked until dawn, touched and kissed...and more.

She felt heat rise to her cheeks at the memory of his hands on her with the waves lapping around their naked bodies, the tangle of coverlets in her bed at The Blue Peacock. She turned away, as if afraid her mother would see the reflection of those nights in her eyes.

"I need to caution you about Nate," her mother said, her voice more tender than Christianne had ever heard it.

"Caution me? About Nate?" Christianne tried to sound incredulous. "He spent half his youth right here at Strawberry Grove."

"If it weren't for the fact that Gavin attended the same Academy of Swordsmanship with Master DuPree, you'd never even have been allowed to meet Nate. Nate's father, the Earl of Fendale, would never have approved of his precious heir being friends with Adam. He never allowed Nate to cross our threshold until Gavin came to live with us."

Christianne thought back, realizing it was true.

"When the lads formed the Knights with Myles Farringdon and Braden Tracey as well, those three connections were too important to risk offense. I'm sure the fact that Adam was included was distasteful to Nate's father."

Possibly so. Christianne had never been fond of the Earl of Fendale, but there was no question that the death of his wife had devastated the old man, and the scandal that now shrouded his only son's future added to his grimness. The absence of his granddaughter must have been hard as well, Christianne thought, picturing Seraphina Rowland again as she had been the night of the birthday fete. She could see the child so clearly, all draped in gauze and flowers, a little fairy bringing her papa a toy soldier, and lisping that she was soon to have a baby brother... Seraphina haunted Christianne. How much more painful must it be for the girl's grandfather to have the nursery echoing in silence like a tomb?

Her mother's voice gentled. "You can't know what it is like for someone like Nate. To have your 'duty to your name' hammered into your head from the time you can walk. You carry around the weight of your ancestors, your station in society. Do you remember the governess you had for such a short time? The one we hired when your father took me to Italy?"

"The one that bolted poor Eliza in that awful metal brace so she couldn't get humpbacked from hunching over her books? I'll wager she never forgot us! I put blacking in her tea. Made her teeth look as rotten as her heart."

"Your heritage is like iron bands wrapped around you so that you can't bend—"

"Or think for yourself? Decide your own future because of a debt you owe people who've been moldering in the grave since Agincourt? You're of noble blood, and so was Papa. Perhaps not stretching quite so far back as the Rowlands, but—"

"You know that the choice your father and I made to be together altered all of our futures. Our children's in more ways than I truly comprehended."

"Kings have bastards all the time, and everyone bows to them."

"Your father was not a king. Besides, it is different for girls. It grieves me more than you'll ever know that you and your sisters are suffering now because of our choices. But I do not regret my life with your father. How could I ever regret loving him? Or the beautiful, headstrong children we made?" Her mother cupped Christianne's cheeks between her hands. "But I have paid a price. One was losing my parents and brothers and sisters. Another, losing my childhood friends."

Had Papa been enough to fill that void? Christianne wondered. He'd still belonged to that privileged world he'd grown up in. As a man, that was possible. He could have a mistress and children by her. Scandal couldn't taint him in the way it had the rest of them.

"I've never told any of you children that Augusta Rowland was a dear friend when I was a girl."

"Nate's mother was your friend?" Christianne looked up in surprise. "I didn't know."

"Of course, she couldn't speak to me after the scandal. Her parents and her husband would not tolerate our continued friendship. Once Gavin came to live with us, Fendale relented enough to let Nate visit. Augusta would send little gifts with Nate to show she hadn't forgotten me. A basket of flowers, some fresh vegetables, small tokens. At first, I thought it was just her way of being polite. Then she sent a basket of gingerbread men. I remembered the two of us stealing down to the kitchen during holidays, and her cook letting us put raisin eyes and buttons and icing smiles on our little people. I'd made a cravat on one of mine with white frosting. One of the gingerbread men she sent had a cravat. I knew she was trying to tell me that she hadn't forgotten. Eventually, she began writing to me, letters she slipped out without her husband knowing. I replied, using Gavin's stationery. It was a ruse that he approved."

Gavin, who had always stitched things together, shielding them from society's barbs and from financial ruin as well after their father's death. What might have happened to the Slades if he hadn't survived the rise of Charles Stuart and the Bonnie Prince's fall?

"When Augusta wrote to me, she was able to share things she could not tell anyone else. She adored Seraphina. That child was the light of her life. Then someone—someone cruel, someone vengeful—someone eager to hurt her—told her that Sera was not Nate's child. Nate's father was so enraged, it scared her. His illustrious name means far more to him than mere humans. Ask him, and he'll tell you. Individually, we each are but a flash on the stage of history, but the name Rowland lives on."

Christianne thought of Nate, the grim set of his jaw.

He'd said much the same about his father's rigid adherence to duty. She could picture Seraphina Rowland's fairylike face, her golden curls, those remarkable, haunting violet eyes as she handed Nate the toy soldier the night of his birthday fete.

Nate had sent little Sera away from Harlestone that night, so soon after Eugenie's body had been found. She'd thought it was heartless. But was it possible Nate feared his father's wrath as his mother had? What if he'd sent the little girl away to protect her? Possibly even to save her life?

Seraphina was a girl. A daughter. She couldn't inherit the title Rowland prized so greatly. But if Eugenie had given birth to a son, everything Nate's father clung to with holy fervor would have passed to the child—and be lost to the Rowland bloodline forever.

Christianne remembered the little girl lisping. *It is for that boy who will go into the army one day, like you did.*

"I'm only telling you this because you must be very careful," her mother warned. "I'm not blind. I've seen the way you and Nate look at each other. I fear these past weeks might have meant more than a mere visit to wherever you have gone. Did Nate take you somewhere—"

"No. I left on my own. He was furious when he found me. He did his best to get me to come home, but I wouldn't until..." Her voice trailed off. "I wanted to find whomever has been attacking him with those handbills. There was a clue I followed, but I failed. It was only chance that Nate found me."

"Thank heaven he did. Yet, I worry for both of you. It would be one thing for you to defy society's censure for your love as your father and I did. But if you and Nate do so, you might be in far more danger than either of you realize. Someone strangled Eugenie Rowland to be certain an unworthy heir wouldn't be the next Lord Harlestone. No one except Nate and the babe's father could know for certain that it wasn't his child. If the mere chance that a bastard might inherit the title drove someone to commit murder, the possibility that you, born out of wedlock yourself, would be linked to the Rowland family tree, might ignite that same fury. I don't know who struck down Eugenie and her unborn child. But what if that murderer would do the same to you?"

Ice trickled down Christianne's spine. She swallowed hard, remembering Eugenie's ghastly expression, her mouth wide in a silent scream. Horror had been imprinted on her delicate features as surely as the circlet of bruises that ringed her swanlike throat.

"I know you want me to be safe," Christianne said, "but loving Nate is a risk I had to take. It's a risk you would have taken, too."

Her mother looked down at the emerald Papa had given her in lieu of a wedding ring.

"Mama, may I ask you something?"

"Anything, my brave girl."

"Was it worth it? The love you had for Papa? You were happy together, weren't you?"

Her mother hesitated. "Much of the time," she said softly. "But it was painful, too. Your father could still move about in the world I left. Our set could understand why he would betray a merchant's daughter, a wife so far beneath him in station. But they would never forgive me. I wouldn't trade our time together, but it came at a price. Now, as I watch you and your sisters come of age, I realize we're not the only ones who paid it. I want your eyes to be open to that if you are considering the same arrangement."

"I love him."

"I know. But Nate is not your father. He'd suffer

being ostracized himself, but I doubt he would allow you to suffer because of him."

"I'm not you. Nate isn't Papa."

"But the world beyond these doors is still the world. And it is harsher than you know."

$\mathcal{N}$ate couldn't go home to Harlestone Hall. Not yet. He'd closed the door on his physical relationship with the woman who'd given him his life back, and the thought of seeing his father while that loss was so fresh was unthinkable. Nate felt raw to the bone and the last thing he wanted was to be pressured about marriage.

With every turn of the coach wheels, the aftermath of Culloden played in his mind—the hospital ward a haze, men screaming in pain. The voice of the shattered youth that had been in the bed beside his echoed in Nate's memory. *How do you go on when you know you'll never be whole again?* And then, Nate's answer: *You take a first step, no matter how much it hurts. Then you take another.*

He'd have to do that now. Take the first step to build whatever his life would be without Christianne, and that meant facing another wound.

Seraphina. For weeks now, the exquisite sketches Christianne had given him had been on his mind, haunting even his sleep. Now, he needed to face whatever this meant, to see for himself what the child needed, and what he needed, and determine what healing might be found between them.

As his coach rumbled up to the Kettering estate, he wondered if Sera would even recognize him after so long. The coach shuddered to a halt and he glimpsed children playing on the grounds, laughing, romping, wrestling with glee. Seraphina stood alone. She was clutching a daisy in her hand, the heart of the flower as gold as her hair, her expression solemn and sad. He'd helped to put it there.

He wanted to rap on the coach roof, tell the coachman to drive on. Instead he climbed down from the equipage, stretching a body stiff from travel and the night of sleeping on the ground with Christianne in his arms.

If he had other children, would it ease Seraphina's loneliness? Would he be able to open his heart to her more fully?

It's not your fault your mother and I made a mess of our marriage, he wanted to tell her, but he could only do his best to *show* her—if she'd let him.

At that moment, Seraphina looked toward him. Violet eyes held his gaze.

"Papa?" she asked, uncertain.

"Hello, Seraphina." His throat felt tight as he walked toward her.

"Did you bring Caval?"

"No. Shall I bring him next time?"

At first she looked eager, then shook her head. "I don't think Aunt would like it. You look very sad, Papa," she said. He couldn't imagine what pricked the little girl to edge closer to him. The hope that she might offer comfort? The knowledge that he was the only parent she had now? An unsatisfactory parent, and yet...

"I would imagine you are sad, too."

Sera fretted her lower lip. "I miss Mama."

"I know you do. I miss her, too." It wasn't a lie. He missed seeing Eugenie in the pony cart with Seraphina, and the way her face always lit up when the little girl came into the room. His wife had been like the flowers surrounding Sera, easily crushed, and the war had trampled over her as savagely as it had the idealistic young officer Nate had been.

"Willie says that I might have another mama soon. Lady Beresford."

It startled Nate that rumors about his encounters with Olivia had reached so far.

"Lady Beresford's boys play with Willie. He says they'd be my brothers then."

"Did he?"

"I always wanted a brother. But the angels took mine back to heaven with Mama before I even got to hold him."

"I'm sorry."

"Lady Beresford doesn't have any girls at all. She said she'd like to play dolls and doesn't have anyone to teach embroidery to. She stitched the most cunning little flower on Bobo's bonnet."

Nate looked down at the doll he'd given Sera years ago, saw the bright flower on the faded little bonnet. He drew in a deep breath, touched by Olivia's kindness. What had his father said when he'd put Olivia on his list of prospective wives? She was dependable, mature, with no girlish notions of romance. It would be a partnership they would build together. He would help her run the estates that Alexander would take charge of when he reached his majority, and she could smooth over Seraphina's entry into society when the time came, scandal fading beneath Olivia's respectable, calm guidance. Olivia had been proven fertile, and could bear the heir Nate needed to continue his own family legacy.

There was no reason *not* to wed Olivia, except that he was in love with Christianne.

But, then, how many aristocrats could marry for something as plebian as love?

"Do you like Olivia?" Nate asked.

Sera tipped her head to one side, considering. "Yes. But she's not as pretty as Mama. And she doesn't know how to sword fight."

"What?"

"Misty does."

"Misty? Who on earth is that?" He smiled at the lop-sided doll in her arm.

"Not Misty, like clouds. Mistress Tia who brought the painting lady here. She showed me how she fought with sticks and beat her brothers. She laughed and laughed."

Mistress Tia...Tianne. Nate felt an uncomfortable knot in his throat, able to picture the scene so well. Christianne, far from the confines of The Blue Peacock, her hair a tousled mass of curls, romping with the children here. How he missed her already!

"She said it was only right that she be the one to teach me sword fighting. You taught *her* when she was a little girl. She's going to come back soon so we can practice. Papa, maybe you could help, too."

"Perhaps," he said, something fragile awakening inside him.

The child ran off to retrieve two sticks that were leaning against a tree. One had a red ribbon tied on it, the other a blue ribbon.

His heart squeezed as he took one in his hand. At the end of the hour, he sank down on a chair.

"Are you happy living with your aunt?" he asked,

tentative. "Or would you like to come back to Harlestone Hall?"

She clutched Bobo tight. "I could come home? Today?"

"I have some things to prepare, but yes. I'll bring you home, soon." He needed to be sure it was safe and there had to be time to piece back the parts of himself he'd left with Christianne. Was that even possible?

Yes. He'd done it before when all seemed lost. He'd do it now. He thought of Christianne, her face when she gave him the drawings. Wouldn't bringing Seraphina home be one way of honoring the love he and Christianne had shared?

He'd make Harlestone a home for this child who had seen so much pain. Maybe she was that first step to the life *after* the love he'd known. As he'd told the young soldier. *Take the first step...then another...*

Even if it hurt like hell.

CHAPTER 28

$\mathcal{N}$ ate had been avoiding his friends. It was true that he'd had more than his share of estate business to deal with in the six weeks since Gavin and Adam had returned. His father had lists from here to Brighton of roofs to be mended, fields planted, boundary disputes to mediate, and the never-ending messes to untangle on Olivia's estate. Nate had had the nursery revamped.

But being busy wasn't the only reason he'd stayed away from the Slades. Just the thought of seeing Christianne without touching her was torture. And Gavin and Adam would be spending most of their time with the family now that they'd returned.

Only at night, when Nate lay alone in his big bed, did he let himself remember what it felt like to have Christianne's lips trailing over his skin, her teeth nipping his neck, her hand teasing its way down his body.

What the hell was he going to do?

He knew damned well what duty dictated. Olivia, so grateful for his help, needing him... Her sons Alexander and Richard gazing up at him with that adoration young soldiers had once lavished on him. Alexander, so eager to please.

The time they spent together had shown Nate just how it might be, the pride a father might take in a son.

And Nate had promised to bring Seraphina home. Did she fear he'd renege on his promise?

"I haven't seen my mother this happy since Father died," Alexander had confided when Nate had gone over the plans for the grist mill.

She did seem happy. She deserved to be so. Could he be content, building a family with Olivia? If he did, would it dull the pain of losing Christianne? Or could it be the barrier that would keep him from making love to her again?

"IT WORKED! IT WORKED!" Alexander leapt with pure joy as the stream sent the water wheel turning.

"You're a wonder, Nate!" Olivia laughed. "I don't know what Alexander and I would do without you!"

She flung her arms around him. She felt warm and womanly. But she was not Christianne. Did she feel his body tense? He didn't know. She pulled away, looking abashed.

"It was Alexander's idea. I just helped him implement it."

Olivia smiled, her eyes shining. "Have you heard from Sera? Did the new draperies I helped you order arrive? The little unicorns embroidered on the cloth should delight any little girl."

Why couldn't he just ask her? Will you marry me? But every time he tried to force the words out, Christianne's face rose in his mind.

"Will you stay for dinner? I had cook make your favorite," she looked up at him, so hopeful.

He'd far rather dine here than listen to his father harangue him about marrying. It only made him more resistant. "You know how I love your cook's pheasant," Nate said.

Olivia was smiling when hoofbeats thundered up the road.

He frowned, seeing Vickers ride toward them, his horse lathered. The footman looked the way he had after his scouting party had been ambushed at Prestonpans.

"What is it?" Nate asked, urgently.

"My lord, there's been an accident."

Christianne? His first thought.

"It's your father," Vickers gasped, wiping sweat from his brow. "He was out riding and his horse fell on that old bridge."

Nate's stomach dropped. "How bad is it?"

"If Master Salway hadn't happened upon him, we might not have known he was injured until it was too late."

Nate thought of the sharp exchange he'd had with his father last night over dinner when the earl had pressured him about marrying Olivia. The idea of those words being the last between them was more painful than he could bear.

He felt a hand on his arm. "Oh, Nate, do you want me to come?" Olivia asked. "I have skill at nursing and I'm so very fond of your father."

As he is fond of you, Nate thought.

"Best let her accompany you, my lord," Vickers said. "Master Salway went for the doctor, but there's no telling how soon he'll find him."

"Olivia, I'd appreciate the help," Nate said.

Alexander had already fetched Nate's horse. Nate swung up.

"I can ride pillion," Olivia said. "I've done so before." Alexander lifted his mother up behind Nate. Olivia wrapped her arms around Nate's waist.

"Alex, fetch my medical kit and come as quick as you can," she said.

Alex nodded and Nate kicked Excalibur into a gallop.

"I hope we're not too late," Olivia murmured.

Was he? Nate wondered. What if he never had the chance to mend the rift that had grown between him and his father in the time since his mother's death?

~

CHRISTIANNE BUSTLED about a room crowded with her sisters, gowns spread over every surface, the traveling trunk on the floor. "Adam will be here in a few hours, and you'll have to have decided what to pack."

The whole household had been in an uproar since Adam had come with the invitation. *The Earl of Fendale requests the honor of your presence at a celebratory dinner and hunting party to celebrate his delivery from a perilous accident.* It was addressed to *Gavin Carstares, Earl of Glenlyon, Master Adam Slade, and Miss Christianne Slade.*

"Perhaps that blow to the head Fendale took six weeks ago damaged more than Nate realized," Adam had teased. "The fact that he's invited me to Harlestone is shocking enough. But inviting Christianne as well? I'd never have believed it if I hadn't seen the invitation with my own eyes."

Christianne had barely been able to think in the whirl of preparations that followed. It had been two months since she and Nate had made love under the stars, but it seemed like an eternity.

She'd missed Nate more every day. She'd written him and received a few brief notes in return. Yet it wasn't the same as hearing his voice, seeing the devilish curl of his lip, feeling the warm brush of his breath right before he kissed her.

"For heaven's sake, you and Eliza are pinging around here like bees trapped in a bottle!" Maria complained as she and Laura bent over Christianne's jewelry casket, holding earrings up and comparing various pairs in the mirror. "It's just a visit with Nate and his awful father!"

"Perhaps it's something wonderful," Eliza said, flashing Christianne a conspiratorial grin. Christianne smiled back. She and Eliza had whispered late into the night after Nate's coach had disappeared down the lane. She had told Eliza everything—almost. That Nate had kissed her. Taken her to bed.

"If I were writing this story, this celebration would be the perfect time for the hero to go down on one knee," Eliza said. "Perhaps Nate's father had a change of heart. It happens when people face death, I'm told. Or maybe Nate simply said he was marrying you no matter what and the old earl had to accept it. What a wonderful scene that would make in one of my stories!"

Hope fluttered under Christianne's breastbone. If Nate had been feeling nearly the longing she'd felt, then wasn't it possible he'd decided to follow his heart? "Fendale would have to *have* a heart in order to change it," Christianne said, not wanting to get her hopes up.

"Why else would the earl ask *you* to come?" Eliza insisted. That was the one question Christianne couldn't answer. "Gavin and Adam will be there, too," Eliza said. "Maybe Nate will ask *them* for your hand."

What had his last letter said, written the week before his father's accident? He'd gone to see Sera, and was preparing things to bring his daughter home. *You are the one who gave Sera and me this chance,* he'd written so tenderly. *There is so much I want to say to you if only I could see you face to face. Just know that I will treasure those drawings—your gift to us—forever.*

She could picture it all in her head. Nate declaring his love, asking her to be his wife, Sera's mother. She could teach Sera to laugh again, to romp and play and run to her father and not be afraid.

Eliza was just about to shut the traveling case when Lydia Slade entered the room. Christianne was struck by how beautiful their mother still was. Fine lines marked creamy skin and pale blue smudges were visible beneath thick lashes, but her eyes held a flicker of hope she couldn't quite conceal. Mother knew about the kind of love Christianne felt for Nate. The passion, and the pain.

"Mama, I thought you had a megrim," Laura said, crossing to their mother and touching her brow as if checking for fever.

"I'm fine," Lydia said. "I have something for Christianne to take on her visit to Harlestone Hall." She held out a faded velvet box. "Would you like to borrow my emeralds?"

Eliza gasped. Laura's eyes went wide. One of the great delights of childhood had been when their mother had shown them the exquisite matched set of jewelry inside, though she rarely had a formal enough occasion to wear them.

"Really?" Tears burned Christianne's eyes.

"Your father gave them to me the night he asked me to marry him. Before everything went wrong." Her mother gathered Christianne in her arms. Her voice trembled. "Perhaps they will bring you luck."

CHAPTER 29

It didn't seem possible that the last time Christianne had visited Harlestone Hall, Eugenie Rowland had been murdered. The estate was as imposing as ever, with its well-laid-out gardens, exquisite maze of boxwood hedges, and the evocative wing of the old castle where she'd spent magical hours with Nate, exploring quests from the legends they loved.

She couldn't wait to revel in his company again. There were times she felt as if her mind was turning to *blancmange* since she'd left the salon. She missed the spirited exchange of ideas, the freedom to say what she thought and the excitement of never knowing what the new day would bring. Most of all, she missed the possibility that on any night, Nate's noble resistance might crack again, and perfect, honorable Galahad would surrender to the need that thrummed ever more insistently between them. A flush warmed her breasts at the memory of his big hands cupping her flesh. *Maybe tonight they'd rediscover that passion…*

Providing no other "emergencies" came up to draw Nate away, she thought in frustration. She'd counted the minutes until she could see Nate's face again and perhaps steal one of the kisses she craved, but they were met by his footman Vickers instead.

"The Earl of Fendale sends his apologies for not welcoming you himself," Vickers said, bowing to Gavin. "He and Lord Harlestone have gone to settle some dispute over grazing rights. They will see you when you all come down for dinner."

Disappointment filled Christianne, and despite Gavin's offer to take her to visit the Harlestone stables, she lingered in her room, listening for noises in the hall in hopes Nate might steal up to see her as he returned. At last, she'd donned a forget-me-not-blue gown and her mother's emeralds and waited until Adam and Gavin came to escort her down to join a dozen other guests.

Nate was already conversing with his cousin, Salway, and other people, some of whom had attended the ill-fated birthday celebration. His eyes grew wide when he saw her. But then, seeing him was a jolt to her as well. Nate, her Nate, seemed so different in this formal setting. He had a stern cast to his features that made her wonder if his leg was aching, his shoulders tense beneath amber velvet, his waistcoat embroidered with gold thread. Rich brown breeches clung to muscular thighs, and his neckcloth fell in pristine waves under a chin set so rigidly that it seemed his jaw might crack.

When they'd discovered Jessamyn's connection with the printer and the handbills meant to ruin Nate, she'd hoped the information might drive the haunted look from his eyes. Especially since the printer's daughter had affirmed that Jessamyn had sailed to the colonies. But Nate looked more on edge than ever.

She hoped he would come and greet her, but the old earl reached Christianne and her brothers first. Nate's father was much changed since the day she'd seen him in the tension-filled courtroom at the inquest. His hair had gone white, his bones like knife-blades in his face. Was the accident more serious than they'd been led to believe? Or was he ill with some cancer eating his flesh? There was an almost frenzied brightness to his ice-blue eyes.

"Glenlyon, I hope your diplomatic mission to the Netherlands was successful," Fendale said, taking a pinch of snuff.

"It was, thank you."

One of Fendale's brows arched up. "Adam, I heard that you accompanied your brother."

"I did."

"I was rather astonished that you both left England, what with your sisters to look after. One never knows what mischief they can get into."

"We are hardly in leading strings, my lord," Christianne said, trying to read the old man's expression.

"Better that you were, Miss Slade." The earl gave a rare laugh. "It is once girls leave the nursery that trouble begins. Ah, excuse me. I see that our neighbors have arrived from the Beresford estate. I must greet them."

He walked away just as Nate was able to limp across the room to join his friends. "Gavin, Adam. Good to see you." Christianne saw Nate's cheeks flush as he shook their hands.

"It's been far too long," Adam said. "I kept expecting you to turn up on our doorsteps as you usually do after such a trip. I had the bottle of port ready."

"I've been tied up with estate business. Then, my father was injured." His gaze shifted to her. "Even this dinner was a surprise."

"A pleasant one, I hope," Christianne said.

"Of course, it's always good to see you." His gaze clung to hers long moments and she prayed her

292

brothers couldn't detect that slight roughness in his voice, the intimacy they'd shared.

"I've been hoping for a chance to speak to you especially, Christianne. Perhaps after dinner?"

"I would love that," she said.

"From your letter, it sounds as if you've had an eventful time while we were away," Gavin said. "It's good news that you discovered the woman behind that libelous campaign against you. I'm hoping to learn more about how you did so."

Christianne smiled at Nate. No one could ever know it had been Christianne who'd unearthed Jessamyn's part in the effort to ruin Nate. It was enough that Nate was safer because of it.

"There's not much to tell. Jessamyn Smith has apparently fled to the colonies. There have been no more handbills scattered about. I'm grateful to know who was behind the slander, but the greater mystery remains. Jessamyn had an accomplice—that man in the mask who dropped the handbills outside The Blue Peacock long ago. The pages with that unique scent. I still don't know how he and Jessamyn are connected or if that has anything to do with Eugenie's death."

"Perhaps Eugenie discovered something dangerous, and was silenced," Gavin mused.

Nate frowned and Christianne saw his father motioning to him from across the room. "I must see to my other guests." He looked at Christianne. "I'll speak to you later?"

"I'll look forward to it." She smiled at him, imagining that time alone. Perhaps if she was rid of her brothers, Nate would return and they could steal away. "Gavin and Adam, go mingle with the crowd and I'll do so as well," she urged. Her brothers wandered off, to her relief. But before Nate could return, Salway Rowland intruded, his eyes hooded, with a hint of mockery, as if he were remembering her time at the salon.

She couldn't see Nate's cousin now without remembering the proposition he'd made. She resisted the impulse to tug the ruffle around her neckline a little higher.

"Good evening, Mistress Slade," he said, sketching her a bow. "I've not seen you since our last encounter in London. I hope all is well with you."

"It is, thank you. And with you?"

"I've been dealing with some delay involving a ship hauling cargo for my sugar plantation. I hope to sort it out soon."

"Ah, no wonder you seem distracted. How is Deborah Musgrove?" she ventured, hoping to either gain information or drive him away. "Her husband said that you were a frequent visitor at Musgrove Place."

"She mentioned you had called without notice." Salway licked his lips, his gaze dipping down to the emeralds pillowed on Christianne's breast.

"We went to ask her about the fan Eugenie was carrying the night she died," Christianne said. "It was painted specially with Seraphina as spring and Eugenie as well. But a section was torn out of the center. We hoped she might be able to tell us who the image was. Perhaps it had some connection to the murder and the father of Eugenie's child?"

Salway shrugged. "It's more likely that Eugenie had rapped the knuckles of one of her admirers one to many times and the fan tore. Or that it caught on something when she fled the room after Nate was so abominable to her."

Christianne's temper sparked. "That's not fair."

"Isn't it?" A bitter edge clipped Salway's voice. "Cousin Nate seems to have come through the whole affair unscathed and landed in a much better place."

"How can you say that after all he's been through?"

"While he was in London the *grieving widower* appeared happier than I've ever seen him—even before he lost his leg at Culloden Moor. When I made my weekly visit to Seraphina the other day, he rode up unexpectedly. I'd brought the child a charming toy horse, but she ran to him and forgot I was even there. I believe that the change in their relationship is because of you."

"I hope so." Warmth blossomed in Christianne's chest. "He deserves happiness and so does she."

Salway looked over to where his uncle and a cluster of other guests had gathered.

"I see Glenlyon and Nate are speaking to Olivia Nasby and her son," Salway observed.

"Young Alex hangs on Nate's every word." The lanky youth reminded Christianne all too poignantly of Gavin at that age, the weight of his responsibilities heavy on his shoulders. Her empathetic brother would understand the fatherless boy in a way few people could.

Olivia laid a hand on Nate's sleeve and smiled up at him. Christianne resisted the urge to cross the room and break into the conversation. Of course Olivia would be grateful to the man who was helping to guide her son. Yet, Christianne couldn't help remembering the uncomfortable conversation she and Nate had had on their way from Deborah Musgrove's.

Fendale clapped his hands. "My friends, let us repair to the dining room. I feel as though I've been granted new life!" A smattering of applause broke out.

Gentlemen offered the ladies nearest them their arms as the company moved toward the dining room door. Salway crooked his elbow toward Christianne.

"Will you do me the honor?"

She glanced across the room. Nate was too much the gentleman to abandon Olivia and cross the room to claim Christianne, and her brothers were nowhere in sight. She laid her hand on Salway's arm as if touching a snake and let him lead her into the dining room. Her eyes were fixed on Nate escorting Olivia in, Alex walking on his mother's other side, jabbering away.

The Jacobean dining table was laden with a repast worthy of a king. Branches of silver candles glistened, their flames reflected in china emblazoned with the crest, awarded by William the Conqueror for the Rowlands' contribution at the Battle of Hastings. Footmen in green and gold livery stood at attention, ready to serve. She smiled at Vickers, who was pouring wine into crystal goblets. Christianne took her seat between her brothers, far from the head of the table where the earl and Nate presided over the company, Alex on one side of Nate, Olivia on his other. Christianne tried to engage in animated conversation with those nearby while stealing glances at Nate's place at the table, hoping to catch his eye. But those moments were rare, his shoulder often turned away from her so he could lean close to catch Olivia's soft voice beneath the soft clink of silverware and the hum of conversation. Worse was seeing Olivia smiling up at him.

When the last course was done, Lord Fendale motioned to the footmen who hastened around to refill glasses, until everyone's goblet was filled to the brim.

The earl cleared his throat. "As you know, I have gathered you here to toast my recovery from a most unfortunate accident. But I am also eager to celebrate the fact that we have found the identity of the troubled young woman who sought to destroy my son's good name."

People around the table looked up in surprise.

"Soon we will find the perpetrator who murdered Lady Harlestone," the earl continued. "But there can be no doubt that it is not my son."

"As if anyone who knew Nate could've believed such rot for a second," Adam grumbled.

"Now, I ask for your attention as I give special thanks to the one person who did more to clear Nate's name than anyone else," Fendale's voice boomed. "Miss Christianne Slade."

Christianne froze with shock as every eye at the table turned to hers. She had not realized anyone besides Nate knew of her full involvement. Even her brothers had no idea. Fendale's lip curled with pleasure as if he reveled in her confusion.

The earl flicked his lace cuffs to fall around his age-spotted hands. "I confess, it is hard to imagine a gently reared woman going to such extreme measures."

"When it comes to Christianne, I'd believe anything," Adam said. "Though I can't imagine what she discovered in Bath."

"Bath?" The earl's gaze sharpened, a hawk diving in for the kill. "What does Bath have to do with it? She managed this feat in London."

"London?" Adam echoed, his brow furrowing.

Gavin stared at Christianne. "I don't understand. Weren't you in Bath with Kitty's family?"

"N-not exactly."

Nate cut his father off, his eyes stormy. "Father, speak no more of it. You're making Miss Slade uncomfortable."

"I can understand why," Fendale said, his ice-cold eyes piercing Christianne's. "The lady's involvement was far from wise—leaving the bosom of her family to seek work in one of the most notorious salons in London."

Bile rose in Christianne's throat as he continued.

"Of course, one must wonder what she did to earn the trust of the patrons while she was at The Blue Peacock."

Nate sprang to his feet. "Father, that is enough!"

But it was too late. Gasps and a buzz of whispers erupted at the table, men eyeing Christianne with avid curiosity, doubtless imagining what she'd done to wheedle information out of the patrons there, while their wives regarded her in horror and swept their gowns as far away from her, as if she might contaminate them.

Adam's dark brows crashed together over eyes. "You were at The Blue Peacock?" he growled under his breath.

"How would you even know about the clues we'd followed to that salon?" Gavin stared at her, bewildered.

Lord Fendale rapped upon the table, like a judge bringing them to order. "Well, if you do not wish to discuss Miss Slade's little escapade, Nathaniel, perhaps we should talk about a more propitious announcement. A trifle earlier than planned, but I hope you will forgive me."

Nate paled. "Father, not yet. I've had no chance to—"

"No need to delay when we have all of your dearest friends together at our table. Come May, Harlestone Hall will be hosting a wedding!"

Christianne felt a swooping sensation in her stomach. She touched her mother's emerald necklace, a sense of doom falling over her.

"Three months hence, my son and heir will make this lovely lady his bride. Stand up, Olivia, dear."

She wanted Nate to leap to his feet again, to say his father was lying or meant it as a jest. Surely Nate would never set her up for this public breaking of her heart. But when Nate's gaze locked with Christianne's, his eyes filled with pain and regret.

She grasped Gavin's arm. He looked at her in surprise as her fingers dug deep. She lifted her chin, refusing to give Nate's father the satisfaction of seeing that his words were a knife in her heart. But she could tell that he knew.

"In the weeks after my accident, Olivia cared for me more tenderly than any daughter could," the earl said with fatherly pride. "I vow, she saved my life." He turned to Olivia, and she smiled up at him with such tenderness it turned Christianne's stomach. "I hoped over a decade ago to welcome you into the family, Olivia. The only way you could make yourself dearer to me is to supply me with grandsons as handsome as your Alexander and Richard. They are such strapping boys!" His cold blue gaze bored into Christianne for a moment, then shifted to Gavin with a dark sense of triumph.

"As Nathaniel's best friend, perhaps you'd care to make a toast, my Lord Glenlyon?"

Gavin peered down at Christianne, and the empathy in her brother's eyes almost undid her. He looked from her to Nate, Gavin's eyes shadowed with understanding and pain. Gavin's long fingers curled around the stem of his crystal goblet, as footmen moved among the guests, filling the glasses with wine.

"To Nate," Gavin said, his voice thick. "One of the finest men I've ever known. And to Olivia. You've both suffered losses. As you forge this new family together, may you find happiness."

A round of applause and toasts rang out around Christianne, the guests thronging about the engaged couple. Christianne felt a hand curve under her elbow —Adam, looking thunderous. "Let's get out of here," he growled.

"No." Christianne wasn't going to run. Let Nate face her. She wouldn't give Fendale the satisfaction. She wouldn't melt into the background like Olivia would if the tables were turned. She didn't hide from storms. She charged into them head-on.

Time and again, she caught Nate looking at her from across the room. She could tell he was torn up inside. Did anyone else notice the bleakness in his face when his gaze found hers?

Adam and Gavin stood on either side of her, Adam flexing his fists, his ebony gaze flashing. "You were at The Blue Peacock that whole time?" he demanded under his breath.

"You never went to Bath?"

"I found who was behind those slanderous handbills, didn't I?" Christianne insisted. "You said you'd have gone to the salon yourself if you could."

"Damn me, I shouldn't have opened my blasted mouth! But even I never imagined you'd be reckless enough to do such a thing."

"I'm glad I did it. Even now." She squared her shoulders. "I wouldn't give up the time I got to spend with Nate."

"With *Nate?*" Adam's eyes burned like coals. "Nate *knew* you were at The Blue Peacock? He was supposed to watch over you while we were gone."

"What did you expect Nate to do? Drag me out by the scruff of my neck?"

"Yes! That's what I would have done!"

"He could have tried it. I would only have run back to The Blue Peacock the instant his back was turned." She thrust out her chin. "It wasn't for him to decide. It wasn't for you to decide."

"Anything could have happened to you there! You've seen the women who have left lives in establishments like Marguerite Charbonneau's, to seek fresh beginnings at Angel's Fall. Heard their stories."

"It's not a brothel! There are liaisons struck up, I know. But only if the woman chooses."

"Some of the men who go there aren't accustomed to hearing the word 'no,'" Gavin warned more gently.

Christianne swiped a curl back from her cheek. "They would have had hard work of it, trying to push themselves on me. Nate was in my room almost every night."

"In your bedchamber?" Adam growled, the tone more dangerous than any roar could be.

Her cheeks burned as the memories washed over her. Nate, stripped to his shirt sleeves, the muscles of his arm rippling as he lifted a glass of claret to his lips. The intimate way he'd bent over her at the table as they'd examined the fan. The thrill that had pierced to her core as his breath brushed warm on the nape of her neck. His mouth on hers, fired with a hunger neither one of them could control. His muscles flexing as he lay atop her, driving himself deep.

Adam's eyes narrowed. "You hoped for something more, didn't you? And tonight that devil of an earl…"

"What's done is done, Adam," Gavin cut in quietly.

Adam rounded on him, fierce as the mercenary soldier he'd once been. "She could've been *killed!*"

But she hadn't been. Only barred from the life she longed for in a way only Adam could understand. Christianne couldn't bear her brother's shattered gaze. She swept off in a swirl of rustling petticoats, and headed for the other side of the room. She caught a glimpse of Adam starting after her, then jolting to a halt, held by Gavin's hand. She could hear Gavin's voice behind her, the tones filled with regret as deep as her tempestuous brother's.

"Let her go."

But where could she go? She wanted to go to Nate as she always had, to tell him her troubles, be held in his arms, have him tease her in the way only he could, lifting her spirits. She wanted to burrow against the hard wall of his chest, and feel their heartbeats match rhythm, pretend that this night had never happened. That they could go on as before in those precious weeks at The Blue Peacock, that magical space in time when he'd been hers alone, when their closeness had seemed so right, as if it would always be that way.

As she walked through the room, she locked gazes with Nate. Saw the anguish in his face before he shuttered it away. She walked out onto the terrace and leaned against the bannister there. Caval was standing vigil on the lawn, waiting for Nate to appear just like Christianne had waited for Nate her whole life long. When Caval saw her, the deerhound bounded up the stairs, tail wagging until he drew near enough to sense her grief. Caval stood up on his hind legs and ever so gently put his great paws on her shoulders. Christianne sank down, and the dog curled up against her and licked her cheeks. For the first time, she let the tears flow. "Caval...how could Nate do this?" she wept into the deerhound's rough coat. "You'll have to look after him now."

CHAPTER 30

Christianne wasn't sure how long she'd been out on the terrace, hoping against hope that Nate might slip away to join her, explain how this nightmare had come to be. But when she finally heard footsteps behind her, she turned to see Olivia Nasby silhouetted against the glow of the sweeping French doors. Bitterness welled up in Christianne.

Nate's prospective bride looked every inch a lady, all calm waters and gentle breezes. Her gown was silver satin, the burgundy-hued underskirt a latticework of silver twined with pale pink roses.

Every instinct in Christianne wanted to make excuses and rush away, but her pride wouldn't let her. She curled her fingers in Caval's coat and stood even more erect.

"I've been looking for you, and hoping for an opportunity to talk to you alone," Olivia said. "Lord Fendale was wrong to speak so freely of what you did," she looked almost fierce for a moment, "but I'm so grateful to you for all you've done to clear Nate's name. It was very brave of you."

"Nate is important to…to my family."

Olivia crossed to one of the rose bushes in a stone

303

pot. She looked as lovely and delicate as one of the blossoms. "Nate has told me so much about you over the years," she said, trailing a hand over a pink bud. "I was an only child, like Nate. I would have loved to have a family like yours to be a part of. Nate has told me that Eugenie didn't feel quite the same way when they were married. I hope that...maybe, in time, I can become like your family, too."

Christianne swallowed hard, and angled her face away. "Nate will hardly need us anymore. You'll be busy making your own family."

The thought filled her with desolation. After the passion she and Nate had shared, he would never feel comfortable bringing Olivia to Strawberry Grove. Besides, it would be torture for Christianne to see the intimate touches, the private glances between husband and wife—and in time, Nate Rowland's babe in another woman's arms.

"I can see you have doubts I'm sincere, but I assure you, Nate and I will welcome the company," Olivia said with a smile. "We won't be newlyweds in the way I imagined when I was smitten with Nate during my coming out. We are past racing pulses and desperate passions."

Nate is not, Christianne wanted to protest. The feel of his hands was branded on her body, the hunger, as his body arched above hers like storms and lightning and wild, tempestuous seas.

"The practical side of marriage can be sweet, too," Olivia reasoned, and Christianne wondered if she was trying to convince herself. "My boys need a father to show them what a man should be."

"There's no finer man than Nate Rowland." Christianne's voice cracked.

"Also, there are certain things a man isn't equipped for. Nate needs someone who can ease Seraphina's entry into society. It's unfair that a child should have to pay for the mistakes of a parent. No one understands that better than you."

Her empathy rankled. "If one cares to bother with society," she said.

"I didn't mean to offend," Olivia said, lowering her eyes. "I just...just want to spare Seraphina the pain of being excluded."

Christianne thought of the little girl, standing on the Kettering lawn, so alone. "I know you'll be able to do all of that, and be a brilliant political hostess like my sister-in-law Rachel," Christianne said. "You understand Nate's world, the policies he's fighting for, the charities he champions. He'll never have to fear that you'll burst out and say something awkward, and set the whole house of cards tumbling down."

Olivia twisted the betrothal ring on her finger. The Rowland crest was etched in the gold setting. The diamond flashed. "I will make Nate a good wife," she said softly. "I wouldn't have accepted his proposal if I thought otherwise. I promise I'll do my best to make him happy."

Christianne's lips trembled. She swallowed back her tears. "He doesn't *need* someone to make him happy. He needs someone to *challenge* him, to push him beyond his limits. Not—not tiptoe around him and treat him like an invalid because of his leg. Promise me...promise me..." She hated the sob that choked her.

"Oh. Oh, Christianne..." Olivia's eyes welled up with tears.

She knows, Christianne realized with a jolt. Olivia knew that Christianne loved him. Knew that the thought of Nate being trapped into that bland existence broke her heart. Christianne couldn't bear the pity in the other woman's eyes. She turned and fled, Caval galumphing by her side. Nate was made for the kind of deep love and passion the other Knights had found, she wanted to cry. How could Nate settle for less?

~

WHENEVER THE KNIGHTS had come to Harlestone Hall, they had slipped away from the rest of the company and convened in the old part of the castle. Their own "Tintagel." That was where Nate went now. He'd hoped to find Christianne there. She'd loved the place when he'd shown it to her. The ashlar stone walls, the arched arrow slits, the books of legends and chivalric deeds and weapons hanging on the walls.

Instead, he found Adam ranging the room like a tiger and Gavin grim and looking so damned disappointed that it was worse than Adam's rage.

"I need to find Christianne," Nate said, but before he could walk out of the room, Adam swung his massive fist. Nate grabbed the edge of the table to keep his balance, but didn't try to block the blow. Pain exploded in Nate's jaw. It didn't hurt half as much as knowing how he'd broken their trust.

Gavin stepped between the two men. "Breaking Nate's jaw isn't going to help," he told Adam, "though I understand the impulse." He leveled Nate with his steely gray gaze. "You *knew* Christianne was at The Blue Peacock all that time?"

"Yes." Nate rubbed his jaw and met Gavin's gaze steadily. "Beat me to a pulp later if you wish. I wouldn't blame you. But right now I have to find Christianne." The need to see her, try to explain, was wildfire inside him. The pain in her face when his father had made the announcement had been worse than the surgeon's saw biting into his thigh, and he knew damned well this wound would never heal.

"Haven't you done enough damage?" Adam raged.

"Did you know she was poking about for information about someone trying to destroy you? Someone who may well have been so set on doing so that they'd already murdered Eugenie?"

"I didn't know what she was doing until she was already at The Blue Peacock."

"You knew the danger she was in there," Adam accused. "Why, Nate? Why didn't you drag her home or summon us back to do so? Gavin and I would have set the road afire behind us to reach Christianne if we'd known."

It was true. All it would have taken was a word in the ear of Marguerite regarding "Tianne Evelake's" true identity and Christianne would have been on her way back to Strawberry Grove. But while he was trying to plan the best course forward, something had shifted.

He'd felt more whole in those hours with Christianne than he had since the day he'd ridden onto the field at Culloden Moor. More alive than he'd felt since he'd realized his marriage was a tragic mistake. The thought that he'd lost that private time with Christianne forever reminded him of when he'd lost his leg. But this time, something even more vital was being severed.

"Stand aside," Nate said. "This is between Christianne and me."

"You know she's fancied herself in love with you since she was in short skirts," Adam insisted.

"I know."

"How could you take advantage of her that way?" Adam's voice cracked. "I trusted you."

Nate's voice softened, rough and low. "What would you say if I told you I'm in love with her as well?"

"You're...what?" Gavin stared at him. "You're marrying Olivia."

"I'm in love with Christianne. I have been...longer

than I could admit, even to myself. I know I should regret the weeks we spent together. But I'd be lying if I said I did."

"My God, if you could have seen her face!" Adam fumed. "You're breaking my sister's heart. Duty be damned!"

"You might never understand why I have to do this, but Gavin will."

"The hell he will!" Adam snarled. "After what our parents suffered because of this same notion of duty and aristocratic bloodlines. Christianne's blood is every bit as blue as any Rowland's. You don't deserve her!"

"You're right." A vise tightened around Nate's heart. "Out of my way, now. I have to find her."

"Stay the hell away from my sister," Adam warned. "I mean it. There's no excuse for what you've done. You knew she was in love with you and you led her on. You gave her a taste of a life she's longed for, when you knew she could never have it. But she believed in you so much she thought her precious Sir Galahad would find a way to make it happen."

Gavin stepped over to Adam, put an arm around his brother's shoulders. "I think it's best if you stay away from all of us, for everyone's sake." Gavin's words struck Nate like a blow.

"What are you saying?"

"You need to build a bond with your new wife and children," Gavin said. "Being around us will only make that harder—for Olivia, Christianne, and for you."

Adam scowled. "Frankly, I don't give a damn how much you suffer this time after what you did to my sister. I'll see you in Hell for this."

Nate turned away, his voice low in his throat. "I'm already there."

THE EVENING SEEMED ENDLESS, but at last the company withdrew to their separate bedchambers, congratulations on the upcoming nuptials echoing down the hall. Christianne's room was at the farthest end of the corridor. She'd been pleased when the servants had showed her to the room, imagining that Nate had placed her in the relatively secluded place so that he might slip in later, and that they could share the privacy she'd come to love during her time at the salon. She'd missed him since she'd left The Blue Peacock, his absence during the evening hours leaving her lonely in a way she'd never felt before.

Now, she would never share those precious, intimate hours with Nate again.

She said goodnight to her concerned brothers at her door, despite their offer to come in and talk over the evening's events. She couldn't endure another minute of the worried light in Gavin's eyes or Adam roaring like a lion with a thorn in its paw. She'd had the maid help her undress. She'd donned her nightshift, then wrapped herself in a dressing gown of deep green. Only once she'd dismissed the servant did she gently consign her mother's emeralds to their velvet case, knowing for the first time what her mother must have felt, closing away the life she'd hoped for in a tomb of black velvet.

Alone, she finally gave her emotions free rein. She paced the room, alternating between rage and heartache as the sounds of the house grew quieter and quieter, until at long last, night's hush enveloped the manor house.

She remembered the eve of Nate's first wedding, how she'd slipped down the hall in her nightshift. She'd been so innocent then, believing that stating a truth that was so obvious to her would be enough. *This is wrong. Don't marry her...* But it wasn't that simple. It never had been.

She was startled by a sudden sound at the door, the quick rap, rap, the pause, then a third. That knock had made her heart quicken when she'd heard it at the salon. Now, her chest clenched at the sound she feared she'd never hear again.

She crossed to the door and opened it a crack. Nate held a candlestick in one hand, the glow casting the haggard planes of his face in shadow. He looked as if he'd fought a battle in the time since the dinner guests had disbursed. A bruise darkened his chin, the ribbon that had bound his hair into a queue was gone, the caramel-colored waves fell about his angular cheekbones.

He'd shed his frock coat and waistcoat, his black breeches accenting his narrow waist and hips and the length of his muscular thighs. He'd torn off his neckcloth at some point and opened the fastenings of his collar, baring the hollow of his throat.

"Let me in," he whispered.

She had wanted to confront him, yet now, she wasn't sure she could bear what he had to tell her.

"Please," he begged. He curled his fingers around the door so that she'd have to pinch them if she closed it. Part of her wanted to slam the door, hard. But she stepped back and motioned for him to enter. With a glance down the hall, he stepped past her, his arm brushing the front of her nightshift, grazing the tips of her breasts beneath the dressing gown.

She bit her lip, remembering those times he had touched her there, caressing her sensitive flesh. But she wouldn't let the grief and loss overwhelm her. She faced him, tipping her chin up, defiant. But this was Nate, who always saw through her anger to her pain.

"How could you?" she demanded, trying to quell the

tremor in her voice. "How could you invite me here tonight, knowing you were going to announce your engagement to another woman?"

"I didn't know my father had invited you. The betrothal wasn't supposed to be announced yet. My father had no right to do it."

"And yet, you are engaged." She forced the words from a raw throat. "When were you planning to tell me?"

He looked away. "I don't know."

"Exactly when did you ask her?"

"After my father's accident. I thought he might die."

"He looked just fine tonight. In fact, he was gloating while he told the whole company about my time at The Blue Peacock."

"He had no right to do that, either. And he *will* answer for it. But this isn't about my father. It's about *us*."

The way he said the word tore at Christianne's heart.

"It was wrong of me not to tell you about the betrothal right away," he told her, "but I couldn't bear the idea of things changing between us."

She gave a bitter laugh. "Marriage to another woman is sure to do that."

"These past months with you have been the sweetest of my life. I knew they were fleeting, but I just couldn't let you go. The time we spent at The Blue Peacock, truly alone… It kills me to think I won't be able to do so again."

"So you weren't honest. I never thought you were a man to resort to deception."

"Neither did I, until I realized that I'd never be able to touch you or kiss you…"

"How can you do this, Nate? Marry a woman you don't love? You *know* what love can be. You've seen it in

Gavin and Adam and Myles. Is that what you have with Olivia?"

"You know it's not," Nate said, low. "But Olivia and I have practical needs the other can fill."

"*Practical* needs? Like the ones that forced my father to marry a woman he didn't love? I saw the heartache that caused my whole childhood. Don't let your father do to you what my grandfather did to my parents."

Nate raked his hand through his hair. "The decision your father made wasn't so simple. If the Glenlyon estate had fallen into ruin, all of the tenants would have faced disaster. They would have been evicted from their homes, their businesses and farms and livelihoods stripped away. I've seen whole villages emptied, families turned out of their cottages. You've seen children from those families, too. Babes mothers and fathers had to abandon on the steps of foundling hospitals so they won't starve. The estate Olivia's husband left has been decimated by a thieving steward. It's not only Alex's inheritance that hangs in the balance. The Rowland lands do as well. My father won't be at peace until I have a son. After the mess I made of my marriage to Eugenie, and the scandal I brought down on our heads, I owe him that."

"Is that what he told you?" Christianne demanded. "What about what you owe yourself?"

A trapped light came into Nate's eyes. "Even if I wanted to change this now, I can't. The betrothal was announced."

"By *your father*," Christianne railed. "He *meant* to box you in. And he wanted *me* to be there when he did it. I saw the way he looked at me. As if it didn't matter my heart was breaking, or your life was being ruined, as long as he got his way. Olivia may be kinder than Eugenie, but she will never understand you the way I do.

The way you understand me, the shining bits and the sharp edges."

Nate's face twisted in anguish. "You'll never know how sorry I am. When I realized what Father was going to do, I wanted to lunge across the table and stop him. But I couldn't humiliate Olivia by taking him to task before the guests. I couldn't abandon her sons and the people on her estates."

"So you abandon *yourself*? The world is changing. You've been in the salon enough to know that is because people push against the old ways."

Nate raked his hand through his hair. "Some of those ways need to change. But honor still matters. Duty."

Christianne glared at him. "You're so anxious to save the world, Nate. When do you get to save Galahad?"

Nate wheeled away from her, limping to the window. He braced his arm on the wall, and leaned his head into the crook of his elbow. Long seconds passed, silence, seeming to stretch into eternity. At last, he turned back to her, his cheeks damp with tears.

"*You* saved me, Christianne," he said. "Those nights we spent together... You made me whole again. The man I was before Culloden. Before Eugenie." Nate crossed to her, reached out, and took her in his arms. He pulled her tight against him, his voice raw. "You're everything to me." His voice broke, the truth wrung from his heart. "I love you, Christianne."

"But not enough." She pulled away. It felt like tearing her heart in two. She crossed to the door, opened it. "You need to leave now."

Nate walked toward the door. She memorized his face, the way the left side of his mouth always curved up just a whisper. The way his gaze held hers. That bond that had linked them, like a cord between their hearts.

"I'll be gone first thing in the morning," she said. "I can't stay here any longer." She drew a deep breath. "I tried to stop you from marrying the wrong woman once before. But I was younger then. Now I know sometimes you can't save the person you love, no matter how much you want to. Sometimes they have to save themselves."

$\mathcal{N}$ ate stalked into his father's bedchamber without knocking. The old earl sat up in the bed where he'd lain for so many weeks, seeming on the verge of death, but now he looked triumphant.

"Nathaniel. I've been expecting you, but grew weary of waiting. I assume you are here to reprimand me because of my eagerness to share the joy of your engagement. We must hasten our discussion along, for at my age, and frail health, I need to get sleep."

"And that was what this whole dinner was about, wasn't it? To put Christianne Slade beyond the pale by exposing the fact that she spent time at the salon and to force my hand with Olivia?"

"You seemed to find Olivia amicable enough when you asked her to marry you."

Had he? He could scarce remember during those days his father seemed to fight for his life. She'd barely left his father's side for a week. Nate had found her sleeping in a chair beside the bed, holding his father's age-spotted hand. She'd looked so tired, Nate had curled his fingers over her drooping shoulder. "How can I ever thank you for all you've done for us?" he'd asked softly.

She'd sighed and leaned her cheek against Nate's hand. "I think your father has been terribly lonely since your mother died. I've been lonely, too."

His father's eyes had fluttered open at that moment, and the vulnerability in them made Nate's breath snag. "Please, Nate. For all of us. It's time..."

He'd never know if his betrothal to Olivia had given his father the strength to fight his way back to life. But marrying Olivia had seemed like the right thing to do at the time. Until he saw Christianne again.

He'd never forget Christianne's face the moment his father had announced the engagement. The disbelief, then the pain and betrayal was burned into his memory.

"How did you find out about Christianne's time at The Blue Peacock?" Nate demanded. "Even her brothers didn't know her part in finding out who'd been stalking me. Did Salway tell you?"

"It hardly matters." His father waved one hand in dismissal. "I did you a favor announcing the engagement. Christianne Slade is poison now, just like her mother. One more demimondaine of easy virtue."

Nate's jaw clenched. "How dare you! Christianne Slade is the most courageous, loyal woman I have ever known. She's done more to uncover Eugenie's murderer and discover the person trying to destroy me than any magistrate, or Callum MacGregor. I'd think you'd be grateful instead of attacking her this way."

"Of course I am grateful for the chit's efforts on your behalf. Keep your connection to the Slade girl if you choose. A woman like that has a place in a man's life. Stowed away in a little house somewhere, to be visited discreetly."

Nate recoiled at the thought of proud Christianne reduced to such a station in life. But had he already done so when he'd taken her virginity? The memory of the nights he'd spent in her arms surged through him, the wonder of her, so responsive beneath his hands. She'd challenged him, demanded all of the passion he could give her, made him feel more alive than he'd ever been.

"I owed it to Christianne to tell her about the betrothal first. She should never have found out in a crowd of people."

"And give her a chance to work her wiles on you?" His father's lip curled. "I think not. I did what I did for your own good and the good of the Rowland name. It is done. Your engagement to Olivia Nasby has been announced. Before the week is out, all London will know. Are you going to face young Alexander and tell him that you are humiliating his mother before all of society?"

He thought of Olivia's eyes, so hopeful, warm and kind. Alexander, laughing as they worked together on his estate.

"And what about Seraphina?" his father sneered. "Do you think Christianne Slade will gain Eugenie's bastard child entry into society?"

"Sera is coming home. If you ever show that venom in my daughter's presence again, I swear I'll—"

"You'll what, Nathaniel? I am the Earl of Fendale. Everything you are or will ever be comes through me."

"I am nothing like you!"

"So you say. Bring Sera home if you must. As long as Olivia is here as well, the child may live here for all I care. But you will wed Olivia or lose everything that is not entailed. Vast amounts of property and money are not tied to the earldom. They are mine to dispose of as I will."

"Like the lives of your family?"

"Exactly. Now I am weary and we still have a houseful of guests, though I imagine the Slade bastards and Glenlyon will not be among them come morning. I am sure you will explain their absence to your betrothed, who might be wondering what happened tonight. Olivia is a sensitive woman and quite shocked about the Slade girl's wildness, I'm certain. You will calm any nerves she might have—as a good husband should."

That much was true, Nate thought. A husband's purpose was to shield those in his care. Christianne did not want his protection. She'd made that perfectly clear. Sera and Olivia and Alexander did.

$\mathcal{N}$ ate stood at the window of the drawing room. It had been three days since the disastrous announcement of his engagement, the house full of his father's guests. But at last, Harlestone Hall was blessedly empty of all but family at last, or so his father had said before the old man retreated to his bedchamber on Olivia's arm. She'd returned half an hour later and taken her favorite seat near the crackling fire. Her skirts spilled over the eggshell delicate chair as she plied her needle. Only the faint hiss of silk being pulled through the taut fabric in Olivia's tambour broke the silence, grating on his nerves.

"Your father should sleep until morning," Olivia said. "I've never seen him so excited. He reveled in the fact that you've solved the mystery of those awful handbills."

"But not my wife's murder."

"Surely it's only a matter of time. In the meantime, let us turn toward a happier future and begin to plan the wedding."

The wedding. Just the thought of it made Nate's muscles tense with that instinctive resistance he'd felt just the moment before an ill-fated charge. And that was what this would be. He would be forcing himself to move forward, even when every fiber of his being wanted the love he'd walked away from, like so many in the aristocracy forced themselves to do.

Nate's chest tightened at the memory of Christianne's face when last he saw her, the strength and heartbreak, the love he had to walk away from because of the duty that came with wealth and power and station.

I'd trade it all to have Christianne as my wife...

But it wasn't that simple. Was it?

Olivia's soft voice shook him from his musings. "Are you sure you're well, my love? Ever since Lord Glenlyon and the Slades left unexpectedly, you've not seemed yourself."

How can I "seem myself" when I've lost everything that matters? he thought. This breach with Gavin and Adam wouldn't heal, not after he'd broken their sister's heart. But the bleakness of a future without his lifelong friends was not half so painful as the absence of Christianne from his life.

Duty seemed a wasteland now. He'd marched onto the field in battle, killed men in its name. He'd obeyed officers far less capable than he, even when he knew it was a mistake, because they'd ordered him forward. But this...could he condemn Christianne, condemn himself, condemn Olivia to a loveless future? He knew what it felt like to endure a marriage without love. The loneliness and torment of watching even his dearest friends in unions that were forged with love, with passion, with that bond as precious and rare as any Holy Grail.

He knew in that instant that he could never step up to the altar and slip a ring on Olivia's finger without damning them both to unbearable loneliness.

"Olivia, I must—must speak the truth. You are a dear friend. I admire you greatly."

"So you have said."

"I loathe the thought of hurting you, and yet, I can't begin a marriage with a lie. I am not in love with you." The confession wrenched, raw from his throat. "I'm in love with Christianne Slade."

Olivia thrust her needle in the fabric and gasped, a bright drop of blood welling on her finger.

"You hurt yourself," Nate said, drawing a kerchief from his frock coat pocket and offering it to her.

"No, it's—it's a trifling cut." Olivia turned her back to him and set her needlework on the elegant pie crust table beside her. He could see her shoulders tremble. "What are you trying to say?"

"I will be a good friend to you. But if I were to become your husband, I would spend the rest of my life imagining Christianne in your place."

"That is not very flattering."

"If it hurts you this much now, what would it be a year from now? Five years from now? My wife did not love me for much of our marriage. I would not put you through that pain."

Olivia bit her lip, and he saw her throat convulse. He prayed she wouldn't weep. "You know I've always regarded you with tenderness. My sons adore you. The betrothal has already been announced. The look in your eyes that night was painful to see."

"And I regret that more deeply than I can say. It was because I knew this betrothal between us was a mistake. I wasn't ready to make the announcement yet because of Christianne, but my father took that choice away."

"What about my estates?"

"I know that you need help with your estates, and

you shall have it. Alexander is a fine young man. I'll see that he's ready to take the reins when it is his time."

"What if she won't have you? Then might you and I..."

"No."

Tears welled up in her eyes. Nate crossed to Olivia and took her hands. "You are a good woman, Olivia. But I'll not enter into a loveless marriage again."

He could see her gather up the remnants of her pride. "I wouldn't want to be married to you if you love another woman. I deserve better than that."

It was true. And what did Christianne deserve? He'd hurt her terribly. The worst thing was that she hadn't been surprised he was marrying someone else. She was wounded that he hadn't told her first. It had made him feel as if his chest was cracking open.

"I promise, this will be better for all of us in the end," Nate reassured Olivia. "I will just be more of a favored uncle you and Alex can rely on, rather than..."

"A father." Nate's heart ached at the poignant catch in Olivia's voice. "I'm grateful to you for that," she said. "When Seraphina comes of age, I'll help guide her as well, if you and Christianne wish it."

If Christianne *did* manage to forgive him, there was no way to tell how difficult things might become when Seraphina came of age. But Christianne would teach Seraphina things that Olivia never could. She'd teach Sera to be strong, to defy those who would crush her, not to bend to every gust of wind or demand or expectation.

Olivia drew off the ring he'd so recently placed upon her finger. "Your father will be disappointed," she said as she placed it in the center of Nate's palm. "But he will accept it in time, once he sees how happy you are."

Would he? Nate's father had always believed he

knew best for everyone. The reason the Earl of Fendale's marriage had been so successful was that Nate's mother had been malleable in most things. She'd managed her husband with a deft sleight of hand, never outright opposing him. But there would be no way to soften the defiance in Nate's decision.

Nate's jaw clenched, resolute. "My father will have no choice."

~

NATE STEPPED into his father's study. The old man bent over the desk where he'd ruled his estates with the iron fist of a Roman emperor. The bust of Julius Caesar on the pedestal had been carved to resemble his father, an array of armaments displayed, books of military strategy filling shelves in precise order, nothing out of place. There had been a time Nate had been fascinated by this room, as his father regaled him of tales of his ancestors, letting him lift the sword Bernard Rowland had used to cut down the French at Agincourt, the breastplate Reginald Rowland had worn at Tewkesbury, and the helmet Edward Rowland had worn on Bosworth Field.

There was never a time he hadn't felt the weight of his family history on his shoulders. It was too heavy a legacy for one small boy to carry, his mother had chided gently once when he'd failed to meet his father's expectations in some small way.

Today would not be a small deviation from what was demanded by Nate's blood and his station. But it would be the truest step he'd ever taken.

"Sir, may I speak to you?"

His father looked up from the ledger he was examining. "I've been wishing to speak to you as well, regarding the Beresford estate. If we combine—"

"We'll not be combining the estates."

"Nate, I know that you're meticulous about your honor, but you'll be managing the estate until Alexander reaches his majority, and Harlestone should reap some benefits. As Alexander's stepfather and Olivia's husband—"

"But I will be neither of those. That is what I've come to tell you."

"What?" His father's hawk-like countenance hardened as Nate withdrew the betrothal ring from his waistcoat pocket.

"Olivia and I have broken off our engagement. We'll remain friends and I will help guide Alexander, and be happy to offer guidance in sound management in the Beresford estate, but I can't in good conscience marry Olivia when I'm in love with someone else." Nate laid the ring on the desk. It gleamed in the light from the mullioned window. "I intend to ask Christianne Slade to become my wife."

The earl's lip curled. "Have you been imbibing gin? Or perhaps you are a candidate for Bedlam?"

"No. I've been honest with myself at last. Olivia deserves better and so do I, and remarkably, both of us agree on that point."

"So you choose that little trollop, a bastard who has proven she is no better than her whore of a mother."

"Speak of Christianne—or Lydia Slade— that way one more time and I'll never darken your door again."

"You are a Rowland!" His father slammed his fist down on the desk. "I'll not have it, I tell you!"

"Christianne's forebears might well have charged, shoulder to shoulder, with the Rowlands in any number of battles. Her mother is of noble blood, as is her father."

"She's a bastard! You would drag the Rowland name through the muck!"

324

"I'm already suspected of murder."

"Murder is the least of it! You've already given our name to Eugenie's bastard."

"Sera is the granddaughter who brought my mother more joy than either one of us could. You know that it's true. Eugenie was close to Mother as well. We might have been ill-suited in our marriage, but Mother cared for her."

"Your mother always grieved that she had no daughter. She'd have welcomed anyone in a skirt. She had far too generous a heart. Had I not been there to take her in hand, she would have gone running off to Strawberry Grove with you! It's mere good fortune that Eugenie didn't bring forth a son to steal the earldom. God knows who the brat's father was. It might have been the butcher's lad for all we know."

"Eugenie is dead and an innocent babe was never born."

"Don't tell me you were eager to embrace this new child, Nathaniel. I saw your face when she announced that it was coming."

"And I saw *your* face when you announced to the assemblage that I was to wed Olivia. *After* you managed to tear Christianne's reputation to rags under the guise of thanking her for solving the mystery of those handbills."

"I told nothing but the truth."

"I always thought you valued courage above all things. I'd match Christianne's courage against any of these warriors you are so proud of."

The earl sucked in a breath. "Nathaniel, love has nothing to do with marriage among the Quality."

"You and my mother were in love."

"We were fortunate. Our stations were the same. Our fortunes compatible. It was an excellent match for both families. But it wasn't without compromises. A man has earthier needs a gently bred woman should not be burdened with. I spared her from those by taking a mistress."

"Did Mother know?" He could only imagine how it would pain his gentle mother.

"Of course she did." His father shuffled papers on his desk, and Nate saw his jaw work. "Your mother was a reasonable creature. That was why she won my regard. No histrionics, no weeping or tempers or sullen silences. She understood how things were done—*properly*—and was as amiable as Olivia, except...once."

"Once?"

"It is none of your concern," his father said. "But this is. If you do not come to your senses and reconcile with Olivia, I will be forced to take drastic measures."

"I *have* finally come to my senses. As for the rest, you must do as you will."

"I'll strip you of everything within my power. Only part of my estate is entailed. I'll will the rest to Salway."

"I wish him joy of it," Nate sneered.

"I planned to bolster the Rowland holdings with Olivia's estates. I can strip them down as easily."

"I doubt you'd do that. Your pride would never allow you to become a wastrel with all of London watching," Nate told him.

"What about your political career?"

"The risk is mine to take," Nate said in chill accents. "I'd rather be Christianne's husband than prime minister."

The earl shook his fist. "Do this thing, and you're no son of mine."

Nate sketched him a stiff bow. "As you wish."

"You'll regret this!" the earl railed. "I give no quarter."

"Like your friend Butcher Cumberland after Culloden Moor. He left Scotland a wasteland. But there are some spirits you can't kill. Do as you must. I intend to ask Christianne to be my wife."

If she'll have me, Nate thought. *Please, God, don't let me be too late.*

~

THERE WAS a time Nate would have walked through the door to Strawberry Grove without ringing the bell, as sure of his welcome as Gavin and Adam would always be. Today he hoped they wouldn't slam the door in his face.

Even if Christianne hadn't shared the disaster at Harlestone Hall with her mother and sisters, Adam wouldn't guard his tongue. The Slade family had always stood as one. They'd had to when people jeered at them because of their illegitimate birth. This public humiliation was far worse than any of them had suffered before. And Nate had been at the center of it.

He rang the bell and waited, surprised when Clary answered the door, her pointed little face framed by a tidy white cap.

"What are you doing here?" Nate exclaimed.

"Miss Christianne sent to The Blue Peacock for Robin and me. Wanted to get us away from the salon."

"I'm glad."

"No offense, my lord, but no one here wants to see you. There was a mighty uproar with Mister Adam, and Lord Glenlyon brought Miss Christianne home."

"I'm sure they're angry, and I don't blame them, but I have to see Miss Christianne."

"Clary, who is at the door?" Lydia Slade's contralto called from inside.

"It's Lord Harlestone, Madam, here to see Miss Christianne."

Nate heard a rustling of skirts and a murmur of

hostile voices as Lydia and her three younger daughters appeared, tying bonnet strings under their chins.

"Nate." The hurt and betrayal that shone in Lydia's eyes when she saw him was like a blow to his gut. "As you can see, we are just leaving."

He tried to peer past them. "I have to see Christianne."

"I'm afraid that is impossible," Lydia said. "I hear you are to be married."

His cheeks burned. "I've come to make things right."

Eliza's eyes filled with tears. "You can't make this right," she said. "You humiliated her in front of that whole crowd. The whole village is buzzing with gossip. How could you do it, Nate? She risked everything to save you."

"She did save me. I have to tell her face to face."

"A clean break is best considering the circumstances," Lydia cut in.

"Eliza, who's there?" Christianne's voice drifted down the staircase.

"It's me, Nate!" he shouted. "I have to tell you something, and ask you—Please." An ominous silence fell for long moments, then he heard carefully measured footsteps. His throat tightened as she came into view.

Her face had a new, somber cast, her wildness tempered by the harsh lessons these past weeks had taught her. He wanted to gather her in his arms, kiss away her pain. But he'd lost that right—unless Christianne chose to give it to him again.

Vulnerability darted into her eyes for a heartbeat before she shuttered it away. "I'm afraid you've come a long way for nothing," she said.

"I'll stay away after this if that is what you want, but first, I have to talk to you." His throat convulsed, and he fought to steady his voice. "I'm begging you, Christianne."

"All right. Come in." Christianne looked at her mother and sisters. "Go ahead with your walk."

"I don't know..." Her mother hung back. "I could—"

"Mama, Nate and I spent six weeks in rooms alone together. Go."

Nate saw mother and daughter exchange looks, then Lydia gave her bonnet strings one last tug. "Let's go, girls," she said. "We'll be walking around the pond. If you need me, send Robin."

"I will." The new understanding between Christianne and her mother hurt Nate's heart.

Christianne motioned Nate into the house and led him to her father's study. Above the now-deserted desk hung a portrait of Lydia as a young woman, love in her eyes, her future ahead of her. It was easy to see why the old earl couldn't let her go, Nate thought. Is that why Christianne had brought him here? This hard reminder of the price certain choices demanded?

Christianne shut the door. She stood facing it a long moment, her blue-print gown setting off her black curls, her back regal and straight. A queen about to face her executioner. She turned to meet his gaze. "How is Olivia?" she asked.

"Almost as relieved as I am. We called off the wedding."

She went still. "Did you?"

"Marrying for duty's sake is wrong when you're in love with someone else."

"That didn't seem an impediment before."

"I've resisted facing the truth for so long. I numbed myself, closing myself off. I've let the expectations of society and my father rule my life, telling myself I had no other choice. You showed me that I do."

He took Christianne's hands in his, and peered down into her eyes. He could feel her trembling. "I love *you*. I always have, and I was just too tangled up in what

I thought was my duty to know it. Everything true and fine and worthy in my life, I can trace back to you. You've made me want to *be* the man I saw in your eyes," he said fervently. "If you give me the chance, I'll spend the rest of my life trying to deserve you."

She stared up at him, so beautiful. He could tell she was not quite daring to hope.

"Be my wife, Mistress Mayhem," Nate's voice caught. "Grant me the greatest honor I ever hope to achieve."

Joy and fear warred in her face. "I might damage your political career. Society will never accept me."

"The eccentric Lord and Lady Harlestone will be far too happy together to care about that. Think of all the important work we can do with the Foundling Hospital and the Marine Charity. There are countless other causes you and I can champion together. We'll have each other, and our family. And the *right* kind of society as well. Olivia already admires you, and others will, too, once they come to know you. But even if we had only our family, we'd have riches I'd never dreamed of."

"But what about poor Sera? She'll never be accepted into society if you marry me, just as I won't be."

Nate plunged ahead. "Olivia has already volunteered to sponsor her when the time comes if the *ton* still shuts us out, and I've agreed to consult on her estate matters and play the role of kindly uncle to Alexander."

He grasped her hands, his voice ragged with emotion. "Marry me, Christianne! You've made me angry, you've made me fight, you've shown no mercy, and I ask none. I only promise that if you become my wife, I will love you to the depths my heart can reach."

Her dark eyes glistened with tears. "Yes, Nate. I'll marry you. Whatever happens in the world beyond, we'll build our own Avalon."

～

NATE LAY ON THE SETTEE, cradling Christianne in his arms, his lips burned from kissing her, his body aching with the need for so much more.

"I want you so much it's practically killing me," he groaned. "I almost wish we were in your room at The Blue Peacock, just for tonight, so that I could show you how beautiful you are to me, how much I need you. Your body, yes, but more than that. Your wit, your fire, your tenderness." He looked down at her, marveling.

When had his reckless hellion of a Mistress Mayhem grown into this woman who'd awakened his heart, defied society's chains, and claimed her own worth? Or had she always done so? Defying the governesses trying to make her into a lady so that she could follow the lads. Shunning the protected life at Strawberry Grove and venturing out into the world on her own—a dangerous world, perhaps, but a risk she'd taken not only for him, but for herself.

"I'll never regret my time at The Blue Peacock," Christianne mused as she traced light circles on his chest. "Not only because of my time with you. But because of what I learned about myself. I needed to see what I was made of. You and Gavin and Adam got to test yourselves in battle. I wish you hadn't suffered so much because of that, and yet, I don't know if you'd have become the man you are now without that wound. The war, and what came after, made you really *see* Robin and boys like him. It showed you what it felt like to be overwhelmed by forces you had no control over, and what it meant to fight your way back, one painful step at a time."

"Oh, Christianne..."

She touched Nate's face. "I loved a boy when I was a little girl, a warm, funny, mischievous boy. I thought I loved a dashing young cavalry officer who made me dream of passion I didn't yet understand. But I never loved either of those Nates half as much as I love the knight in my arms right now, with all of the scars, all of the mistakes and all of the heartache that made you into the man who defied the world to love me." Her voice caught. "I still hope you will not pay too great a price for it."

Nate's eyes burned, his throat thick with emotion. "Whatever the world chooses to think or do—there is no life for me without you. You always understood me better than anyone, from the time you'd look up at me with those dark eyes. I knew I was no perfect knight. The harder I tried to be one, the more I knew I could never live up to what was expected of me. I could never be the hero you thought me to be." He looked away, regret twisting his features. "I know I disappointed you."

"Only because of Seraphina," Christianne said. "You were betraying her, but you were also betraying yourself. I know you. In the end, you'd never forgive yourself for rejecting an innocent child."

"It was no small thing to withhold love from her because of my own foolish pride," Nate grimaced in self-disgust. "But you showed me that I had to do better. I hated the humiliation of knowing my wife had cuckolded me because I repulsed her with my maimed leg, but my mother adored Eugenie and Sera. It felt cruel to tell her the truth and dishonest not to. But actually, I was being dishonest with myself. I was simply afraid of the truth, for myself and my mother, and certainly for Seraphina."

"From all my mother has said, and from all you've shared about your mother, I believe she would have loved Seraphina the same. You don't stop loving a child because you discover something like this. Not if you truly love them."

"My father claims that the truth broke my mother's heart."

Christianne tapped her fingers against her lips, considering. "I don't believe that," she said after a moment. "Yes, it had to cause her pain, to see you hurt thus, and yet, I think your father's harshness had to hurt far worse. I know someone you could ask."

"Who?"

"My mother. She was friends with your mother before my mother ran off with Father."

"I didn't know that."

"When you started visiting Strawberry Grove, they passed notes occasionally. Just those bits mothers always include when their children go off somewhere without them. *"Please don't feed Nathaniel nuts. They make him bilious."*

She'd wanted to make him smile. The corner of his mouth tipped up. "They do not," he said with feigned outrage.

"I think it was your mother's way of extending a hand to mine without your father knowing. My mother accepted and was grateful. In time, they wrote about other things. Augusta confided how much she'd wanted another child," Christianne continued. "When Seraphina was born, she was so happy. She saw Seraphina as a gift."

"That's what she told me when she first laid Sera in my arms," Nate said. *"You've been given such a gift, Nathaniel. I miss her so."*

"Maybe my mother can show you those letters one day," Christianne said.

"I'd like that," he said, running his finger over Christianne's cheek. He felt suddenly younger, hopeful that his mistake hadn't destroyed his mother after all.

Nate gathered Christianne in his arms, his mouth seeking hers. "Does your jaw hurt?" Christianne asked, touching the purple mark on his face. "I assume one of my brothers is responsible for that bruise."

"Adam has a wicked right hook. I told him he could finish the job after I found you."

"He'll have to control his temper. I intend to kiss you a great deal to make up for this time apart and I don't want you wincing when I do it." She fitted her body to his, as if every curve and line had been made to mesh with his. His tongue gently probed the crease of her lips, and she opened to him, and he explored her mouth, feeling a tenderness that awed him.

"You're a gift, Christianne Slade," he murmured, trailing his lips to her throat. "My beautiful, head-strong, loving Mistress Mayhem."

CHAPTER 33

*I*t was well past dark, the Slade household in an uproar of joy and excitement at the news Nate and Christianne had shared. Overwhelmed with happiness, Nate reveled in the fact that this would truly be his family now. His children would call Lydia Slade Grandmother. Eliza, Maria and Laura would be aunts, and he would do everything in his power to see that they found someone to love them as he loved Christianne, with a devotion that they deserved. Adam and Gavin would forgive him in time, once he showed them how much Christianne would be treasured as his wife.

Now, Nate stood outside the door of Lydia Slade's morning room, the exquisite chamber her lover had made especially for her. He tapped at the door and heard the melodic voice that had enchanted an earl.

"Enter," she called.

Nate did so. He'd come to this sanctum as a boy, to be scolded for some transgression he and Adam had committed. Later, he'd come here as a man who was trying to win pardon for the sons Lydia adored. He'd sat in the green satin chairs to report on his progress, and she'd always made him feel as if he were as loved as any of her wild brood. Now, she looked up from the elegant secretary in the corner where she was supposed to answer letters, accept or decline invitations, and attend to all of the daily correspondence of a noble lady. But there had been no invitations for Lydia, the notorious mistress of the Earl of Glenlyon, and few letters. Nate was suddenly struck by how lonely she must have been.

"You said you wished to see me alone?" he asked. Lydia looked up, the fine lines about her eyes doing nothing to hide their luster. Threads of gray softened the fire of her hair. The aspen-leaf gold of her gown made her seem like the embodiment of autumn, a woman nearing that harvest season of her life when her children were bursting with spring.

Despite the difference in coloring, there was much about her that reminded him of her eldest daughter, a defiance, pride, intelligence and forthrightness, as well as a loathing of injustice.

He wondered if the hot-blooded earl who loved Lydia had ever thought about what their union would cost her. She rose and approached him.

"I hope you have no doubts about how much I love your daughter," Nate said earnestly. "I'm only sorry it took me so long to act on it."

"I'm grateful you had the courage to honor that bond before it was too late." She cupped his cheek in a motherly hand. "I wish you all of the joy you both deserve. Your life will never be boring with Christianne as your wife, but even the challenges will be filled with more love than most people ever experience."

"We were destined to be together from the beginning."

"It was that way between the earl and me. I don't regret the choices I made, but I wish he had dared...well.

It's long past now. Your future is just beginning and I greatly admire you for risking all to have Christianne your partner in it."

"I promise I'll do everything in my power to see that she is happy." He suddenly sobered as he thought of Eugenie and her murderer who'd somehow escaped. "I'll keep Christianne safe."

Lydia's eyes twinkled. "I hope you have better luck at that than I did." She crossed to her desk. "Christianne mentioned that she told you of the letters your mother wrote to me."

"Yes. I was surprised to learn that you and Mother were friends. I never knew."

"No one did. If your father had discovered our friendship, you would no longer have been able to come here. It took a great deal of courage for your mother to strike up this correspondence, knowing how furious your father would have been if he found out. I think she needed someone to talk openly with, things he had forbidden her to speak of. I was honored that she trusted me."

"I'm glad she had you to confide in."

Lydia took up a bundle of letters, tied with a bit of ribbon. "I saved Augusta's letters. They were precious to me. Her life was what mine might have been, if I'd left my lord when he wed another. But there are things that are painful even in the most propitious match. Are you certain you wish to know them?"

Lydia's gaze searched his face, and he glimpsed a sadness there. "Yes, ma'am."

She handed him the letters. He sat down in a chair near the window, took out the first letter, written on his mother's special stationery, and began to read the familiar handwriting.

Am I a poor mother, Lydia? It breaks my heart to see

Nathaniel in pain, but I love this little girl to distraction. Eugenie is not the wife I would have chosen for my son, and yet, I'd not surrender Seraphina for anything. My husband does not feel the same, though. When he discovered the truth about Sera's birth, he went wild with fury. Sera is such a sweet child. I keep hoping he will see that and love her as I do. I suppose I have grown so attached to her because I had a little girl once. My firstborn. She died when Nate was but three years old.

Nate stared at the words his mother had written. "I had a sister?" He looked up at Lydia, stunned. "What was her name?"

"Adaline."

Nate gaped at her. "That is impossible. I..." He stopped, swallowed hard. "When I was a boy, I would talk about—about a little girl named Adaline. I insisted she lived in the nursery with me. My father got furious whenever I mentioned her. He told me it was my imagination. He mocked me. My parents never spoke of the real Adaline. Not once."

"Your father forbade it, and your mother always did what he commanded."

"I must have...have remembered her in spite of him. There were nights my mother would slip into the nursery at Harlestone, and put me to bed. A second bed stood beside mine, and I always tucked a toy elephant in it. When I told her the elephant was Adaline's, she'd help me wrap the covers around it so tenderly. Now I know why."

What had his mother felt, having the little daughter she'd lost obliterated from all memory as if she'd never existed at all? What had it been like for her to hide that huge hole in her motherly heart behind smiles and amiability, not to mark birthdays even in her memory? How many times must she have looked at other girls who would have been Adaline's age had she lived?

Then Seraphina came into her life. A second chance.

"How did Adaline die?"

"Your mother never said."

Nate's jaw set, hard. "I intend to find out."

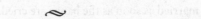

CHRISTIANNE LOOKED up from her throng of sisters as he entered the room, expecting to see the guilt Nate had felt over his mother's decline eased by what he'd learned from her letters. Instead, he looked so stricken, Christianne hurried over to him and took his hand.

"Nate, what is it?"

"I wish I could stay here longer, but there is something I must discuss with my father." His voice was so strange it frightened her.

"Please, tell me whatever is wrong. Your skin is ice cold."

"You remember I told you about the imaginary friend I had as a boy?"

She stared at him, bewildered. "Yes. Adaline."

"She wasn't imaginary. She was real."

Christianne could feel the anger welling up inside him. "Real?" she echoed. "I don't understand."

His face contorted with pain. "Adaline was my sister."

AS SOON AS Nate arrived back at Harlestone Hall the next day, he sought out his father. The old earl was in his dressing room, donning buckskin breeches for his afternoon ride.

"Sir, I need to speak to you alone," he said.

"Can it wait until Trevor arranges my neckcloth?"

"I'm afraid not."

His father nodded toward the door, and the valet bowed and left the room. The earl tugged at his left cuff. "Please tell me that Slade chit had the sense to refuse you."

"Christianne has accepted my proposal. We will be married as soon as the banns are cried."

"Why would she not? To become a Rowland is the highest honor anyone can name."

"Is it? I'm not certain of that anymore," Nate said, every muscle in his body taut. "It is time you told me the truth."

"I have always done so."

"You have not. Lydia Slade showed me letters my mother wrote to her over the years. I stayed up all night reading them. Despite all that had happened between Eugenie and me, Mother never stopped loving her, or loving Sera."

"So much that she started defying me!" Rage contorted his father's face. "Never, in all our marriage had she done so! She changed toward me. I saw it in her eyes. What kind of an unnatural wife chooses a harlot like Eugenie and her bastard over her husband of thirty-five years?"

"You can't make someone stop loving a child on command."

The earl tore free the half-tied neckcloth and flung it away. "Your mother showed no loyalty! She shared things with Eugenie and that Slade woman that should have been sealed within the marriage bond!"

"Like about Adaline?"

His father went ice-white.

"Yes," Nate confirmed. "I know about Adaline. *My* sister. *Your* daughter! I remember it all now. You banished the nurse I adored and hired a new one who didn't know Adaline existed. You struck me when I spoke Adaline's name and convinced me she was a figment of my imagination, that there was something wrong with me."

The earl knotted his fists, the veins standing out on his brow. "It does no good to grieve the way your mother did! Better to cut off the dead limb and cauterize the wound."

"Like my leg?" Nate demanded.

"Exactly!"

"Except I can still feel my missing limb, do you know that?" Nate touched his thigh. "It still aches and burns and itches even though it's not there. Mother's daughter was more a part of her than a leg. You tried to rip Adaline from her heart, but Sera made her whole again. Then you tried to rob Mother again with Sera."

"That child is not of our blood! She's no Rowland! It was all a lie."

"Like the ones you told me about my sister? Tell me the truth."

"No."

"*Tell me!*" Nate demanded. "How did Adaline die? You're the only one who can."

The stony face seemed to crack. His father's eyes glistened. He looked away, seeming lost in a different world. "Bracing air strengthens the lungs," he insisted. "Everyone knows that. I threw open the nursery windows and ordered the nurse to take her for drives in the open carriage."

Something stirred in Nate's memory. He'd always been tucking more blankets around his imaginary Adaline...trying to get her warm. He remembered how high the edge of her bed had seemed when he tried to climb in beside her after Nurse was asleep.

I'm so cold, Nate. He could hear her small, shivery voice, but he couldn't see his Adaline...not her face...

"What was she like?" he asked.

His father stalked across the room to the chair

where he always read, and touched the book that was on the table. *Paradise Lost.* "She was beautiful," he said thickly, "like your mother." He wheeled on Nate, fists clenching. "You say losing Adaline ripped out your mother's heart? What about *mine*? You think I didn't grieve? We had to find a way to go on. Then, Sera came. Those curls were just like our Adaline's. Your mother even brought out all of the little clothes we'd dressed Adaline in. I could almost make myself believe it was Adaline reborn. I felt as if maybe it was a sign my child had forgiven me." His lips twisted with anguish. "But then I found out the truth. Fate was mocking me. Every time I saw Seraphina, I knew it. That bastard child lived, but my daughter, my Adaline was gone."

How had he not seen it? Nate thought numbly. The slow crumbling of defenses his father had built since the death of Adaline. How that had changed him.

The earl ground his fingers against his temple. "But your mother wouldn't hear of us distancing ourselves from the girl by then. She actually threatened to leave me if I sent the child away. It was the one time she truly defied me."

"Then I sent Sera away for you," Nate said. "After Eugenie died." Bile rose in his throat. Had he been any better than his father? Distancing himself from pain? He hadn't wanted to look in Sera's eyes and see how he had failed her. Thank God Christianne hadn't let him keep those walls up and build them higher with excuses.

"Seraphina is coming home where she belongs. As soon as the banns are cried, I am bringing Christianne here as my wife. God willing, we'll fill that nursery with brothers and sisters for Sera to make memories with. You have estates scattered all over England, but Harlestone Hall became mine the moment I was given the title Viscount Harlestone. You have two choices. You can go to one of your other estates and be alone, and nurse your bitterness, or you can be part of our lives." Nate's lip curled. "*If* you have the courage. But if you ever do anything to harm Christianne or Seraphina again, you will answer to me as a man—not as my father."

CHAPTER 34

Strawberry Grove was in an uproar, the Jewel Box awash with every kind of new gown imaginable as an army of seamstresses rushed to finish Christianne's trousseau. She'd been happy to hand the task over to her mother and artistic Maria while Laura and Eliza chimed in with their opinions. "Make sure there are some things that I can move in," had been Christianne's only caveat.

"Even *you* can tolerate a little constriction on your wedding day!" Maria had teased. *Her wedding day.* Every time Christianne thought of it, a shiver of delight went through her. In three days she was going to be Lord Nathaniel Rowland's bride, to be married before all the world in a ceremony at Harlestone Hall's chapel.

For the ceremony, Christianne had chosen embroidery with an Arthurian theme. The satin was the color of mist. Gold and silver threads turned the mystical forest stitched across the folds into a shimmering Avalon. A knight made his way up a long journey on the path, coming home after a difficult quest at last. The peacock blue overskirt would be spangled with stars. The color choices made Christianne smile. They were the same rich tones that draped the walls and windows of the salon where she and Nate had no longer been able to hold back the passion between them.

"This gown is going to be so beautiful." Laura ran her hand over the exquisite design. "But I don't know how they'll ever finish the embroidery in time."

"Gavin has hired an army of seamstresses," Christianne said, warmed by her brother's generosity. The gown was a gift from her brother, who was overjoyed that his sister and best friend were seizing the happiness society had tried to deny them.

Eliza touched the unicorn's embroidered hoof. "It's just like something I would put on one of my heroines," she enthused. "In fact, I believe my countess shall wear one exactly like it in the final scene."

Emotion knotted in Christianne's throat. "Make sure the shoulders are loose enough that I can move. I intend to do a great deal of hugging that day."

"Just wait until *after* the ceremony to hug that hulk of a dog of Nate's you love so much," Maria chided.

"Hug anyone you want, any time you want," Laura said, kissing Christianne on the cheek. "Nate will think you're the most beautiful creature in the world. He's always loved the wildness in you."

It was true. But he'd seen the tenderness there as well, the vulnerability she'd shown so rarely, only to the family who'd grown up together in Strawberry Grove.

Clary came bobbing up, a note in her hand. "Pardon me, but there is a message for Miss Christianne from Lord Harlestone."

"Another love letter," Laura trilled, snatching the missive and pretending to read it. "My darling, your eyes are like pools—"

"You'll have to treat Christianne with more respect when she's a viscountess and mistress of Harlestone Hall!" Maria chided.

Christianne grasped the letter and laughed. "I will be most put out if you do! I want everything to remain just as it is between us. Forever!"

"What does your lover want this time?" Eliza asked. "I swear, he's using more paper than I have on the last three chapters of my novel."

It was true that Nate had written her often as he prepared for her arrival at his estate. Wedding preparations and plans to bring Sera home had consumed his time, along with aiding on the Beresford estate. They'd had little time together, but soon they'd have the rest of their lives.

"Nate is on his way to retrieve Seraphina," Christianne said, joy bubbling up inside her. "He asks me to ride to Harlestone Hall to make certain everything in the nursery is perfect. He wants me to be there when he and Sera arrive."

"I thought you'd agreed that Sera and Nate would have these few days alone," Eliza said.

"I don't blame Nate for changing his mind." Laura smoothed the ribbons trimming a nightgown sheer as mist. "Most men find it daunting to handle a child alone, and Sera and Nate have been estranged. Would you like me to go with you?" Christianne grinned at her youngest sister. Laura could never resist children, and this newest niece was more thrilling to her than any trousseau could ever be.

"You can't come with me this time, but you'll meet Sera soon. As for Sera's room, Nate didn't want anyone to see it before Sera did, not even me. He must have just gotten a case of the jitters."

She loved that he wanted the nursery to be perfect. Christianne smiled, certain that it *would* be as soon as Seraphina and Nate were in it.

"You'll need to take a maid," Maria warned. "As a viscountess, you'll have to be quite proper."

"I don't have the title yet, and, I have no plan to relinquish my freedom even when I do." Christianne tossed her curls over her shoulder. "I have been neglecting Avalon's exercise shamefully. I'm not going to plod along with a chaperone when she needs a good run."

"Mama wouldn't like you going alone," Laura warned.

Christianne grimaced, remembering her mother's warning. *Joyous as this time is, you must stay on your guard. Eugenie's murderer still hasn't been found.*

"Well, Mama is off taking calf's-foot jelly to the blacksmith's wife, so she's not here to forbid me. Nate wishes me to come and welcome Sera home. Just the three of us." The thought that they'd soon be a family warmed Christianne to her core. "I'll bring Felicity. She is the best chaperone I know." Christianne smiled as she thought of the dagger Adam had given her. She'd slip it into the pocket tied under her petticoats so it wouldn't interfere with her ride.

"It may be getting dark when you come home," Laura fretted.

Christianne hugged her sister. "It will be fine. I'm sure when it's time to leave, Nate will see me home."

Wasn't that the real reason Christianne didn't want anyone to come with her? Her body tingled with delicious anticipation as she imagined riding with Nate, stopping at her secret place beneath the oak tree, where they could sample the delights their wedding night held in store.

HARLESTONE HALL GLEAMED from floor to ceiling, the maids teetering on ladders, shining every prism in chandeliers, footmen rolling up carpets to be taken out and beaten free of dust. It was as if all the tragedy of the past years was being banished, leaving everything bright and new.

Christianne smiled as Mrs. Davies bustled in to meet her, the aging housekeeper's black dress covered in an apron, her hair bundled under a mobcap. She looked as bewildered as if Christianne had appeared out of thin air.

"I beg your pardon, Mistress, for not greeting you with proper ceremony. His lordship didn't warn us you were coming to Harlestone today or I'd at least have put on a fresh apron and cap. He's been in such a dither, getting ready for the little mistress to come home that your visit must have slipped his mind."

Christianne's heart swelled with tenderness, knowing how nervous Nate was and how much he wanted Sera's homecoming to be perfect. "I do hope I'm not intruding!" she told Mrs. Davies.

"We *are* in a bit of a whirlwind here, with Miss Seraphina set to arrive and deliveries being made for the wedding. But Lord Harlestone has made it clear that you are to be mistress here, and we are to treat you as such."

Did Christianne imagine the slight disapproval in the housekeeper's tone? Christianne could imagine the discussion Nate had had with the servants. As a rule, members of an aristocratic family's staff were more caught up in the dignity of the household they served than the nobles themselves. Their reaction to an illegitimate viscountess might be masked behind bland faces, but Christianne could imagine what they were thinking.

Let them whisper among themselves, she thought. In time, the prideful among them would learn she wasn't one to be intimidated. But better to begin with honey than vinegar.

"I have always loved this house," Christianne said. "You've tended it many years, haven't you, Mrs. Davies?"

"Since Lady Augusta was a new bride, God rest her soul. I have tried to keep Harlestone Hall to her standards even now that she's gone, but that was hardly possible with Lord Nathaniel's first wife so often gone. Those few weeks the Dowager Countess of Beresford was here, things improved. After sixteen months with three bachelors tracking in dirt and scattering tobacco ash everywhere, it was lovely to have a woman about who understood how to do things properly. I'd hoped to get a great deal done since none of the gentlemen are here today."

"Lord Fendale and Master Salway are not at home?"

"Lord Harlestone went to fetch the little miss and Lord Fendale is at his solicitors making some changes in his will. But Mr. Salway should be back soon. He's ridden over to Beresford's for tea. He's been most solicitous to the poor lady since she and Lord Harlestone parted ways."

Christianne chose to ignore the housekeeper's subtle jab, wondering if Salway was interested in Olivia because of the Beresford estates, or because she'd briefly been Nate's betrothed. She was shaken from her musings by Mrs. Davies' pointed stare. The housekeeper was obviously waiting for a reply. "I am sure Master Salway is welcome company for the Dowager Countess," Christianne said with a forced smile.

"I've never met any man more eager to please than Master Salway." Mrs. Davies pressed a hand to her ample bosom. "After the tragedy with Lady Harlestone, Master Salway went out of his way to comfort his uncle. It touched my heart to see how solicitous Salway was. No one is beneath his notice. When he discovered that my grandson, Walter, adored botany, Master

Salway brought him cuttings of rare flowers from clear across the ocean."

The back of Christianne's neck prickled with sudden suspicion. "Rare flowers?"

"Frangipani, he called them. Outlandish name!"

"That was very thoughtful of Salway. Does Walter still have these flowers? I'd love to know what they smell like."

"They smell just like heaven. Master Salway let me sniff perfume he had made from it on his last trip to the islands. He'd had it distilled for some lucky lady. He told me he keeps a bottle himself just to remind him of the islands at night."

Christianne's fingers curled tight. There had to be some connection between that perfume and the scent on the green feather. Salway had pursued Christianne because Nate wanted her. Now he was paying Olivia court. Wasn't it likely Salway had been Jessamyn's lover after Nate had bedded her?

Mrs. Davies' voice broke through Christianne's racing thoughts. "I'll tell Master Salway that you wish to smell his perfume when he arrives home," the housekeeper said. "Perhaps he might spare a little as a wedding present."

"Oh, no!" Christianne burst out. "That's not necessary." One slip of Mrs. Davies' tongue and Salway could destroy the evidence. If he truly was the masked man who had come to The Blue Peacock, the likelihood that he would also be Eugenie's murderer had to be high as well. He'd been in the garden the night she was killed. All the pieces of the puzzle fit. Christianne had to get into his room before he came home. She scrambled to make a plan.

"As you can see from the note, Lord Harlestone wanted me to look over the nursery before Miss Seraphina returns," Christianne said. "Since no one else is around, I will familiarize myself with the rest of the house as well."

Mrs. Davies' brow puckered in irritation. "I suppose I could stop what I'm doing and give you a tour."

"That isn't necessary. I can see you are very busy, and I've already taken too much of your time. I've been here on several occasions in the past and can find my own way around the house. Just give me your keys."

For a moment, she feared Mrs. Davies would refuse. Christianne risked giving her a teasing smile. "I promise I won't steal the silver."

Mrs. Davies' eyes widened, but after a moment, her mouth set in a prim line. "I would hardly imagine such a thing."

"Then it's settled." Christianne held out her hand. Reluctantly, the housekeeper unfastened the ring of keys at her waist and handed them over.

"If you need anything—" Mrs. Davies began.

Christianne smiled. "I'll know where to find you."

She tried to seem casual as she mounted the stairs to the second floor with Mrs. Davies watching. At the top she pretended to examine a pretty landscape. A soft "humph" of disapproval came from the housekeeper as a maid hastened up with some news about a delivery.

The instant the pair vanished, Christianne scooped up her petticoats and dashed toward Salway Rowland's room. The corridor seemed deserted—the bedchambers already put in order for the morning, and not yet being prepared for night.

Thank God she'd memorized the location of rooms before the disastrous engagement supper, and knew right where Salway's was located. She tried the door, found it locked as Mrs. Davies had said. She fumbled through the ring of keys, cursing the time it took to test each one until finally she heard the metallic click she'd hoped for.

Her hand trembled as she opened the door and slipped inside, shutting it behind her.

Would he really be reckless enough to keep the scent that might reveal him in Nate's own home? Yet, perhaps no one had told him about the link between the scent and the handbills.

A heavy bed from the era of James I was positioned in the center of the room, the bedcurtains faded on the side nearest the window. Rustic paintings of exotic scenes from the island where he'd tended the plantation hung on the wall. An ivory-backed brush, an assortment of snuff boxes, stickpins, powder and scent bottles were laid out in precision on his dressing table.

She rushed over, smelling each bottle of scent in turn. She'd almost given up hope when she spied a small box, the top carved with an exotic bird with a long tail feather. Christianne opened the lid. A small bottle was pillowed on black satin. She picked it, pulled the stopper and held it to her nose. Fragrance swirled in the air, so exotic, so familiar that she almost dropped the bottle. She stoppered the lid, and lifted the silk that lined the bottom of the box, but she already guessed what it was. A mask, and affixed to one side was the broken stub of an iridescent green feather.

She was about to slip it into her pocket when she heard a soft metallic click. She wheeled, the floor seeming to drop beneath her feet.

Salway Rowland stood blocking the door, a pistol in his hand.

CHAPTER 35

"Why, oh, why can you never follow simple instructions?" Salway demanded. "The note stated quite clearly that you were to make certain the nursery was ready to welcome Sera home, but you had to go poking about where you didn't belong. You always were too clever for your own good."

"You weren't clever enough." A rush of adrenaline shot through Christianne as she set the evidence she'd gathered on the bed. The weight of the dagger in her pocket bumped against her hip. "I know you've been behind this scheme to ruin Nate from the beginning. You're the masked lover who visited Jessamyn at The Blue Peacock."

She edged her hand through the slit in the side of her gown, trying to gauge how quickly she could pull the blade free of scabbard and cloth. Not fast enough to avoid a pistol ball if Salway fired straight. But if she rattled his nerves, might he fire and miss?

"Jessamyn was eager to fall into my bed after Nate used and discarded her. I had to promise to take her on exotic adventures, even *marry* her to ensure her cooperation. Not that I would ever lower myself. You, on the other hand, flung yourself into danger for Nate's

353

sake without any hope of reward. Yet you emerged from the flames of ruin and came near to being a viscountess. Quite an astonishing ascent. However, like Icarus, you will plunge to the ground."

"You will never get away with whatever you've planned. Mrs. Davies knows I'm here. There is a house full of servants. Someone is bound to see."

"You underestimate the chaos this wedding has caused. And I have arranged to add to it. I locked that hound of Nate's into the pantry where they've stored the cakes and such. I'm sure the entire household staff is in hysterics by now and we shall be able to exit on the north side of the manor without anyone noticing us."

"Are you going to kill me like you killed Eugenie?"

His lip curled in contempt. "That is what you think? That I killed her?"

"You were in the garden that night. You plotted to ruin Nate."

"I am not a man given to murder lightly," he bristled. "I *had* feared that I was going to have to dispose of Olivia, had her marriage to Nate come to be. Thanks to you, Alex and Richard will not be orphaned. In fact, I might become their stepfather in Nate's place."

"Olivia will never have you," Christianne said, slipping her fingers around the dagger hilt.

Salway shrugged. "Time will tell. At least I will not have to concern myself with Nate's nuptials again. I've devised a plan that will end any chance he will remarry."

Her skin crawled at the pleasure that flooded his face. "I don't understand."

"I have made quite a fortune shipping convict labor to the colonies. You are about to take the place of one Anne Stone and be one more harlot sent to the tobacco fields in Virginia." Scorn twisted his face. "I spent my whole life trying to please Nate and dancing to the earl's tune, but no matter how hard I tried, I was nothing. A poor relation to be used and shoved aside. But all that changed after the night of Eugenie's murder—from then on I was the one in control. I could have anything I wanted."

"Is that why you hoped to bed me? Because Nate wanted me?"

"To deflower you would have been quite a triumph. The woman Nate was desperately in love with? The sister Adam and Gavin adored? It would have repaid them for every slight. I would have kept my part of the bargain I made you as well, and set you up in a salon."

"To see them suffer."

He scowled. "Because I am a Rowland. I keep my word. But you scorned my offer, so another course is necessary. You and Nate would have a dozen babes, the way you're always touching him, even maimed as he is. One was bound to be a boy."

"So you will kill any woman he marries?"

"He'll never marry once you go missing. He'll move heaven and earth, searching for you. You see, I'll make sure he receives hints that you are still alive somewhere and need saving. But he'll never find you. Another woman, lost because of him... Eugenie, Jessamyn, you. Any man would feel as if he were cursed. That should keep even the honorable Nate from doing his duty."

Horror filled Christianne at his hellish plan. "I won't let you do this to him," she swore.

She stiffened, alert to a faint—voices somewhere down the hallway. Nate's deep baritone, so heart-wrenchingly familiar.

Salway must have heard it, too. His eyes went wide. He glanced behind him. Seizing her chance, Christianne yanked the dagger from her pocket.

"Nate! Run!" she shrieked, launching herself at Salway.

She slammed into him, the pistol firing as she knocked him through the doorway into the hall. The gun's report reverberated through the corridors. She grappled with Salway as footsteps hastened down the hall, Nate's uneven gait, the rush of footmen and maids. Salway's hand closed around her wrist like a vise as he tried to force the blade around, the point nudging the soft curve of her belly.

"Salway!" Nate's voice rang out, and in a heartbeat, Salway flew backwards, the two men toppling over in deadly battle.

Christianne shoved herself backwards with her feet, searching for the fallen dagger. She saw it flash—but was it in Salway's hand or Nate's?

A guttural cry of pain, the horrendous sound of tearing flesh as the two men collapsed against each other.

"Nate!" Christianne cried, as Nate rolled to the side.

Blood ran from a wound in Nate's arm, but Christianne's dagger was buried to the hilt in Salway's chest. Nate climbed awkwardly to one knee. His face ashen with torment as he stared at his cousin. "God, Salway... Salway, why?" he demanded. "Christianne warned me about you, but I didn't want to believe... You were... were like a brother to me."

"No. A toady, maybe. Forever in your shadow. Never good enough to be one of your *precious Knights*." He spat the last words.

"Good God. Why do you hate me so much?"

"Everything was so easy for you," Salway gasped. "The perfect heir. Officer. Then I discovered what it meant to have power. Told...your mother Sera is not your child."

Nate's throat constricted in grief. "How could you

do that to her? My mother loved you. I know you cared about Eugenie and Sera."

"Your father...humiliated me...showed Eugenie made a fool of. Drove him mad to be helpless to protect the family name," he managed to say between the shallow breaths of a dying man.

Nate's fingers dug deep into Salway's shoulders. "Did you kill her? God, Salway, tell me. Let this be over."

Salway grasped the lace at Nate's throat and pulled him close. Pain-white lips stretched in a macabre smile. "It will...never be over. Not for you."

Nate heard the death rattle in Salway's throat. "Give Eugenie justice, Salway," he pleaded. "Just one word from you."

"Two words," Salway laughed as he pulled the dagger from his chest. Blood gushed from his wound. "*Paradise Lost.*"

Salway's body went limp against Nate, the rattle of breath silenced. He reached up and closed his cousin's eyes.

Christianne fell to her knees beside Nate, threw her arms around him. He turned into her arms. "Are you hurt?" Nate asked. "Please tell me you're safe."

"Your arm," Christianne choked out. "You're bleeding."

"It's just a scratch. I'm fine. And you?"

"Shaken, but fine. Where is Sera?" Christianne tried to still the tremors in her hands.

"She's safe," Nate assured her. "She was hungry when she arrived, and despite the furor over the wedding, cook had made her favorite sugar biscuits to welcome her home."

He pressed his face against Christianne's breasts and held on to her as if she were the last solid thing in his world. "Salway was my first friend. What the hell happened?"

"Jealousy." Christianne swayed slowly, her fingers stroking his hair. "He let it devour him inside. What did he mean when he said *Paradise Lost*?"

"I don't know," Nate said grimly, his thoughts clearly far away. "But I mean to find out."

Shadows fell over them, the crowd of servants who'd sounded an alarm.

"My lord, we heard a gunshot—" Vickers exclaimed, breathless, then he stared at the slumped body on the floor. "Master Salway!" he gasped.

"He meant to kidnap Miss Slade and fell on the knife," Nate explained. "Someone go fetch Bascombe. Christianne, find Sera. Lock yourselves in the nursery and don't open the door for anyone until I come."

She'd never heard his voice so hard. "Nate, you're scaring me. What is this about?"

His mouth set, grim. "Just do it."

CHAPTER 36

*N*ate walked into his father's chamber, blood staining his arm—Salway's and his own. "What happened?" The earl sat up straighter, his hawk-like eyes narrowing.

"Christianne was nearly kidnapped."

"Kidnapped?" his father echoed. "By whom?"

"Salway. He's dead."

Something flared in his father's eyes. Then it was shuttered away. "He was weak, just like his father. No doubt he killed Eugenie as well."

"He says not."

"Lies! More lies! His father was a liar, too!"

Nate crossed to the table beside his father's favorite chair. How many times since Eugenie's death had he seen his father cradling the book it held, that strange expression on his face? He'd never noticed that the binding tipped just off kilter, as if something had been pressed between the pages.

Veins pulsed in his father's temples as if they were about to burst. "Doubtless he tried to shift blame. Fling anyone into the fire to hide his own crime. He probably even attempted to accuse me!"

359

"No. He didn't say anything about you. He only said two words. *Paradise Lost.*"

His father flushed an alarming red as Nate trailed his fingers over the gilt title. "Don't touch that," he said. "You have no right to pry through my private things!"

Nate opened the book. There, pressed between the pages, was the fragment torn from Eugenie's fan. A delicate painting of his mother's face stared back at him.

As a commander in Scotland, he'd had a sixth sense when an ambush was in the offing. He remembered the sensation he'd felt, the instinctive need to get Sera away from Harlestone at once. He'd been right.

He looked at his father. "My God. Salway was telling the truth. It was you. You murdered Eugenie."

"It was a necessary sacrifice, no different than the choices we're forced to make in battle."

"In *battle?*" Nate's stomach churned with horror. "You strangled my wife, your own daughter-in-law in her own garden."

"I found her weeping in the garden alone after that ridiculous announcement in the ballroom. She told me she knew you were angry, but that you would protect her and the child, no matter how difficult things were between you. You'd never let anything happen to either one of them. She spoke about how Augusta had adored Seraphina. That Augusta had told her about Adaline, how cruel I'd been. How it had been my fault that the girl had died and I'd buried her... her memory as well as her body. But you weren't like me. You were a good man," the earl said with a disgusted air. "So honorable, even if you didn't love her anymore." His eyes like slits, he spat, "I knew she was right. There was nothing I could do to keep that bastard from inheriting when the time came. I had no choice."

The earl was pacing now. "Don't you understand? If that harlot you married had brought forth a son, it isn't the name that is lost. It's the bastardization of the name. The fake heir wouldn't be a 'real' Rowland. He'd be a counterfeit, and that's what I cannot and will not abide! It was my responsibility to see that our bloodline continued at any cost. I would have gotten away with it if Salway hadn't seen me when he was slipping out to meet Deborah Musgrove! He knew the image of the fan that was torn away was my Augusta."

"Why didn't Salway just tell the magistrate? With one word, he could destroy the Rowland legacy forever."

"If I was hung for murder, you would inherit my fortune. But with me alive, the purse strings were wide open. Meanwhile, your reputation was being destroyed. He counted on you not marrying. He'd inherit it all. I think being in control was more important...of me...of you..."

"The portrait on the fan leaf, the one you ripped out. Why?"

"Salway told me Eugenie had had it painted as a gift for Augusta after she learned about Adaline. Augusta as Demeter, Eugenie as Persephone and Seraphina as spring."

"And the child, the shadowy cherub smiling down on them. That was meant to be Adaline, wasn't it?"

"Augusta was mine! She didn't belong there, with the by-blow of that harlot you married! Augusta was a Rowland. My wife."

"And Eugenie was mine. You talk about the honor of the Rowland name? You murdered a helpless woman. She carried our name. Seraphina had already lost the grandmother who doted on her. You left Seraphina motherless."

"A goat would be as fine a mother as that little piece of muslin."

"Eugenie loved Sera more than you ever loved Adaline or me."

Was it poison inherited from his father— pride masquerading as honor—that had made Nate distance himself from his only child? Or had Sera reminded him too intensely of the Adaline he'd lost? Pressing on that unspoken grief? Or had he and Eugenie just been too young and untested when the worst had befallen them? Closing each other out?

It was something Christianne would never have allowed. How many times had she charged into a room, forced him to confront his real feelings, the raw places, the ugliness, the bitterness, lancing wounds instead of letting them fester, hidden until they spread to every part of him, changing who he was?

His father stood up, ramrod straight, his features seeming carved in marble. "What are you going to do, now that you know the truth? You are supposed to protect your family, are you not? I'm the only family you have left."

Nate thought of Strawberry Grove. The Slades and Gavin racing across the grounds as children. He thought of Lydia Slade, how she'd raised her rival's son with her own brood, and come to love him as much as any of those she'd carried in her womb. Every time she'd looked at Gavin's storm-gray eyes and tawny-gold hair, she must have known she was looking at the image of the merchant's daughter who had ruined all of her girlish hopes and dreams.

It had taken immense courage for Gavin to love the Slades. And for Lydia to love Gavin. It could have ended so differently, if either of them had faltered as Nate did.

It's not too late, he could almost hear Gavin say. *It took time for us to love each other, and we had to forgive each other for mistakes we made. And mistakes others made. You decide how the future will unfold.*

"You're wrong. I have the Knights, closer than brothers. I have the Slades, from Mother Lydia to Maria and Eliza and Laura and Adam. I have Seraphina, if she'll forgive me. And most of all, I have Christianne. God willing, we'll soon add children to the nursery so that Seraphina doesn't grow up alone, as I did."

His father's expression shifted, suddenly conciliatory. "Nate, you're my son. My heir. I made a mistake. In a fit of anger, I snapped. She drove me to it! Is that a reason to destroy a man's life? I'm your father."

"I'm Sera's father. Eugenie deserves justice."

"Just… take tonight to consider," his father pleaded. "Think about your next step. Once you make it, you'll never be able to take it back."

"You should have thought about that before you attacked everyone I love." Nate's gut clenched at the thought of the proud man he'd looked up to his whole life, the officer he'd always longed to emulate, standing in the prisoner's dock condemned for murder.

Yet, what kind of father would let his own son suffer in his place, suspected of the murder *he'd* committed. Christianne might have been lost to him as well…and Seraphina, sacrificed to the Earl of Fendale's monstrous pride.

"I know you think that being a Rowland puts you above the law, but it does not. You will have to face the consequence of what you have done."

∼

NATE TRIED THE NURSERY DOOR, but it was locked. He tapped softly, the knock he'd used so often during Christianne's stay at The Blue Peacock.

After a moment, the door swung wide. Christianne stood in the opening, her hand curved around the hilt of a rapier. Nate's heart swelled with love. Christianne. His warrior queen.

"I grabbed this on the way to the nursery," she explained. "I was never so glad of your family's penchant for hanging old weapons on the walls."

Despite everything, Nate forced a smile, knowing Christianne had the quick thinking, the courage and the skill to fight off anyone who tried to harm her or Sera. He remembered the other lads in the Knights laughing indulgently at her insistence that they teach her to wield a sword. He's always known she was serious.

Soon, the threat that had stalked them would be over. Salway would be buried in the churchyard. Nate's father would face the penalty for his crime. And no matter what challenges Seraphina had to meet in the future, she would have a mother ready to do battle for her with swords or wits. A woman who could stand against any foe. A woman who would teach his Seraphina how to fight for herself.

"Is everything all right now?" Christianne asked. "Can you tell me what happened?"

Nate glanced at his sleeping child, then drew Christianne to the far corner of the room. "I found the fragment of Eugenie's fan that was missing," he said softly. "It was pressed between the pages of my father's copy of *Paradise Lost*."

"Oh, Nate."

"It was Mother's favorite poem. I'd seen him with the book so often this year, I'd go to his chamber and he'd be holding the volume. We always sensed that finding the image torn from the center of the fan would be the key to finding her murderer. Now I know. Deborah Musgrove was right. Eugenie had had the scene painted as a gift for my mother. The center panel was my mother as the goddess Demeter, the one who lost her daughter to the god of the dead."

Christianne's eyes widened. "I remember the myth. She grieved so deeply that all the crops died, so Zeus restored Persephone to her mother for six months out of the year. When they were reunited, spring came." She paused for a heartbeat, her voice raw but tender. "Spring. Seraphina."

"My father saw the fan earlier that night and guessed that mother had shared the story about Adaline. He was furious. When Eugenie announced she was pregnant, he knew it was not by me. He realized the coming child might well become Earl of Fendale, and I think his sanity snapped."

"So he followed Eugenie into the garden and killed her," Christianne slid into his arms. "How horrible."

"Salway saw him leaving the scene that night and knew my mother's likeness was in the center of the fan. He deduced the truth and had been blackmailing my father ever since. You warned me about Salway. I absolutely should have listened."

She brushed the lock of hair from his brow, her eyes filled with tenderness. "We see what we want to see, don't we? Especially when it comes to people we care about. Where is your father now?"

"Locked in his bedchamber with Vickers standing guard. I wanted Sera's return home to be so different. How will I ever explain this night to her?"

"We'll do it together. She doesn't need details. I told her that there was an accident and that you and I would make certain she is safe. Come. Look at her, and you'll see how happy you made her."

She took him by the hand, and Nate let her lead him over to the bed where Sera lay sleeping. Beside her on the pillow, lay the miniature portrait of Eugenie he'd had copied for her.

Nate's throat constricted as he saw her little hand curled around the frame's edge. His eyes burned with tears he'd not shed, not for Salway or his father. Not even for himself.

As if she sensed his presence, Seraphina stirred. "Papa?" she breathed, her lashes fluttering open. "Miss Tia promised you'd come... I tried...to stay awake... wanted to tell you..."

Nate bent down to brush one of her curls away from her cheek, just the way his mother had when he was small. "I'm listening."

"I promise to be good. You won't have to send me away...ever again."

"Oh, Sera. This was never your fault. It was mine. I haven't been the papa you deserved, but I promise to do better, if you'll give me a chance."

He reached out, gathered her into his arms. She stiffened just a moment, uncertain. Then she melted into his embrace. She smelled of sunshine and innocence and life beginning again. *Spring.*

"Thank you for my present," she said. "I love Mama's picture. I was starting to forget her."

Like I forgot Adaline, Nate thought. But he hadn't. Not really. He'd carried his sister with him, a tender glow even his father's wrath couldn't extinguish. "I'll help you remember her," he said, burying his face in her curls. "I promise."

Sera's head bobbed, and he felt her drift back to sleep.

Maybe someday, his little girl might learn the truth about her grandfather, her uncle Salway, even her own unconventional birth. The thought filled him with pain. But the truth was better than a life based on erasing what was real. Adaline. His mother's grief. His father's ruthlessness.

With Christianne's courage and fierce loyalty, with

the love of the Slades and Gavin and Myles—the Knights would surround his daughter with a sense of belonging, just as they had done for Nate when he was so wounded. He felt Christianne's hand on his back. That touch almost undid him. Gently, he lowered Sera into her little bed and tucked the covers around her.

"Will you stay with her tonight?" Nate asked.

"Of course."

"I need to wait with my father until Bascombe arrives. My mother would have wanted me to."

A worried line formed between Christianne's brows. "Be careful."

"I will." He kissed her, long and hard, then walked to stand watch over the man who had betrayed him.

~

NATE BRACED himself to enter his father's room, knowing he must keep this long night's appointment with the man who had stolen so much from him. As he slipped through the door, he tried desperately to reconcile the father who had taught him to shoot, to ride and to tend the lands under his protection, with the ruthless murderer who had strangled his pregnant daughter-in-law, and let people believe his son was guilty of the crime. Would he have come forward if Nate had been arrested and gone to trial? Nate would never know.

For the moment, the earl sat with two glasses of wine at the table. The fragment of fan was spread openly on his lap, Nate's mother's smiling face staring up at him.

The old man looked up as Nate approached him. "As you can see, I've been expecting you," he said, gesturing to the glasses. "I knew you'd come to your senses, Nathaniel. I suggest we put this unpleasantness behind us as soldiers must on the battlefield. Momentary madness shouldn't require a man to sacrifice his life."

Nate stared at him, dumbfounded. Could he really believe Nate would go on as if none of it had happened? But then, wasn't that what soldiers had been expected to do since time began? Wade neck deep in blood, then rejoin the lives they'd left behind and somehow be the same men they were before the killing fields?

"I haven't changed my mind," Nate said. "That night in the garden, when you found me with a pistol in my lap, you told me a Rowland must face adversity with courage. You will have to face this."

His father gave him a hard look, then saluted him with the glass. "Then we shall toast my last night at Harlestone Hall."

Nate shook his head. "No. I'll not toast that."

His father examined his glass, swirling the deep red liquid around. "Do you believe in Heaven or Hell?" he asked, taking a drink.

"I don't know."

"I wonder, where do soldiers go? We've already seen Hell, have we not? Or do we create our own at a general's command?"

"Sometimes what we do is necessary," said Nate. "Sometimes it only feels so."

Long minutes passed in silence. "I was proud of you when you excelled in your first commission. Then you returned home, your leg gone. It tore me apart. I did not show it. In her last days, do you know what your mother said to me?"

"No."

"That you had lost your leg, but I had lost my heart." His father slumped in his chair, suddenly seeming decades older and weary. "I didn't lose it. I killed it on purpose after Adaline died."

"I remember her now. So many little things. You had no right to take those memories away from me."

"Memories?" The earl drained the last of his wine. He swallowed hard, wincing as the spirits slid down his throat. "Memories are open wounds. Would God I could forget..."

They sat in silence as the clock on the mantel moved its hands in a slow crawl toward dawn. His father stared down at the portrait of Nate's mother. When, at last the earl stirred, he touched his wife's painted cheek. "I...miss her." His voice was thin, slurred, his breathing shallow, raspy.

Was he having apoplexies? Had his heart seized? God knew he was under enough stress. Nate's brow furrowed as he regarded his father. "Your eyes...they look so strange. And your breathing... Are you all right?"

"Not yet. But I will be. I tried to make things right before...end. Vickers..." His father groped for his pocket, fumbling for something inside it. Nate tried to help him free a document of some kind, but as he did so, something else fell out. A small glass bottle shattered on the floor.

Nate read the label written in an apothecary's hand. *Laudanum.*

The truth struck him like a blow. "No! You can't do this! How much did you take?"

"It is...done." His father clasped Nate's hand. "Stay with me...until...I sleep." Eyelids wrinkled with age drifted shut. Harsh lips contorted, as his father struggled to speak between gasping breaths, squeezing out words Nate had never heard from his lips before.

"I am...sorry..."

CHAPTER 37

*I*t was the next day when Nate found Christianne sitting in the garden. He'd had little sleep, his face haggard and yet he was experiencing a strange sense of peace. He sagged down upon the bench beside her as little Sera and her nurse played in the garden with Caval.

"They've been together from the moment I brought her outside," Christianne told him. "I thought it best to get her out of the house."

"Thank you." Nate took her hand. "I'm sorry I've been delayed so long. Between Bascombe's arrival, dealing with Salway's attack, and everything after..." His voice trailed off. "I thought of sending Vickers with a message, but there was news I had to give you myself. Will you walk with me?"

She cast a tender look at Sera and her nurse then slipped her arm through Nate's and he led her near a bank of roses.

"My father is dead," he said quietly.

Christianne stumbled to a halt. "Dead?" she echoed.

"All my life, I heard tales of Rowlands facing down formidable foes on the field of battle, but in the end, he

370

was too much a coward to face justice for what he'd done. He drained a bottle of laudanum."

She turned toward him. Her wide, dark eyes searched his face. "I don't—don't know what to say. I should say I'm sorry. But I'm not."

Nate looked at Seraphina, playing among the flowers. "Is it wrong to feel relief that your parent is gone? He killed Eugenie. Wiped Adaline from memory and broke my mother's heart. He said nothing when the world accused me of murdering my pregnant wife."

Christianne remained silent, but seized his hand in her warm, strong one.

"The ugly truth is that I'm glad he's gone," Nate confessed. "If he still lived, how could I ever know for certain that you and Sera would be safe?"

"Did he take the laudanum leftover from his accident?"

"Mrs. Davies told Bascombe that my father had her procure a large bottle right after Eugenie was murdered. I think he simply decided that if evidence ever pointed to him, he'd take his own life rather than face trial."

"I don't understand how a father could allow his innocent son to take the blame."

"While I was with you and Sera in the nursery, he drafted his confession and had Vickers and his valet witness it."

"Thank God he did that much."

Nate looked into the distance, pensive, his voice soft. "I had a bottle of laudanum once. I saved it after I lost my leg. I endured the torment of the damned to build up enough to end it all if I couldn't bear it any longer. That was why I locked myself away from Eugenie at first. I scared myself. But I had the Knights to help me find my way through it. And, strangely enough, Salway and my father. But you were the one who made me realize that those shadow parts of me were what made me the man I am now. I'd love to be able to dance with you, my Mistress Mayhem, and teach Sera and the babes we'll one day have to run races like we used to do. But I wouldn't wish any of it back. Not now. That moment on Culloden Moor gave me this life. Gave me you." He paused, looking deep into her eyes.

"We'll not let the darkness of the past take that happiness away from us," he said. "What happens once my father's confession becomes public will be difficult. And I will always wish Eugenie and I had had a chance to cut the tie between us in another way and she could have found the kind of happiness that I have. But each of them chose their own path in the end. I can't change it. You and I can only choose ours. I spent my life wanting to protect everyone around me. Put women, especially, between my shoulder and my shield."

"I remember you saying that." Christianne touched his arm, and he could tell she was thinking of the moment Salway had attacked her.

"But you'd never let anyone do that for you," Nate said, skimming his knuckles along the soft curve of her cheek. "You always had to charge out on your own, sword drawn."

"You are the one who taught me how to fight with a sword." She smiled up at him, mischief and love shining in her eyes. Nate smoothed a curl back from her brow, trying not to think how close he'd come to losing her.

"Maybe, after all this time, we've finally unraveled the mystery of what love can be, my Christianne. You've shown me that we fight better side by side. Together."

*H*arlestone Hall had never seen such a magical celebration for a child's birthday. Colorful flags boasting coats of arms waved gaily in the breeze while a horde of children dueled with wooden swords and shrieked in delight. A clever enchantress in the person of Nate's beloved countess had turned the ponies into unicorns with gilt horns that sparkled in the sun, while knights who sounded remarkably like Vickers and the other footmen, mounted guard, wearing helmets from the suits of armor that had lately adorned the corridors of the illustrious estate. Nathaniel Rowland may have inherited the earldom, yet, Harlestone would always be home to him. Christianne had banished the ugliness of the past. Salway and his father had no power here anymore.

Nate's heart welled up with joy as he watched his wife of three years fly about like a whirlwind, making magic for the daughter she'd embraced as her own. He gazed out across the family that had embraced him with such joy; Lydia, who'd brought his sister back to life, Gavin's growing brood and the boisterous Slades. Nate was as notorious as they were now, with his own wild love story to appall the *ton*.

One day, he would have to deal with the arrogant swells again, when Sera was old enough. But he had no doubt that his formidable countess was up to the challenge. Sera would have Olivia's friendship as well. The bond between Harlestone and the Beresford estate was thriving.

Nate grinned at how lovely Christianne looked, a vision in blue satin as she swept through their guests, making certain everyone from the smallest child to Clary and Robin felt included in the fun and at ease.

Adam Slade strode up and clapped Nate on the shoulder. "You are grinning like a man totally besotted with his wife, Galahad. But you know the kind of mischief my sister loves to stir up. Have a care when you see that glint in her eye."

It was true, Nate thought, and he couldn't wait to see what she did next. She'd filled his life with surprises, laughter and passion. "I thought I knew what it was to love Christianne when I wed her. But every time I think I can't love her more, she surprises me."

"She's outdone herself today, that's for certain," Adam said, gesturing to a magnificent creation the village blacksmith had crafted—a stone with a sword thrust into its center.

"She's been conspiring with our blacksmith for months now to add that to our garden."

"At least it will keep the children occupied for years."

Adam smiled fondly as Gavin's son took a turn at the test, his golden locks shining. Adam's black-haired boy and Myles Farringdon's chestnut-haired brood shouted encouragement. "The lads have been wearing themselves out since they arrived, trying to claim King Arthur's crown."

"They might have been us thirty years ago," Gavin chuckled as he strolled up. "Who could ever imagine the trials that lay ahead of us, or the treasures we would win."

Gratitude filled Nate as he watched Christianne pin a gilt crown onto Sera's golden curls. She'd healed wounds far more crippling than his maimed leg, and had given him a life and love he'd thought far beyond his reach.

At eleven, Seraphina had blossomed, her shyness easing in the delicious chaos that had upended the staid halls of the Rowland family. She would never be as heedless or confident as the tiny brother and sister who adored her, but she would forever have the first place in her father's heart. The love Nate and his daughter shared was a testament to courage and trust and forgiveness. The greatest gift Christianne had given them both.

"I believe I'd better retrieve my littlest princess before she makes off with Sera's crown," Nate said. "Adaline can't resist anything that glitters."

"She's already divested one of the unicorns of its horn," Adam laughed.

At two years old, Adaline Rowland was as determined as her mother had ever been, and Sera could deny her nothing.

But before Nate could intervene, Christianne scooped up their daughter and delivered the child to her husband. "I believe it is time for the queen of the day to attempt to pull the sword from the stone, my love," Christianne said.

"Come to Papa, Adaline." Nate held out his arms, and his little daughter launched herself into his embrace. Christianne kissed his cheek, her lips warm with delicious mischief, her dark eyes alight with merriment. Now and forever, his irrepressible Mistress Mayhem...

Christianne crossed to the sword in the stone and

clapped her hands. "Step back, noble knights. It is time for Seraphina to take her turn."

"I don't think she can do it, Aunt Christianne," Gavin's son protested. "It's not that—that girls aren't clever, but it's a matter of force, you see."

"We *shall* see, won't we?" Christianne's eyes danced as she led her daughter to the center of a gathering crowd.

"I think they're right," Seraphina confided softly. "I don't think I'm strong enough."

Nate watched Christianne caress Seraphina's cheek. "Sometimes wits are more important than brute strength. Your father taught me that when I was your age." She glanced at Nate, and the love he saw there awed him.

Baby Arthur squealed from his aunt Eliza's arms, waving his plump hands at his sister. Sera waved back to him, her cheeks pink as she stepped up to the stone. She glanced at Nate, uncertain.

"Go on, sweetheart," Nate urged. "You are stronger than you know. I am sure of it."

She walked around the stone, examining the sword, and he could almost hear the cogs in her mind whirring. She grasped the hilt and pulled once. Twice.

Then he saw her frown as she studied the decorations emblazoned on the hilt. A miniature Excalibur and an enameled shield. Evelake... Galahad's shield. Sword and shield. Wasn't that what Nate and Christianne had been to each other?

Sera's eyes shone as she pressed the two engravings together, grasped the hilt of the sword in the stone more firmly, and pulled. The sword slid free, the force tumbling her backward.

"It was a *puzzle!*" Sera burst out, her violet eyes wide as she stared at her prize in disbelief.

Myles Farringdon's son bowed low to Sera, a grin

brightening his face. "You've bested us all, milady," he said, reaching out a hand as the other children crowded around, whooping their congratulations. Adaline scrambled down to fling herself at her triumphant sister.

Christianne went to Nate and put her arms around her husband's waist. Nate drew his wife close, reveling in the warmth of her body and imagining the passion night would bring.

"I don't believe I've ever seen a cadre of boys more stunned," Christianne teased.

"I have. The first time you divested me of my sword. I wish I'd realized then that you'd already stolen my heart." Nate kissed her lavender-scented hair. "I always dreamed of being the knight errant, rescuing my lady fair. I didn't know that I would be the one in need of saving. You made all of this possible, Christianne Rowland. The laughter, the hope, this Avalon we've created."

He saw her smile, sensed her mind was far away. "What are you thinking, love?"

"I'm thinking of the tapestry you had made as my wedding gift, the dark forest full of dragons and Sir Galahad trying to reach the maid in the castle. There was a time no one believed we could weave our lives together. Now it shines like that tapestry woven of golden threads."

"Threads both dark and light," Nate said, remembering the dangers they had faced. "Yet this life we're weaving together will only grow more beautiful with time."

"Yes," Christianne said, her ebony eyes aglow.

"We'll make it so together," Nate said, his lips pressed against her hair. "My own Mistress Mayhem, the mistress of my heart."

THANK YOU!

Thank you so much for reading Saving Galahad. If you enjoyed reading this book, please consider giving a review or star rating to help other readers make a choice. It's one way to support authors and is much appreciated!

If you'd like to stay in touch, I'd love to have you join my newsletter, where I feature giveaways, information about new releases coming up, special sales on my books-- and books I'm looking forward to reading myself! I'll post about other fun goings on as well-- like my latest adventures in the kitchen and my favorite recipes. You can sign up here: www. KimberlyCatesBooks.com

It's so much fun to connect with readers. If you 'like' my Kimberly Cates Facebook Author Page. I'll be posting "Behind the Book" tidbits, interesting insights into history and some posts about the 'real me'-- adventures about moving to a new state for the first time in my life, discovering the beauty of California, my efforts to make space ships out of cardboard boxes for my grandchildren, finding the perfect yarn store and how I juggle multiple pseudonyms and time periods without (at least so far) losing my mind.

THANK YOU!

I'd love to have you visit me on Pinterest, where I have Pinterest boards for each of my books, featuring historical artifacts, images and fun things that pertain to each novel.

Also, if you are in the mood for an historical novel, I'd love for you to check out my Ella March Chase titles!

As always, I send my kind regards and appreciation to you, my readers. Thank you for your support and encouragement! May your world be filled with "happily ever afters!"

Kimberly

ABOUT THE AUTHOR

When Kimberly Cates was in third grade she informed her teacher that she didn't need to learn multiplication tables. She was going to be a writer when she grew up. Kimberly filled countless spiral notebooks with stories until, at age twenty-five, she received a birthday gift that changed her life: an electric typewriter. Kimberly wrote her first historical romance, sold it to Berkley Jove, and em-

Kimberly Cates

barked on a thirty-year career as an author. Called "a master of the genre" by Romantic Times, her thirty-three bestselling, award-winning novels are noted for their endearing characters, emotional impact and their ability to transport the reader to the mists and magic of the British Isles.

Kimberly has also penned historical romances as Kimberleigh Caitlin and contemporary romances under the pseudonyms Kimberly Cates and Kim Cates.

ALSO BY KIMBERLY CATES

ROGUES, RAKEHELLS AND REDEMPTION:

Culloden's Fire Series

Gather the Stars

Angel's Fall

Crown of Dreams

Crown of Mist

Morning Song

Saving Galahad

Celtic Rogues Series

Black Falcon's Lady

The Black Falcon's Christmas

Her Magic Touch

Briar Rose

Stealing Heaven

Lily Fair

The Raider Series

The Raider's Bride

The Raider's Daughter

To Catch a Flame

To Chase the Storm

AMERICAN WEST

Only Forever

FUTURE RELEASES:

Restless is the Wind

Contemporary Romance:

Fly Away Home

Historical Fiction:

The Queen's Dwarf by Ella March Chase

The Virgin Queen's Daughter by Ella March Chase

Three Maids for a Crown, a story of the Grey sisters by Ella March Chase